Praise for
AMERICAN ROYALS

"With love and rivalries, a heady pre-wedding atmosphere, and a country's future poised to change, *American Royals II: Majesty* is **an indulgently fun escape.**" —*Shelf Awareness*

"McGee skillfully juggles each woman's narrative, framing their struggles with plenty of pomp and circumstance and the challenges of living very public lives. Add in a dramatic finale that packs in all the feels, and you've got **a royal winner.**" —*Kirkus Reviews*

"McGee's sequel is **just as gripping as the first.**" —*SLJ*

"Imagine a world where Meghan Markle is the queen of the United States of America. . . . *American Royals* is the next closest thing." —*Teen Vogue*

"Relatable, believable, fantastical, aspirational, and **completely addictive.**" —Sara Shepard, #1 *New York Times* bestselling author of *Pretty Little Liars* and *The Perfectionists*

"With elegance, saucy secrets, and forbidden love, *American Royals* is **fast-paced and utterly charming.** Katharine McGee's prose sparkles, capturing the glamour and pressures of an American monarchy." —Kendare Blake, #1 *New York Times* bestselling author of the Three Dark Crowns series

"*Crazy Rich Asians* meets *Gossip Girl*. It's easy reading, but the quality of writing from Katharine McGee is sublime. . . . [An] **addictive new modern fairytale.**" —Yahoo Lifestyle

"More than two centuries later, the House of Washington still rules . . . with **forbidden love and *Gossip Girl*–esque drama** included." —*theSkimm*

MAJESTY
AMERICAN ROYALS II

BY KATHARINE McGEE

American Royals
American Royals II: Majesty
American Royals III: Rivals

MAJESTY
AMERICAN ROYALS II

KATHARINE McGEE

This is a work of fiction. All incidents and dialogue, and all characters with the exception of some well-known historical and public figures, are products of the author's imagination and are not to be construed as real. Where real-life historical or public figures appear, the situations, incidents, and dialogues concerning those persons are fictional and are not intended to depict actual events or to change the fictional nature of the work. In all other respects, any resemblance to persons living or dead is entirely coincidental.

Text copyright © 2020 by Katharine McGee and Alloy Entertainment
Cover art copyright © 2020 by Carolina Melis

All rights reserved. Published in the United States by Ember, an imprint of Random House Children's Books, a division of Penguin Random House LLC, New York. Originally published in hardcover in the United States by Random House Children's Books, a division of Penguin Random House LLC, New York, in 2020.

Ember and the E colophon are registered trademarks of Penguin Random House LLC.

Visit us on the Web! GetUnderlined.com

Educators and librarians, for a variety of teaching tools, visit us at RHTeachersLibrarians.com

Produced by Alloy Entertainment
alloyentertainment.com

The Library of Congress has cataloged the hardcover edition of this work as follows:
Name: McGee, Katharine, author.
Title: Majesty / Katharine McGee.
Description: First edition. | New York : Random House, [2020] | Series: American royals ; 2 | Audience: Ages 12 and up. | Summary: In an alternate America, tensions are high as Beatrice prepares to become the country's first queen, while Princess Samantha and Prince Jefferson struggle to decide what their futures might hold.
Identifiers: LCCN 2020008034 (print) | LCCN 2020008035 (ebook) | ISBN 978-1-9848-3021-0 (hardcover) | ISBN 978-1-9848-3022-7 (ebook)
Subjects: CYAC: Kings, queens, rulers, etc.—Fiction. | Princesses—Fiction. | Princes—Fiction. | Love—Fiction. | Courts and courtiers—Fiction.
Classification: LCC PZ7.1.M43513 Maj 2020 (print) | LCC PZ7.1.M43513 (ebook) | DDC [Fic]—dc23

ISBN 978-1-9848-3024-1 (trade paperback)

Printed in the United States of America
5th Printing
First Ember Edition 2022

Random House Children's Books supports the First Amendment and celebrates the right to read.

Penguin Random House LLC supports copyright. Copyright fuels creativity, encourages diverse voices, promotes free speech, and creates a vibrant culture. Thank you for buying an authorized edition of this book and for complying with copyright laws by not reproducing, scanning, or distributing any part in any form without permission. You are supporting writers and allowing Penguin Random House to publish books for every reader.

For John Ed,
who said he'd never get one

MAJESTY
AMERICAN ROYALS II

PROLOGUE

The morning had dawned dreary and gray, with a mist that hung over the streets of the capital. It was, the media correspondents all agreed, appropriate weather for a funeral.

They stood behind a velvet rope to one side of the palace doors, swapping cigarettes and breath mints, hurriedly checking their lipstick in their phone screens. Then the palace's main gates swung open to admit the first guests.

So many of them had come, from every last corner of the world. Emperors and sultans, archdukes and dowager queens, even a cardinal sent by the pope himself. There were members of Congress and aristocrats, from the highest-ranking dukes through the simple life peers—all of them here to honor His Majesty George IV, the late King of America.

Clad in somber black dresses and dark suits, they filed through the doors and into the massive throne room. There was no other space in the capital that could accommodate three thousand guests.

A series of rifles fired a military salute over the river, and the funeral procession turned onto the final avenue toward the palace. Silence fell, as dense as the lingering mists. Media crews stood up a bit straighter, cameramen fumbling to adjust their lenses.

No one spoke as a cluster of figures appeared through the haze: eight young men of the Revere Guard, the elite corps of officers who protected the Crown, providing the Sovereign's Final Escort. Between them they bore a coffin draped in the red, blue, and gold of the American flag.

Most of the Guards stared resolutely forward. But one young man—tall, with light brown hair and shadowed blue-gray eyes—kept glancing back over his shoulder. Perhaps he was getting tired. The funeral procession had crisscrossed the streets of the capital all morning. As the crow flies, the distance measured less than two miles, yet the winding route had taken several hours to complete. It had been designed that way on purpose, so that as many citizens as possible might get one last moment with their former king.

It was still hard to believe that King George was really gone. He had only been fifty when he died, after a sudden and tragic battle with lung cancer.

A few paces behind the coffin walked twenty-two-year-old Princess Beatrice—no, the people reminded themselves, she was a princess no longer. Upon the death of her father she had become Her Majesty Beatrice Georgina Fredericka Louise, Queen of America. The title would take some getting used to. America had never been ruled by a queen, until now.

When the procession reached the palace gates, Beatrice dropped into a curtsy before her father's casket. A chorus of insect-like clicks rose up from the cameras as the photographers hurried to capture the iconic image: of the new, young queen, curtsying for the very last time.

BEATRICE

Six weeks later

Beatrice had never heard the palace so silent.

Normally its halls echoed with noise: butlers giving orders to footmen; tour guides lecturing groups of students; ambassadors or ministers chasing after the Lord Chamberlain, begging for an audience with the king.

Today everything was still. Dust sheets hung over the furniture, emitting a ghostly glow in the half-light. Even the crowds that usually thronged the main gates had melted away, leaving the palace stranded, an island in a sea of empty sidewalks and trampled grass.

Behind her, Beatrice heard her mom getting out of the car. Sam and Jeff had elected to stay at the country house another night. When they were younger, the three siblings used to go there together—in a dark SUV, watching movies on its dropdown TV—but Beatrice could no longer ride in the same car as her sister. The monarch and the first in line for the throne weren't permitted to travel together, for security reasons.

She'd only made it halfway across the entrance hall when her heel snagged on an antique carpet. She stumbled—and a firm hand reached out to steady her.

Beatrice looked up into the cool gray eyes of her Revere Guard, Connor Markham.

"You okay, Bee?"

She knew she should reprimand him for using her nickname instead of her title, especially in public, where anyone might overhear. But Beatrice couldn't think properly with Connor's hand on hers. After all these weeks of distance, the feel of his touch sparked wildly through her veins.

Voices echoed down the hallway. Connor frowned but took a swift step back, just as two footmen turned the corner, accompanied by a man with grim features and salt-and-pepper hair: Robert Standish, who'd worked as Lord Chamberlain for Beatrice's father, and now for her.

He swept a formal bow. "I'm sorry, Your Majesty. We weren't expecting you until tomorrow."

Beatrice tried not to flinch at the title. She still wasn't used to *Your Majesty* being directed at her.

The footmen began moving from room to room, whipping away dust sheets and tossing them in a pile. The palace sprang to life as ornate side tables and delicate brass lamps were hurriedly uncovered.

"I decided to come back early. I just . . ." Beatrice trailed off before saying *I just needed to get away*. This past month at Sulgrave, the Washingtons' country estate, was supposed to have been a getaway. But even surrounded by family, she'd felt alone. And exhausted.

Each night Beatrice tried to stay awake as long as she could, because once she fell asleep the dreams would come. Horrible, twisted dreams where she had to watch her father die, over and over again, and know that it was her fault.

She had caused her dad's death. If she hadn't shouted at him that night—hadn't threatened to marry her Revere Guard and renounce her position as queen—then King George might still be alive.

Beatrice bit back a sigh. She knew better than to let herself think like this. If she did, her mind would sink like a stone, deeper and deeper into a well of grief without ever touching bottom.

"Your Majesty." Robert glanced down at the tablet he carried with him at all times. "There are a few things I'd like to discuss. Should we head up to your office?"

It took a moment for Beatrice to realize that he meant her father's office. Which belonged to her now.

"No," she replied, a little forcefully. She wasn't ready to face that room—and all the memories trapped inside it. "Why don't we talk in here?" she added, gesturing to one of the sitting rooms.

"Very well." Robert followed her inside and pulled the double doors shut behind them, leaving Connor in the hall.

As she perched on a striped green sofa, Beatrice darted a glance at the three bay windows that overlooked the front drive. It was a nervous habit she'd picked up after her father's death: to study the windows of each room she walked into. As if the natural lighting might help her feel slightly less suffocated.

Or as if she was looking for an escape route.

"Your Majesty, your schedule for the upcoming week." Robert held out a sheet of paper, embossed with the royal crest.

"Thank you, Lord Standish," Beatrice said, and paused. She'd always addressed him by his full title, ever since she'd met him as a teenager, but now . . . "May I call you Robert?"

"I would be honored," he said obsequiously.

"In that case, you must start calling me Beatrice."

The chamberlain gave a throaty gasp. "Oh, no, Your Majesty. I would never presume to do such a thing. And I would suggest," he added, "that you never make an offer like that again, certainly not to anyone in a service position. It simply isn't appropriate."

Beatrice hated that she felt like a chastened schoolgirl, like she was seven years old again and her etiquette master had snapped a ruler over her knuckles as punishment for a sloppy curtsy. She forced herself to study the paper in her lap, only to look up in confusion.

"Where's the rest of my schedule?"

The only events listed were low-stress public appearances—a nature walk outside the capital with a conservation group, a meet-and-greet with the local Girl Scouts—the sort of goodwill-generating events that Beatrice used to do as heir to the throne. "I should have an audience with each of the party leaders in Congress," she went on. "And why isn't a Cabinet meeting scheduled for Thursday?"

"There's no need to dive into all of that right away," Robert said silkily. "You've been out of the public eye since the funeral. Right now, what the people need from you is reassurance."

Beatrice fought off a sense of disquiet. The monarch was meant to govern, not run around shaking hands like some kind of mascot for America. That was what the *heir* to the throne was for.

But what could she say? Everything she knew about this role she had learned from her father. Now he was gone, and the only person left to advise her was Robert, his right-hand man.

The chamberlain shook his head. "Besides, I'm sure you'll want to spend the next few months planning the wedding."

Beatrice tried to speak, but her throat seemed to have glued itself shut.

She was still engaged to Theodore Eaton, the son of the Duke of Boston. But in the past month, each time she'd started to think of Teddy, her mind had violently shied away. *I'll figure it out when I'm back*, she'd promised herself. *There's nothing I can do about it now.*

It had been easy to let herself forget about Teddy at Sulgrave.

None of her family members had spoken of him. They hadn't spoken much at *all*, each of them wrapped up in their own private grief.

"I'd prefer not to focus on the wedding just yet," she said at last, unable to hide the strain in her voice.

"Your Majesty, if we start planning now, we can hold the ceremony in June," the chamberlain argued. "Then, after your honeymoon, you can spend the rest of the summer on the newlyweds' royal tour."

Might as well say it all at once, Beatrice thought, and braced herself. "We're not getting married."

"What do you mean, Your Majesty?" Robert asked, his lips pursed in confusion. "Did something . . . happen between you and His Lordship?" Beatrice drew in a shaky breath, and he lifted his hands in a conciliatory gesture. "Please, forgive me if I'm overstepping. To do my job effectively, I need to know the truth."

Connor was still standing out there in the hallway. Beatrice could picture him: frozen in the Revere Guard stance, his feet planted firmly, a hand near his holstered weapon. She wondered, with a bolt of panic, if he could hear them through the closed wooden doors.

She opened her mouth, ready to tell Robert about Connor. It shouldn't be hard; she'd had this very conversation with her father—had marched into his study and informed him that she was in love with her Revere Guard—the night of her engagement party to Teddy. So why couldn't she say the same thing now?

I need to know the truth, Robert had insisted. Except . . . what *was* the truth?

Beatrice didn't know anymore. Her feelings for Connor were tangled up in her feelings about everything *else*, desire and regret and grief all painfully intertwined.

"I'd agreed to get married while my father was still alive,

because he wanted to walk me down the aisle," she managed. "But now that I'm queen, there's no need to rush."

Robert shook his head. "Your Majesty, it's *because* you are queen that I suggest you get married as soon as possible. You are the living symbol of America, and its future. And given the current situation . . ."

"The current situation?"

"This is a period of transition and uncertainty. The nation hasn't recovered from your father's death as easily as we might have hoped." There was no inflection, no emotion in Robert's tone. "The stock market has taken a hit. Congress is at a stalemate. Several of the foreign ambassadors have handed in their resignations. Just a few," he added, at the expression on her face. "But a wedding would be such a unifying occasion, for everyone in the country."

Beatrice heard the subtext beneath his words. She was now the Queen of America—and America was afraid.

She was too young, too untried. And most of all, she was a woman. Attempting to govern a country that had only ever been led by men.

If there was instability in America right now, *Beatrice* was the cause of it.

Before she could respond, the room's double doors swung open. "Beatrice! There you are."

Her mom stood in the doorway. She looked elegant even in her travel clothes—slim-cut navy pants and a pale blue sweater—though they fit more loosely than they used to. Grief hung over her shoulders like a weighted cloak.

When Queen Adelaide saw Robert, she hesitated. "Sorry, I didn't mean to interrupt."

The chamberlain rose to his feet. "Your Majesty, please join us. We were just discussing the wedding."

Adelaide turned to Beatrice, a new warmth in her voice. "Have you and Teddy set a date?"

"Actually . . . I'm not sure I'm ready to get married." Beatrice shot her mom a pleading glance. "It feels too fast. Don't you think we should wait until we've had time to grieve?"

"Oh, Beatrice." Her mom sank onto the couch with a heavy sigh. "We'll never be done grieving. You know that," she said softly. "It might sting less with time, but that doesn't mean we'll ever stop feeling the loss. We'll just get a little better at carrying it."

Across the room, Robert nodded in vigorous agreement. Beatrice tried to ignore him.

"We could all use a source of joy, of *celebration*, right now. Not just America, but our family." Adelaide's eyes gleamed with yearning. She had loved her husband with every fiber of her being, and now that he was gone, she seemed to have pinned all that emotion onto Beatrice—as if Beatrice and Teddy's love story was the only source of hope she had left.

"We need this wedding now more than ever," Robert chimed in.

Beatrice glanced helplessly from one of them to the other. "I get that, but—I mean—Teddy and I haven't known each other very long."

Queen Adelaide shifted. "Beatrice. Are you having second thoughts about marrying Teddy?"

Beatrice looked down at the engagement ring on her left hand. She'd been wearing it all month, out of inertia more than anything. When Teddy had first given it to her, it had felt wrong, but at some point she must have gotten used to it. It proved that you could get used to anything, really, in time.

The ring was beautiful, a solitaire diamond on a white-gold band. It had originally belonged to Queen Thérèse over a hundred years ago, though it had been polished so expertly that any damage was hidden beneath all the sparkle.

A little like Beatrice herself.

She realized that Robert and her mom were both waiting for her reply. "I just . . . I miss Dad."

"Oh, sweetheart. I know." A tear escaped her mom's eye, trailing mascara forlornly down her cheek.

Queen Adelaide *never* wept—at least, not where anyone could see. Even at the funeral she'd locked her emotions behind a pale, resolute stoicism. She'd always told Beatrice that a queen had to shed her tears in private, so that when it came time to face the nation, she could be a source of strength. The sight of that tear was as startling and surreal as if one of the marble statues in the palace gardens had begun to weep.

Beatrice hadn't been able to cry since her father's death, either.

She *wanted* to cry. She knew it was unnatural, yet something in her seemed to have irreparably fractured, and her eyes simply didn't form tears anymore.

Adelaide wrapped an arm around her daughter to pull her close. Beatrice instinctively tipped her head onto her mom's shoulder, the way she had as a child. Yet it didn't soothe her like it used to.

Suddenly, all she noticed was how frail her mom's bones felt beneath her cashmere sweater. Queen Adelaide was trembling with suppressed grief. She seemed fragile—and, for the first time Beatrice could remember, she seemed *old*.

It splintered what was left of Beatrice's resolve.

She tried, one last time, to imagine being with Connor: telling him that she still loved him, that she wanted to run away from her life and be with him, no matter the consequences. But she simply couldn't picture it. It was as if the future she'd daydreamed about had died with her father.

Or maybe it had died with the old Beatrice, the one who'd been a princess, not a queen.

"All right," she said quietly. "I'll talk to Teddy."

She could do this, for her family, for her country. She could marry Teddy and give America the fairy-tale romance it so desperately needed.

She could let go of Beatrice the girl, and give herself over to Beatrice the queen.

NINA

Nina Gonzalez tensed as she drew a wooden block from the increasingly precarious tower. Everyone at the table held their breath. With excruciating care, she placed the Jenga piece atop the makeshift structure.

Somehow, it held.

"*Yes!*" Nina lifted her hands, letting out a whoop of victory—just as a pair of blocks slid off the stack and clattered to the table. "Looks like I spoke too soon," she amended with a laugh.

Rachel Greenbaum, who lived down the hall from Nina, swept the fallen blocks toward her. "Look, you got FIND A HAT *and* CELL BLOCK TANGO!"

They were playing with King's College's famous "Party Jenga" set, covered in red Sharpie. It was the same as regular Jenga, except each block was inscribed with a different command—SHOTSKI, KARAOKE, BUTTERFINGERS—and everyone had to follow the rules of whatever blocks they knocked down. When Nina had asked how old the Jenga set was, no one knew.

It was the last weekend of spring break, and Nina's friends were hanging out in Ogden, the café and lounge area beneath the fine arts building. Because of its location, Ogden mostly attracted the theater kids, which had always surprised Nina, since it served cookies for *free*.

"FIND A HAT is easy. You just wear some object as if it's a hat," explained their other friend Leila Taghdisi. Nina obediently folded a paper napkin into a triangle before setting it on her head.

"And for CELL BLOCK TANGO, you have to leave your phone out for the rest of the game so we can all read your texts." Leila shot Nina an apologetic glance. Her friends knew how private Nina was about her personal life—and her relationship with the royal family.

But Nina had resolved that this semester she would be *normal*. So, like any normal college student, she pulled out her phone and set it on the table.

Rachel sighed. "I can't believe our first day of spring quarter is on Monday. I'm nowhere *near* ready for the start of classes."

"I don't know, I'm kind of glad to be back." Nina was actually excited about school again, now that she could walk around campus without being tailed by paparazzi. She still garnered a whisper here or there—still occasionally saw her fellow students looking at her for a beat too long, their brows furrowed in confusion, as if they thought they'd met her but couldn't remember where.

But it was a massive improvement over the nightmare she'd been living earlier this year, when she was dating Prince Jefferson.

People had remarkably short memories for this sort of thing. And after the earth-shattering, world-altering news of the king's death, Nina's brief relationship with Jeff was the last thing on anyone's mind. The world had clearly forgotten her and moved on, to Nina's immense relief.

"Not me. I never wanted to leave Virginia Beach," Leila chimed in. "If we were still there, we'd be out on the sand right now, watching the sunset and eating Nina's addictive guacamole."

"It's my mamá's recipe. The secret is in the garlic," Nina explained.

She was so grateful that Rachel had dragged her on that trip. It was nothing like the vacations Nina had gone on as a guest of the Washingtons: the rental house had been run-down, with no air-conditioning, and she'd had to sleep on a sofa in the living room. Yet she'd loved it. Sitting there with the other girls on her hall, drinking cheap beer and telling stories over a beach bonfire, had felt infinitely more satisfying than all the five-star royal travel.

"Sadly, I can't offer you guacamole." Jayne, another of their friends, emerged from the café's kitchen, balancing a tray in her oven mitts. "But these might help."

The three girls immediately tore into the cookies. "Have I mentioned how glad I am that you work here?" Nina asked.

"Instead of at the library with you?" Jayne and Nina were part of the same work-study program, which required them to get jobs on campus in exchange for the funding of their scholarships.

"Your baking talents would be wasted at the library. These are delicious," Nina replied through a mouthful of cookie. Her mamá would have scolded her for talking with her mouth full, but she wasn't at home right now—or at a stuffy royal reception, either.

Jayne set the cookies on the counter before pulling up a chair. She didn't bother taking off her school-issued apron, which was printed with the mascot of King's College: a knight in a shining silver helmet. "That's me, the gourmet chef of slice-and-bake."

Nina's phone, still at the center of the table, flashed with a new text. Rachel eagerly snatched at it, then slid the phone over. "So far, your texts are boring."

It was Nina's mom. *Are you coming over for dinner sometime soon? I'll make paella!*

Nina's parents, Julie and Isabella, lived in a redbrick townhome a few miles away. It was a grace-and-favor house: a property that belonged to the royal family and was leased rent-free to those who served them—in this case, Nina's mamá Isabella, who had once worked as the late king's chamberlain and was now Minister of the Treasury. Nina tried not to be bothered by the fact that Sam's family, *Jeff's* family, owned the house she'd grown up in.

In the aftermath of her breakup with Jeff, Nina had spent a lot of time at home. It was just so comforting, eating her parents' cooking and sleeping in her childhood bed. Avoiding the curious glances of her college classmates.

But she had more friends now, had carved out a place for herself. She no longer felt a desperate need to escape.

Thanks, Mom, but I'll stay on campus for now, she typed in reply. *Love you!*

Rachel crumbled the remains of her cookie over a napkin. "Next time we should sneak in a bottle of wine, make this a drinking game."

"You know I can't drink on the job," Jayne protested.

"You can't get *caught* drinking on the job. There's a difference," Rachel said cheekily, and everyone laughed.

They kept on playing, the Jenga tower growing increasingly, dangerously high. Rachel knocked over a tile labeled FOREIGN AUDITION, which apparently meant that for the rest of the game, she needed to speak in an accent. Undeterred, she launched into a story about a guy she'd recently met, her accent veering wildly between Eastern European and French.

Nina stretched her arms overhead. She felt tired, but in a lazy, contented way.

"Anyway, he just texted to ask me out," Rachel was saying.

"Accent!" Jayne scolded.

"My apologies," Rachel corrected, in the most atrocious

Cockney voice Nina had ever heard. "So, do you guys think I should say yes?"

She held out her phone, its plastic case covered in cartoon pineapples. The other girls obediently leaned forward to study the profile picture: an artsy black-and-white shot of a guy whose lip was pierced in at least six places.

"He seems pretty different from Logan," Nina ventured, naming Rachel's ex-boyfriend.

"Exactly!" Rachel had dropped the accent, but this time no one admonished her. "Different is what I'm *looking* for right now. You should know the feeling, after what happened with you and Jeff."

Nina stiffened, though some reluctant part of her acknowledged the truth in Rachel's words.

She'd met the royal twins over a decade ago, when her mamá began working as the king's chamberlain. She and Princess Samantha had been best friends ever since, as close as sisters.

Then, last year, Nina had started secretly dating Sam's brother. It had worked so well when it was just the two of them—but once the rest of the world found out, she'd become the target of nationwide abuse.

That was the thing about royalty: it was as polarizing as a magnet. For years Nina had watched people pass judgment on Sam without even knowing her, instantly deciding that they either hated or adored her, that they wanted nothing to do with her, or that they would use her for their own ends.

Once Nina dated Jeff, the same thing had happened to her.

She'd tried to ignore the ugly online comments and paparazzi's catcalls. She'd told herself that she could handle it all, that Jeff was worth it. Until his ex-girlfriend Daphne had confronted her, revealing that *she* had orchestrated the abuse: she'd planted a photographer outside Nina's dorm room and sold their relationship to the tabloids.

When Nina tried to talk to Jeff about it, he'd taken Daphne's side.

She'd seen him only once since the breakup, from across the room at his father's funeral. Then the Washingtons had left for Sulgrave, and Nina had finished out her winter quarter and gone to Virginia Beach, trying valiantly to wipe Jeff from her memory. Though it was pretty hard to forget your ex-boyfriend when he was your best friend's brother—and the most famous man in the country.

"I'm sorry, Nina," Rachel went on. "But we both need to branch out from that frat-boy crowd. Just think of all the types of guys we haven't even *begun* to explore! Musicians, upperclassmen . . ." She cast a pleading glance at the other girls, who hurried to chime in.

"Those cute TAs who bike here from the grad quad," Leila offered.

"Or artistic writer guys," Jayne exclaimed. "Like the ones you'll meet in your journalism class!"

"I'm not taking journalism so that I can meet guys," Nina reminded them.

"Of course not," Rachel said easily. "You're taking journalism so that *I* can meet guys."

Nina snorted. "Fine," she conceded. "I'll try to *branch out*, whatever that means."

"I'm just saying you should put yourself back out there, go to a party with us every now and then. Come on, Nina," Rachel pleaded. "Your new look is too good to be wasted on the library."

Nina brushed her fingers through the ends of her newly short hair, which now fell to just above her shoulders. Her head felt curiously light without the weight of all those tresses. She'd done it on impulse after the breakup: she had needed, desperately, to change something, and this was as drastic a change as she could make short of getting another tattoo.

Now when Nina looked in the mirror, she found a new and startling version of herself. The bones of her face had become more prominent, her brown eyes gleaming brighter than before. She looked older, stronger.

The Nina who'd spent years pining after Jefferson—who'd contorted herself into someone she didn't recognize, hoping to win acceptance as his girlfriend—was gone. And this new, fiercer Nina knew better than to get her heart broken by anyone. Even a prince.

When her phone buzzed with an incoming call, Nina assumed it was one of her parents, until she looked over and saw Samantha's name. She pulled it quickly into her lap.

Rachel's eyes cut toward her. "Everything okay?"

"Sorry, I need to take this." Nina rose to her feet, shrugging into her denim jacket, and headed out the double doors of the café.

"Sam. How are you?" She immediately winced at the question. Of course Sam wasn't doing well; she was *grieving*.

"Tired. I'm ready to be home." The princess's tone was normal—brave, even—but Nina knew her well enough to hear the emotion behind it. Sam wasn't nearly as tough as she pretended to be.

"When do you get back?" Nina asked, tucking her phone into her shoulder.

"Actually, we're on the road now."

Nina hated how her mind fixed on that *we*. She imagined Jeff sitting next to his twin sister, hearing Sam's half of the conversation.

"Jeff is here, but he's asleep," Sam added, guessing her friend's thoughts. "With headphones on."

"I—right. Okay."

It hurt to think of Jeff: a dull, lingering sort of pain, as if Nina were pressing on a bruise that hadn't yet healed. Things between them had ended so abruptly. One minute they'd been in the palace ballroom, twined in each other's arms, and then later that night their relationship was just . . . *over*.

Part of Nina wanted to hate him—for allowing Daphne to push them apart, for letting their relationship crumble instead of fighting for it. But she couldn't stay that angry with a boy who'd just lost his father. She wished she felt brave enough to ask Sam how Jeff was doing, except she didn't trust herself to say his name.

There was a rustling on the other end. "Come on, Nina, tell me everything. What's happened with you since—" Sam broke off before saying *since my dad died*. "Since I've seen you," she amended.

They both knew that this wasn't the normal dynamic of their relationship. Normally Sam was the one who kept talking: debating and theorizing and telling stories in her winding, roundabout way, which was always more satisfying than if she'd told them start to finish. But today, Sam needed Nina to be the one who filled the silence.

Nina's heart ached. When someone was hurting like this, there was nothing you could say to make it better. The only thing you could do was hurt alongside them.

Still, she cleared her throat and attempted an upbeat tone. "Did I tell you I chopped off my hair?"

Sam gasped. "How many inches?"

"I'll send you a picture," Nina assured her. "And I just got back from a spring break trip with some friends from my dorm. You would have loved it, Sam. We rowed kayaks down the coast, and found this tiki bar that served half-price frozen drinks . . ."

She sank onto a bench as she talked. Various students passed, heading to their dorm rooms or to meet friends for ice cream at the Broken Spoon.

"Nina," Sam finally asked, with uncharacteristic hesitation, "I was wondering . . . would you come to the Royal Potomac Races with me tomorrow?"

Nina went very still, her heart thudding. Hearing that silence, and knowing exactly what it meant, Sam hurried to explain. "I understand if you can't be around Jeff. It's just my first public appearance since—" She broke off, then forged ahead. "Since my dad's funeral, and it would mean a lot to have you there."

How could Nina possibly say no to a request like that?

"Of course I'll be there," she promised.

And just like that, she thought with weary resignation, she was headed back into her best friend's world—the world of the American royals—all over again.

DAPHNE

Daphne Deighton had never really liked the Royal Potomac Races. They were just so *loud*, so unapologetically common. Really, what else could you expect from a free public event?

Thousands of people had gathered along the Potomac, transforming its riverbanks into a brightly colored fairground. Families picnicked on beach towels; girls in sunglasses posed for pictures that they hurried to post online. Long queues had formed behind the scattered bars that sold mint juleps. The bars inevitably ran out of ice after the first few hours, yet people kept on lining up to purchase warm bourbon with a few sodden pieces of mint.

Thankfully, Daphne never ventured to those sections of the river. There was another side to the Royal Potomac Races, one that still enforced a sense of hierarchy, of exclusivity. After all, the truly important people weren't about to watch the races from a dirty picnic blanket.

Near the colorful pennants of the finish line, behind ropes and stiff-lipped security, lay the massive white tents of the private enclosures—capped at the very end by the Royal Enclosure itself, open only to the Washington family and their invited guests.

Unlike the other tents, where low-ranking aristocrats and businesspeople strode around in plastic name tags, no one in the Royal Enclosure wore a *badge*. It was tacitly assumed that if you were here, you must be someone worth knowing.

And Daphne knew them all. She could trace the tortuous maze of the Washington family's relationships, which tangled over the entire globe. She doubted anyone else could tell Crown Princess Elizabeth of the Netherlands (the king's cousin) from Lady Elizabeth of Hesse (an aunt on his mother's side) from Elizabeth the Grand Duchess of Romania (surprisingly, no relation).

That was the difference between Daphne and all the other beautiful girls who'd set their sights on Prince Jefferson over the years. In Daphne's experience, most beautiful girls tried to skate through life relying on nothing but their looks. They lacked brains, or hustle—while Daphne had more than enough of both.

A volley of trumpets sounded, and everyone in the crowd glanced expectantly downriver, to where the pennants of the royal barge snapped against the sky.

Sunlight sparkled on the Potomac, setting its pewter waters afire. Daphne's eyes automatically zeroed in on Jefferson, who stood next to his twin sister, one hand lifted halfheartedly, though he wasn't quite waving. The wind stirred his sleeves, ruffled his dark hair. At the front of the boat, a fragile smile on her face, was Beatrice.

The riverbanks erupted in applause and whistles. People shouted at Beatrice, or, just as often, at Jefferson. Parents hoisted children onto their shoulders so they could catch a glimpse of the new queen.

A song began to play over the loudspeakers, and the cheers quickly died out. For a moment all Daphne heard were the opening notes of the music, above the hiss of wind and the steady rumbling of the barge's motor. Then thousands of voices wove together as everyone began to sing.

From shore to shore, from sea to sea
Let our beloved nation ring
With cries of love and loyalty
Our hearts we pledge to you, our queen

Until now, the lyrics had always ended in *our king*; the rhyme of *ring* and *queen* didn't work quite as well.

The barge pulled up to the dock, and the Lord Chamberlain stepped forward to help the royal family disembark. All the courtiers on the lawn quickly fell into bows or curtsies. In their pastel dresses and seersucker suits, they looked like an indolent flock of butterflies.

Daphne didn't rush. She sank down as gracefully as a flower drooping, and held the pose for a long, slow moment. She'd taken ballet as a child, and at times like this she was every inch a dancer.

When she finally stood, Daphne skimmed her hands over the front of her dress, which followed the enclosure's strict rules and hit at precisely knee-length. It fell around her legs like peach sorbet. Atop her glorious red-gold hair she'd pinned a custom-made fascinator, the same delicate shade as her gown. It was so nice to wear color again, after all the weeks she'd spent dressing somberly, observing the official mourning period for the late king.

Though, to be fair, Daphne also looked striking in black. She looked striking in everything.

She made her way to where Jefferson stood, atop the grassy embankment that sloped liltingly to the river. When he saw her, the prince nodded in greeting. "Hey, Daphne. Thanks for coming."

She wanted to say *I've missed you*, but it felt too flirtatious, too self-centered, after everything Jefferson had been through. "It's good to see you," she decided.

He stuffed his hands into his pockets. "It feels a little weird to be here, you know?"

Daphne didn't feel weird at all. If anything, she felt that she and Jefferson were back where they were meant to be: with each other. After all, their lives had been intertwined since Daphne was fourteen.

That was when she'd decided that she would marry him, and become a princess.

For over two years everything had gone according to Daphne's plan. She'd thrown herself in Jefferson's path, and soon enough they were dating. He adored her, and, just as crucially, America adored her—because Daphne had won them over, with her gracious smiles and her soft words and her beauty.

Until Jefferson had abruptly ended things, the morning after his graduation party.

Another girl might have accepted the breakup and moved on. But Daphne wouldn't admit defeat. She *couldn't*, not after the lengths she'd gone to for that relationship.

Now, thankfully, the prince was single again. Though he wouldn't be for long, if Daphne had anything to say about it.

Didn't Jefferson see how easy things would be if he followed her plan and asked her out again? They could attend King's College together this fall—he'd taken a gap year, which meant he would enter with Daphne's class—and then after they graduated he would propose, and they would get married in the palace.

And finally, at long last, Daphne would be the princess she'd been born to be.

"I'm so sorry about your father. I can only imagine what you're going through." She reached for his arm in a silent gesture of support. "I'm here if you want to talk."

Jefferson nodded absently, and Daphne lowered her hand.

"Sorry, I just . . . there are some people I need to say hi to," he mumbled.

"Of course." She forced herself to remain still, her expression placid and unconcerned, as the Prince of America walked away from her.

Bracing herself for endless small talk, Daphne bit back a sigh and began to circulate through the crowds. She caught sight of her mother across the lawn, chatting with the owner of a department store chain. How typical. Rebecca Deighton was nothing if not an instinctive judge of people she could use.

Daphne knew she should go over there, flash her perfect smile, and charm yet another person into being on Team Daphne. She glanced back at Jefferson—and froze.

He was talking to Nina.

It was impossible to hear them over the low roar of the party, but that didn't matter; she could see the pained, pleading look in the prince's eyes. Was he asking Nina to forgive him for the way he'd treated her . . . or for a second chance?

What if Nina decided to give him one?

Daphne tore her gaze away before anyone caught her staring. She strode blindly into the cool shade of the tent, past delicate tables topped with pyramids of flowers, all the way to the ladies' room at the back.

She braced her hands on either side of the sink, forcing herself to take slow, shaky breaths. She was curiously unsurprised when, moments later, a pair of footsteps sounded behind her.

"Hello, Mother," she said heavily.

Daphne watched as Rebecca prowled through the restroom, making sure the row of stalls was completely empty before she turned back to her daughter. "Well?" Rebecca snapped. "He's talking to *that girl* again. How could you let that happen?"

"I was with him, but—"

"Do you realize how much it cost to *be* here this afternoon?" her mother cut in. At times like this, when she got upset, the old Nebraska twang slipped back into her voice. As if she'd forgotten that she was Rebecca Deighton, Lady Margrave, and had slipped back into her old persona—Becky Sharpe, lingerie model.

Daphne knew her parents had gained access to the Royal Enclosure the tacky way, by underwriting the regatta itself. And while the higher-ranking, wealthier aristocrats probably hadn't flinched at the amount, the Deightons felt every penny they spent. Acutely.

"I'm aware how much it cost," Daphne said quietly, and she wasn't just talking about the check her family had written. Not even her parents knew everything Daphne had done in her attempts to win Jefferson—and to keep him.

For a moment the two women just stared at each other in the mirror. There was a guarded wariness to their expressions that made them look more like enemies than mother and daughter.

Daphne could almost hear the gears of her mother's mind turning. Rebecca was never hampered by obstacles for long; she didn't think about what was, but what *could* be. Everyone else lived in reality, but Rebecca Deighton occupied a shifting shadow-world of infinite possibility.

"You'll have to get rid of her," her mother concluded, and Daphne nodded reluctantly.

Nina had loved Jefferson, *really* loved him, and that made her a more dangerous opponent than any of the aristocratic girls at court, with their sterile, cookie-cutter beauty. Daphne could outwit and outshine those girls any day. But someone who genuinely didn't care about Jefferson's position—who, in fact, loved him in spite of it—that was a real threat.

"I know you'll think of something." Her mother turned on one heel so fast that her skirts fluttered around her.

As the bathroom door clattered, Daphne began fumbling through her leather clutch. Her hands shaking only a little, she quickly dabbed concealer beneath her eyes and touched up her waterproof mascara. She felt like an Amazonian warrior, arming herself before battle.

When she was done, she stared into the mirror—at her high arched brows, her full lips, the vivid green of her thick-lashed eyes—and let out a breath. The sight of her reflection always calmed her.

She was Daphne Deighton, and she had to keep moving relentlessly, ruthlessly, constantly forward—no matter what, or who, stood in her way.

SAMANTHA

It was hard for Princess Samantha to enjoy the Royal Potomac Races this year.

Usually she loved them. Not for the reason some people did, because they were a chance to see and be seen: the first event of the spring social calendar, marking the return of galas and parties after a winter of hibernation. No, Sam had always enjoyed the races for their energy. They were so brash, so utterly *American*, with an infectious, carnivalesque sense of excitement.

But this year the colors felt dull, as if her senses were muted under a thick blanket. Even the band sounded strangely out of tune. Or maybe *she* was the one out of tune.

Everywhere she looked, all she saw was the achingly conspicuous space where her father should have been.

Sam remembered how once, when she was little, she'd told her dad that she wanted to grow up and be as strong as the rowers. "But you *are* strong," he'd replied.

"As strong as what?" Sam had never understood why people used adjectives without defined parameters. "Strong as a lion? Stronger than Jeff?"

King George had laughed, leaning down to drop a kiss on the top of her head. "You are as strong as you need to be. And I am prouder of you than you'll ever know."

Sam blinked rapidly at the memory, wrapping her arms

around herself despite the afternoon sun. Then she saw a familiar blond head across the crowds, and her breath caught.

He was as gorgeous as ever in a linen jacket the same shocking blue as his eyes. A matching pocket square, monogrammed with his initials, completed the look. Sam would have teased him for the absurd preppiness of it, if every cell of her body weren't aching at his nearness.

She'd never meant to fall for her sister's fiancé. When she'd met Teddy Eaton, the chemistry between them had been instant and electric. Neither of them had known that he was intended for Beatrice. Sam had tried, after that, to stay away from him . . . but by that point it was too late.

When Teddy saw her heading toward him, an instant of surprise, or maybe even pain, flickered over his features, but he quickly smoothed it over with a smile—the same way Beatrice always did. Sam shivered a little at the thought.

She hadn't heard much from Teddy this past month, but she'd assumed he was keeping his distance out of respect for her grief—that when they saw each other again, everything would fall back into place. Now she couldn't help fearing that his silence meant something else.

"It's so good to see you," she breathed, once she'd finally reached his side. Her voice was hoarse with longing. This was the closest they'd been since her father's funeral.

"Samantha."

At his distant, formal tone, her smile faltered. "What is it?"

"I thought—I mean, I wasn't sure . . ." Teddy studied her face for a long moment; then his shoulders sagged. "Beatrice hasn't told you?"

Dread pooled in her stomach. "Told me what?"

He ran a hand helplessly through his hair; it fell back in the same perfect waves as ever. "Can we go somewhere alone, just the two of us? We need to talk."

At the mention of going somewhere alone, Sam's heart

had lifted, only to seize in fear when she heard *we need to talk.* The four most ominous words in the English language.

"I . . . all right." Sam shot Teddy an anxious glance as she led him around the corner, into a narrow passageway between the Royal Enclosure and Briony, the next tent over. There was no one in sight, just a few humming generators that fed air-conditioning into the tent through fat cords.

"What's going on?" Sam dug her heel anxiously into the mud.

Teddy's expression was shadowed with remorse. "I'm kind of glad the queen didn't tell you. I guess . . . it's best you hear this from me."

Sam felt her muscles quietly tensing, her body caving inward as if readying for a blow.

"We're getting married in June."

"*No,*" she said automatically. It couldn't be. The night of her engagement party, Beatrice had pulled Sam out onto the terrace and confessed that she was calling off the whole thing. She was going to talk about it with their dad, come up with a plan for telling the press.

Except they'd lost him before Beatrice had time to do any of that. And now that she was queen, Beatrice clearly felt obligated to go through with this ill-advised engagement.

"So it meant nothing, when you said that we were in this together? Teddy, you *promised!*" And so had Beatrice.

Sam should have known better than to hold her sister to her word.

Teddy's fists clenched helplessly at his sides, but when he spoke, his voice was oddly formal. "I'm sorry, Samantha. But the queen and I have agreed."

"Stop calling her *the queen!* She has a name!"

He winced. "I owe you an apology. The way I've handled all of this . . . it hasn't been fair to Beatrice, and especially not to you."

There was something so stubbornly honorable about his confession that Sam couldn't help thinking how right she'd been when she'd told Beatrice—in a fit of pique—that she and Teddy deserved each other.

"It's not fair to you, either!" Sam cried out. "Why are you *doing* this?"

He looked down, fiddling with a button on his blazer. "A lot of people are counting on me."

Sam remembered what he'd said in Telluride, which felt like a lifetime ago: that the Eatons' fortune had evaporated overnight. Marrying Beatrice, gaining the support of the Crown, would save his duchy from financial ruin. Because it wasn't just about Teddy's family: the Eatons had supported the Boston area—had been its source of financial stability, its largest employer—for over two hundred years.

Teddy, who'd been raised as the future duke, felt obligated to take that responsibility onto his shoulders.

"You shouldn't get married because you think you *owe* it to the people of Boston," Sam said heatedly.

Teddy looked up to meet her gaze. His eyes were more piercingly blue than normal, as if confusion, or perhaps regret, had deepened their color. "I promise you that I'm not doing this lightly. I have my reasons, and I'm sure your sister does, too."

"If she really has to rush down the aisle, tell her to pick someone else! There are millions of guys in America. Can't she marry one of *them*?"

Teddy shook his head. "You know it doesn't work like that. Beatrice can't go and propose to someone else. It would make her seem fickle and capricious."

The truth of it hit Sam like a sickening blow. Teddy was right. If Beatrice broke off her very public engagement and began dating another guy, it would just fuel the attacks of all those people who were already cheering for her to fail.

America would start to wonder: If Beatrice couldn't even make up her mind about her personal life, how on earth would she make decisions about the country?

"You can't seriously be going through with this," she insisted.

"I know you don't understand—"

"Why, because I'm just the *spare*?"

At some point Sam had taken a step forward, closing the distance between them, so they were now standing mere inches apart, their breathing ragged.

"That's not what I meant," Teddy said gently, and the red-hot anger pounding through her veins quieted a little.

"You're really doing it," she whispered. "You're choosing Beatrice." The way everyone always did.

"I'm choosing to do the right thing." Teddy met her gaze, silently pleading with her for understanding, for forgiveness.

He wasn't about to get either. Not from her.

"Well then. I hope the right thing makes you happy," she said caustically.

"Sam—"

"You and Beatrice are making a huge mistake. But you know what? I don't care. It's not my problem anymore," she added, in such a cruel tone that she almost believed her own words. "If you two want to ruin your lives, I can't do anything to stop you."

Pain flickered over Teddy's face. "For what it's worth, I really am sorry."

"It's worth *nothing*." She didn't want Teddy's apologies; she wanted *him*. And like everything else she'd ever wanted, she couldn't have him, because Beatrice had laid claim to him first.

She whirled around and stalked back toward the party, grabbing a mint julep from a passing tray. At least now that she was eighteen, she could legally drink at these events instead of sneaking away from the photographers to chug a beer.

Sam squinted, scanning the crowds in search of Nina or Jeff. The sun felt suddenly overbright, or maybe it just seemed that way through the haze of her tears. For once, she wished she'd done as her mom asked and worn a hat, if only to hide her face. Everything had begun spinning wildly around her.

Hardly knowing where she was going, she wandered down to the riverbank, where she sank onto the ground and kicked off her shoes.

She didn't care that she was getting grass stains all over her couture dress, that people would see her there, alone and barefoot, and gossip. *The party princess is back,* they would mutter, *already drunk, at her first public outing since her father's death.* Fine, she thought bitterly. Let them talk.

The water lapped softly among the reeds. Sam kept her eyes fixed furiously on its surface so she wouldn't have to see Teddy and Beatrice together. But it didn't stop her from feeling like a stray puzzle piece that had gotten lost in the wrong box—like she didn't fit anywhere, or with anyone.

"Here you are," Nina said, coming to sit next to Sam.

For a while the two of them just watched the boats in silence. Their oars were a blur of water and fractured light.

"Sorry," Sam mumbled. "I just . . . I needed to get away."

Nina pulled her legs up, playing with the fabric of her long jersey dress. "I know the feeling. I actually just talked to Jeff."

Sam sucked in a breath, glad to be distracted from her own problems. "How did it go?" she asked, and Nina shrugged.

"It was awkward."

Sam glanced over, but Nina plucked a blade of grass and began to tie it into a bow, avoiding her gaze. Maybe she'd noticed that Daphne Deighton was here, too.

"He probably wants to try and be friends," Sam ventured.

"I don't know *how* to be friends!" Nina reached up to fiddle with her ponytail, then seemed to remember her hair was shorter now. Her hand fell uselessly to her side. "I'll obviously keep running into him, since he's your brother, but I can't pretend that nothing ever happened between us. It's not normal to have to keep seeing someone after you've broken up with them! Is it?"

"I don't know." Sam had never really been through a normal breakup, because she'd never had anything resembling a normal relationship. She let out a breath. "But I guess I'm about to find out. I just saw Teddy."

Her voice raw, Sam explained what he'd told her: that he and Beatrice were going through with the wedding.

"Oh, Sam," Nina said softly when Sam had finished. "I'm so sorry."

Sam nodded and tipped her head onto Nina's shoulder. No matter what happened, she thought, she would always be able to do this—to close her eyes and lean on her best friend.

BEATRICE

When Beatrice stepped into her father's office, she saw that nothing had been touched since he died.

All his things were in their usual places on his desk: his monogrammed stationery; a ceremonial gold fountain pen; the Great Seal and its wax melter, which resembled a hot glue gun but emitted liquid red wax instead. It looked for all the world like her dad had just stepped out and might return again at any moment.

If only that were true.

Beatrice had thought she was used to being the focal point of everyone's attention. But she hadn't realized how much worse it would get once she became queen. It wasn't fair that she'd been granted just six weeks to process the loss of her dad, only to be shoved back into the national spotlight. But what choice did she have? The mourning period was officially over, the endless carousel of court functions swinging back into motion. Already Beatrice's schedule was packed with events: benefits, charity appearances, even an upcoming gala at the museum.

And she wasn't ready. Yesterday at the races, when the national anthem had played, she'd automatically opened her mouth to join in, only to remember belatedly that she couldn't sing it anymore. Not when the song was directed at *her*.

Her position always left her feeling this way—that she was most alone when she was most surrounded by people.

At the creaking sound of footsteps, her head shot up.

"Sorry." Connor winced as the floor once again groaned beneath his feet. That was the thing about living in a palace; two-hundred-year-old floorboards did not keep secrets.

He closed the door and leaned against it. "I just . . . I wanted to check on you."

Guilt twisted in Beatrice's stomach. She'd been avoiding Connor—or at least, avoided being *alone* with him, since he was always nearby: hovering in the wings of her life while she occupied center stage.

He still didn't know that she and Teddy were really getting married. She needed to tell him, and soon; the palace was planning to announce the wedding date later this week. But every time she started to bring it up, she found herself dodging the subject like an utter coward.

"I'm just tired," she murmured, which was true: she still wasn't getting much sleep.

"Don't do that. You don't need to be strong with me, remember?" Connor crossed the distance between them and gathered her into his arms, pulling her close.

For a moment Beatrice let herself relax into the embrace. Somehow she always forgot how much taller he was until they stood like this, her face nestled into the hollow at the center of his chest.

"I'm here for whatever you need," Connor said into her hair. "You don't have to be the queen around me, you know. You can just be *you*."

"I know." It was easy for Beatrice to be herself around him, and maybe that was the problem. Maybe with Connor she was too *much* of herself, and not enough of a queen.

She twisted out of his embrace, her eyes lifting to meet his. "Connor—there's something I need to tell you."

He nodded, clearly alerted by her change in tone. "All right."

The entire world seemed to fall still. Beatrice was suddenly aware of every detail—the feel of her silk blouse over her collarbones, the dust motes slanting in the hard afternoon light, the devotion in Connor's eyes.

He wouldn't look at her like that again, not once he found out what she'd agreed to. Beatrice took a deep breath, and let the truth fall painfully into the silence.

"Teddy and I are getting married in June."

"You—*what?*"

"The engagement isn't just for show. It's . . . we're really going through with it."

Connor recoiled. "I don't understand. The night of the engagement party, you two agreed that you would call off the wedding as soon as it was appropriate. What happened?"

My father died, and it's all my fault.

"I'm queen now, Connor." The words seemed to strangle Beatrice as they floated up out of her lungs. "It changes things."

"Exactly! Now *you* can change things, for the better!"

Hearing that excitement, his belief in her, nearly undid her. "It's not that simple. Just because I'm queen doesn't mean that I can rewrite the rules." If anything, she was more bound by the rules than ever before.

Connor caught her hands in his. "I love you, and I know that we can figure this out. Unless . . . unless your feelings have changed."

Tears stung Beatrice's eyes. "You want me to say it? Fine, I'll say it! I *love* you!" she burst out, so viciously that she might have just as easily been saying *I hate you*. "But that isn't *enough*, Connor!"

"Of course it's enough!"

He spoke with such conviction, as if the truth of his

words was self-evident. As if loving her was as simple and uncomplicated as the fact that the sun rose in the east and set in the west.

But their relationship had never been simple. From the very beginning they'd been sneaking around, living on scattered moments together: the secret brush of Connor's hand over her back as she slid into a car, their eyes meeting in a crowded room and lingering a beat too long. The late nights when he slipped into her bedroom, only to leave before dawn.

Even now, no one knew about them except Samantha, and Sam had no idea who Connor *was*, only that Beatrice loved someone who wasn't Teddy.

For months, Beatrice had told herself that those stolen moments added up to something worth protecting. But she knew now that they weren't enough.

She thought with a dull pang of what her father had said the night she told him that she loved her Guard. That if she pulled Connor into this royal life, he would eventually come to hate her for it—and, worse, he would come to hate himself.

There was a cold wind coming off the river; Beatrice had to stop herself from going to shut the window. "This obviously wasn't an easy decision. But it's what's best. For both of us."

"Why are *you* the one deciding what's best for both of us?" Connor said roughly. "When you're making choices about our future, I want a damn vote!"

Before she could answer, he grabbed her by the shoulders and kissed her.

There was nothing gentle or tender in the kiss. Connor's body was crushed up against hers, his hands grasped hard over her back, as if he was terrified she might pull away. Beatrice rose on tiptoe, digging her fingers into his uniform.

When they finally pulled apart, they were both breathing heavily. Beatrice's hair fell in damp wisps around her face. She looked up and saw the quiet anguish in Connor's eyes. He knew her well enough to know that she didn't normally kiss like that—with such wild, desperate abandon.

He understood that she'd been kissing him goodbye.

"You really mean this, don't you," he breathed.

"I do," Beatrice told him. It struck her that those were the words of the wedding service, words that normally swore eternal love. And here she was, using them to tell Connor that he should leave her forever.

His jaw was tight, but he managed a nod. Beatrice almost wished that he would shout, call her cruel names. Anger would have been so much easier to bear. *Anything* would have been easier than this: the knowledge that Connor was in pain, and she had caused it.

"In that case, Your Majesty, please accept my resignation. I'll be leaving your service. And this time, I won't be coming back."

He paused as if waiting for her to protest, to beg him to stay, the way she had once before.

Beatrice said nothing. She couldn't ask Connor to remain here as her Guard while she married Teddy.

If she asked it of him, he might say yes. And he deserved so much more than that.

"I understand." To her surprise, she spoke as if nothing was wrong, even though she hurt so much—deep inside her, in the hollow, lonely place she never let anyone see.

Connor's gaze met hers, as cool as a mountain lake under gray skies. "I'll go inform the head of security."

Beatrice felt cold all over, yet she was sweating as if she'd come down with a fever. She watched, curiously immobile, as Connor turned back to cast one last glance over his shoulder.

"Goodbye, Bee."

When he was gone, Beatrice made her way numbly around her father's desk. She still wasn't crying. She felt like a frost had settled over all her emotions and she would never feel anything again.

She paused behind her father's chair, her hands resting lightly on its back. She'd never sat in it before, not even when she and the twins used to sneak in here as kids, to steal lemon candies from the secret drawer and spin the enormous globe. For some unspoken reason, sitting at the king's desk had felt as utterly off-limits, as sacrilegious, as climbing onto his throne.

Slowly, Beatrice pulled out the chair and sat.

DAPHNE

"Mademoiselle Deighton." The French ambassador sailed forward to greet her with an easy double kiss, one for each cheek. He was handsome, and a shameless flirt; the French never sent anyone who wasn't.

"*Bonsoir*, Monsieur l'Ambassadeur." She flashed him a brilliant smile, grateful for all her years of high school French.

It felt like half of court had turned out for tonight's event at the George and Alice Museum, or the G&A, as everyone called it. In celebration of Beatrice and Teddy's engagement, the museum was opening a new exhibit titled ROYAL WEDDINGS THROUGH THE AGES.

Daphne's eyes cut across the room to where Jefferson stood with Samantha. He still hadn't said hello. Aside from their brief exchange at the Royal Potomac Races, Daphne hadn't really spoken to him since that day at the hospital—when she sat there with Jefferson, waiting for good news that had never come.

The prince was grieving, Daphne reminded herself: he needed his space. Yet she couldn't help worrying. What if he was no longer interested in her? Or, worse, what if he was getting back together with *Nina*?

Unlike Daphne, Nina could show up at the palace whenever she wanted, ostensibly to see her best friend. But who could say whether all those visits were to see Samantha . . . or her brother?

Daphne redoubled her efforts in the direction of the French ambassador: smiling her perfect smile, laughing her brightest laugh, being the most intoxicating, glittering version of herself.

Delighted, the ambassador introduced her to several of his colleagues. Daphne heard the click of a photographer's camera to her left. She sucked in her stomach but pretended she didn't notice, because she didn't want the moment to look staged.

When people all over the capital opened the society pages tomorrow, this was the image they would see—the prince's ex-girlfriend charming government officials with ease, just as a princess should.

Sometimes Daphne felt that only at moments like this, when she was somewhere public, did she truly exist. That she wasn't real unless someone else's eyes were on her, unless she was being *seen*.

Eventually she murmured her excuses and headed toward the bar. Her dress, a silk chiffon that shifted from burnished bronze at her shoulders to soft gold at the hem, billowed out behind her as she walked.

Daphne ordered a soda water with lime, then deliberately arched her back and leaned her forearms onto the bar's surface, turning to her most flattering three-quarter angle. She looked as if she didn't have a care in the world, as if she were completely unaware of the party and its hundreds of influential guests.

It was an old party trick of hers, from when she'd first started attending royal events. She would make sure everyone noticed her, then deftly extricate herself from the group, making it easy for Jefferson to come find her alone. It worked every time.

The prince inevitably wanted what everyone *else* wanted. That was just human nature, and it was especially true for royalty.

At the sound of footsteps behind her, Daphne allowed herself a small, triumphant smile. He'd come faster than she'd expected.

Slowly, sensually, she turned around—only to realize that Jefferson hadn't come to find her. It was his best friend, Ethan Beckett.

Daphne quickly blinked away her confusion. She hadn't been this close to Ethan since the night of Beatrice's engagement party.

Or really, the morning after.

"Hey, Ethan," she said, as normally as she could manage.

He leaned against the bar next to her. The cuffs of his blazer were folded back, revealing his strong, tanned wrists. "You seem to be having quite the night."

There was something sardonic in his tone, as if he knew precisely what lay behind her wild display of charm, and was amused by it.

Daphne flicked a glance back at the dance floor, but she'd lost sight of Jefferson in the crowds. Where had he gone, and *who* was he with?

She felt Ethan's gaze on her and glanced back up. An idea began to take hold in Daphne's mind, stubborn and burrlike: an idea so simple that it was either brilliant, or deeply foolish.

"Ethan," she asked sweetly, "can we talk?"

"Am I mistaken, or isn't that what we're doing now?"

"I meant alone."

Ethan stared at her for a moment, then held out an arm in a careless display of chivalry. "Sure."

"Thank you." She had no choice but to place her hand over his sleeve. And there it was again, the way her whole body sparked to alertness at his touch.

Daphne realized that even though she'd *slept* with Ethan—twice—they had never actually held hands. Her fingers itched to lace themselves in his, just to see what it felt like.

She let go of Ethan's arm as if it were burning.

"This way." Daphne started toward the archway that led out into the rest of the museum. Ethan gave a resigned sigh but followed.

Long ago the G&A had been a train station, until the new, longer trains that ran on electricity had rendered its platforms obsolete. It was King Edward II who'd decommissioned the entire thing, turning it into an art museum instead, and naming it after his grandparents. Out here in the main causeway, you could still see traces of the old rail station: the grand curves of the mezzanine where travelers once sat gossiping over their morning espressos, the brick entrances to the train platforms, which now led guests to impressionist paintings. The ceiling soared overhead, its iron supports swooping up in a series of elegant arches.

Daphne didn't break stride until they were halfway down the hallway. Finally she paused at a statue of a man on horseback—a Roman emperor, probably, or one of the Washington kings. Whoever he was, his horse had reared up onto its hind legs, as if the man meant to trample anyone who stood in his way.

Daphne knew the feeling.

She glanced in all directions, making sure they were alone, before she ventured a smile in Ethan's direction. "Sorry to drag you away from the party, but I was hoping to ask a favor."

His brows shot upward. "Really? You're coming to *me*, after—"

"I don't like it either," she interrupted, before he could say it out loud. "I just . . . I don't have anyone else."

Ethan crossed his arms warily. "What do you want, Daphne?"

"I need you to keep Nina Gonzalez as far from Jefferson as possible."

She saw him tense at her words and hurried to elaborate. "It shouldn't be difficult; you both live on the same campus. Can't you help me get her out of the picture?"

Ethan paled. "You can't seriously mean—after Himari—"

"I'm not saying you should *hurt* her!" Daphne hissed. She hated what she'd done to Himari Mariko: her best friend, who'd been in a coma since last June. "I just want you to spend a little more time with her," Daphne explained. "Keep tabs on what she's up to."

Ethan's voice was flat. "I see. You're asking me to sideline Nina while you try to get Jeff back."

Daphne nodded. "She's Samantha's best friend; she's going to keep showing up at royal events. I need you to distract her."

She'd forgotten what a relief it was, talking with Ethan. There was no one else with whom she could speak such blunt, unadorned truths. Being with him felt like taking off her shoes after a long and painful night of standing.

"I'm curious," Ethan said sarcastically. "When you came up with this plan, how exactly did you think I was going to *distract* Nina?"

Daphne bristled at his tone. "Invite her to some parties, join her study group, *flirt* with her for all I care. The important thing is that she stays far from the palace, okay?"

Ethan's eyes flashed. "Shocking, I know, but I doubt Nina would be interested in me."

"Then *make* her interested! Come on, it should be easy. Don't you remember what Nina was like on vacation? All she ever did was *read*. I'm sure she'd respond to some big romantic gesture." Daphne paused, trying to remember everything she knew about Samantha's best friend. "She's always dreamed of visiting Venice. She collects M&M's from foreign countries. She works in a *library*, for god's sake."

Daphne took a step closer, close enough that she could have kissed Ethan in half a heartbeat. He stiffened as she rose on tiptoe to whisper in his ear.

"Unless, of course, you think it's too much of a challenge."

He drew back, shaking his head. "Sorry, you can't bait me into this one."

Heat flooded her face, but before she could argue, he'd caught her hands in his.

"Forget Nina. Forget *Jeff*," he said roughly. "Daphne—you and I have been running these circles around each other for years. Aren't you ready to quit pretending?"

"I'm not pretending anything." The words came out in a whisper.

"Let's do this, you and me. For real this time." And with that, he leaned down to kiss her.

Daphne had known, when she'd dragged Ethan out into the hallway, that something might happen between them. But she hadn't bargained on this—this eager, treacherous rush of feeling that made her press her body forward, her arms darting up to circle his neck. She felt like she'd been on a torturous low simmer for months, and now she was finally alive again.

Some dazed part of her mind imagined saying yes. Giving up on Jefferson, giving in to this gravitational pull between her and Ethan. That world seemed to momentarily exist, as insubstantial and iridescent as a soap bubble, before it vanished.

Daphne tore herself away and stumbled back, adjusting the straps of her dress. There was a long, weighted silence.

"Daphne," Ethan said at last. "I can't wait for you forever."

"I never asked you to wait for me," she snapped.

Something like hurt flickered over his face, but it quickly disappeared, replaced by his usual indifference.

"Right. Instead you asked me to *spy* on Nina, so you could start dating my best friend again." Ethan turned away. "This time, you'll have to find someone else to do your dirty work."

"I'll make it worth your while!"

Daphne had cried out without thinking, out of desperation. She saw Ethan freeze, then glance warily over his shoulder at her. "What do you mean?"

"I can give you something," she said recklessly. "Money, or favorable coverage in the press, or . . ."

Ethan stared at her for a long moment, so boldly that Daphne felt herself squirm beneath his gaze. The sounds of the party felt impossibly distant.

"I'll need a title," he decided. "Someday, when you're a princess, you'll make it happen."

"Of course," she told him, relieved that now they were bargaining. There was nothing Daphne loved more than a good negotiation.

"I want to be a duke," he added.

Daphne almost laughed at the sheer audacity of it. "They haven't awarded any new dukedoms since the nineteenth century. You know that."

"A marquess, then." Ethan sounded as though he was enjoying himself.

"A viscount."

"An earl."

"Done." She gave a crisp, businesslike nod. "You keep Nina away from me and the prince, and eventually I'll make you an earl."

"Okay, then." Ethan relaxed into his usual languorous grin. "As always, Daphne, it's a pleasure doing business with you."

Daphne watched him head back to the reception hall,

wondering at the odd pang of disappointment she felt now that this moment with Ethan—this confrontation, or verbal sparring, whatever it was—had ended.

She took a breath, pasting on her usual dazzling smile before starting back toward the party.

SAMANTHA

The reception hall of the G&A museum was a crush of people.

The guests smiled and laughed, posing for the photographers, raising their voices over the sound of the string quartet in the corner. Now that June 20 had been officially confirmed as the wedding date, people seemed incapable of talking about anything else. They eagerly gossiped about what they would wear, or who might not get an invite, or what lucky designer would make Beatrice's gown.

Sam hated them for being so gullible and stupid, for buying into the absurd charade of Beatrice and Teddy's relationship. Couldn't they tell that it was all for show, each detail choreographed by the palace's PR team?

Yet the entire nation seemed to have erupted in wedding fever overnight. Sam had seen it everywhere. Restaurants were naming new dishes and cocktails after the couple; dozens of fitness studios already claimed to offer Beatrice's pre-wedding workout routine. Even tonight Beatrice and Teddy were the guests of honor, for the museum's opening of a new exhibit on royal weddings.

If only Nina had agreed to come with her. But when Sam had asked, Nina had begged off, claiming she was busy. Which Sam had silently translated as *I don't want to see Jeff.*

She ran her hands over her dress, a whimsical all-lace affair with an asymmetrical hem, and scanned the crowds in search of her brother. Instead Sam saw Beatrice across the reception hall.

As usual, Beatrice was surrounded by a cluster of people. In her hyacinth-blue dress, a smile pasted on her face, she looked like a beautiful porcelain doll. That was Beatrice, perpetually acting. Sam had never been any good at statesmanship, because she wasn't any good at artifice. She tended to do and say exactly what she meant, the very moment she thought of it.

Beatrice's eyes darted up to meet Sam's. For an instant, her picture-perfect mask slipped, revealing the real Beatrice—a young woman who looked uncertain and achingly alone.

Sam took a single step forward.

Then something caught Beatrice's attention, and she glanced away. Sam followed her sister's gaze—to Teddy.

Sam watched, utterly oblivious to the rest of the room, as Teddy made his way to her sister. His tie was the same shade of blue as her dress, making them seem like a matched set. He said something charming—at least, Sam assumed it was charming, from the way everyone laughed—and placed his hand lightly over Beatrice's.

Sam drew in a sharp breath and stumbled back. Her eyes burned, yet she wasn't crying. She needed to get *out* of here, far from Beatrice and Teddy and all the rest of them.

She wove blindly through the crowds and pushed open a door marked STAFF ONLY. A server looked up, startled. "Excuse me—I mean, Your Royal Highness—" He was pushing a catering cart, and Sam heard the unmistakable clink of jostling wine bottles.

"Don't mind me," she muttered. The startled waiter had barely registered her words before Sam had lifted a bottle of sauvignon blanc from the cart. Then she was sailing past him, through a heavy unmarked door and into the spring night.

A narrow balcony wound around the side of the museum. Still clutching the wine bottle in one hand, Sam draped her elbows onto the railing. The iron felt blessedly cool against her feverish skin.

Below her stretched the capital, a jagged quilt of light and dark. It had rained that morning, and headlights flickered through the haze, making the cars seem to float above the shimmering pavement. The scene blurred disorientingly in her vision.

She hadn't realized how much it would sting, seeing them together. *I don't care*, she thought furiously. *I hate them both. Beatrice and—*

There was a brief struggle in her chest, pride warring with affection, but at her core Sam was a Washington, and pride won out. It didn't matter that once upon a time she'd thought she was in love with Teddy.

He wasn't her Teddy anymore. He was just another face in a room full of strangers.

In choosing Beatrice, or duty, or whatever he wanted to call it, Teddy had proven that he was just like the rest of them. He was part and parcel of this whole stuffy institution, which had never understood or valued her.

Sam's hand closed around the railing so tight that her palm hurt. She glanced down and saw that the iron was carved with a pattern of tiny faces: woodland sprites laughing in a sea of leaves and flowers. It felt like they were mocking her.

Letting out a ragged cry, she lifted her satin heel and kicked the medallion in the center of the railing. When it didn't budge, she gave it a few more kicks for good measure.

"I don't know what that railing ever did to you," remarked a voice to her left. "But if you need to attack it, at least set down the wine first."

Slowly, Sam turned to look at the tall, broad-shouldered young man who stood a few yards away.

She had a feeling she'd met him before. He wore an expensive gray suit that set off his deep brown skin, though his tie was askew and his shirt untucked, giving him a decidedly rakish air. When his eyes caught hers, he grinned: a cool, reckless grin that made Sam's breath catch. He looked a few years older than she was, around Beatrice's age. Sam felt something in her rise to the challenge of his dark eyes.

"How long have you been lurking out here?" she demanded.

"Lurking?" He crossed his arms, lounging carelessly against the railing. "I was out here first. Which makes *you* the intruder."

"You should have said something when I came outside!"

"And miss that epic royal tantrum? I wouldn't have dreamed of it," he drawled.

Sam's grip on the railing tightened. "Do I know you?"

"Lord Marshall Davis, at your service." He bent forward at the waist, executing a perfect ceremonial bow. The words and the gesture were elegant, the type of thing any nobleman might have done when meeting a princess, yet Sam sensed that he didn't mean a word of it. There was an irreverence to the gesture, as if Marshall had exaggerated his courtesy in contrast to her own undignified behavior.

He rose from his bow, his mouth twitching with suppressed laughter, just as his name clicked in Sam's memory. Marshall Davis, heir to the dukedom of Orange.

Orange, which spanned most of the western seaboard, hadn't joined the United States until the nineteenth century. Marshall's family wasn't part of the "Old Guard," the thirteen ducal families knighted by King George I after the Revolutionary War. In fact, Marshall's many-times-great-grandfather had been born into slavery.

Daniel Davis was one of the thousands of formerly enslaved people who sought their fortunes out west after abolition had set them free. He fell deeply in love with his new home, and when Orange revolted against Spain, he became a key figure in its war for independence. Daniel was such a popular general that when the fighting was done, the people of Orange clamored for him to lead their new nation. And so—just as a century earlier George Washington had become King George I—Marshall's ancestor was named King Daniel I of Orange.

Twenty years later, Orange gave up its status as an independent kingdom to join the United States: meaning that the Davises, once kings, were now titled the Dukes of Orange. They weren't the first Black aristocrats—Edward I had ennobled several prominent families after abolition—but they were former royalty, which made them the most newsworthy.

Sam knew that Marshall was a stereotypical West Coast playboy, who surfed and went to parties in Vegas and was always dating some Hollywood actress or vapid aristocrat. Come to think of it, hadn't he been invited to last year's Queen's Ball as a potential husband for Beatrice? Though given his reputation, Sam doubted her sister had danced with him all that long.

Marshall nodded at the wine bottle, interrupting her thoughts. "Would you mind sharing, Your Royal Highness?" Somehow he made even her title sound like a source of amusement.

"I hate to disappoint you, but I forgot a corkscrew."

Marshall held out his hand. Bemused, Sam passed him the bottle. Moisture beaded along its sides.

"Watch and learn." He reached into his pocket for a set of keys before jamming one into the cork. Sam watched as he twisted the key in quick circles, gently teasing the cork from the neck of the bottle, until it emerged with an eager *pop*.

She was impressed in spite of herself. "Nice party trick."

"Boarding school," Marshall said drily, and handed her the sauvignon blanc. Sam hadn't brought any wineglasses, so she went ahead and drank straight from the bottle. The wine had a crisp tartness that settled on the back of her tongue, almost like candy.

"I've always wondered if the stories about you are true." Marshall caught her eye and grinned. "I'm starting to think they are."

"No more or less true than the stories about you, I imagine."

"Touché." He reached for the bottle and lifted it in a salute.

They passed the wine back and forth for a while. Silence thickened around them, light leaching from the sky as night settled its folds around the capital. Sam felt her thoughts turning brutally, relentlessly, back to Beatrice and Teddy.

She would show them. She didn't know how she'd show them, but she would do it—would prove just how little either of them mattered to her.

Next to her, Marshall rocked back on his heels. He was always moving, she realized: shifting his weight, leaning against the railing and then away again. Perhaps, like Sam, he felt constantly restless.

"Why are you hiding out here instead of enjoying the party?" she demanded, curious. "Are you avoiding a clingy ex-girlfriend or something?"

"Well, yeah. Kelsey's in there." When Sam didn't react to the name, Marshall let out a breath. "Kelsey Brooke."

"You're dating *her*?"

Sam wrinkled her nose in disgust. Kelsey was one of those starlets who all looked the same, as if they'd been mass-produced by a factory line specializing in doe eyes and big boobs. Her fame had skyrocketed this year when she'd starred in a new show about witches on a college campus who used their powers to save the world—then made it back in time for sorority parties, where they fell into doomed romances with mortals. The whole concept sounded pretty dumb to Sam.

"I *was* dating her. She broke up with me last month," Marshall replied, with an indifference that didn't fool Sam.

He shifted, and the fading light gleamed on a pin affixed to his lapel. It reminded Sam of the American flag pin her dad always used to wear.

Following her gaze, Marshall explained, "It's the official Orange state logo." The pin depicted a bear, its teeth pulled back in a menacing growl.

"You have grizzly bears in Orange?"

"Not anymore, but they're still our mascot."

An old, familiar instinct stirred within Sam. Knowing that she was being difficult, and deliberately provocative, and a little flirtatious, she reached out to unfasten the pin from his jacket. "I'm borrowing this. It looks better on me anyway."

Marshall watched as she pinned the bear to the bodice of her dress, perilously close to her cleavage. He seemed torn between indignation and amusement. "You should know, only the Dukes of Orange can wear that pin."

"And *you* should know that I'm entitled to wear anything you can wear. I outrank you," Sam shot back, then blinked at her own words. She'd said nearly the same thing to Teddy last year—*I outrank you, and I command that you kiss me.* And he had.

"I can't argue with that logic," Marshall replied, chuckling.

Sam's pulse quickened. Her blood seemed to have turned to jet fuel, her entire body buzzing with recklessness. The pain of seeing Teddy with Beatrice felt muffled beneath this new, sharp emotion. "Let's go back inside."

Marshall set the bottle down with deliberate slowness; Sam noticed that it was nearly empty. "Right now?" he asked. "Why?"

Because it was fun, because she wanted to stir up trouble, because she needed to do *something* or she felt like she would implode.

"Think of how furious it'll make Kelsey, seeing us together," she offered, but something in her tone must have given her away.

Marshall's eyes lit on hers in a long, searching look. "Which of your exes are *you* trying to make jealous?"

"He's not my ex," Sam replied, then immediately longed to bite back the words. "I mean, not technically."

"I see." Marshall nodded with maddening calm, which somehow made Sam even more defensive.

"Look, it's none of your business, okay?"

"Of course not."

Silence fell between them, more charged than before. Sam wondered if she'd revealed too much.

But Marshall just held out an arm. "Well then, Your Royal Highness, allow me the pleasure of being your distraction."

As they headed back into the party, he let his hand slide with casual possessiveness to the small of her back. Sam tossed her head, her smile blazing, relishing the low hum of gossip that arose when people saw them together. She forced herself to look up at Marshall, to keep herself from searching the crowds for Teddy. She didn't want him thinking that she'd spared him a moment's consideration.

If she spent the rest of tonight with another future duke, Teddy would see just how little his rejection had hurt her—that he'd never really mattered to her at all.

NINA

Nina shifted on her stomach, turning the page of the book that lay open before her.

She and Rachel were out in the Henry Courtyard, the vast lawn around which most of the freshman dorms were clustered. Everyone seemed determined to take advantage of the sunshine: sprawling on picnic blankets, blasting music from portable speakers. A few yards away, Nina saw a group of students eating brownies straight out of the pan. She had a feeling that they contained a little more than sugar.

"Are you seriously trying to read right now?" Rachel demanded from her neighboring beach towel. "Jane Austen can wait."

Nina shook her head in amusement, but marked her page and sat up. "Actually, it's *Jane Eyre*."

"Austen, Eyre, they're all full of tortured romance and you love it." Rachel bit her lip as if unsure whether to continue. "Speaking of which, I noticed you didn't go to the museum event last night."

The whole premise of the gala, the opening of a new exhibit on royal weddings, felt strange to Nina. As ridiculous as it was to pity the Washingtons, she did feel a little sorry for them, that their lives were so shamelessly commercialized. That their personal milestones—their birthdays, weddings, funerals—were never private, but instead became a media frenzy. And then all their clothes and invitations were displayed in museums for public consumption, so that everyone in America could feel like those moments belonged to *them*, too.

"I didn't really want to go." *And run into Jeff again,* she didn't need to add.

Nina hadn't known what to expect when she saw the prince at the races last weekend. Half of her still wanted to slap him across the face for defending Daphne that night at the engagement party, and the other half wanted to pull him into a hug and murmur how sorry she was about his dad.

Of course she hadn't done either. The only way to survive that kind of encounter was to keep it as civil and short as possible.

She'd seen the confusion on Jeff's face when she'd greeted him like a near stranger. But Nina needed that emotional distance for her own protection. She wasn't a good enough actress to pretend that she and Jeff were "just friends" again.

Instead Nina had followed the court formula for surface-level conversations; she certainly knew it well enough, after all these years of being Sam's best friend. When Jeff said hello, she'd bobbed a curtsy, murmured her condolences, and made polite conversation about the weather and the races before excusing herself and walking away in relief. The whole exchange had taken two, maybe three minutes.

Yet she'd spent hours replaying it in her mind. No matter how determinedly she told herself that she was over Jeff, her heart hadn't quite gotten the message yet.

A series of gongs echoed through campus: the Randolph clock tower, which famously marked noon and midnight with thirteen chimes instead of twelve, the result of a senior prank that had never been corrected.

"That's my cue." Nina stood, brushing stray bits of grass from her cropped jeans.

"You're leaving?" Rachel protested.

"I have Intro to Journalism in twenty minutes."

Rachel reached across the blanket to grab her friend's copy of *Jane Eyre*. "You can't go, I'm holding your homework hostage!"

"No worries, keep the book. You could even try reading it," Nina teased.

Rachel flopped dramatically back onto her towel and placed the novel over her face. Her curls formed an unruly pillow behind her. "I'll just nap instead. This makes a nice sunshade."

"Good thinking," Nina agreed. "Now the story will sink into your brain through sheer osmosis."

She heard Rachel's answering laugh, muffled beneath the heavy book.

Nina headed down the paved walkway toward the center of campus, passing dozens of people as she walked: sorority girls in printed T-shirts, prospective students on a campus tour. To her relief, none of them spared her a second glance. The afternoon sun filtered through the filigree of leaves overhead, dappling campus in a green-gold light.

For some reason, her eyes kept drifting to a dark-haired boy ten yards before her. She could only see the back of him. But something—his sculpted calves, the bold, brisk way he walked—intrigued her. She found herself oddly curious to see his face.

Her heart picked up speed as the mystery guy turned toward Smythson Hall, which was so overgrown with ivy that it looked like it had sprouted organically from the ground itself. He was headed toward the same first-floor classroom that Nina was. She quickened her steps to catch up. He reached for the door—

Nina skidded to a halt, nearly biting her tongue in shock. It was Ethan Beckett. Jeff's best friend.

She felt her face turning a mottled shade of red. Why hadn't she recognized Ethan? They'd spent plenty of time together over the years, though it was always around the royal twins. Their paths had never crossed at school before.

"*You're* in journalism class?" she blurted out.

"Nina. Nice to see you, as always." He flashed his usual cavalier smile and held open the door for her. She avoided making eye contact as she slid past him to head inside.

Facing the whiteboard were at least thirty desks, arranged in rows. The room hummed with the overlapping conversations that always came after a school break.

Nina settled into a desk on the far right. Maddeningly, Ethan ignored all the empty chairs to take the one next to her. He nodded at her short hair. "I like the new look."

"It was time for a change." Nina tried to inject the statement with an air of finality, to indicate that he shouldn't feel obligated to keep chatting, but Ethan didn't take the hint. He leaned forward, bracing an elbow on his desk and angling toward her.

"So, Intro to Journalism," he mused. "To be honest, I hadn't expected to see you here. I'm surprised you'll go anywhere near journalism, after what the media—"

Nina hissed through her teeth, cutting him off. She glanced furtively around the room, but everyone else was absorbed in their own discussions.

"I'm trying to put all that behind me," she said tersely. The last thing she wanted right now was to revisit what the paparazzi had done to her family.

When she saw that Ethan was still looking at her, Nina sighed. "I'm taking this class because I'm trying to get a minor in creative writing, and this counts as a departmental credit. I want to be a writer someday," she added, feeling oddly self-conscious at the admission. "Not that I've composed anything longer than a high school newspaper article."

"Give yourself some credit. You used to write all those

plays that you and Sam would perform out on the lawn by the pool." Ethan's eyes glinted with amusement. "Some of them were actually kind of funny."

Nina couldn't believe he remembered those. "I'm going to pretend that was a compliment," she replied, with a touch of sarcasm.

The door swung open, and a woman with deep brown skin and a bright smile entered the room. Lacey Jamail: the youngest staff writer ever hired by the *Washington Circular*.

"Welcome to Intro to Journalism. Your first assignment will be done in pairs," the professor said without preamble.

Everyone instantly broke out in conversation. Nina cast a quick glance around the room, but Ethan had already turned her way.

"Partners?" he asked.

"Sure," Nina agreed, with less reluctance than she would have guessed.

Professor Jamail began explaining the assignment, waving her dry-erase marker like a baton as she spoke. Nina hurried to scribble down her words.

When class ended forty minutes later, she closed her spiral notebook and tossed it into her shoulder bag, only to find that Ethan was lingering near her desk.

"Are you headed to the library?" he asked.

"Actually, I was going to the student center for lunch."

"Sounds good." Ethan fell into step alongside her.

"I—okay." Why was he suddenly acting like they were old friends? Sure, they'd known each other for years, but they'd never spent any time together without the twins there, too. Had *Jeff* asked him to check on her?

Nina used her meal points to pay for a sandwich, then found Ethan at a table near the window. As she sat down, he slid a bag of peanut M&M's toward her. "These are for you."

Now she *definitely* thought Jeff was involved. How else could Ethan have known about her love of M&M's?

"You aren't going to eat?" she asked, grabbing the M&M's. It looked like Ethan hadn't purchased anything except the candy.

"I had lunch in the dining hall earlier. But I'm happy to get a pizza if you're one of those girls who feel self-conscious about eating alone." He lifted an eyebrow. "Based on the way you used to put down waffles at the ski house, I don't think you are."

Nina rolled her eyes. "Let's just get started. Do you have any ideas about who we should interview?" Their assignment was to coauthor a profile piece about someone on campus.

Ethan draped an arm over the back of his chair. "Can't we talk about something else, at least until you're done eating?"

She took a slow bite of her turkey sandwich. "If you think I'm going to do all the work on this project, you're wrong."

"*You* do all the work?" Ethan flashed a cheeky grin. "I thought *I* was the one doing all the work. I'll have you know my GPA is a three-nine."

Nina felt guilty for assuming he was a slacker. "Then why did you want to be partners with me?"

"You thought I wanted to be partners just so I could mooch off your assignment?"

"Not to brag, but I kick ass at assignments."

Ethan let out an amused breath. "Maybe I just wanted to spend some time with you, Nina. I mean, we've known each other since we were kids, but we don't actually *know* each other well at all."

She set down her sandwich and leaned her elbows forward onto the table. "What do you want to know?"

"I'm curious what really happened between you and Jeff," Ethan said carefully.

Nina didn't dignify that with a response—but she didn't

look away, either. She held Ethan's gaze, her eyes blazing, until he was so discomfited that he glanced down at his lap.

"Sorry. That was out of line."

"It was," she said flatly.

"It's just that I'm worried about Jeff. And he won't talk about your breakup with me. He won't talk about anything, really, since . . ."

Nina tried to grab hold of her anger again, but it had warped and mutated beneath a sudden wave of sympathy. When she thought of Jeff, her mind no longer went automatically to the night they'd broken up. Now all she saw was the look on his face at the Royal Potomac Races: a bewildered, searching look that had quickly faded, as if he'd been about to smile at her, then remembered that he'd lost her, too—on top of losing his dad.

The truth was, Nina had been longing to talk about Jeff for weeks, but there was no one she could really discuss him with. She didn't want to worry her parents; they were still shaken after that whole paparazzi nightmare. Rachel had only met Jeff once, so she didn't have any real insight into the situation. As for Sam—it had been hard enough to begin with, talking to Sam about her own brother. Now it seemed the height of selfishness, to bring this up while Sam was grieving. Nina's romantic dramas felt small and unimportant next to everything her best friend had been through.

It felt a little strange, talking about this with Ethan, but he *did* know Jeff better than anyone. Maybe he would understand the strange paradox of Nina's feelings.

"Things were never simple with me and Jeff after the news of our relationship got out," Nina began. "It was fine when it was just us. But once everyone knew, so many things kept getting in the way." *Primarily, Jeff's ex-girlfriend.*

"The media really put you through hell, didn't they."

The usual sarcasm had evaporated from Ethan's tone, and

to Nina's surprise, he seemed the handsomer for it. A bit of earnestness added depth to his brown eyes, smoothed away his careless smile.

"The thing is, I didn't realize how much our breakup would impact my relationship with Sam, too." Nina sighed. "I should have known better than to date my best friend's brother. Clearly *you* know better," she added, glancing back toward Ethan. "You never made a move on Sam, all these years."

He scoffed at that. "Trust me, Sam isn't my type."

"What *is* your type?"

The question had come out oddly flirtatious, but to her relief, Ethan didn't seem to notice. "It's complicated enough being Jeff's best friend. I don't need to add another Washington relationship to the mix."

"I know what you mean," Nina admitted. "Honestly . . . sometimes I wonder why Sam and I are still friends."

She felt a stab of disloyalty, saying this to Ethan. But then, who else *could* she talk about it with? Ethan was the only person who understood how it felt, being inextricably bound to the royal family without actually being one of them.

"Why do you say that?" Ethan asked. Not judgmental, but simply curious.

"We just don't make *sense* as best friends." She paused, searching for the right words to explain. Nina's parents had taught her to be skeptical, and practical, whereas Sam hurtled forward without ever asking questions. Nina hardly dared to want things, and Sam always seemed to want enough for two people.

"We have next to nothing in common, except the fact that we've known each other since we were six."

"But that's just it—you've known each other since you were six," Ethan argued. "You don't need to *be* similar to your friends, not when you have so many years of shared history. Besides, your friendship is probably stronger because of all the ways you're different. Jeff and I aren't all that like each other, either."

"Really? You seem pretty similar to me."

"In some ways, sure." Ethan shrugged. "But Jeff is *actually* as easygoing as he seems, while I'm just pretending. Also"—he lowered his voice conspiratorially—"I secretly hate the way the royals travel."

Nina raised an eyebrow skeptically. "You don't like staying at five-star resorts, with a small army of staff?"

"I'll admit there are perks." Ethan waved away her words. "But I'd rather travel without the royal press pack, without even an itinerary. Just wander around with a backpack and a passport."

"Is that why you're taking Intro to Journalism? To be a travel writer?" Nina asked, curious.

"I thought we'd agreed that I took Intro to Journalism so I could hang out with *you*."

Nina laughed and took another bite of her sandwich, wondering why she'd always been so irritated by Ethan's sarcasm in the past. She was beginning to sense that Ethan wasn't the type of person you could get to know at first glance. You needed a second glance, and then a third.

Which she had never given him. Because he'd always been standing next to Jeff, and when Jeff was around, she'd never had eyes for anyone else.

Nina winced at the realization that she'd treated Ethan as dismissively as everyone had always treated her—when they'd stared through her as if she were a pane of glass, to focus on Sam.

She held out the bag of M&M's as a peace offering. "Want some?"

"Careful what you offer; I might eat the whole bag," he warned, reaching for the candy.

"And—Ethan? Thank you. For talking about all of this, I mean."

"Of course," he said gruffly. "It's not like anyone else would understand."

BEATRICE

"I'm not sure," Beatrice repeated, the same thing she'd said a dozen times already. She stared at the mirror, where the wedding gown—long-sleeved, with a voluminous tiered skirt—was reflected back at her. She looked like a stranger.

Queen Adelaide cast an apologetic glance at the designer before turning to her daughter. "Why don't you walk around a little, see how it feels?"

Beatrice sighed and took a few steps forward. She wished Samantha were here, if only to hear the sarcastic commentary she would have provided on all these dresses. Except Sam had gone completely MIA. Normally Beatrice wouldn't have given it another thought; Sam frequently skipped the events on her official schedule. This time, though, Beatrice knew her sister was punishing her for announcing her wedding date.

In typical Sam fashion, she was acting like she didn't care—Beatrice had seen her at the museum gala, flirting outrageously with Lord Marshall Davis as if to prove something. But when Beatrice had tried to talk to her later that night, her sister had slammed the door in her face.

Sunlight slanted through a stained-glass window on the opposite wall, turning the wooden floor into a dancing carpet of color. They were in the throne room, which had temporarily transformed into the official headquarters for Beatrice's Wedding Dress Search. Footmen had carried in massive trifold mirrors and a seamstress's platform, as well as an enormous screen so she could change in privacy. The palace had even closed for tours, which only fanned the nation's speculation about what might be going on today, and whether it was about the wedding.

Beatrice would have preferred to do all this at the designers' ateliers. But apparently it was too risky: someone might see her, and leak the secret of which fashion houses were in contention to make what people were already calling the wedding dress of the century. As it was, the designers had still been forced to sign lengthy nondisclosure agreements, and drove in long, circuitous routes to the palace in unmarked cars.

Honestly, Robert was treating her gown like a state secret that needed to be protected as vigilantly as the nuclear codes—codes that Beatrice still didn't know.

There were so many things she *should* be doing right now: studying the latest congressional report, composing speeches, arranging her first diplomatic visit. Anything, instead of standing here like a human mannequin while designers whipped various gowns on and off her body.

Over the past week, whenever Beatrice had tried to do her *actual* job, some obstacle had always arisen. Her schedule was too crowded and she needed to wait; the timing wasn't right and she needed to wait. Robert kept telling her that—wait, wait, *wait*—but what was she waiting *for*?

She glanced over at him. "Robert, can you set an audience with the new Senate majority leader? I should meet with him, now that he's been nominated. And we'll need to begin planning my speech for the closing session of Congress." It was one of the government's oldest traditions that the monarch opened Congress in the fall, and closed it before the summer recess.

Beatrice's heart quelled a little, at the realization that she would dismiss a Congress her *father* had opened just ten months earlier.

Robert shook his head. "Your Majesty, I'm afraid that isn't possible. You cannot meet with Congress until after you are crowned. It would be unconstitutional."

Beatrice knew the Constitution backward and forward, so she knew that, technically speaking, he was right. The article in question had been written out of a very real eighteenth-century fear: that if the succession were ever in doubt, contenders to the throne might bully their way into Congress and attempt to take over the government.

"I can preside over the closing session as long as Congress invites me," Beatrice reminded him. That invitation, another archaic tradition, was one of the many checks and balances that the Constitution had established between the three branches of government.

The chamberlain glanced at Queen Adelaide for support, but she was chatting with the gown's designer. He turned back to Beatrice with an oily smile. "Your Majesty, you will deal with countless congressional leaders over the course of your reign. They are fleeting and temporary, coming and going every four years. What difference does it make if you miss a single session?"

"It makes a difference because it's the first congressional ceremony of my reign." Didn't he see that?

"Your Majesty," Robert cut in, and now there was a distinct note of warning in his tone, "it would be best if you waited to meet with Congress until after your wedding to His Lordship."

She felt like she'd been slapped across the face. The coronation of a new monarch always took place a year after the previous monarch's death, which meant that Beatrice wouldn't be crowned until *after* her wedding. She'd thought it was just another tradition, but she realized now that Robert didn't want her addressing Congress—or really, doing anything involved in the governance of America—as a young woman on her own.

He wouldn't really approve of her until she had Teddy at her side.

The chamberlain glanced back down at his tablet, as if he expected Beatrice to drop the issue. Something in that gesture, in the sheer dismissal of it, made the air burn in her lungs.

"I need a minute," she announced.

Ignoring everyone's disapproving frowns, Beatrice hurried out into the hallway. Her new Guard, thankfully, didn't follow. Unlike Connor, who would have caught up with her in a few steps, put his hands on her shoulders, and asked how he could help.

Connor. Beatrice clutched great handfuls of her dress to keep from tripping as she hurtled around a corner. She felt like she was trapped in one of her nightmares, running away from something without ever being able to run fast enough—

She froze, her white satin heels sinking into the rug, as she caught sight of Teddy.

He immediately threw a hand over his eyes. "Sorry, I didn't mean to see you in your wedding dress. That's bad luck, right?"

"Don't worry. This is *not* going to be my dress," she heard herself say.

Slowly Teddy opened his eyes and took in the volume of her ivory skirts. "Oh, good. I didn't know it was *possible* to cover a dress in so many ruffles."

To her surprise, Beatrice smiled. She glanced uncertainly down the hallway. "Were you here to see someone?"

"You." Teddy cleared his throat. "I mean—I wanted to give you this," he said, and she realized he was holding out a brown paper shopping bag.

Before she could answer, Queen Adelaide's voice sounded

behind them. "Beatrice, are you all right? We're getting behind schedule."

Some strange impulse seized hold of Beatrice. Before she could second-guess herself, she'd thrown open the nearest door, which led to a narrow linen closet. Teddy cast her a puzzled look, but followed her inside.

When he pulled the door shut behind him, the overhead light clicked off.

"What's going on?" he whispered into the dimness.

Beatrice felt hot and prickly with embarrassment, and maybe with adrenaline. Had she really just *run away* from her mom? It was the sort of spontaneous, heedless thing that Sam usually did.

"I needed a hiding spot."

"Fair enough," Teddy replied, as if her explanation made sense.

Beatrice slid to the floor and hugged her knees. Her gown poufed up around her in a sea of petticoats and flounces. After a moment, Teddy lowered himself to sit next to her.

"I was going to save this for when we had a little more space, but you clearly need it now."

He held out the bag, and Beatrice pulled it into her lap. Inside was a recyclable takeout box marked with a familiar *D* logo. "Were you in *Boston* this morning?" she breathed, incredulous.

"I had it couriered."

She tore open the box to reveal an enormous butterscotch brownie, as big as the bricks that lined the walkway outside the palace. "How did you know?"

"You told me, that night at the Queen's Ball. You said that Darwin's brownies were the only thing that got you through exams. I figured, with everything that's going on, you could use a little de-stressing right now."

For a moment Beatrice just stared at him, caught off guard

by his thoughtfulness. She couldn't believe he'd remembered a throwaway comment she'd made months ago.

"I didn't get the wrong thing, did I?" he asked, seeing her hesitation.

In answer, Beatrice grabbed the plastic fork and stabbed eagerly into the brownie. It was gooey and sweet and reassuringly familiar.

When she looked over, she saw that Teddy was staring at her, a corner of his mouth lifted in amusement. "I don't think I've ever seen you look so . . . unroyal," he admitted.

"There's no elegant way to eat a Darwin's brownie, and it's never stopped me before." Beatrice held out her fork. "Want to try it, before I devour the whole thing?"

She'd made the offer automatically—it was what she would have done with Jeff, or Sam, or, well, *Connor*—but when Teddy hesitated, she realized what she'd said. There was something decidedly intimate about eating from the same fork.

"Sure," he replied, after a beat. "I need to see if it lives up to the hype."

As she passed him the brownie, Beatrice's knee brushed against his beneath the ivory spill of her skirts, and she quickly pulled it back. Teddy pretended not to notice.

"This is a pretty good hiding place," he observed. "Did you come here a lot when you played hide-and-seek?"

"Actually . . . when I was little, I read that fantasy series about the wardrobe. I once searched every last closet in the palace, hoping I'd find a doorway to another world."

Beatrice wasn't sure why she'd confessed that. She blamed the cool oaken silence of the linen closet, or the fact that she was alone with her fiancé—instead of surrounded by people, as they usually were—and he was being so unexpectedly *nice*.

"You went looking for magic doors to Narnia?" Teddy asked.

She tried not to be hurt by his surprise. "I know, no one ever thinks of me as the imaginative type."

While Samantha and Jeff had run all over the palace, pretending they were pirates or knights or adventurers, Beatrice was in etiquette lessons or working her way through an endless reading list. Their childish impulses had been indulged; hers had been quietly denied.

No one wanted their future monarch to waste time *playing*. She was meant to be duty-bound, as plodding and obedient and steady as an ox at the plow.

It was hard not to wish, sometimes, that life had cast her in a different role.

"That's not what I meant," Teddy said gently. "I just . . . I used to want to escape into a fantasy world, too."

Of course, Beatrice thought. Teddy knew what it was like to grow up under a heavy set of expectations. He had reasons of his own for agreeing to this engagement, probably reasons that had to do with his family.

He certainly wasn't marrying her because he loved her.

"Teddy—what are we *doing*?"

"Right now we're sitting on the floor of a closet, in the dark. Though I have to say, I still haven't figured out why."

She shook off a bizarre desire to laugh. "I meant the wedding," she clarified. "We can still call off the whole thing."

Teddy was silent for a moment.

"Is that what you want?" he said at last.

Beatrice couldn't remember the last time anyone had asked her that. People asked her plenty of other things: whether she could attend their charity dinner, or could she turn toward their camera for a photo, or would she recommend their cousin for a position in the royal household. It felt like she couldn't even walk through the palace without being trapped in a small hail of requests.

But no one asked what she *wanted* anymore. As if the moment she'd become the queen, she'd stopped having any sort of desires at all.

Beatrice realized with a sick sense of guilt that she'd done the same thing to Teddy. In all her anguish over what the wedding was costing her, she hadn't even considered what he was giving up.

He'd cared about Samantha, and Sam had feelings for him, and still Beatrice had asked him to go through with this. She longed, suddenly, to broach the topic, but she felt like she'd forfeited the right to discuss Samantha with Teddy.

"I just—I doubt this is what you thought your wedding would be like," she said hesitantly.

Teddy shrugged. "I never spent any time thinking about my wedding until this year," he told her. "Did you?"

"Actually . . . when I was little, I thought I was going to get married at Disney World."

She felt Teddy struggling to stifle a laugh. Color rose to her cheeks as she rushed to explain.

"When I was five, I begged my parents to take me to Disney World. The girls at school had all been talking about it. . . ." And she had wanted, desperately, to fit in with them, to actually follow the conversation at the lower school lunch table for once.

"We had to go after the park closed," she went on. "We couldn't be there with the other guests, for security reasons. And—"

"Wait, you got to ride Space Mountain with *no lines?*" Teddy cut in.

"Please, five is too young for Space Mountain. Though I did ride the spinning teacups so many times that it gave my Revere Guard motion sickness," Beatrice recalled, and Teddy chuckled. "When I saw the castle that night, all those princess characters were there. And I don't know, I guess I knew I was a princess, and I figured that was where princesses got married."

Beatrice didn't admit that she hadn't recognized the women

in colorful ball gowns as fictional characters. She hadn't seen any of their movies—so she'd assumed they were real princesses, as she was.

"A Disney World wedding," Teddy said slowly. "Are you sure it's not too late to change locations? The look on Robert's face alone would be worth it."

Beatrice chuckled at that—but as the laugh traveled out of her chest, it transformed into a single, ragged sob. Then somehow she was laughing and weeping at once, crumpling forward and hiding her face in her hands.

She didn't expect Teddy to reach for her.

He wiped away the tears on first one cheek, then the other, his thumb brushing ever so lightly against the damp fan of her lashes. Beatrice's breath caught as his hand cupped around her face, his palm cradling the back of her neck. She was startled by how much she wanted to close her eyes and lean in to him.

Some part of her felt guilty for that desire, as if it was a betrayal of everything she'd felt for Connor.

Except that she and Connor were over, and it had been weeks—months, really—since anyone had touched her like this. Aside from those few frantic kisses the afternoon he left, Connor had hardly even dared to hug her since her dad died. Beatrice hadn't realized how desperately she had craved this: the simple human comfort of feeling another person's skin on hers.

"Beatrice . . ." Teddy pulled his hand away, as surprised by his gesture as she was. "If we really are doing this, I want to ask you something."

"All right." She leaned back, and her gown rustled with the movement, a dry sound like wind raking through autumn leaves.

"Will you be honest with me?"

Whatever Beatrice had expected, it wasn't this.

"Look—I know there will be things you don't want to share," he hurried to add. "Some things you *can't* share, because of who you are. When that happens, I'd rather you just admit that you can't tell me something, instead of feeling like you need to lie. And I swear that I will do the same."

The room had become very small and still. Beatrice's heart pounded against the rigid corset of the gown.

She wondered what secrets Teddy was trying to keep from her. Was he worried she would ask him about his history with Samantha? Or was he asking this for *her* sake, because he somehow knew about her and Connor?

Whatever his reasons, Beatrice saw the wisdom in Teddy's request. He was right.

There might not be love between them—but there *could* be trust, if they built it. And trust might allow for privacy, even secrets, but never for lies.

"I agree. Let's always tell each other the truth."

Teddy nodded and stood, holding out a hand to help her to her feet. His grip was warm, and steady, and firm.

For some reason, Beatrice thought back to the day she'd proposed. She remembered how utterly strange Teddy's hand had felt in hers.

It didn't seem quite so wrong, this time.

10

DAPHNE

Daphne was very quiet as she browsed the rack of silk tops, her ears straining to catch the conversation of the women behind her. She didn't dare alert them by turning around, so she couldn't see their faces, but she sensed from the quiet intensity of their voices that they were discussing something scandalous.

She hadn't come to Halo, her favorite boutique, with the express intent of eavesdropping—but Daphne had long ago learned to keep her ears and eyes open.

If she learned something good, she could pass it to Natasha at the *Daily News*. Daphne had been slipping her gossip items for years now, in exchange for favorable coverage from the magazine. Or, if it was *really* good, Daphne might even find a way to use it for her own ends. Like that time years ago, before she and Jefferson were dating, when she'd caught Lady Leonor Harrington in a back stairwell with one of the palace security guards.

Daphne had assured Lady Harrington that she would keep the secret—but had also gently suggested that the noblewoman sponsor her application to the Royal Ballet Guild, notoriously the capital's most exclusive charity group. Then Daphne had convinced the security guard to let her into the palace a few times at big events, when no one would notice an extra guest.

That was the thing about secrets. You could trade them over and over again.

Her phone vibrated in her quilted purse. Daphne reached to silence it, hoping it wouldn't startle the gossiping women—but when she saw the name on the caller ID, her mouth went dry.

Himari Mariko *couldn't* be calling, because Himari had been in a coma for almost a year. She'd fallen down the palace's back staircase the night of the twins' graduation party, in what everyone thought was a tragic accident.

Though Daphne knew it was her fault.

Her skin crawling with trepidation, she accepted the call. "Hello?"

"It's me."

Hearing Himari's voice in her ear was like communing with a ghost.

Daphne took a step back, bracing her hand on a table of folded silk shorts. "You woke up."

"Just this morning," Himari said. "And starting tomorrow I can have visitors. Will you come?"

There was something wet on her face; Daphne reached up to wipe it away, surprised to find that she was crying. That a *real* emotion had awoken beneath the countless false ones that she wore so beautifully. The sheer force of it hit her like a blow.

"Of course," she whispered, already halfway out the door.

After all this time, Himari was back. Her best friend, her confidante, her partner in crime—and maybe her downfall.

♛

The next morning, Daphne strode down the long-term care ward of St. Stephen's Hospital, a gift basket clutched in her arms. She nodded at various doctors and nurses as she passed, but beneath her usual demure smile, her mind was whirling.

She had no idea what to do now that Himari was awake. Should she walk in the room and beg for forgiveness, or go instantly on the attack? Maybe she could offer Himari a sort of bargain: give her something she wanted, in exchange for keeping the secret of what had really sent her into a coma that night.

It had all started last spring. Himari had caught Daphne and Ethan together, and threatened to tell Jefferson what she knew. Daphne had pleaded with her to calm down, but her friend refused to listen. She clearly wanted to break up Daphne and Jefferson, then make a play for the prince herself.

Cornered and desperate, Daphne had slipped a couple of ground-up sleeping pills into Himari's drink. She'd meant to scare her a little, convince her to let the whole thing go. Never in a million lifetimes had Daphne anticipated that her friend would climb a staircase in her dazed, disoriented state—only to fall right back down.

Daphne wished she could take it all back. The next morning, she'd almost marched down to the police station and confessed, just so she'd be able to talk about it with someone. As it was, there was only one person she *could* discuss it with, who knew the sordid truth of what she'd done. And that was Ethan.

All year, while Himari was in a coma, Daphne had kept on visiting her. Not because it made her look good—her usual motivation for doing things—but because she wanted to, desperately. Seeing Himari was the only way to stave off the guilt that threatened to consume her.

Daphne paused at the door marked with a laminated name card: HIMARI MARIKO. Gathering the frayed strands of her courage, she knocked. When she heard a muffled "Come in," she pushed open the door.

And there was Himari, propped up against a pillow in her narrow hospital bed. Her cheekbones jutted out more sharply than before, and a tube still snaked under the blankets to clamp the skin of her forearm, but her bright brown eyes were open at last.

Time seemed to stretch and snap back over itself, like the cherry-flavored gum the two of them used to chew between classes at school.

"Himari. It's so good to see you. Awake, I mean," Daphne said clumsily. She held her breath: waiting for a string of invectives, for Himari to throw something at her, or maybe scream for a nurse.

Nothing happened.

"I would say that I've missed you, except I feel like I saw you last week." Himari's voice sounded lower than it used to, a little scratchy from months of disuse, but there was nothing cold or distant about it. She nodded at Daphne's outfit and, unbelievably, smiled. "You look great, as usual. Are high-waisted jeans really back? I *need* a pair."

For a moment Daphne just stood there in dazed shock. Himari was talking the way she used to: before Jefferson, and Daphne and Ethan's secret, had come between them.

"Here, this is for you." Daphne recovered enough to hold out the gift basket. She'd spent all of yesterday filling it with Himari's favorite things: flowers and tea, the new fantasy novel by her favorite author, the macarons she loved from that bakery all the way in Georgetown. Himari reached for it and began sorting through its contents with her usual charming greed.

"Let me help," Daphne offered as Himari pressed her face into the flowers and inhaled. There was an empty vase on a table; she carried it to the bathroom and filled it with water before arranging the bouquet inside.

The hospital room felt different from all the times Daphne had visited. Now its sterile surfaces were cluttered with personal items, stuffed animals and foil balloons on sticks and a stack of magazines. Daphne smiled when she saw that Himari was drinking water out of the cartoon-printed thermos she used to sip her morning green juice from. The room even *sounded* better, the medical equipment emitting a cheerful erratic beep, rather than the soulless refrain of someone unconscious.

Daphne set the flowers on a nearby table, then pulled a chair forward.

"What are you doing?" Himari scooted over, creating space on the bed. "Head wounds aren't contagious, I promise."

Daphne couldn't see an easy way out. She climbed up next to her friend, the way she used to back when they would hang out in Himari's room, trading stories and secrets and laughing until their chests hurt.

"My nurses said you visited every week," Himari went on. "Thanks for doing that. You're such a loyal friend."

Did those last two words have a sarcastic bite? Daphne couldn't really tell. It was still so surreal, hearing Himari speak at all.

"We were all worried about you, Himari. That fall . . ."

"Did you see it?"

"I—what?"

"Did you see me fall?"

The air seemed to drain from the room. Daphne looked over, meeting her friend's gaze. "I was at the party, but no. I didn't see you fall."

Himari tugged absently at her sheets. "The doctors said there was a low dosage of narcotics in my system. As if I'd mixed vodka and NyQuil, or something."

"Really?" Daphne replied, with admirable calm. "That doesn't sound like you."

"I don't get it either," Himari insisted. "And what was I going upstairs for?"

Was this a trap, or did Himari truly not know? Daphne didn't dare answer with the truth. She decided her only option was to answer a question with a question.

"You don't remember?"

Some of the tension seemed to drain from Himari's body. "No. It's so bizarre. I remember everything else: god, I remember the name and title of every last person at court. But the days leading up to the accident are a complete blank."

A complete blank. Relief swept through Daphne. If Himari didn't remember, it would be like none of it had ever happened: Daphne sleeping with Ethan, the blackmail, the night of the fall.

Or—what if Himari was only *pretending* to have forgotten? She might be acting like this to draw Daphne close, and carry out some greater revenge scheme.

"I'm not surprised you remember everyone at court," Daphne said carefully. "You and I spent weeks combing through *McCall's Peerage* before our first royal function."

Himari smiled at that. To Daphne, at least, it looked genuine. "I still can't believe we made note cards for that. We were such dorks."

Back then, neither of them had mattered in the vast hierarchy of court. Himari's parents possessed an earldom, so they ranked higher than Daphne's, who were a second-generation baronet and lady. But Himari's older brother would inherit their title, while Daphne, at least, was an only child.

Both girls had been nobodies, and each wanted desperately to be *some*body. It was what had initially drawn them to each other—their shared impulse to climb.

Daphne hadn't realized at the time what that kind of wanting could do to someone, how dangerous it could make them.

"If you don't remember falling," she asked, "what *do* you remember?"

"The last thing I remember is our French exam! When I woke up, my first thought was that I had a calculus final today, and I needed to make sure I brought my calculator to school."

Daphne listened hard, searching for any hint of hesitation or falsehood in Himari's words, but she didn't hear any.

"Our French exam? That was at least a week before the graduation party." And before Himari's birthday: when Daphne ended up with Ethan, and Himari saw them in bed together.

Before Himari threatened Daphne with the secret, and Daphne decided to fight fire with fire, and everything escalated so horribly out of control.

"It could be worse. I could've lost months instead of days," Himari pointed out. "Though I guess I *have* lost months, given that a year of my life has disappeared."

"I'm so sorry," Daphne replied, because there was nothing else to say.

"I didn't believe my parents, you know." Himari was still holding the gift basket, fiddling with the cellophane wrapper around a soy candle. "When I woke up and heard the date, when they told me that the king had died, I didn't believe it."

Daphne swallowed. "A lot happened while you were in the hospital."

"I know, you're about to graduate! Next year, I'll have to be a senior all alone." Himari sighed dramatically, looking so utterly like her old self that Daphne almost smiled.

Suddenly, she remembered a time back in freshman year—before she was dating Jefferson, because no one would dare do something like this now—when a junior named Mary Blythe started a rumor that Daphne had gotten plastic surgery. On her nose, her boobs, everything.

Daphne had forced herself not to acknowledge the rumor. She knew that the more vocally she protested, the more people would believe it was true.

Himari, however, had created a fake email address and reached out to Mary, posing as a recruiter for a reality dating show. She'd convinced Mary to record an embarrassing audition video—which Himari then played during a school assembly.

"What?" she'd exclaimed, in answer to Daphne's stunned look. "No one gets to mess with you."

Himari was a little scary that way. There was no one as fiercely loyal to her friends—or as utterly merciless to her enemies.

If only Daphne knew which category she fell into now.

"So what have I missed?" Himari pulled her legs up beneath the blankets. "Catch me up on everything that's happened in the past year."

"Beatrice is queen," Daphne began, but Himari interrupted.

"I know *that*! Tell me about you and Jeff," she pleaded. "Why does everyone keep saying you might get back together? When did you break up in the first place?"

"He broke up with me last summer," Daphne said cautiously. "For a while he dated Nina Gonzalez. Samantha's friend."

Himari's eyes widened in recognition, and she barked out a laugh. "*That* girl? Seriously?"

This time, Daphne couldn't hold back her smile.

She hadn't realized how much she'd missed having someone to confide in. For years, Himari had been the first person Daphne went to with any sort of news—good news, bad news, news that didn't really matter at all.

But ever since the accident, Daphne had been holding these sorts of conversations with Himari in her head: asking her questions, guessing how Himari might have replied. This was precisely the reaction she had imagined, when she'd wondered what Himari would've said about Nina.

Himari reached into the gift basket for a box of chocolate truffles and popped one into her mouth, then passed Daphne the box. "Tell me the whole story, from the beginning."

11

SAMANTHA

Samantha walked down the palace hallway with willfully slow steps. She trailed her fingers over every tapestry, scuffed her feet on the carpets, the way she'd seen children do when their parents dragged them on a palace tour. She felt maddeningly like a child right now, receiving a summons to meet with Lord Robert Standish.

She'd only been to Robert's office twice before. Once a few years ago, when that paparazzo got the infamous photo of her skirt riding up. And then last spring she'd been called there with Jeff, after Himari Mariko fell down the stairs at their graduation party.

Neither occasion had been especially pleasant.

The Lord Chamberlain worked on the second floor, just outside Beatrice's study—so that he could monitor the queen's visitors, a bright-eyed Cerberus guarding her time. Sam was grateful to see that her sister's door was firmly shut. She'd done a fantastic job avoiding Beatrice for the past couple of weeks, and had no intention of stopping now.

She knocked at the chamberlain's door, then reluctantly slipped inside to take a seat.

Robert was seated at his desk, dressed as usual in a charcoal-colored suit. It was the only thing Sam had ever seen him wear. She'd occasionally caught herself wondering whether he ever took it off, or maybe his closet was simply full of them, dozens of matching gray pants and jackets lined up in tidy little rows.

She made an impatient noise, but Robert didn't look up. He kept on typing, as if to punish her for her tardiness.

Perched on his desk was an arrangement of red roses, along with golden daylilies and blue delphiniums. The whole thing was disgustingly patriotic. Sam reached up to pluck one of the flowers, rolling it back and forth. It was as dusky blue as a midsummer sky, as Teddy's eyes.

She crushed it between her fingers, then let it fall to the floor.

"You're nineteen minutes late," Robert said at last. Sam found it strangely irritating that he'd said *nineteen* instead of *twenty*. He shook his head with a resigned sigh. "Your Royal Highness, I set this meeting so that we could discuss your new responsibilities as first in line for the throne."

"There's no need for me to go through all the training that Beatrice did," Sam said automatically. "It's not like I'm ever going to *rule*."

This—being first in line for the throne—was the highest Sam would ever rank. Once Beatrice had children, the entire family would engage in a silent game of musical chairs, bumping everyone down a spot in the order of succession. The more kids Beatrice had, the more obsolete Sam would become.

Even *Teddy* had upgraded to Beatrice, the instant he'd gotten a chance.

"I'm certainly not suggesting that you prepare to be *queen*. Beatrice isn't going anywhere." Robert was clearly so appalled by the suggestion that he was startled into omitting her title, for once.

"Good, then we agree." Sam rose to her feet. "There's no need to waste your time preparing me for a role I will never fill. Especially when neither of us wants to be here."

"Sit down," Robert snapped, and Sam sank sullenly back

into her chair. "We aren't here to train you as a future monarch. Besides, the only person qualified for that sort of preparation is Her Majesty herself." Robert was the type of person who said *Your Majesty* as if the title belonged to him, or at least as if it lent him a secondhand glamour.

"Then why are we here?" Sam demanded.

"Our discussion today will focus on your new role as heir to the throne. You are a representative of the Crown now."

"But . . . wasn't I always?"

Robert's sneer deepened at her ignorance. "As princess, you were a representative of your family. But now you are the heir apparent—the queen's next in line, should anything go wrong. You have *level-one security clearance*." He gestured to the alarm on the wall. It was one of many scattered throughout the palace, all of them protected by biosecurity, so only a handful of people could activate them. A handful of people that now included Sam.

"I'll expect you to carry out the same schedule of social engagements that Her Majesty used to fulfill as the heir," Robert went on. "Including the Royal Derby, the queen's garden parties, the US Open—tennis *and* golf—the Baltimore Flower Show, the Chelsea Art Fair, the Fourth of July celebrations, hospital benefits, and, of course, anything related to the military."

At first Sam thought he'd merely paused, that he would keep on listing events until either she interrupted or he went hoarse. But the chamberlain only looked at her in unmistakable challenge.

"Well, if that's all," she said, with forced lightness.

"It's a hundred and eighty events per year." When he saw her eyes widen, Robert nodded. "Which is why we have a great deal of work to do to make you into a princess."

Sam's face went hot. "I *am* a princess," she reminded him.

Robert spoke slowly. He clearly relished this opportunity to show how little he thought of her. "My apologies, Your Royal Highness. I meant that you need to start *behaving* like one."

Sam hid the sting of hurt she felt at his words. She thought of all those hours she and her siblings had spent in the downstairs drawing room with their etiquette master. He'd droned on about how to greet visiting dignitaries, and the varying depths of a curtsy, and the order of precedence in every aristocratic house, because god forbid she insult someone by addressing a junior family member before a senior one. Beatrice, of course, had nodded with childish seriousness and taken notes. Even Jeff had paid halfhearted attention. While Sam had spent the entire time staring out the window, daydreaming.

Eventually the king and queen had given up, and let Sam run wild. She was simply too much effort to teach.

"With Her Majesty's upcoming wedding, your family will be under more scrutiny than ever before." Robert tilted his head, considering her. "You'll need an escort, of course, as the maid of honor. I'll find someone suitable."

"What?" Robert wanted to pick out her *wedding date*?

His eyebrows rose. "I'm sorry, did you have someone in mind? I wasn't aware that you were seeing anyone."

Sam thought of Teddy, and her jaw hardened. She tilted her head up defiantly. "I don't need a date. I'm perfectly happy to go to Beatrice's wedding alone."

"Unfortunately, that's out of the question. You'll need to help lead the opening dance." Robert made an expression that was probably meant to be a smile, though it resembled a grimace. He began organizing papers on his desk, arranging their stacks into careful right angles. "I'm afraid we have to conclude today's meeting. I really wish we'd had more time, but since you were nineteen minutes late, we'll have to pick back up on Thursday."

"You want to meet *again*?"

"It's crucial that we begin meeting several times a week. We have a great deal of material to cover."

Sam felt her own anger rising to meet his. "You should know that you're wasting your time."

"Because you refuse to cooperate?"

Of course Robert assumed *she* was the problem. He didn't know what it was like growing up in a sister's shadow—fighting for years to be taken seriously, only to realize that fighting would never get her anywhere.

The nation had never *wanted* to like Sam. Wasn't there an old saying, that nothing drew people together like a common enemy? Well, if Americans could agree on one thing, it was their disapproval of Princess Samantha.

"It doesn't matter how hard we try," she said, unable to keep the bitterness from her voice. "I'm the least popular member of my family. America has *never* cared what I do. They aren't about to start now."

She marched out of Robert's office before he could answer, letting the door click shut behind her.

As Sam turned down the hallway, she fumbled in her pocket for her phone. She started to call Nina, to see if they could meet up later—but a familiar voice emanated from the palace's two-story entryway, halting her in her tracks.

Standing at the foot of the curved staircase was Lord Marshall Davis. He was gesticulating wildly as he argued with a footman. And he was wearing full ceremonial dress.

"Marshall? What are you doing here?" Sam hadn't known when she would see him again, after they said goodbye at the end of the museum party.

He looked up in evident relief. "Samantha! I came to see you, actually. I need my lapel pin back."

Sam flushed as she remembered the proprietary way she'd

grabbed that pin, fastening it to her dress before dragging Marshall into the party. It had all been impulsive, fueled by obstinate pride and that bottle of wine. *Think before you act, Sam*, her father always used to say. But Sam had a tendency to act first, leaving the thoughts—or, often, regrets—for later.

She braced her palms on the stair railing and leaned forward, trying to sound nonchalant. "You didn't think to text?"

"You never gave me your number." Marshall started up the stairs, taking them two at a time, the same way Sam did.

He was wearing the peers' ceremonial robes: crimson wool trimmed in gold lace, complete with a cloak that tied at the throat with a white satin ribbon. They looked absurd on him. The robes had been designed centuries ago, back when the leaders of most duchies had been old white men. Marshall was so tall and imposing that he made the outfit look ludicrously like a Halloween costume.

"I can't believe you came here on your way to . . . where are you going?"

"Swearing-in of the new Chief Justice." He glanced down ruefully at his robes. "Believe it or not, I only just realized the pin was missing."

"Don't you have an extra?"

"Did you lose it?" Marshall sighed. "I've lost it too. I wore it on a dare, once, and it fell out on the streets of Vegas. It actually wasn't at the casino, but at the In-N-Out we stopped at when—"

Sam cut him off with a groan. "Chill out, okay? I have your jewelry."

Marshall didn't rise to the bait. He just smiled and said, "Where is it?"

"In my room."

To her surprise, he followed her down the hall, his red velvet cloak streaming out behind him. Historical portraits glared at them from the walls: statesmen with powdered wigs and pointed beards, women in pearl necklaces layered six strands deep. Marshall's outfit wouldn't have looked out of place inside one of the paintings.

Sam wondered what he was wearing underneath the robes. She glanced over at the broad expanse of his chest with an idle spark of curiosity.

Marshall's eyes met hers. Aware that he'd caught her staring, she hurried to ask a question. "Why are you the one here representing Orange? Isn't your grandfather the active duke?"

Most peers looked forward to ceremonial occasions like this. It was one of the few chances they had to put on these dusty old robes—and stare down their noses at all the commoners who didn't have the right to wear them.

"He's been sending me as his proxy a lot lately. He says he hates the cross-country flight. Not that I actually *do* anything," Marshall added under his breath.

"What do you mean?"

"Even when the dukes are all assembled, I'm only there to help fill out the room. I can't actually speak or vote. Being a proxy literally means that I'm a body filling a seat—a very good-looking body, obviously." He flashed his usual cocky smile, but Sam sensed that his heart wasn't in it. She surprised herself by answering with a truth of her own.

"I know the feeling. No one ever wants me to be anything *but* a body—a smiling, waving, tiara-wearing body."

"Would it help if I said you look great in a tiara?" Marshall offered, and Sam rolled her eyes.

"The tiara isn't the problem. It's the rest of it that I can't stand."

"If it makes you feel better, I'm not the smiling-and-waving type either."

"But at least you have a *purpose*! You'll get to rule someday!"

He seemed surprised by her reply. "In forty years, maybe. For now, there's nothing for me to do except sit around and wait."

"Welcome to life as the spare. It's a job full of nothing," Sam said drily.

"You, doing nothing? I find that hard to believe." Marshall's mouth twitched. "Just think of all the buildings you haven't yet kicked."

"Look, can you please forget about that?"

Sam hated that Marshall had caught her in that moment. She felt more exposed, somehow, than if he'd seen her naked.

"Absolutely not," he said mercilessly. "The American princess taking out her frustrations on a national monument? It's one of my most treasured memories."

"Then you'll be next," Sam warned, and he laughed.

As she pushed open the door, she saw Marshall cast a few curious glances around her sitting room. Unlike the rest of the palace, Sam's suite was an eclectic clash of styles and colors. Brightly colored rugs were strewn over the floor at odd angles. Against one wall, an ornate grandfather clock—which Sam's ancestor Queen Tatiana had brought from Russia, its hours marked with gorgeous Cyrillic numerals—stood next to a table that was hand-painted in bright green turtles.

Sam headed to her desk and pulled out the top drawer. An assortment of objects clattered inside: old lipsticks, earring backs, a pearl button that had fallen off her leather gloves. At the center of all the disorder was the enamel bear pin.

"See? I told you I hadn't lost it!"

She reached for the fabric of his robes. Surprise flickered in Marshall's eyes, and she realized belatedly that he hadn't expected her to pin it *on* him.

Sam's hand fell abruptly from his chest.

"Here, let me." Marshall reached to hook the pin in place. It was made to be worn like this, Sam realized: not pinned against the drab backdrop of a suit, but atop the scarlet robes, where it gleamed like liquid gold.

She took a step back, struck by the immediate physicality of Marshall's presence. He no longer looked ridiculous in the robes at all. If anything, the other peers would look ridiculous next to *him*.

"So, did it work?" she asked, recalling why she'd taken the pin in the first place. "Did we make Kelsey jealous?"

"I don't know. Haven't heard from her." Marshall shrugged. "What about you and your mystery guy?"

"He saw us," she said evasively.

When she'd walked into the reception hall arm in arm with Marshall, Sam hadn't dared look over at Teddy. But she felt certain he'd seen them together. Everyone at that party had seen them, because she and Marshall were, if nothing else, gossip-worthy. And they'd been making a bit of a scene.

Thinking of it gave her a rush of hot, vindictive pleasure that quickly evaporated.

Teddy was going to *marry* her sister. And no matter what Sam did, there was no way she could hurt him worse than he'd hurt her.

"Thanks, Samantha. I'll see you around," Marshall said cheerfully, and started toward the door.

Sam swallowed, remembering what Robert had said: that protocol demanded she bring someone to the wedding.

"Marshall. What if we kept going?"

He glanced back at her, caught between curiosity and confusion. Sam hurried to explain. "I have to bring an escort to Beatrice's wedding. It could be you."

His brow furrowed. "You want *me* to be your date to your sister's wedding?"

"Why not? You already have the outfit, after all."

Again Sam had that disconcerting sense that Marshall could see right through her.

"This is still about that guy, isn't it? You think bringing me to your sister's wedding will make him jealous?"

"Well . . . yes," she admitted. "But it works both ways! Think of how upset Kelsey will be. She'll *definitely* want you back."

"Because she'll be upset that I'm dating someone more famous than she is?"

"Because girls always want what they can't have," Sam retorted, and bit her lip.

That wasn't the reason she liked Teddy, was it? She wanted him because she *cared* about him, not because he was off-limits.

Yet a small, terrible part of her wondered if that had been part of his appeal. After all, Teddy was the only thing of Beatrice's that Sam had ever managed to take for herself. Even if it hadn't lasted.

"I'm dreading this wedding," she went on, glancing back up at Marshall. "It's everything I hate: protocol and ceremony and stuffy old traditions, all rolled up into one massive event. Like always, I'll be scrutinized and criticized no matter what I do. And like always, nothing I do will really matter at all."

She heaved a breath. "I understand if you don't want to get involved. It's just—it would be nice, to go through all this with someone I can actually stand."

"Someone you can actually stand," he repeated, an eyebrow lifted. "When you give me such glowing compliments, how could I refuse?"

"Sorry, did I bruise your precious masculine ego?" Sam scoffed. "Look, Marshall, you and I want the same thing—for our exes to realize they made a mistake. That won't happen unless they pay *attention* to us. And if there's one thing we're both good at, it's attracting attention."

Marshall had a reputation, and she had a reputation, and in her experience, gossip always added up to something greater than the sum of its parts. The two of them together were far more buzzworthy than anything they could do on their own.

"You're not just asking me to be your wedding date, are you," Marshall said slowly. "You want to really sell this. Make everyone think I'm your boyfriend."

"Hollywood celebrities manipulate the press like this all the time," Sam insisted, though she wasn't actually sure it was true.

"What's your plan, exactly? We hold a press conference, tell everyone we're dating? Become Samarshall?"

"Or Marshantha. I can be the second half," Sam replied, without missing a beat. She was relieved when Marshall laughed at that. "And there's no need for a press conference. We can just attend a few events together, let the paparazzi catch us holding hands, get people talking about us. By the time we go to the wedding, Kelsey will be begging you to get back together!" *And Teddy will regret ever letting me go,* she thought acridly.

"You may be right . . . but I'm not sure it's worth the beating I'd get from the press," Marshall said, his eyes fixed on hers. "Whenever someone in the royal family dates a person of color, things get ugly. Remember how people reacted when your aunt Margaret dated the Nigerian prince? And he was a future king. Not to mention what they did to Nina when she dated your brother," he reminded her. "If people think we're dating, I'm the one who's going to take the heat for it, not you. That's just the way things are."

Sam's stomach twisted. When she'd suggested this plan to Marshall, she hadn't been thinking about his race at all. She'd just thought that Marshall was famous—or rather, *infamous*. And it hadn't hurt that he was tall and objectively good-looking. Perfect revenge-dating material.

She'd been with lots of guys before, and plenty of them

hadn't been white, but she'd been able to keep most of her romantic entanglements from the media—probably because they never lasted beyond a single weekend. This was the first time she'd be dating someone so publicly. Now, as she recalled the anguish Nina had gone through when she was with Jeff—the paparazzi hounding her family, the hateful online comments—Sam realized what she was asking of Marshall.

She nodded, feeling slightly ashamed. "I'm sorry. Of course, I wasn't thinking."

"I'm sure you can find someone else who'd be interested in your . . . offer," Marshall replied.

"Please, just forget I ever—"

"Then again, I'm not sure I want you to find someone else."

Sam looked up. There was a fleeting glimpse of emotion on Marshall's features, but it quickly vanished beneath his usual careless smile.

"Are you saying that you're okay with this?" she pressed. "Even if it puts you under the microscope?"

He shrugged. "Why not? I've never dated a princess before. For real or for revenge. Or for . . . well, whatever this is."

Sam held out a hand. "So . . . we have a deal?"

Marshall eyed the gesture with amusement. "Oh, no need to shake on it. I trust you, Sam. I *can* call you Sam, right?" he added cheekily. "Or would you prefer something else? Babe, or sweetheart, or what about *Sammie?*"

Sam made a choking noise. "Under no circumstances can you use any of those names."

Marshall grinned, flipping his cape out behind him like a character in an old-fashioned play. "Okay, then. See you later, honeycakes."

Sam grabbed a pillow from her couch and hurled it at his head, but he'd already shut the door behind him.

BEATRICE

Beatrice hurried down the front steps of the palace, her Guard at her heels. "Sorry," she exclaimed when she saw Teddy at the front drive, standing next to a red SUV. "I didn't mean to be late for our meeting."

His mouth quirked at the corner. "Beatrice, this isn't a *meeting*. I asked Robert to block some time on your calendar because I wanted to hang out."

"Oh—okay," Beatrice breathed. She hadn't just *hung out* with someone—no agenda, no stated purpose—since college, unless you counted all the hours she'd spent with Connor.

"No worries." Teddy walked up to the passenger side and held open the door. He clearly planned on driving her *himself*.

To Beatrice's surprise, her protection officer frowned but merely said, "I'll tail you guys."

Beatrice slid into the passenger seat and buckled her seat belt over her floral silk dress. She couldn't remember the last time she'd gotten to sit in the front of a car.

"Are you hungry?" Teddy asked, as he pulled out of the palace's main drive. "I was thinking we could go to Spruce. You love their kale salad, right?"

Actually, Beatrice had never liked Spruce. It was too loud, full of media people and models all vying to be noticed. The last time she'd been there was for an interview she'd done last summer.

"Wait a second," she said, as comprehension dawned. "Did you read my profile piece in *Metropolitan* magazine? Were you *studying up* on me?"

Teddy flushed, his eyes fixed on the road. "I don't usually plan a date without doing a little recon."

There was a funny silence as they both realized he'd used the word *date*.

"For the record, I only ordered the kale salad that day because I couldn't get a burger," Beatrice went on.

"Why not?"

"A burger isn't interview food. Too messy," she said regretfully.

Teddy glanced over, his eyes bright. "If there's one thing I know, it's burgers. But we're *not* getting you the one at Spruce. I mean, they put *brie* on it."

"What an abomination," Beatrice agreed, smiling.

Teddy chuckled and turned up the music, some indie rock band that Beatrice didn't recognize. "I'm so glad you see sense."

It wasn't until she saw the bright lights of the drive-through that she realized Teddy was taking her to Burger Haus.

"I grew up on these," he admitted, before pulling up to the intercom and ordering two cheeseburgers. Beatrice was amazed by the efficiency of the system. Seeing her expression, Teddy chuckled.

"Beatrice. Have you ever eaten fast food?"

"Of course I have! Just not from a drive-through." She glanced down, smoothing her dress over her thighs. "We ate at McDonald's as a family at least once a year when I was a kid. Our press people alerted the tabloids ahead of time, so they could plant photographers at nearby tables. They always used them in that section, 'Royals: They're Just Like Us.'"

"Then you haven't really eaten fast food," Teddy told her. "Everyone knows it's impossible to enjoy a burger when paparazzi are watching you eat it." He was trying to sound lighthearted, but it didn't quite work. Beatrice wondered if she'd frightened him—if he was coming to realize what he'd signed on for, agreeing to marry her.

They reached the drive-through window, and a woman with a high ponytail looked up at them. Her eyes widened as she squealed in recognition.

"You're Theodore Eaton! The Dreamboat Duke!" When she saw who was in the passenger seat, her face grew even redder. "Oh my god, Your Highness—I mean Majesty—" She sank into a startled curtsy, still holding a container of fries in one hand.

Normally Beatrice would have acknowledged the woman with a gracious smile. But she was out in a car without her Guard, about to eat a burger without worrying about how unflattering it might look in photos. Actually, no one was taking her photo at *all*. The prospect filled her with a childish excitement.

"Really? You think I look like the queen?" she said, and winked.

Later, when he'd dropped her back at the palace's entrance hall, Teddy cleared his throat. "Before I go, there's something I've been meaning to ask you," he ventured. "My parents were wondering—would you come to Walthorpe for a weekend?"

Visit Teddy's childhood home. Beatrice was surprised at the flicker of anticipation she felt at the prospect of learning more about him.

"I'd love to," she agreed.

Teddy broke into a relieved grin. "Okay, great," he said, thumbs looped into his pockets. "Well . . . I should get going.

You need to rest your throwing arm for tomorrow's big pitch."

Oh, right. Beatrice had almost forgotten that tomorrow she was scheduled to throw the first pitch at National Stadium. It was a long-standing tradition in American baseball that the monarch opened one of the first games of the season.

"You've practiced, haven't you?" Teddy added, at the look on her face.

"I was just planning on tossing it underhand. I mean, the whole thing is ceremonial. Won't everyone just want me to hurry up and throw the ball, so the real game can begin?"

"You can't *toss* it." Teddy sounded horrified. "Beatrice, America judges people based on their throwing ability. As if your first pitch represents what kind of ruler you'll be."

"Great," Beatrice said darkly. "Now when I throw it in the dirt, I'll get booed off the field."

"We won't let that happen," Teddy promised.

"What do you plan to do, teach me to throw a baseball between now and tomorrow morning?"

"That's exactly what we're going to do. Don't worry, you're in good hands," he assured her. "I was captain of my high school baseball team. And I was the pitcher."

"I thought you were captain of your *football* team."

"Yeah, I was that too," he said easily.

"What else were you, prom king?" When Teddy didn't protest, Beatrice threw up her hands in exasperation. "Oh my god, you *were*. You're literally Mr. America! No *wonder* that woman called you the Dreamboat Duke!"

"*Please* don't use that name," Teddy groaned. "Now come on, we're wasting moonlight."

Half an hour later they were out on the palace's back lawn. A few moths fluttered nearby, their wings glimmering a silvery purple. The night was cool, but the air had a soft, expectant quality that held the promise of summer.

With the help of a footman, Teddy had tracked down some of Jeff's high school athletic gear. He rifled through the box, grinning triumphantly when he emerged with a baseball and a pair of old gloves.

Pulling on the catcher's mitt, he headed past her and crouched onto the balls of his feet. "Okay, show me what you've got, Bee."

She froze. Only two people had ever used that nickname. "Where did you hear that? Calling me Bee, I mean." She wondered if Sam had told him, or if he'd come up with it himself. After all, it *was* the first syllable of her name.

"You don't like it?" Teddy gave a puzzled frown, and Beatrice shook her head.

"No, I like it. I just—I haven't heard anyone say that in a while."

Taking a deep breath, she threw the baseball. It veered wide to the right of Teddy's face. When he tossed it back to her, she held up her glove, fumbling to catch it, but missed.

"Okay, so you can't catch," Teddy said bluntly, as she scrambled to grab the ball from the ground. "But that doesn't matter, because you won't have to catch tomorrow. Our problem is that you throw like—"

"Don't you dare say 'like a girl,'" Beatrice cut in, and he laughed.

"Please, I know better. You should see Charlotte's fastball." He shook his head. "I was *going* to say that you throw like you've never held a baseball before."

Teddy took off his glove and walked back over, to stand behind her. "Let's try this again: slowly, one step at a time. I'll talk you through the whole thing."

Beatrice hardly dared breathe as his hands settled on her waist.

"First of all, you're too far forward." He put a slight pressure on her hips, turning her, then wrapped his arms around her and closed his hands over hers. Beatrice was suddenly and acutely conscious of every place their bodies touched.

"Start with the ball at chest level. Now lift your left hand and point toward your target." As he spoke, Teddy kept his hands on Beatrice's arms, guiding her carefully through the motions. His breath sent shivers down the back of her neck.

When she finally threw the ball, it went farther and straighter than it had the first time. "That was better!" Beatrice cried out in triumph, and turned around.

Teddy's magnetic blue eyes were fixed on hers. He shifted, and for a breathless moment Beatrice thought he was going to kiss her. Instinctively she tipped her face up—but nothing happened.

He's my fiancé, she realized, with a dazed sort of shock. Of course he was, she *knew* that, yet the knowledge struck her now in a way that it hadn't before.

It was as if, all this time, she had known that she was marrying Teddy Eaton, son of the Duke of Boston. But only now did she fully appreciate that she was marrying Teddy Eaton, the man.

"Yep, that was better," Teddy agreed, and smiled at her—not the picture-perfect smile she'd seen a thousand times, but a new, disarming smile, unguarded and infectious.

It was his *true* smile, Beatrice realized.

And for the first time since she'd lost her dad, she was smiling her own true smile, too.

13

NINA

Nina clattered down the staircase of an off-campus house, her flapper dress swaying with the movement. She reached into her purse to check her phone one last time, in case any of her friends were ready to leave the party, too.

And, Nina admitted to herself, in case she'd heard from Ethan.

They'd been texting all week. At first they were just coordinating logistics for their journalism project, but the conversation had quickly spun out from there. Now they checked in daily, even if it was nothing but a distracting emoji sent during class.

Texting was the easy part. When they were texting, Nina felt certain that she and Ethan weren't doing anything wrong; they were just old friends who'd happened to reconnect at college. When they were texting, she could control her responses down to the last comma.

It was when she saw Ethan in person—the day they'd grabbed lunch after class, or the afternoon they'd studied together at the library, passing a bag of Swedish Fish back and forth as Ethan hummed along to some song on his headphones—that everything felt muddled.

Nina still hadn't told Sam that she'd started hanging out with Ethan. She'd meant to . . . but when she'd gone to the palace yesterday, Sam had announced that she and Marshall

Davis were in a *fake relationship*, which was such startling and confusing news that Nina couldn't think about anything else.

"I don't like this," she'd warned, when Sam explained her plan. "Making Teddy jealous is a terrible reason to go out with someone. And has Marshall considered what the tabloids will say about him, once you announce your so-called relationship?"

Nina's skin prickled at the thought of all the vile things people had written about her. Sure, Marshall was wealthy and noble, so he wouldn't get the "tacky commoner" or "she's a nobody from nowhere" comments that had chased Nina. But he would still be a person of color publicly dating a member of the royal family.

Sam's expression had softened at Nina's words. "We talked about that, actually. Marshall told me he's okay with it."

"Then he doesn't realize how ugly it's going to get," Nina had snapped.

It wasn't just about Marshall, although Nina did think he'd signed on for more than he'd bargained for. Nina was also worried about her friend.

Sam was incapable of doing anything halfway. She threw her whole heart into every decision she made, and it usually ended up hurting her. Pretending to date Marshall could only cause her pain.

Nina's thoughts were interrupted as a group of rowdy, jostling boys spilled out the doors of Rutledge House. Ignoring their laughter, she slid her phone back into her purse, only to pause at the sound of her name.

"Nina—hey!" Ethan detached himself from the group and crossed the street to meet her. He took in her outfit and smiled. "I should have known you'd be at Gatsby Night. You can't resist the chance to live out a novel."

Nina shook her head, causing her feathered headpiece

to slip lower on her brow. "Actually, I don't like *The Great Gatsby* all that much."

"Really?"

"Jay plans his entire life around Daisy, and she's not even that great!" Nina exclaimed. "What kind of relationship is that? In real life, no one would make the person they loved *social climb* to prove their worth."

A shadow darkened Ethan's eyes, but he just glanced down the road. The streetlamps cast pools of lemony light on the pavement. "Are you waiting for someone?"

"Actually, I was just heading home—"

"Let me walk you."

Before she could say anything, Ethan was jogging back over to the group of guys. "I need to walk my friend home," she heard him say, and for some reason the term startled her. But why should it? She and Ethan *were* friends. What else could they be?

They started back toward the freshman dorms in a companionable silence. The familiar spires and faux-Gothic towers of campus always looked slightly different at night. Nina would catch herself noticing details she'd never seen before—a weeping stone angel, a wisp-thin row of trees—and wondering if they'd always been there, or had only sprung to life now that the sun had set. She hugged her arms around her chest, surprisingly glad that Ethan had come with her.

He glanced over, catching the motion, and picked up his pace. "Are you cold?"

"Yeah," Nina said, though she felt something else, too: a subdued, half-eager feeling that she didn't dare examine closely.

Ethan's phone buzzed, breaking the silence. When he glanced at the screen, a funny expression—excited and uncertain and wary all at the same time—flickered over his features. He declined the call, then typed out a quick text, holding the phone so Nina couldn't see it.

"You can take that if you want," she felt the need to say, but Ethan shook his head.

"It's fine."

Something about his tone made Nina wonder if the call had been from a girl—if Ethan had planned to see someone else tonight, and instead was here with her. It was a strange, but not unpleasant, thought.

They reached the entrance to Nina's dorm. This was the very spot where Jeff had kissed her, the night they were spotted and the photo ended up in the tabloids.

Pushing those memories aside, Nina fumbled in her purse, just as Ethan's stomach emitted a loud growl.

"You hungry?" she asked, laughing.

He gave an unselfconscious shrug. "I could eat."

"Thanks for walking me home." She pushed open the door to her entryway, and to her surprise, Ethan followed her inside, heading up the stairs in her wake.

"What kind of pizza do you like?" he asked, tapping at his phone. His eyes sparkled with mischief, in a way that almost reminded Nina of Sam.

"It's okay, I don't want any," she said unconvincingly.

"Pizza isn't a *want*; it's a *need*." Ethan paused, his gaze searching hers. "Unless you want me to go."

Well . . . friends were allowed to late-night eat together, weren't they?

"Pizza sounds delicious," she amended. "Mushroom, please."

He let out an indignant breath. "It's a pizza, not a salad. I'll get pepperoni."

"If you weren't going to listen, why did you bother asking?"

"Because I assumed you had better taste than to want *vegetables*. Fine," he compromised, "we'll do half and half."

Nina unlocked her door. Ethan immediately went to sit in her desk chair, tipping it back onto its hind legs. He glanced around her room, his eyes resting on each detail in turn—the collage of photos above the bed, the lip balms and pens scattered over her desk—as if he was trying to figure her out. Nina suddenly longed to know what conclusions he'd drawn.

"It's funny," Ethan mused. "Of all the people we knew, you were the last one I expected to come to school here."

Nina climbed onto her bed, pulling a blanket over her lap. "Really?"

"I guess I always thought you'd go to school far away. Out of the country, even." Ethan sighed. "Sometimes I wish *I* had."

"It's not too late. You can do a semester abroad somewhere," she pointed out.

"But in the meantime, I'm still here, still . . ." He gave a shrug, as if to say, *Still tied up in the lives of the royal family.*

"Where would you go? London?"

"Why do you assume that? Because I wouldn't need a foreign language?" At Nina's guilty look, Ethan chuckled. "I'll have you know, I do speak Spanish."

"So, Salamanca?"

Ethan's eyes slanted away, as if he wasn't quite certain he wanted to share this. "Actually," he mumbled, "if I studied abroad, I always secretly wanted it to be in Venice."

"Venice?" Nina blinked, startled. "That's where *I've* always wanted to go."

"Because it's the city of romance?"

"You're thinking of Paris." She leaned onto one hand, tracing the waffle pattern of her blanket. "I've always been fascinated by Venice. The whole city is *sinking*, settling down into the water one centimeter at a time. There's nothing anyone can do to stop it, so they just keep going about their business as normal. As a tourist you feel lost in it all, but it doesn't really matter because every road in the city leads back to the piazza. And eventually you'll find your way back there, to sit at a café and watch the sun set over the water . . ."

"I didn't realize you've been to Venice," Ethan said slowly, and Nina felt her face grow hot.

"I haven't. I've just read about it."

A knock sounded on the door: their pizza delivery. Nina answered it, then turned back to Ethan, the box in one hand. "You might as well sit over here," she surprised herself by offering.

"Sure." Ethan flopped easily onto the bed, then shifted so that he sat facing her, the pizza box balanced picnic-style between them. Nina almost groaned aloud as she bit into her slice.

"I told you that you wanted pizza." Ethan sounded inordinately pleased with himself. He'd already inhaled his first slice and was grabbing a second.

Nina tried, and failed, to conceal her amusement. "I hate to contribute to your oversized sense of self-importance, but yes, you were right."

She hadn't expected it to feel so natural, sitting here with Ethan, on her *bed*.

"So," he asked, "why didn't you go to school in Venice, if you've read so many books about it that it sounds like you *have* been there?"

"I don't know. Maybe . . ." This was hard to admit, but Nina forced herself to say it. "Maybe I was being cowardly. I've never traveled that far from home before." She folded her pizza over on itself so she could take another bite. "It's okay. Venice isn't sinking all that fast; it won't have changed much by the time I get to see it."

"But that's not the point of studying abroad," Ethan argued. "You don't go to Venice because *it's* changing; you go because *you* would change, living there. When you came home you would see everything in a new light. You would notice things—and people—that you hadn't paid attention to before."

There was a significance to his words that made Nina wonder if he was talking about the two of them. If he noticed *her*, now, even though he hadn't before.

She set the half-empty pizza box on the edge of her desk. "That was . . . surprisingly profound, for a late-night pizza conversation."

"Pizza and philosophy, my two specialties." Ethan grabbed her pillow and placed it behind his head, then leaned back with a contented sigh.

"You can't steal my pillow!" Nina cried out.

"I need it more than you do. My head weighs more," he argued. "It's full of beer and profound thoughts."

She tried to pull at the corner, but it didn't budge. "A gentleman would never do this," she scolded, laughing.

Ethan's eyes were still half-closed. "Sorry, I used up all my gentlemanliness walking you home."

"Give it *back!*" Nina tugged at the pillow, just as Ethan yanked it from behind his head and threw it at her.

"Oops," he said cheerfully.

Then they were whacking each other with the pillow, just like when they were little and would all chase each other around the palace, shrieking with delight, with Sam always in the middle of the melee, leading the great girls-versus-boys joust of pillows.

Eventually they leaned back, both of them breathing heavily. Nina felt almost sore from laughing so hard. The laughter was still fizzing through her, dissolving into a bright, heady afterglow.

Suddenly, she realized how very close her face was to

Ethan's. Close enough that she could see each freckle that dusted his cheeks, could see the individual lashes curling over his deep brown eyes.

He reached out to tuck a loose strand of hair behind her ear.

Nina's entire being centered on that point of contact, where his skin touched hers. She knew she should move, should remind Ethan that this wasn't fair to Jeff and they needed to call it a night. Yet she couldn't bring herself to say Jeff's name, and break the magic that seemed to have spun itself around her and Ethan.

Ethan's touch grew firmer, his hand moving to trace the line of her jaw, her lower lip. The air between them crackled with electricity. Very slowly, as if he wanted to give her time to change her mind—which she didn't—he brushed his lips against hers.

Nina leaned deeper into the kiss, her grip tightening over his shoulders. She felt heat everywhere they touched; his hands seemed to singe her very skin.

Ethan abruptly pulled away, his breathing ragged. "I should get going," he muttered, sliding off her bed.

As the door shut behind him, Nina fell back onto her bed and closed her eyes, wondering what the hell had just happened.

14

SAMANTHA

When Sam saw that the ballroom was still dark, she heaved a dramatic sigh. She had meant to show up late to this stupid wedding rehearsal, but it would seem that Robert had outsmarted her, and sent her a schedule with a false start time.

She wondered if he'd done the same to Marshall. Last week, when she'd informed Robert that Marshall was her wedding date, the chamberlain had sniffed in disapproval. "He'll need to attend rehearsals. Please make sure he shows up," Robert had said ominously.

"Fine," Sam had snapped, though she wasn't sure she could *make* Marshall do anything. He was like her in that regard.

She sank onto a velvet-upholstered bench and stared at the painting on the opposite wall: a full-length oil portrait of their entire family, the type of formal, choreographed picture that was intended for the pages of future textbooks.

In the portrait, Queen Adelaide was seated with four-year-old Jeff in her lap. Light danced over the latticed diamonds of her tiara. The king stood behind them, one hand on the back of the chair, the other resting on Beatrice's shoulder. Sam's breath caught a little at the sight of her dad. It felt like she was looking through a spyglass that sent her back in time, to before she'd lost him.

She glanced to the opposite side of the painting, where she stood, detached from the rest of her family. It almost seemed like the rest of them had posed without her, and then the artist had painted her in at the last minute.

"Do you remember sitting for that?"

Sam glanced up sharply. Beatrice hesitated, then sat next to Sam: warily, as if unsure whether she might bite. She was wearing a long-sleeved dress that buttoned at the wrists, which looked especially elegant next to Sam's frayed jeans.

"Sort of." Sam remembered the hypnotic sound of the artist's pencil, remembered being so impatient to see herself—to witness this transformation of blank canvas into an image of *her*—that she kept trying to wriggle from her mom's lap. When Adelaide had snapped at her, the artist had suggested that Sam and Jeff trade places. *Don't worry if she won't stand still; I'll fix it in the painting,* he'd assured the queen. *That's the benefit of oil portraits: they're more forgiving than photography.*

She remembered seeing reprints of that portrait in the palace gift shop, and realizing that complete strangers were paying money for images of her family. That was the first time that Sam truly understood the surreal nature of their position.

"I miss him," Beatrice murmured. "So much."

Sam looked over at her sister. Right now she didn't seem particularly majestic. She was just . . . Beatrice.

"I miss him, too."

Beatrice's eyes were still locked on the painted figure of their dad. "This doesn't even *look* like him."

"I know. He's way too kingly."

The George who stared back at them from the portrait was grave and resolute and stern, the Imperial State Crown poised on his brow. No one could doubt that he was a monarch.

But Sam didn't miss her monarch; she missed her dad.

"He always made that face when he put the crown on. Like the weight of it forced him to be more serious," Beatrice mused.

"So do you. You have a constipated crown face," Sam deadpanned. At her sister's expression, she huffed out something that was almost a laugh. "I'm *kidding!*"

"Ha-ha, very funny," Beatrice replied, though she ventured a smile.

Sam realized that this was the most they'd spoken in weeks. Ever since the Royal Potomac Races, she'd gone back to avoiding her sister, the way she had for so many years. Beatrice had made a few attempts at reconciliation—had knocked at the door to Sam's room, texted asking if she could get lunch—but Sam had answered them all with silence.

She glanced over at Beatrice, suddenly hesitant. "Nice pitch at the Generals game, by the way."

"You saw that?"

The surprise in her sister's voice melted Sam's animosity a little further. "Of course I saw. Didn't you know it's a meme now? It's pretty badass."

"Thank you," Beatrice said. "I . . . I had some help."

Sam started to answer, only to fall silent as Teddy turned the corner.

And just like that, the fragile moment of truce between the Washington sisters was shattered. Everything Sam wanted to say would have to remain unspoken. The way it always did in their family.

There was a moment of chagrin, or maybe regret, on Teddy's face, but it quickly vanished. "Hey, Samantha," he greeted her, as easily as if she had never been anything to him but his fiancée's little sister.

Sam braced herself for a wave of longing and resentment, but all she felt was a dull sort of weariness.

They were saved from further conversation by the arrival of everyone else: Queen Adelaide and Jeff, followed by Robert. The chamberlain gestured for Beatrice to lead them all into the ballroom—as if it were crucial that they follow the order of precedence, even in a casual setting. This was precisely why Sam had always hated protocol.

"Thank you all for being here," Robert began. "I know it might seem early to be rehearsing, but we can't afford any mistakes. We'll have two *billion* people watching the live coverage of the ceremony."

The wedding of Sam's parents had been the first royal wedding broadcast on international television, a decision that had been controversial among the Washington family. *People watched it in* bars, Sam's grandmother always said, her voice hushed with disapproval.

"And I thought it best that we all meet before your weekend in Boston," Robert added, with an ingratiating nod toward Beatrice. "That way you can review the schedule with His Lordship's family and let me know if they have any preferred changes."

Sam hardly heard her sister's reply, hardly registered her mom chiming in, saying that she would be down in Canaveral this weekend and would they give the duchess her love. Sam had focused with relentless cruelty on those four words: *your weekend in Boston.*

Teddy was bringing Beatrice home to Walthorpe.

He'd moved on from Sam to her older sister. Which was fine by Sam, since he meant nothing to her, either. All it had been was a stupid flirtation, and now it was over.

Robert was still droning on about something—most likely etiquette—while Sam edged closer to her brother.

"It's just us this weekend," she whispered, with a nod toward Beatrice and Teddy. "Should we have people over?"

Back in high school, they had often thrown parties when

their dad left town. It was as if, once the monarch had gone and the Royal Standard was lowered from the flagpole, the palace stopped feeling like an institution and started feeling like their *house*.

Jeff blinked. "You want to throw a party, after what happened last time?"

Sam winced at the memory. "Himari's fall was an accident. And besides—she's out of her coma!" Sam had seen the news; it was all over social media. "Come on, Jeff, we could all use some cheering up right now."

Not to mention, it would show Teddy how little she cared that he and Beatrice were being all couple-y up in Boston.

"Okay. Let's do it," Jeff whispered.

"What are you two conspiring about?" their mother demanded.

"Nothing," the twins chorused. It felt so much like old times again that Sam had to bite her lip to keep from laughing.

Robert cleared his throat, a pompous, grating sound. "As I was *saying*, today we will be practicing the opening moments of the reception. After their entrance, the newlyweds will begin the traditional first dance to 'America, My Homeland.'"

At his words, Beatrice and Teddy made their way onto the ballroom's polished wooden floor.

"Following the first chorus, the family members will join in, as dictated by tradition." Robert nodded at Queen Adelaide. "Your Majesty, His Grace the Duke of Boston will lead you onto the dance floor. As for His Highness Prince Jefferson . . ." Robert turned pointedly to Jeff. "You still haven't told me the name of your date."

Jeff flashed a blithe, careless smile. "I'm waiting until the last minute. It's more fun to keep everyone guessing."

Sam wondered if her brother had anyone in mind. There was always the possibility he would do what the world expected of him, and get back together with Daphne.

She hoped not. It certainly wouldn't be easy on Nina, seeing Jeff and Daphne together again.

"Samantha," Robert said now, omitting her title, though he'd used it for everyone else. "You said that you've invited Lord Marshall Davis. Where is he?"

Sam was inordinately pleased by how startled Teddy looked at the news. Even Beatrice, who never revealed her emotions, widened her eyes in surprise.

"I'm sure he's on his way," she began, though she wasn't at all sure. But somehow, right on cue, the doors to the ballroom were flung open.

Marshall crossed the room with bold, easy strides and came to stand next to Sam. "Sorry, I hope I didn't hold things up too much."

It was the most unapologetic *sorry* that Sam had ever heard. Which meant a lot, coming from her.

Robert pursed his lips in disapproval. "Now that we're all here, let's begin." He swiped at his tablet, and the opening notes of "America, My Homeland" played on the speaker system.

It really was a dour song, Sam thought, feeling almost sorry for Beatrice. At least when *she* got married, she would get to choose the music for her first dance.

Marshall draped an arm over her shoulders in a casual gesture. "Hey, babe."

Sam nestled in closer, letting her head tip onto his shoulder. "I told you not to call me that," she murmured—and gave his side a pinch.

Marshall didn't even wince. He just caught her hand with his, lacing their fingers. "Oh, snookums, I have a younger sister. You're going to have to do better than that to send me running."

"*Snookums?* Seriously?" Sam tried to tug her hand from his grip, but Marshall held it fast.

He began brushing his thumb in lazy circles over her knuckles. It was distracting enough that Sam fell still. She let her gaze drift to where Beatrice and Teddy were floating through the steps of the dance.

She hated to admit it, but they looked good together. When Teddy spun her on her toes, Beatrice's dress even fluttered out a little, hinting at how much better the real dress would look. The exertion seemed to warm her, so that by the time they'd reached the first chorus, her cheeks were flushed with a delicate pinkness that made her look . . . happy.

Robert turned around with a clucking noise. As Jeff headed to the other side of the ballroom—dancing with their mother, who was standing in for his date, whoever *that* would be—Marshall tugged Sam onto the dance floor. He clasped her right hand firmly in his left, settling his other hand on her hip. She fit into his arms with surprising ease.

The music slid into a bleak, lonely-sounding bridge, and Marshall groaned. "How do they expect us to dance to such a depressing song?"

"Just shut up and do as you're told," Sam snapped, a little disconcerted that his thoughts so closely mirrored hers. "I'm starting to worry that you're more trouble than you're worth."

He smiled at that. "No one will believe we're dating if you keep saying what you *actually* think. Especially about me."

"But you make it so easy to insult you," Sam tossed back, even as she realized that Marshall was right. She'd never been this brutally honest with a boy before—because she'd never entered a relationship knowing it would go nowhere. Honestly, it was kind of liberating.

"Look, I know we said we'd go on our first public date next week," she went on, "but Jeff and I just decided that we're having a party on Saturday. You should come."

Marshall's grip on her waist tightened. "Ah, so your

mystery guy is going to be there. And you need me to strike fear and jealousy into his heart."

No, but I'll post such fantastic pictures that he'll have no choice but to see them, and realize I've moved on. "I can invite Kelsey, if that's what you're asking," she offered.

"Kelsey rarely leaves LA. She only came to that museum party because she was filming a commercial the next day."

"I thought you said you hadn't talked to her," Sam replied, and he gave a wry shrug at being caught.

"We didn't talk. I just . . . saw her post about the commercial online."

"*Marshall!*" Sam hissed. "You haven't unfollowed her? That's the first thing you're supposed to do after a breakup!"

"Sorry if I don't rush to take your advice. I know that when it comes to relationships, you're infinitely wise and mature," he said drily, and Sam rolled her eyes.

"Just promise you'll come to the party, okay?"

"Sure," he agreed, surprising her. "When in my life have I turned down a party?"

"I—okay. Thanks." Sam was suddenly distracted by the way Marshall's hand drifted lower, to settle over the curve of her spine.

Really, dancing was a strange social phenomenon. Here she was, so close to Marshall that they could talk without being heard, close enough that she could smell the clean, laundered scent of him. Yet everyone seemed determined to pretend that it was just like any other court ritual—that it wasn't intimate or physical at all.

Her next step landed her foot squarely on his. She stumbled back, but Marshall tightened his grip on her elbow to steady her.

"I know this won't come naturally to you, but you could try following my lead," he offered.

"This is what I hate about ballroom dancing. Why should *you* be the one to lead, anyway?"

"Because I'm taller. Obviously." Marshall's lips twitched. "Also, I have more durable shoes. They're built to be stepped on by even the sharpest of high heels."

"It was your fault," she insisted, though she was biting back a smile. "You were in my way."

They danced for a few more minutes in silence. But when Marshall started to angle them on a diagonal, Sam shook her head. "What are you doing? This is the three-step turn!"

"That comes later. First it's the chassé."

She dug her heels in, her shoes squealing in protest on the hardwood floor.

"Samantha! The chassé comes first!" Robert shouted. Sam could hear his frustration from across the ballroom.

She started to shrug off the criticism the way she always did, but to her shock, Marshall drew to a halt, right there in the middle of the dance floor.

"Sorry, Lord Standish; it was my mistake. I led Samantha astray."

Robert grumbled to himself, but waved aside the apology.

Marshall turned back to Samantha, a hand held out expectantly. Slowly, a bit startled, she placed her palm in his.

"Did you just take the fall for me?"

"That's what fake boyfriends are for, isn't it?"

"I . . . you didn't have to do that."

Marshall shrugged as if it was no big deal. Maybe to him, it wasn't. "I did, actually. I know what it's like to be someone's punching bag."

There was a note in his voice that made Sam want to ask what he meant. A *real* girlfriend would have—or, rather, a real girlfriend would have already known.

"Thank you," she said simply.

They went through the rest of the dance without speaking. Sam tried to concentrate on the steps—the promenade; the standing turn; the full spin, when she twisted into Marshall's arms and then uncurled slowly. She focused on that, to keep herself from wondering about him.

Suddenly the music was slowing down, the song reaching its final dramatic crescendo. Before Sam had quite registered what was happening, Marshall pulled her into a low, dramatic dip. Her entire weight was cradled on his right arm. Sam imagined she could hear his heartbeat echoing through her own body.

"That was a good start," Robert called out, tapping away at his tablet. "But we have a bit of work to do. Let's do the whole thing again, from the top."

Then Marshall was lifting her back up—slowly, his eyes still fixed on hers. Sam struggled to breathe. She felt herself flush from her neck all the way to the roots of her hair.

"Not bad, my little ham Sam-wich," Marshall murmured, effectively shattering the tension between them. Sam rolled her eyes and detangled herself from his arms.

As they resumed their places, she told herself that her elevated heart rate was from the physical exertion. It definitely had nothing to do with the fact that, for a moment there, she'd thought Marshall was about to kiss her.

DAPHNE

The gates of Washington Palace had been designed for maximum visual impact, carved with intricate scrollwork and interlocking Ws. As Daphne and Himari gave their names to the security guard and he waved their taxi through, Daphne felt that there was something gratifying about all the grandeur.

She loved an imposing door or gate, provided she was on the inside.

"How do you feel?" she asked, when they'd gotten out of the car. Himari was uncharacteristically quiet.

The girls had seen each other nearly every day since Himari had been discharged from the hospital. At first they'd remained at the Marikos' house, flipping through magazines, making up for an entire year's worth of lost conversation. Then, at the doctor's recommendation, they'd slowly returned to their old activities: getting their nails done, or strolling down the sidewalks of Hanover Street, admiring the window displays.

"I'm a little nervous. But mostly excited." Himari nodded at the stoic-looking footman who gestured them through the front doors and toward the back lawn.

Daphne nodded, though she felt uneasy. "I'm just surprised your parents agreed to let you come."

"My doctor wants me to get back into my old routine, to help rebuild my neural recognition networks. The more

I act like my old self, the better chance I might remember everything I've forgotten." Himari saw Daphne's concerned look, and sighed. "If it makes you feel better, I promised my parents that I'm not drinking, not even a sip. Since I still have no idea what happened last time."

Whenever Himari made comments like this, Daphne worried her friend was baiting her, trying to trap her into saying something incriminating. So she said nothing. Then again . . . Himari wasn't even glancing her way.

It was that enchanted twilight hour when the sun was just setting, and for an instant, the sky became as dazzling as noon. It illuminated the terraced flower beds, their white mountain laurels scattered over the ground like handfuls of snow. In the orchard beyond, Daphne could see that the cherry trees had exploded into bloom.

Their steps crunched over the gravel as they followed the other guests toward an enormous white tent. Daphne recognized it as the same tent that the palace erected for the monthly garden parties—dull afternoon affairs, with flat champagne and cherry tarts. Seeing that familiar setup at night was strangely exhilarating. It lent everything a touch of mischief, made them all feel like children who were sneaking out past curfew, and might get away with it.

When they walked in, Daphne immediately caught sight of Ethan across the tent, and looked away. She hated that she could so easily pick him out of a crowd—that she knew the contours of his body, even from a distance.

"Oh my god," Himari whispered. "Is that *Marshall Davis* with Sam?"

Daphne followed her friend's gaze. Sure enough, the future Duke of Orange was standing there next to Samantha, his arm slung carelessly around her waist. "That's a new development," she mused. Though it honestly shouldn't have surprised her, given what reckless partiers they both were.

As she and Himari headed farther inside, there was a distinct lull in conversation. People began elbowing their neighbors, pointing out in hushed whispers that Himari had arrived.

Daphne reflexively reached up to loop an arm through her friend's. "Are you okay? Want me to take you home?"

"No." Himari bit her lip in indecision. She didn't look vengeful or dangerous at all; she looked . . . vulnerable. "I just—I didn't expect everyone to stare so much."

Of course, their classmates all knew that Himari had woken up: after emerging from a ten-month coma, she was something of a celebrity. She'd told Daphne that a few reporters had even called her house, asking for an exclusive interview, but Himari's mother had turned them down. "We don't talk to the *media* in this house," the Countess of Hana had replied, with cool disdain. She still subscribed to the old aristocratic belief that if your name appeared in the paper, it meant something had gone horribly wrong.

"Don't worry. Five minutes from now everyone will be focused on whatever stupid thing Samantha and Marshall do next," Daphne said firmly. "Besides, if people are staring, it's because you look fantastic."

Himari choked out a laugh. "My mom said the same thing. I guess months on a liquid diet will do that."

"I meant your clothes," Daphne replied, amused.

"Oh, I texted Damien an SOS this afternoon, and he brought this by. I couldn't go out in any of my old things. They were all hopelessly out of fashion," Himari said dramatically.

Unlike Daphne—who recycled outfits as often as she could get away with it, who accepted free gifts from up-and-coming designers because she couldn't afford new jewelry—Himari had never worried about money. Even now she was wearing a lavender jumpsuit and matching sequined clutch that Daphne had seen on the mannequin at Halo just yesterday.

There was a swirl of excitement nearby. Daphne turned to see Prince Jefferson standing a few yards away. He was wearing a white golf shirt that made him look especially tan, and smiling that eager, boyish smile of his, the one that most of America had fallen desperately in love with.

"Jefferson," she breathed, as she and Himari both curtsied at the same time, to exactly the same depth.

The prince waved away the gesture. "Please don't. I always hate it when people do that."

"It's nothing," Daphne started to say, but Himari interrupted.

"Jeff, when girls curtsy, we aren't doing it for you. We're doing it for *us*."

Daphne stiffened, wondering if her friend was being flirtatious, but Himari only added, "I like making people scurry out of my way. And the bigger my dress, the farther they have to scurry."

Laughing, the prince pulled Himari into a hug. "This is exactly why I've missed you," he joked, then stepped away, his tone becoming more serious. "Himari, I really am sorry. I don't know what happened that night, but it happened at *our* party. Sam and I feel terrible."

"It wasn't your fault," Himari assured him, and Jefferson smiled, relieved.

Of course it wasn't Jefferson's fault, Daphne thought. It was *hers*. She wished she could get the same absolution from her friend—but she knew she never would.

He nodded toward a table laden with drinks. "I'm thirsty. You guys coming?"

Now that Jefferson had broken the ice and talked to Himari, everyone else was surging forward. They began peppering her with questions: How was she feeling? Did she dream all those months? What was the first thing she said when she woke up?

Daphne hesitated. Jefferson had stepped ahead, the crowds

parting before him as he walked, but Himari lingered, reveling in the sudden flurry of attention. She met Daphne's gaze. For a moment, something flickered in Himari's eyes, but then she gave a little jerk of her chin to say, *Go ahead.* Daphne hurried to catch up with the prince.

It was her first time alone with him since the Royal Potomac Races, though Daphne had done her best to keep tabs on him. She was pretty sure he still hadn't invited a date to Beatrice's wedding.

And he hadn't been spotted with Nina, either, though Daphne knew better than to make assumptions. Just because they weren't together publicly didn't mean that nothing was going on in private. Last time, Jefferson and Nina had been hooking up for weeks before Daphne—and then the media—found out.

And wasn't Ethan supposed to be handling the Nina situation for her? The few times Daphne had checked in, he'd replied with vague one-line answers. Then, last weekend, she'd lost patience and dialed his number—only for Ethan to decline the call.

You can quit with the harassment. I'm with Nina right now, he'd texted, before she could try him again.

Daphne had felt an odd pang of surprise that he was out with Nina so late on a Saturday, though that was precisely what she'd asked of him. *Good,* she'd replied curtly.

She didn't care what Ethan did, as long as he kept Nina far from the prince, clearing the way for Daphne to make her move.

"This is a great setup," she said now, coming to stand behind Jefferson. "How did you get the tent?"

He rummaged beneath the table for a bag of ice cubes and scooped some into a red plastic cup. It always amused Daphne that he and Sam were some of the richest teenagers on earth yet still insisted on drinking out of those cups like regular college students. "Oh, the tent isn't for us. There's a garden party tomorrow," he replied mischievously.

Jefferson poured soda over the ice before handing the cup to Daphne. She loved that he hadn't even needed to ask: that he just made her drink, the way he always had.

Then again—being the perfect, well-behaved girlfriend hadn't really worked out for her last time. Daphne had a feeling that *Nina* drank at parties.

"You forgot the vodka," she said lightly.

"Right—sorry." Covering his surprise, Jefferson poured some into her cup. Then he grabbed himself a beer and led her away, toward the far corner of the tent and into a temporary bubble of privacy.

"It's going to be a rough cleanup, getting rid of all this before tomorrow's party," Daphne observed, kicking one heel behind the other.

The prince shrugged. "We'll be fine as long as nobody does anything stupid. Myself included."

"You, do anything stupid?" she teased. "Like that time you played darts, and were so off target you hit the painting of Lord Alexander Hamilton on the other side of the room?"

"Hey, I hit him right in the eye. You *could* say that I have awesome aim," Jefferson protested. "Or what about the time I led everyone on a tour of the dungeons, and accidentally locked us all inside?"

"You keep calling that room a dungeon, but it's just a basement."

"There's also the party we had over winter break sophomore year, when Ethan and I unpacked a box of Fourth of July sparklers. That was the night I met you, actually," Jefferson reminisced, in a softer tone.

Daphne smiled. "I thought those sparklers were a terrible idea, but I still lit one. I guess I wanted to impress you."

The prince spun his beer bottle in one hand. "I remember

seeing you out there on the terrace, laughing and holding that sparkler. The way it lit up your face... I thought you were the most beautiful girl I'd ever seen."

For some reason, Daphne remembered what Ethan had told her earlier this year. *Jeff doesn't know you like I do. All he sees is what you look like, which is a damn shame, because your mind is the best thing about you. Your brilliant, stubborn, unscrupulous mind—*

Daphne swept that thought forcibly aside. Why was she thinking about Ethan right now, anyway?

"Then you dropped that sparkler on the grass, and everyone started shouting," Jefferson went on, chuckling.

As if any of that had been an accident. "I tried to stamp out the fire with my heels!" Daphne recalled.

"Luckily for you I was right there. With a beer."

"And I shouted at you not to, because I thought beer would feed the fire even more!"

"Nah, that's just liquor," Jefferson pointed out. "Beer works as a firefighting tool. After all, it's mostly water."

"You were sixteen," she teased. "Two years too young to be drinking one."

"It's not my fault that most things worth doing are against the rules," he replied with an easy grin.

Daphne knew this was her moment to make a play for him. But she couldn't be obvious about it; the last thing she wanted was for Jefferson to feel *pursued*. She had to lead him onward without him ever even realizing.

"Didn't we stay up so late that we went out for breakfast?" she asked, as if the night hadn't been etched in her memory. Flush with victory, Daphne had lingered at the palace until nearly dawn, when the only people left were the twins' closest friends. She'd wanted nothing more than to go home and collapse onto her duvet, but she'd forced herself to rally. There was no telling when she might get another chance like this.

So Daphne had brightened her eye makeup and reapplied her lip gloss. She'd opened a bottle of champagne, though she had no intention of drinking any—the pop of the cork always made things seem *festive*—and then, as everyone was passing the bottle around, she'd asked, "Should we go get some breakfast?"

"You're right; we ended up at the Patriot!" Jefferson exclaimed, naming the bar at the nearby Monmouth Hotel. "I haven't had those hash browns in ages."

"Me neither," Daphne said nostalgically, almost wistfully. "After tonight, I'll need that kind of carb-fest to recover."

She was always doing this with Jefferson: laughing in delight when he proposed something, as if it was his idea and not one that she'd quietly led him to. Skirting him around topics she would rather avoid, finding ways to bring up the ones she did. She *managed* him, the way she always had, and always would.

"You know what, we should go tomorrow," Jefferson said, and Daphne smiled as if the suggestion surprised her.

"You don't think you'll be sleeping in?"

"Who knows if I'll sleep at all!" Jefferson pulled his phone from his pocket. "Look, I'm setting a ten a.m. alarm right now."

"Then let's do it," she agreed, and shifted just a little closer to him.

Though he could be wildly adventurous, Jefferson also craved familiarity and routine. Which was why Daphne would win him in the end. She was the first, most public, and most addictive of all his habits. And she didn't intend to let him forget it.

They talked for a while longer, but it was impossible not to lose someone at a party like this, so Daphne was unsurprised when Jefferson's old rowing team interrupted them. They descended on him in a pack, rowdy and good-natured and already drunk, shouting that they needed him for a round of shots. Daphne smiled indulgently and let them drag him off.

When she found Himari again, her friend's eyes flashed with concern. She pulled Daphne aside, lowering her voice. "Daphne—Nina Gonzalez is here."

Daphne looked across the tent to where Nina stood uncertainly next to Sam and her new boy toy, or whatever he was. "I had a feeling she'd show up." Now Daphne really needed to find Ethan and make sure he was sticking to their plan.

"She'd better stay far away from Jeff," Himari exclaimed. "Honestly, I still don't understand how they started dating in the first place. How could he have gone from *you* to *her*?"

"Exactly," Daphne replied, feeling vindicated for the first time in months.

Himari grimaced. "I can't decide which is worse: her black fingernails or those weird feather earrings. Do you think she made them herself?"

"Out of what, a pigeon?" Daphne replied, and her friend snorted.

"Are we sure Jeff didn't fall and hit his head that night, too?"

It was such a transparent effort to cheer her up that Daphne's chest swelled with gratitude. And she knew then that her friend wasn't playing her—that Himari truly didn't remember what happened the night she fell. Daphne knew it with an instinctive, bone-deep certainty, the way you know that you need to breathe in order to live. She just . . . *knew*.

At the realization, Daphne felt some long-missing piece of her click into place.

There are no second chances in life, her mom had always told her. *You'd better do everything right the first time, grab hold of every opportunity, because you won't get another one.*

Yet through some extraordinary twist of fate, Daphne was

actually *getting* a second chance. Time had rewound itself to a year ago, before she and Himari had their falling-out, before everything went so horribly wrong.

Daphne wasn't accustomed to feeling grateful. In her mind, she was entitled to everything she had, because she'd worked so damned hard for it. She bargain-shopped and charmed people, clawed her way up the social ladder and defended every inch of gained ground. She came up with elaborate schemes, and when those fell through, she *always* had a backup plan.

Now, for the first time in her eighteen years, Daphne Deighton felt humbled, because she'd received a gift that she truly didn't deserve.

"I'm so glad you're okay," she said hoarsely, and pulled Himari in for a quick, fierce hug. "I really missed you."

After all this time, she had her best friend back.

BEATRICE

Beatrice unzipped her cocktail dress and fell back onto the four-poster bed of her guest room at Walthorpe, blinking up at its canopy. The red fabric was shot through with threads of gold, making her feel like she'd floated inside a sunset.

Their day in Boston had been a whirlwind. She and Teddy had done several official appearances—a photo op at city hall, a reception at Harvard Medical School—because of course, Beatrice never got an *actual* day off.

Yet she didn't mind so much anymore, now that she wasn't doing these events alone. It was such a relief to walk into a room and know that she only had to talk to half the guests, because Teddy would take the other half. Then, afterward, she and Teddy would spend the car ride comparing notes about the people they'd met, laughing at what someone had said.

When they'd gotten to Walthorpe, Beatrice had braced herself for a big, formal dinner, full of cousins and godparents and perhaps even neighbors. To her relief, the only other people at the table were Teddy's parents and his two younger brothers; his little sister, Charlotte, was out of town.

Beatrice loved the way the Eatons teased each other, the sort of good-natured teasing that hit *almost* too close to home, before they rushed eagerly to each other's defense. They told her about Teddy's high school years and Charlotte's softball league and the last time they'd hosted a royal visit, over twenty years ago, when Beatrice's dad had run the Boston Marathon. "They brought you with them, did you know that?" Teddy's mom stated, her eyes twinkling. "They refused to travel without you, so here you were, cradle and all."

Beatrice hadn't realized how desperately she needed to hear stories like that. Stories from *before*.

Forcing herself to sit up, she began tugging the various pins and clips from her updo, a low chignon that the palace hairdresser had styled that morning in the capital. She sighed in relief as her hair rippled over her shoulders in a wavy dark curtain.

As she rose to her feet, still wearing nothing but her cream-colored underwear and strapless bra, Beatrice realized that she didn't know where the closet was. She'd hardly been in this room before dinner; one of the attendants had unpacked for her, and laid out her dress on the bed.

There was a door to the right of the fireplace. That had to be it. Tucking her hair distractedly behind one ear, Beatrice turned the handle to pull it open—

And found herself face to face with a naked Teddy Eaton.

Beatrice gasped and stumbled back. She reached frantically for the dress that still lay on her bed and held it over her chest like a robe, closing her eyes.

"I'm sorry, I didn't mean to— I was looking for the closet—"

"It's fine, Bee. Really." His voice was thick with amusement. She dared a look, and saw that Teddy had thrown a towel around his waist. He must have just stepped from the shower; his hair was damp, rivulets of water dripping down his body. Steam curled in from the bathroom.

"Why do I have a door that leads to your room?" Beatrice's blood thrummed against the surface of her skin. She tried to avert her eyes, to keep from staring at him—he was still shirtless—but that only made her more flustered.

Teddy fought back a smile. "Haven't you been in an

Edwardian-era house before? A lot of them had rooms with connecting doors, for . . . ease of movement," he finished tactfully.

Great. She was in a bedroom that had, literally, been designed for Teddy's ancestors' late-night rendezvous with their lovers.

Beatrice tried to shift the dress so that it covered as much as possible, but it felt very flimsy.

"Actually, I'm glad you stopped by," Teddy went on, as casually as if she'd popped over for a coffee. "I wanted to see how you were doing."

"Let me put some clothes on first," she suggested, and he laughed in agreement.

When she was safely dressed in black leggings and a button-down sweater, Beatrice knocked at the connecting door. "Teddy?" she called out, tentatively pushing it open.

"Come in." His voice sounded from inside the closet.

Teddy's room was nearly a mirror image of her own, except that his bed was more modern. Beatrice didn't see any framed pictures, or posters, or any other intimate touches. It all seemed as bland and impersonal as her own room was, back at the palace.

She drifted to the desk along one wall, probably because it was where *she* spent the most time, and was oddly gratified to see that the same must be true for Teddy. This space actually felt lived-in, with a hoodie strewn over the back of the chair, stray ballpoint pens arranged next to a pair of cordless headphones. A leather tray held stacks of official-looking documents.

Beatrice didn't mean to snoop—but when her eyes traveled over the papers, the words *payment inquiry* jumped out at her from the top.

Lord Eaton, the notice read, *we are respectfully touching base regarding your loan from Intrepid Financial Services. We have indicated our desire for repayment on several occasions. . . .*

Her breath caught as she turned page after page, finding more of the same: *Lord Eaton, regarding your pledged donation to Massachusetts General Hospital, the board would formally like to enquire when we can expect payment. . . . We are hoping to resolve the issue of your outstanding loan as soon as possible. . . . Lord Eaton, this document confirms the sale of your home at 101 Cliff Road . . .*

Teddy stepped into the room, pulling his arms through a charcoal Henley. "Sorry, it took me a while to find a pair of jeans that fit. Most of the pants in there must be Livingston's; they're *way* too short on me—" He broke off at the expression on Beatrice's face.

"Sorry. I wasn't trying to look through your things," she said awkwardly, gesturing to his desk. "But what is all this?"

Teddy ran a hand through his hair, making it stick up like the quills of a porcupine. Beatrice fought back an unfamiliar desire to reach up and smooth it.

"I mean—of course—you don't have to talk about it if you don't want to," she added, stumbling over the words. "We did agree that we could keep secrets from each other."

"It's okay; you deserve to know." Teddy sighed. "My family is on the brink of financial ruin."

Beatrice nodded; she'd guessed as much from the content of those letters. "This is why you're marrying me, isn't it?"

"I . . . yes. Marrying you is the best thing I can do for the duchy."

She looked away, blinking rapidly. This shouldn't have surprised her; she'd known Teddy had his reasons for going into this engagement. But it stung, hearing the reality of their situation stated so bluntly.

Teddy explained that the Eaton family fortune, once one of the largest in America, had evaporated in a series of poor investments. For the past several years, the family had been frantically delaying the inevitable: selling off family heirlooms and tracts of land, including their house in Nantucket. But they couldn't hold back the tidal wave much longer.

"It wouldn't matter if it was just us," Teddy said softly. "But there are so many people whose livelihoods, whose *lives*, depend on us. The people whose mortgages we bought, because they couldn't afford to carry one on their own. Or the hospital—ten years ago my grandfather pledged them a hundred million dollars, to be paid out over the next few decades. Now they've done an expensive renovation, bought whole wings full of new equipment, because they're *counting* on that pledge being fulfilled. What are they going to do when we tell them we aren't good for it?"

Beatrice nodded numbly, mechanically. She of all people understood what it felt like, to be responsible for the well-being of strangers.

"I know you're overloaded with requests," Teddy was saying. "And there's a lot more to America than Boston. Please don't think I'm asking you to assume these debts. All I meant was that by marrying you, I'm helping to buy us some time. Banks tend to hold off on seizing assets when they belong to relatives of the royal family." He attempted a smile, but by now Beatrice knew him well enough to see that it wasn't a perfect fit.

She stood very still, her mind sifting through everything Teddy had told her. Outside the open window, crickets lifted their voices in a soft chorus.

"Of course I'm assuming your family's debts," she decided. "Personally, if necessary. These are my people, too. I'm not about to let them lose their jobs and homes." She let out a breath. "And I'll buy back your Nantucket house."

"You don't need to—"

"It'll be my wedding present to you." Beatrice looked down at the carpet. "It's the least I can do, given that you're marrying me because you *have* to, not because you want to."

She hadn't meant to say those last words, but there they were.

Teddy took a sudden step closer. "That's unfair, coming from you."

"*What?*"

"Come on, Beatrice," he insisted, in a tone she'd never heard him use before. "You're the one who's in *love* with someone else."

The words fell like heavy stones into the space between them. She blinked. "How did you . . ."

"Samantha told me, the night of our engagement party. She said that you were calling off the wedding because you loved someone else."

Beatrice's mouth had gone dry. There was something surreal about hearing Teddy mention Connor, as if she'd stepped into the distorted reality of her dreams.

Every instinct in her screamed to deny it—to shrink from revealing anything personal, the way she'd always been taught.

But Teddy had told her the truth about his secrets. Didn't she owe him the same?

"The guy I was talking about—he's gone," she confessed. "He left court. He was . . ." She trailed off before giving any more details, but Teddy didn't press her. Instead he asked a question she hadn't expected.

"Do you still love him?"

Beatrice blinked. "That isn't . . ."

"I think I have a right to know." Teddy's voice scraped over the words. "I deserve a little warning if you're going to spend the rest of our lives hating me."

"Why would I hate you?" she repeated, startled.

"Because I'm not *him!*"

An uneasy silence followed his words. Beatrice sucked in a breath, feeling disarmed. She forced herself to meet Teddy's impossibly blue eyes.

"I did love him," she said at last. "But now . . ."

Now when she thought of Connor, he seemed out of reach, as if she were trying to snatch at a shadow that rippled on the surface of water. As if all she had left were memories of memories.

"I don't know anymore," she whispered. "And really, it doesn't matter; I'm never going to see him again." She hesitated—but here they were, laying all their ugly truths on the table, and she was surprised at how urgently she wanted to say this. To acknowledge the silent obstacle that kept looming between them.

"Unlike you and Samantha," she added.

Neither of them had mentioned Sam until now, as if they both knew it would be easier to pretend Teddy had never been involved with her.

"Look, Bee, I'd be lying if I said I never had feelings for your sister," he said uncomfortably. "But that was *before*, okay?"

"Before *what?*"

He held out a hand, then lowered it, as if he'd thought better of the gesture. "I just . . . I guess I thought it was you and me now."

The simplicity of that statement made her fall still.

Again Beatrice had the sense that there was something archaic and fine about Teddy, something that belonged in another century. Surrounded by all the other people of court—who made promises they never intended to keep, who operated out of pure self-interest—he shone like real gold in a sea of cheap imitation metal.

Beatrice reached for Teddy's hand, tugging him toward her. He looked surprised, but didn't pull away.

"You're right. From now on, it's you and me."

As she spoke the words, she felt them becoming true.

SAMANTHA

"Nina!" Sam exclaimed, realizing they'd hardly seen each other all night. She pushed her way through the center of the tent, where she'd been dancing with Jeff and his friends—which was probably why Nina had kept her distance.

When she'd caught up to her best friend, Sam flashed a bright, exuberant grin. "I need some air. Come with me?"

"What about Marshall?" Nina asked.

Sam glanced to where Marshall stood near the bar, recounting some anecdote amid gales of laughter. Everyone looked distinctly sloppier than they'd been when they first arrived, their hair disheveled and their smiles too wide.

All night, Marshall had been playing the role of her boyfriend with robust enthusiasm—spinning her on and off the dance floor, charming her friends with his outrageous stories, calling her a series of increasingly obnoxious names like *schmoopy* and *pumpkin bear*.

Everything he did, Sam realized, was larger than life. It wasn't just his sheer physical size, though that might be part of it. But Marshall seemed to inhabit every moment to the fullest. He even *laughed* more deeply than anyone Sam had ever known, the type of hearty belly laugh that people joined in simply for the sake of hearing it.

"He'll be fine on his own," Sam decided.

She led Nina out of the tent, past the laughter and music

bursting from its edges. The palace loomed up to their right, its glass windows catching the moonlight, so that the massive building seemed to be winking.

Past an avenue of drooping locust trees, on the other side of a gated stone wall, was the Washingtons' pool house—originally built by King John as a home for his mistress, though everyone pretended to forget that. Now the ornate pillars and carved stone balcony looked out over an Olympic-sized pool.

Sam kicked off her shoes and sat along the edge, letting her bare feet trail in the water. It felt pleasantly warm; someone must have turned on the heater, knowing that the twins were having a party tonight. Wind rippled over the surface, creating a thousand shadows that chased each other over the water.

"Okay," Sam began as Nina sat down next to her. "What's up with you?"

Nina shifted guiltily. "What do you mean?"

"You've got that look. Like there's something you want to talk about, but you don't know how to bring it up." Sam tugged halfheartedly at the hem of her white dress, which was shorter than she remembered, then gave up and looked over at her friend.

"There *is* a guy," Nina admitted. "But it's complicated."

Sam nodded. "Good! You were overdue for a rebound."

"Actually . . . it's Ethan."

"Wait. Ethan *Beckett*?"

She listened as Nina explained that she and Ethan had started hanging out after they did a project together for journalism class. Then, last weekend, he'd walked her home and kissed her in her dorm room.

"Have you seen him since?" Sam asked, and Nina winced.

"He didn't come to journalism yesterday. I don't . . . What if he's trying to ghost me?"

"He's probably freaking out," Sam said patiently. "You're his best friend's *ex*, and he likes you."

Nina looked up, hopeful. "You think he likes me?"

"If he didn't like you, he would have showed up to class and acted like nothing happened. Instead he's hiding, hoping you'll be the one to make the next move. Ugh, *men*." Sam flicked a hand dismissively. "Now you're the one who has to decide—was it a one-time thing, or do you like him?"

The answer was immediate. "I like him."

Sam leaned back on her palms on the flagstone terrace. "You do realize that things would have been so much cleaner if you'd moved on to someone new. I mean, someone *outside* our group of friends."

"No one else would get it!" Nina exclaimed. "Ethan understands what it's like being an outsider within the royal family."

"You aren't an outsider!"

"Sam, you know I love being your best friend. But no one ever appreciates what it means. They either judge me for it, or envy me for it," Nina explained. "All I'm saying is that Ethan gets it because he's been through the same experience."

Sam hated how complicated she made things for her friend. Growing up alongside Sam had put Nina in a constrained and bizarre situation, one foot in each world without really belonging to either.

"Okay," she breathed.

"So you approve?"

"First of all, you don't need anyone's approval for your romantic relationships. Even mine," Sam said emphatically. "But for the record, I'm fine with you and Ethan. Besides," she added, "I'm not exactly in a position to judge."

Nina let out a strangled laugh. "We make quite the pair. You're faking a relationship, and I'm hiding from my ex-boyfriend, plus his best friend, who I *kissed* last weekend."

"These are massive problems," Sam agreed. "Clearly, the only solution is to sneak into the kitchens and eat Chef Greg's raw cookie dough."

Nina smiled. "You know, that does sound like a solution."

They started to clamber up from the ground, but before they could move, Sam heard the soft creak of the gate being opened.

"There you are, snickerdoodle! Hey, Nina," Marshall added. "You ladies look comfortable. Should I bring the party to you?"

"Actually, I'll catch up with you guys later." Nina stood. "There's something I need to do."

Sam would have argued, but she had a feeling that Nina was going to look for Ethan, so she just nodded. "See you later."

When Nina had left, Marshall turned to Sam with a lifted eyebrow. "Did I scare her off?"

"She doesn't like you," Sam said blithely, and Marshall snorted. "I mean, she doesn't like what we're doing. She thinks it's a bad idea, faking a relationship."

His eyes widened. "Seriously? You told her?"

"Nina is like a sister to me!" Sam glared at him. "She would *never* blow our cover. She'll take my secrets to the *grave*."

Marshall threw up his hands, chuckling. "Okay, jeez. You're talking like the characters from *Pledged*."

Sam was oddly irritated by the reference to Kelsey's show. "That's insulting," she said haughtily. "My vocabulary is leagues above their garbage dialogue."

"Fair point. No one watches *Pledged* for the banter." Marshall came to sit next to her, clasping his hands around his knees. "Nice pool," he added. "It's almost as big as the one at our Napa house."

"A giant pool in a drought-prone region? No *wonder* everyone in Orange likes you so much!"

He smiled appreciatively. From somewhere in the vicinity, a bird called out a few notes of song, then fell silent. Sam kicked listlessly at the water.

"Jeff and I used to come out here all the time when we were kids," she went on, almost to herself. "We were always racing, or playing pirates, or whacking each other mercilessly with pool noodles."

She wasn't sure when the competitive streak between her and Jeff had begun. Maybe it came from being a twin, feeling that she and her brother were always jostling for attention, for space. Or maybe because the entire world kept reminding her that she mattered so much less than Beatrice. Whatever the reason, Sam was constantly challenging Jeff to something—bungee jumping or a ski race, beer chugging or even their childhood games of Candyland.

Marshall smiled. "My sister Rory used to make up these elaborate pool games that involved floating basketballs and relay races and more rules than anyone could keep track of. Sometimes I think she changed the rules mid-game just to ensure that she'd win." His eyes lit on Sam. "You two would get along."

"Oh, yeah," Sam agreed. "If I was playing pool games against a varsity swimmer, I would definitely cheat."

"I play water polo, actually. That's where my broken nose came from."

She looked over at Marshall's profile. His nose did have a slight bend, but in a serious, Roman way. "Your nose is distinguished," she decided. "It has character."

"Try telling my family that. My mom must have tried a thousand times to get me to quit. She said water polo is the sport of hooligans."

"Has she *seen* ice hockey?" Sam quipped, and he barked out a laugh.

The heavy spring darkness closed around them, the only

illumination coming from the lights embedded in the sides of the pool. Sam's toes, painted a bright watermelon pink, glowed beneath the surface of the water.

"I don't know why I thought you were a swimmer." She cast him another sidelong glance, her voice ringing with amusement. "Didn't you challenge the Duke of Sussex to a swim race in Vegas?"

"It was the Duke of Cambridge, actually, and *he* challenged *me.*" Marshall's eyes gleamed at the memory. "When the paparazzi got wind of it, his younger brother was the one who took the fall."

"That's what the spare is for, isn't it?" Somehow the question came out with less bitterness than usual.

Marshall didn't contradict her. "I guess the British didn't want to hear about their future king betting on a late-night swim race, especially not against a notorious hedonist like me."

The words were cavalier, yet something in them made Sam wonder if Marshall was growing as tired of his party-boy image as she was of hers.

"So, who won? I assume you upheld our national honor before the Brits?"

His mouth tugged up at the corner. "What happens in Vegas stays in Vegas."

"Oh my god," Sam cried out. "He *beat* you, didn't he?"

Marshall seemed to be struggling against an outraged protest. "I'd had a lot of beers that night, okay? And I didn't have my swim cap—"

"Of course, your *swim cap,*" Sam said knowingly. "I suppose the duke was more aerodynamic, since he's balding?"

"I tried to challenge him to a rematch, but he wouldn't accept!"

She burst out laughing, and then Marshall was laughing too: that low, rumbling laugh of his. It seemed to weave a hushed spell around them.

"You want to head back?" Marshall said at last, rising to his feet.

"Sure." Sam nodded—but before she could stand, Marshall put his hands on her back and shoved her into the pool, dress and all.

She gave a startled yelp as she tumbled forward. Then the water closed over her head, and everything was suddenly hushed, and languid, and warm.

Sam shot back up into the moonlight, spluttering as she whirled on Marshall. "I can't *believe* you!"

"Oops," he said brightly, and held out a hand to help her out.

"Thanks." Sam leaned forward, reaching for his hand. Then she braced her legs on the side of the pool and yanked Marshall into the water alongside her.

He broke the surface with a powerful kick and shook his head, spraying water droplets from his close-cropped dark curls. Sam sensed that it was a habitual movement, something he'd done a thousand times during water polo games. He was still wearing his button-down and jeans, and the fabric of his wet shirt clung to the muscles of his arms, settled distractingly in the curve of his throat.

A slow, eager grin curled over his face. "Oh, you're going to pay for that."

Sam squealed in delight as he lunged toward her. She kicked frantically back out of his reach, the two of them chasing each other in an exhilarating zigzag. The pool echoed with their splashing laughter.

Marshall caught her ankle and began dragging her back toward him. Sam sucked in a breath as they slipped, wrestling, under the water. He kicked them forward, holding Sam tight against him, though she was no longer trying to escape.

Suddenly their faces were close, their bodies intertwined.

Sam could see each individual water droplet in the fan of his eyelashes, glittering like liquid stars.

Marshall must have felt the shift in her, because he went still, too.

It was shallow enough for Sam to stand, yet she stayed where she was, floating in a strange, enchanted sort of stillness. Her dark hair fell riotously over one shoulder, like a mermaid's. One of Marshall's hands had looped beneath her legs, the other braced behind her back, yet his hands seemed to drift over her with only a whisper of a touch.

Marshall reached up, tucking back one of her damp curls. Then he brushed his lips lightly over hers.

All too quickly he'd moved on, tracing teasing kisses along her jawline, nipping at the flushed skin below her ear. Sam circled her fingers around Marshall's neck, trying to catch his mouth with her own. His grip on her waist tightened.

Finally his lips found hers again. Sam kissed him back urgently, feverishly. She had shifted, her legs wrapped around his torso, her bare thighs circling the wet scratchy denim of his jeans. His palms slid farther, to settle on her lower back. They seemed to scorch her everywhere they touched—

At the sound of raucous shouts, her head shot up.

She twisted out of Marshall's arms and looked behind her, to where the gate to the gravel path stood wide open. A flock of partygoers had spilled onto the terrace and were staring at Sam and Marshall's tangled forms with hungry curiosity. Sam caught the unmistakable flash of photos being taken.

Before the party, she had instructed the front drive not to bother with collecting everyone's phones the way they usually did. The head of security had argued, of course, but the only person who outranked Sam, and could countermand a direct order from her, was in Boston right now. Sam had *wanted* her guests to take a lot of pictures tonight—preferably pictures of her and Marshall that would make Teddy burn with jealousy.

It looked like her wish had come true.

Sam lifted her eyes to meet Marshall's, but she didn't see shock or outrage or even regret on his face. All she saw was a guarded sort of amusement. And the realization hit her like a blow—he'd been facing the right direction, had seen all those people. That kiss hadn't been for Sam's benefit, but for theirs.

Sam forced her lips to bend into a smile. She let go of Marshall, stepping back and adjusting the straps of her dress as if she hardly noticed she was wearing it.

"Nice work," she said softly. "We put on a good show, didn't we?"

She managed to inject the words with her usual cavalier nonchalance. It wasn't hard. Sam was very good at pretending that things didn't matter to her.

She'd been doing it for most of her lifetime.

18

BEATRICE

"Where are you taking me?" Beatrice followed Teddy across Walthorpe's back lawn, toward a wooden, barnlike structure that she'd assumed was a garage.

"You'll see," he replied, with that eager dimpled smile that seemed to light up the room.

It struck Beatrice that something fundamental in their relationship had shifted. This walk out to the barn was not at all the same as when they'd walked into Walthorpe together just a few hours ago—before they'd shared such secrets with each other.

Before Teddy had said, *It's you and me now.*

He led her up a narrow staircase, then paused on the landing. "That bedroom in the main house is where I sleep, but this has always felt like my *actual* room," he explained, and pushed open the door.

The top floor of the barn had been converted into what could only be described as a rustic media room. Somehow the space felt vast and cozy at once, with the barn's high vaulted ceilings and exposed wooden beams. Before a massive TV sat an enormous L-shaped couch of brown suede, and on that couch, playing a video game, were Teddy's two brothers.

"Hey, man." The younger one, Livingston, glanced up at Teddy's arrival, his eyes widening when he saw Beatrice. He quickly elbowed his brother and jumped to his feet. "Oh—sorry, we didn't realize you were coming up. I mean—"

"It's okay. Please don't feel like you have to leave." Beatrice hated that she had this effect on people, that she couldn't walk into a room without everyone immediately registering, and reacting to, her presence. She wondered how it would feel to be anonymous. To meet someone and actually get to *introduce* herself for once.

Lewis and Livingston exchanged a glance, then shrugged and resumed their game.

Beatrice wandered over to a black-and-white poster of Half Dome that hung on one wall. "Have you been there?" she asked, turning to Teddy. She'd always wanted to hike all the way up to the peak, but the one time she'd been to Yosemite, her schedule hadn't allowed it.

"A few summers ago, but that wasn't why I bought the poster. I wonder . . ." Teddy lifted the frame, revealing a jagged, fist-sized hole in the wooden planks. Beatrice could see the building's insulation coiled beneath.

"Yep. It's still here." Teddy sounded buoyant, and a little proud. "A dry-ice rocket exploded too soon," he added, for her benefit.

Lewis chimed in from the couch. "I told you we'd get away with it! That was six years ago and Mom *still* has no idea!"

"Sounds like you guys had fun up here," Beatrice teased.

"What about you?" Teddy asked. "Surely you went through a rebellious phase at some point—got caught smoking in the cherry orchard, broke a national artifact or two."

"I once knocked over a vase that my great-grandmother brought from Hesse," she offered. It wasn't especially scandalous, but she couldn't tell Teddy about her *real* "rebellious phase"—when she'd been in a secret relationship with her Revere Guard. "I tried to glue the pieces back together, but the housekeeper caught me."

"How did you break it?"

"Long story." It had been Sam and Jeff's fault, actually, as so many things were. "My dad grounded me for two weeks. Not for breaking the vase, he told me, but for trying to hide what I'd done. He said that monarchs need to always own up to their actions. Especially their mistakes."

Teddy looked over sharply, clearly worried she might cry. But to Beatrice's surprise, and relief, she was actually smiling at the memory. It was nice to know that she could think of her dad and feel happiness, mixed in with all the sorrow.

"Can I get you something?" Teddy wandered to the corner, where a few wooden cabinets were built into the wall. He paused. "I don't even know what your drink of choice is."

"Um . . ." Champagne at formal receptions, wine at state dinners. "I'm fine with whatever's around," she hedged, but Teddy must have heard the truth in her tone.

"It's okay if you're not a big drinker."

He was right. Beatrice always limited herself to one, maybe two drinks per night at events like that. "Not really. I can't afford to get drunk and publicly make a fool of myself." Hearing her own words, she realized how ridiculous they sounded. "Although . . . I don't see why I can't have a drink right now."

"Sure," Teddy said, smiling. "If you want to *privately* make a fool of yourself, your secret is safe with me."

He said it in a lighthearted tone, but Beatrice heard the truth in his words. She did feel safe with Teddy. She knew, with an instinctive certainty, that she could trust him.

"All we've got is beer." Teddy knelt to explore the contents of the liquor cabinet. "And some kind of grapefruit vodka, which has Charlotte written all over it."

It might be deeply un-American of her, but Beatrice had never really liked beer. "I'll try the grapefruit thing," she decided. "It can't be worse than the cherry brandy they always serve after state dinners."

Teddy lifted an eyebrow but didn't argue, just turned back toward his brothers. "Does anyone remember if we have plastic cups in here?"

She came over to help him look, opening and closing various cabinets in rapid succession. "Here we go," she exclaimed, finding a shelf with a few stray coffee mugs. She reached for one and held it out toward Teddy, realizing as she did that it was a custom-made mug, the kind you could order from an internet photo site. It was emblazoned with a picture of Teddy and a long-limbed blond girl.

"Who's this?" she asked, angling the mug so that her fiancé could see.

He reddened all the way to the tips of his ears. "That's my high school girlfriend, Penelope van der Walle," he mumbled. "She made that for me—it's so embarrassing. I didn't even realize it was still here. Sorry," he added, shooting a murderous glance toward his brothers. Neither of them spoke, but their shoulders shook with silent laughter.

"I see," Beatrice said evenly. For some reason, the thought of Teddy with that doe-eyed girl made her feel hot all over. In a surprisingly territorial way.

Teddy hurried to put the cup back on the shelf. He grabbed a navy mug that said NANTUCKET and reached for the vodka, but Beatrice, her actions fueled by some emotion she couldn't understand, had already grabbed it. She filled the coffee mug nearly to the brim.

"Drink that slowly, okay?" Teddy eyed her heavy pour with a flicker of trepidation. "It's meant to be mixed with soda water and lime."

Beatrice took a sip—and kept drinking. "You're wrong," she insisted, when she'd drained at least a quarter of the cup. "This is delicious."

They wandered over to the couch. Lewis and Livingston

were still engrossed in the game, their animated football players racing around a cartoon field. "We used to play this all the time in high school," Teddy reminisced.

"But weren't you on a *real* football team back then?" Beatrice asked. "Didn't you want to play something else?"

"It's different when it's a video game. Totally unrelated skill set," Livingston explained, and held out the controller. He looked like a younger, stockier version of Teddy, with the Eatons' trademark blond hair and blue eyes. "Want to play? We could do two on two, me and you versus Lewis and Teddy."

Beatrice hesitated. "I've never played."

"That's why you're on my team. I'm the best player here; I can cover your mistakes," Livingston declared. His brothers each made a low "ohhhh" sound at the challenge. But when Beatrice still hesitated, he backtracked. "Or you can play with Teddy, of course."

She took another sip, then set her mug on the coffee table. A new lightness had stolen into her head, casting everything in a delightful golden glow.

"No, you're right. I want to play with you, against Teddy," she decided. "I want to see the look on his face when we completely destroy him."

There was some hollering and heckling at her declaration, a few good-natured jokes at her fiancé's expense. Teddy shot her a taunting grin. "What do you say, Bee, should we bet on it?"

"Absolutely," she said, feeling reckless. "What are the terms?"

Teddy's eyes met hers, and heat coursed through her; not the tickling warmth of the vodka but something wilder and more dangerous. Beatrice wondered if he was going to bet her a kiss.

She wondered what she would say, if he did.

"We could do a round of truth-or-dare," Teddy suggested. Another high school game that Beatrice had never played.

"You're on," she said, more bravely than she felt.

It took a few minutes for Beatrice to get the hang of the game. But her competitive nature quickly took over; and soon she was perched on the edge of the couch, shouting just as loud as the boys as she stabbed frantically at her controller. Time seemed to stretch out indeterminately, all her energies focused on that massive screen.

With only a few minutes to go, she and Livingston were about to win—until Teddy's receiver caught Lewis's pass and sprinted into a touchdown, just as the clock ticked down to zero.

It took a moment for Beatrice to realize that the room had erupted in shouts of excitement and outrage, and that hers were loudest of all. She put down her controller, feeling self-conscious.

"Hey, you played great." Livingston knocked his fist against hers in congratulations.

"Thanks." No one had ever fist-bumped her before. No one had ever given her a *night* like this before, either—a night of pretending she was any ordinary person.

Teddy clearly knew her better than she'd realized.

"So," he said, turning to her with a half smile. "Truth or dare?"

"Truth?" After the truths they'd already shared tonight, it sounded easy to go ahead and share one more. Certainly easier than whatever wild dare Teddy and his brothers might come up with.

"What would you be, if you weren't the queen?"

If she weren't queen. Beatrice's brain could hardly wrap itself around the notion. The only time she'd allowed herself the luxury of imagining it, she had wanted a future with

Connor. That felt like very long ago, now. And besides, Beatrice realized, that dream was built around someone else.

It was time she dreamed something for *herself*. What would she, Beatrice, do if she had the freedom to choose? If she stopped listening to people like Robert Standish and actually did what *she* wanted, for once?

"I'd go on a backpacking trip, all over the world."

Lewis leaned his elbows onto his knees with a puzzled frown. "But haven't you been all over the world?"

"Sure, inside ballrooms and stuffy conference rooms! I've never traveled like a *normal* person." Beatrice's words were faster now, more urgent. "I want to learn to skydive. And scuba dive. And make a dry-ice bomb!"

The boys laughed at her declaration. "Let me get this straight," Teddy summarized. "You want to throw yourself out of a moving plane, and learn how to make holes in your wall."

Beatrice nodded vigorously. "Yes, exactly! That all sounds *fun*."

"You're so much cooler than the magazines make you sound," Livingston remarked, then immediately winced. But Beatrice knew what he'd meant.

Teddy nodded at his brother's words. "I know. Isn't she?"

♛

"You okay?" Teddy started down the stairs next to Beatrice. It was late; Lewis and Livingston had gone back to the main house a few hours ago, leaving the two of them alone.

"I'm *fantastic*," Beatrice declared—but at the bottom of the staircase, she halted. A low, whimpering sound came from across the barn, tugging at her heartstrings. Beatrice set out in search of it.

"Bee?" Teddy asked, trotting to keep up.

At the end of a hallway, a yellow Labrador lay surrounded by a squirming, playful pile of puppies. They tumbled over one another in blithe confusion.

Beatrice sank to her knees on the dusty ground, and one of the puppies started toward her. She sighed contentedly as it crawled onto her lap.

"You didn't tell me that your family has dogs." Her new friend set its paws on her shoulders and began licking her face, little exploratory kisses as if to figure out who she was. Beatrice couldn't help it; she laughed. The kind of easy laugh that floats through your body like magic.

Her chest almost *hurt* from it, as if she'd been compressing that laugh inside her since before her father died.

Teddy knelt down next to her. "I didn't realize that we still did. I mean, I knew Sadie had her puppies a couple months ago, but I thought we'd have given them away by now."

"Is Sadie your dog?"

"She's everyone's dog. She pretty much has the run of this place."

"I'm in love." Beatrice turned a pleading face to Teddy. "Can we keep him?"

She'd said *we*, not *I*. But she meant it. Beatrice wanted to take care of this puppy with Teddy, together.

"Beatrice . . ."

"We can't leave Franklin here!"

Teddy sighed, but she saw that he was smiling, and felt something catch within her at the sight of that smile. "You've already named him," he observed.

"A patriotic American name. *And* a smart name." She tightened her arms around Franklin. "Please?"

"All right." Teddy held out a hand to help her to her feet.

Beatrice had expected him to put up more of a fight. "Really?"

"It's not easy for me to tell you no."

Ignoring his hand, Beatrice rose to her feet, still holding Franklin tight to her chest. "Because I'm the queen."

"No. Because when you look at me like that, I can't say no to you. I don't *want* to."

"Oh" was all she managed.

As they walked back toward the house, Teddy looped an arm around her waist to keep her from stumbling. The vodka was really hitting her, wasn't it? She remembered something the Russian ambassador had once told her—that being drunk on vodka was the only true drunk. That while beer and wine muffled and muted your emotions, vodka revealed them.

Perhaps his words were true. As she and Teddy walked back across the moon-drenched grass, their shadows stretching before them, Beatrice no longer felt confused.

"Shhh," Teddy whispered as they slipped through the back door.

"*You* shhh!" she shot back. "You're the one making all the noise!"

He took Franklin from her arms. "Beatrice, you've had a lot to drink."

"Don't worry," she said emphatically. "I assure you, I always behave in a matter befitting the Crown."

Teddy snorted back a laugh and led her up the stairs. Beatrice found herself so unexpectedly grateful for him. She'd never done this before, never trusted anyone enough to just . . . keep drinking. She'd always been so terrified of doing or saying the wrong thing.

When they reached her room, Teddy grabbed a box from the closet and set Franklin down in it. "We'll get a real crate in the morning."

Beatrice kept trying to undo the buttons of her sweater, but her fingers no longer seemed to work properly. "Can you help with this?"

"Yeah," Teddy said hoarsely. "Sure."

She stood there quietly, swaying a little on her feet. Teddy's hands fumbled for a moment, almost as if he was nervous, but then he unbuttoned the sweater, from her throat all the way down to the hem, and helped slide it off her shoulders. Underneath she was wearing nothing but a whisper-thin tank top.

"Let's get you into bed." Teddy pulled back the covers for her. Beatrice obediently sat down—but before he could walk away, she closed a hand over his arm.

"Don't go. I can't sleep."

"After all that vodka, I bet you will," he said lightly.

"*Please.* Ever since my dad died, I've had these nightmares." Her throat felt raw; she swallowed. "Please just stay, for a little while."

He nodded and walked around to sit on the opposite side of the bed, like some kind of sentinel.

"You can lie down, you know."

He hesitated. "Just until you fall asleep," he compromised, and stretched out on his back.

Moonlight edged around the brocaded drapes over the window. Beatrice could barely see the planes of Teddy's face. There had always been so much distance between them, so much ceremony and formality. She had grown used to looking at him without actually *seeing* him.

But now, Beatrice let her eyes travel unabashedly over him.

The only word for Teddy's body was . . . well, *beautiful*. His bones were long and gracefully drawn, his muscles flowing over them in taut smooth lines. He was still wearing his long-sleeved shirt, though its hem rode up a little at his stomach, revealing the carved outline of his abs.

Beatrice propped herself on one elbow, watching the rise and fall of his chest, the beat of his pulse, as rapid as her own.

Sensing her gaze, Teddy turned on the mattress to face her. In the dim light his eyes seemed to have turned a deeper shade of blue, almost cobalt. She heard his breath catch, and the sound made Beatrice feel curiously brave.

She shifted forward and pressed her lips to his.

Perhaps out of surprise, his mouth opened beneath hers, letting her tongue brush up against his.

She and Teddy had kissed plenty of times: PG-rated, chaste, performative kisses at engagement parties and official events. Kisses that were meant for America, not for the two of them.

This was something else entirely.

Suddenly, somehow, Beatrice was next to Teddy, curled up against the warm length of him. Her arms snaked around his shoulders to pull him closer. She could feel the rapid pounding of his heart.

She tugged impatiently at his shirt, trying to pull it over his head, but Teddy tore himself away. A small groan of disappointment slipped from Beatrice's lips.

"We can't do this," Teddy said hoarsely.

Beatrice sat up, letting her hair fall in a tumble around her shoulders. Unsatisfied desire clawed at her insides. She braced her hands on the mattress, tangling them in the sheets to ground herself. She felt dizzy and aching and hot and cold all at once.

"We're going to be married, you know," she reminded him, with irrefutable logic.

"We can't do this *tonight*," he amended.

"But I want you," she added, drunk enough to speak baldly.

"Bee—you're too drunk to make this kind of decision. No matter how much we both might want it," he added, in a softer tone.

Some part of Beatrice wondered if she should feel embarrassed for throwing herself at Teddy. Yet she didn't. Perhaps because Teddy made everything feel so steady, so clear.

Falling in love with Connor had been a breathless, heart-stopping whirlwind. While this—whatever it was between her and Teddy—didn't stop her heart or crush the air from her lungs.

He made her pulse race *faster*, made it *easier* to breathe. As if she'd been trapped in a sealed room and now someone had finally thrown open a window.

Teddy had started to move off the bed, but Beatrice shook her head. "Stay. Just to sleep," she pleaded. "I wasn't lying about the nightmares."

He hesitated, but leaned back onto the pillows.

Beatrice yawned and nestled herself against him, her head tucked onto his chest. Teddy shifted one arm carefully around her, playing idly with the strands of her hair; as if this weren't strange or new or unusual, as if they'd done it a thousand times before. Within minutes Beatrice's breaths had evened out, and she drifted to sleep, safe in the circle of his embrace.

For the first time in months, she slept through the night.

NINA

Nina started toward the palace's front drive with weary resignation.

When she got to the party tonight, she'd been so worried about Ethan—and what she would say once she saw him—that for once she hadn't really panicked about the prospect of running into Jeff.

All week she had been replaying that kiss in her head. She'd been too nervous to text Ethan, figuring that this was the type of conversation they should have in person. Then, when he hadn't shown up at journalism class, she'd assumed he was avoiding her: that he wanted to pretend the whole thing was a drunken mistake and move on.

But what if Sam was right, and he was only staying away out of loyalty to Jeff?

Nina sighed when she saw the line that snaked around the front steps, unruly partygoers all waiting for one of the palace's courtesy cars. This always happened when the twins' parties ended too abruptly.

Earlier, after her talk with Sam, she'd gone back to the party and circled the dance floor in search of Ethan. But then Sam and Marshall had decided to go and make out in the pool, and now the party was rapidly disintegrating. Nina had offered to stay the night—so she would be there when

Sam had to face tomorrow's social media firestorm—but Sam kept insisting that this was precisely what she'd *meant* to do. She was acting like none of it bothered her, but Nina knew better.

She blinked, startled, when moonlight glinted on raven-dark hair at the front of the portico.

"Ethan!"

Before she could think better of it, she'd stepped off the sidewalk and was trotting down the driveway toward him. He paused, one hand poised on the car door, to glance uncertainly back at Nina.

"Hey," she breathed, tucking a strand of hair behind one ear. She felt tentative and eager and uncertain all at once, as if she were standing on the edge of a precipice and wanted desperately to jump off.

"Can I get a ride? I mean—we're going to the same place, right?"

After a beat of hesitation, Ethan stepped aside, holding open the door for her. "Sure. Of course," he said gruffly.

"Thanks." Nina slid into the backseat, and Ethan followed.

"King's College," he told the driver.

The car turned obediently out of the driveway, and here they were, the two of them alone at last.

As they reached the edge of John Jay Park, light flickered over the tinted windows, the sharp beams of other cars' headlights crisscrossing the lazy glow of streetlamps. A tense, taut silence stretched between them.

"I was looking for you tonight," she said at last.

"Really?" Ethan gave one of his usual careless shrugs. "It was a crowded party. That tent *definitely* isn't meant for the kind of dancing I saw inside."

"Come on, Ethan, don't act like we aren't—like we didn't—" She flushed, but went on with more certainty. "We should talk about what happened last weekend."

"Nina . . ." There was a note of warning in his tone, but something else, too, that sounded almost like yearning.

"Ethan, I *like* you."

Nina hardly recognized herself. Sam was always the one who wore her emotions on her sleeve, while Nina usually poured every ounce of energy into concealing those feelings, even from the people who actually needed to hear them.

Yet here she was, professing her feelings for Ethan—and the words had come out so easily, as if they'd been shaken loose from deep within her.

"I like you, too."

At those words, Nina looked over, trying to catch his gaze in the darkened car. But his features were inscrutable as ever.

"I know it's weird, and a little complicated—"

"More than a little," Ethan said under his breath.

"But I also know that I don't feel this way very often." Only once before, in fact. Nina shoved that thought aside. "I understand if you can't go there, because of Jeff. But for what it's worth, I've really liked hanging out with you lately. Last weekend . . ." Nina's pulse was going haywire. She realized that she was drawing a line in the sand—that they could have gone on pretending that last weekend was a drunken mistake, until now.

She took a deep breath. "I think there's something here, and whatever it is, I want to give it a shot."

Was it wrong of her to feel this way about Ethan when she had loved Jeff for so many years?

But that was the thing—she had loved Jeff since they were children, and her love for him had never really matured. It had always been a little girl's love. Nina had never even questioned *why* she loved Jeff; she had just taken it as a given.

If she hadn't been blinded by Jeff in all his dazzling princely glory, she might have noticed Ethan so much sooner.

She felt him shifting, sliding into the middle seat between them. His eyes blazed as if he was searching for something in her face.

Whatever he saw made him reach some decision, because he leaned away. "You shouldn't want to be with me," he said heavily. "There's no need for you to get wrapped up in all my mess. If you only knew . . ."

"Knew what, Ethan?" she exclaimed, frustrated. "That you're irritating and insufferable and also smart as hell? That you're my ex-boyfriend's best friend, and being with me would violate some kind of bro code? That you gave me the most intense kiss of my life and then went completely silent all week?" Nina clenched her hands tighter in her lap. "I already know all that, and I'm *still here!*"

Ethan hesitated. Nina could feel the weight of his conflicted emotions, and for an instant, she wondered if she should be worried. Then he leaned forward, and her concerns evaporated.

"I want to try this, too," he said hoarsely. "No matter how complicated or selfish it is of me to say that."

He reached for her hand, lacing their fingers. Even in the darkness, Nina could see that he was smiling.

"What?" she demanded.

"The most intense kiss of your life?" he repeated, sounding unmistakably smug.

Nina's heart pounded against her rib cage. "To be absolutely certain, I'd need another data point," she said, and now she was smiling, too. "For scientific accuracy."

"Well, if it's for the sake of science," Ethan agreed, and leaned in to kiss her.

Nina stopped worrying about how reckless and wrong this was, or whether it would hurt Jeff, or whether she was making a mistake. There wasn't room in her mind to think of anything but Ethan.

20

SAMANTHA

Unsurprisingly, Sam was summoned to her mother's study the next morning.

When she knocked at the door, Robert Standish answered. He gave Sam a disdainful nod before settling into a wingback chair. Queen Adelaide—wearing a cream-colored top and a loose scarf, her hair tucked behind her usual crocodile headband—sat behind her desk, scrolling in silent shock through her tablet.

The queen's study was in the opposite wing of the palace from the monarch's, a holdover from previous centuries, when couples had married for political alliances and wanted to spend their days as far from each other as possible. It was a smaller, more intimate room, with pale blue wallpaper and delicate furniture. Queen Adelaide, like most royals, still corresponded by hand; Sam saw that her desk was littered with notes, from Sandringham and Drottningholm Palace and Peterhof and the Neues Palais.

"Well, Samantha," her mom began. "When I planned to leave town this weekend, I certainly didn't expect that I would have to fly back this morning because lewd photos of my daughter are all over the internet." She held up her tablet, her voice low and vicious as she read various headlines aloud. "'Princess Wet and Wild.' 'A Bad Heir Day.'"

In the photos, Sam's legs were wrapped around Marshall's

waist, his hands splayed on her lower back. She hadn't been wearing a bra, and the soaking white halter dress clung to her with all the modesty of a wet tissue. She might as well have been photographed naked, given how little was left to the imagination.

Sam waited for a flush of outrage, but all she felt was a weary disappointment. She'd *expected* her so-called friends to leak images of her and Marshall. And they had surpassed even her expectations.

"Look at this one!" Her mother brandished the tablet before her like a weapon, her face red with disappointment. "'Party Princess Pool Porno.'"

"That's bad alliteration. I expect better from the *Daily News*," Sam replied, with more levity than she felt. Robert let out an aggrieved sigh.

"*Samantha!*" Adelaide slammed her fist on her desk, startling all of them. Even the dust motes that floated in the morning sunlight seemed to jump at the noise. "What were you thinking, letting yourself get caught half-naked like this?"

"I was fully clothed!" At least, technically speaking. "Besides, we were only kissing. You know we have plenty of ancestors who did worse—people who had flagrant affairs with ladies-in-waiting or gentlemen of the bedchamber. And they were *married!*"

"Yes, but they weren't stupid enough to get photographed." Her mom slid the tablet forward in disgust.

"Only because photography hadn't been invented yet."

Sam's eyes flicked to the hundreds of comments cluttering the space below the article. The headlines might have been focused on Sam, but she saw with a sinking feeling that far more of the comments were about Marshall than about her. Some were so overtly racist that they made her stomach turn.

Marshall had been right when he said that *he* would take the heat for their relationship, not Sam.

Queen Adelaide ground her teeth. "What on earth possessed you to let your guests keep their phones? You know better than to trust a group of that size. Especially if you were planning on kissing Marshall Davis, of all people!"

"What do you have against Marshall?" Sam thought of those comments and drew in a slow, horrified breath. "Is it because he's *Black*?"

She saw a fleeting expression of agreement on Robert Standish's face, and wished she could slap it right off him.

"Samantha. Of course not," her mother replied, startled and clearly hurt. "It's his reputation I'm worried about. He's too wild and reckless. And he's always partying with *celebrities*," she added, with a touch of disdain. Adelaide had never understood people who *chose* to live in the spotlight, when the Washingtons only did so out of a sense of duty.

Sam scowled. "If you disapprove of him, then why did you put him on the list of potential husbands for Beatrice?"

"Partying aside, Marshall is a very eligible young man. Orange is one of the wealthiest and most populous duchies in the nation. And you know the monarchy has never tracked as well in West Coast popularity polls," her mom said matter-of-factly. "It would've been a smart move, bringing someone from Orange into the royal family." She sighed. "But I never really expected Beatrice to fall for Marshall. It was pretty clear to everyone that their personalities wouldn't mesh."

Sam clenched the carved armrests of her chair. "I guess this means you want me to stop seeing him?" She strove for nonchalance, but the ragged edge to her voice betrayed her.

Robert cleared his throat, a soft "hem-hem" that grated on Sam's nerves. "On the contrary," he replied, speaking up for the first time. "We've consulted with the PR teams, and decided the best approach is to accelerate the relationship between you and His Lordship. It will help us spin this not as a scandal, but as a gross intrusion upon the privacy of two young people in love."

"You . . . what?"

"The only way to salvage this situation is to double down on your relationship."

Sam's mind careened back to last night—to that stupid, ill-advised performance of a kiss. Why had she ever thought this was a good idea?

"His Lordship will remain in the capital," Robert was saying. "You'll do a few joint appearances; have dinner at high-profile restaurants, the type of places where people will sneak photos of you and post them all over the internet. There will be *no more* public displays of affection beyond hand-holding," he added sternly. "And then, next month, you'll go to Orange for their annual Accession Day festivities. Her Majesty will be attending as well, since it's the hundred and fiftieth anniversary of Orange joining the union."

Sam ran a hand through her hair; it was still frizzy, and smelled of chlorine. "The thing is, Marshall and I only just started dating. I can't turn it into a serious relationship overnight."

"But *I* can," Queen Adelaide said firmly. "I just got off the phone with Marshall's grandfather, the duke. He was as distressed about these photos as I was. It's all settled." She nodded crisply, as if to say, *That's that.*

"I don't know if Marshall will want me in Orange with him. . . ." They may have agreed to act like boyfriend and girlfriend until the wedding, but Sam wasn't sure how Marshall would feel now that their families were stage-managing their relationship.

"I believe he'll agree once his grandfather speaks to him."

Sam heard the meaning beneath Robert's words. *Your feelings on this matter are immaterial. You are both going to do as you're told, for the good of the Crown.*

"We can't afford any more negative publicity," he added. "Your relationship with His Lordship *needs* to go smoothly—at least until the wedding. Afterward, you're free to break up, of course." He gave a narrow smile. "We'll just release a statement that things didn't work out, but you're still friends."

Robert clearly assumed her relationship with Marshall wouldn't last. Sam hated that she would prove him right.

"Fine, I'll make sure we stay together through the wedding. God forbid anything overshadow Beatrice's big moment," she said sarcastically.

Her mom's eyes flashed. "Samantha, Beatrice never baited the press like you did last night."

"Sorry I'm not as perfect as she is," Sam snapped.

"Perfect?" her mom repeated. "All I'm asking for is *acceptable*. Daphne Deighton didn't grow up in a palace, but she has a better understanding of appropriate behavior than you do!"

"Then maybe I should get Daphne to teach me how to be a princess!"

Queen Adelaide pursed her lips. When she finally spoke, her words were cold and without inflection. "I expected better of you, Sam. And you know who else did? Your father. He would have been *appalled* by your behavior last night."

Sam stood up, scraping the chair so violently on the floor that it nearly tipped over. "Well then, sorry I'm such an epic failure."

It was immature, but she couldn't resist slamming the door behind her as she stormed out of her mom's study. The hallway's crystal light fixtures swayed in response, shards of light shuddering wildly over the walls.

How *would* her dad have reacted, if he were here right now?

Hey, kiddo. I love you, he would have murmured, the moment she walked into his office. *Do you want to tell me what happened?*

He would have let her explain, never interrupting or

condescending. Even when Sam was young he'd always made time for her, listened to her childish concerns with utter seriousness. Then, instead of dictating terms, he would have asked, "How do you think we can fix it?" And they would have come up with a solution together.

It wasn't fair of her mom to claim that he would've been ashamed of Sam—to use him as a weapon to win a fight.

But then, it really wasn't fair that they had lost him at all.

If only Sam could go back in time, request a do-over, push some cosmic PLAY AGAIN button like in a video game. She would do everything differently. She wouldn't act out to get attention, wouldn't waste time on Teddy. Most of all, she would tell her dad how much she loved him.

Sam didn't even bother alerting security to her departure. As she swept out the palace's front gates, she heard the guards' startled protests, their radio messages back toward headquarters about a princess on the loose. To his credit, her Revere Guard, Caleb, only asked once where they were going. When she didn't answer, he just kept walking doggedly alongside her.

On the streets, a few tourists squealed at her sudden appearance, or turned to each other and whispered, "Look, there she is! Can you believe it, after last night?" They cried out her name, shoving their phones forward to snap photos of her. Sam flashed them a peace sign as she turned the corner onto Rotten Road—*route du roi*, it had been called in Queen Thérèse's time, "the king's route," which had somehow devolved in English into *rotten*.

Past an enormous trash bin was a door that read THE MONMOUTH HOTEL: STAFF ENTRANCE.

The Washington twins had been coming to the Patriot—the cozy, unassuming taproom at the back of the boutique hotel—since they were sixteen: always walking in this way, through the back. They loved it here. The atmosphere was casual enough that no one ever bothered them, and if they drank too much they could, literally, stumble around the corner home. One time when she'd stayed out past curfew, Sam had tried to climb the palace's outer wall to sneak back in. She'd ended up with bruises on her butt for weeks.

She cast a quick glance around the room, with its dark-paneled walls and scattered knickknacks: an old American flag behind glass; a set of beer caps arranged in the shape of the royal crest; a Revolutionary War sword, mounted firmly to the wall in case anyone tried, unadvisedly, to use it.

The bar was nearly empty right now, just a few hotel guests reading newspapers, which made sense given that it was barely noon. The brunch crowd were all in the glamorous dining room at the front of the restaurant—though Sam and Jeff had long ago convinced the bartender to let them order brunch back here, in the peace and quiet.

With uncharacteristic nervousness, Sam took a seat and pulled out her phone. Her screen was lit up with dozens of messages. She swiped past most of them, zeroing in on her thread with Marshall.

7:08 a.m.: *Hey, are you okay?*

An unfamiliar warmth blossomed in her chest. No one except Jeff and Nina ever checked in on her like this.

Sam knew it was her fault. She kept people at a distance, held them back with her breezy attitude and her attention-seeking clothes and her repeated insistence that she didn't *need* any help, thank you very much. And then Marshall had come along, and had somehow seen her barricade for what it was—because he'd built one of his own, too.

Her breath oddly shaky, she tapped out a reply. *I'm so sorry about everything.*

His response was immediate. *I'm the one who should apologize. I pushed you in the pool, after all.*

I'm still sorry. People said some really ugly things about you in the comments. Sam hesitated, her fingers paused over the screen, then added, *Have you talked to your family?*

There was a long pause, as if Marshall was debating what to tell her. *There are some protesters outside Rory's apartment. But the police are already clearing them out*, he added quickly. *It's nothing she hasn't handled before.*

It made Sam slightly nauseous that Marshall's family took this kind of vitriol as a given. She wanted to scream at all those anonymous people, logging on to their computers and writing nasty comments simply because they liked being hateful.

Sam swiped at her phone to pull up a gossip site, and stared again at the photos—at how her tanned, freckled arms looked next to Marshall's brown ones. Underneath that skin they were the *same*, a frame of bones supporting a tangle of nerves and muscles and a steadily beating heart. It seemed ridiculous that anyone should care what color wrapped around it all.

She wished she knew how to make things better. Except . . . maybe, in some small way, she and Marshall were doing just that.

If they kept up this relationship, the entire world would see Marshall in a place of honor at a royal wedding: dancing the opening song, standing next to the Washingtons in official photos. Sam was aware how powerful that kind of imagery could be—maybe even powerful enough to change the national discourse.

But at what cost to Marshall and his family?

I'll understand if you want to call the whole thing off, she forced herself to write, pulling her lip into her teeth.

Nope. The media attention sucks, but it's worth it.

Sam's heart gave a strange lurch. She began tapping at the screen, but before she could reply, another text appeared from Marshall.

Kelsey texted this morning. Your plan was genius.

She leaned back on the barstool to catch her breath. Right. This was all just for show.

Of course I'm a genius, she managed, striving to match his irreverence. *Btw, next time we make out, can we face the other way? I want to make sure the photos get my good side.*

Sam stared at her phone, but there was no immediate answer. She turned it over, shoved it away from her, leaned her chin in her hand, then impatiently flipped it back over. The three little dots of the typing bubble had appeared on Marshall's side of the conversation.

Sure, he replied. *Lucky for you, both my sides are gorgeous.*

Sam sent an eye-roll emoji, then tossed her phone forcefully into her bag.

Her eyes caught on a girl sitting across the bar, in sunglasses and a green dress with wispy sleeves. She'd hunched her shoulders forward, deflecting attention, though no one seemed to pay her any mind.

"Daphne?"

The other girl removed her sunglasses with obvious reluctance. "Hey, Samantha," she said, and glanced down at her phone.

"You're waiting for someone," Sam realized. Of course, girls like Daphne didn't sit at the bar of the Patriot alone. The way Sam did.

"No. I mean, I *was* waiting for someone, but he probably isn't coming."

"It was Jeff, wasn't it?" When Daphne didn't answer, Sam knew she'd guessed right. "Hey, if it helps, I guarantee he's not in any shape to be out right now. Not that I'm doing much better."

To her surprise, Daphne made a strange spluttering sound that was almost a laugh. "I should have known not to make plans with your brother the morning after one of your parties."

"In that case, want to join me?"

Sam didn't know what had prompted her to ask. It felt like a violation of her friendship with Nina to sit here with Jeff's *other* ex-girlfriend. Although . . . just last night, Nina had insisted that she liked Ethan.

And right now, Daphne didn't seem like her usual shiny, perfect self. She seemed as disappointed at being stood up as any other girl, and Sam liked her the more for it.

"All right." Daphne slid down from her barstool and moved to the one by Sam. She crossed her ankles, her hands folded in her lap, the way photographers always asked Sam to sit for her formal portraits. Actually, it looked quite regal.

The bartender came over, his smile carefully polite. He was far too professional to reveal that he knew who they were, or that Sam had been all over the headlines that morning. "What can I get for you ladies?"

"*Coffee*," Sam groaned just as Daphne murmured, "A cappuccino, please, extra dry."

When the bartender turned aside, Sam glanced curiously at Daphne. "So, I saw you talking to Jeff at the party."

"For a while," Daphne said carefully.

"Are you guys getting back together?"

"I don't know." Now Daphne was the one looking meaningfully at Sam. "I mean, I keep wondering if Nina is still in the picture . . ."

So, Daphne was fishing for information. Sam hesitated, feeling suddenly protective of her best friend. She wasn't about to tell Nina's secret—but she also didn't want it to seem like Nina had been waiting around all these months, pining uselessly for Jeff.

"Actually, Nina has moved on," she said carefully. "She's into a guy at school."

There was a funny note in Daphne's voice as she replied, "Oh, you mean Ethan?"

Sam was too hungover, and too confused, to hide her surprise. "How did . . ."

"I saw them together last night," Daphne said easily, and Sam nodded. She hadn't realized things with Nina and Ethan had worked out, and in such a public way that Daphne had seen them. Then again, Sam had been pretty distracted toward the end of the party.

The bartender returned to deliver their coffees. Sam was too impatient to wait for cream or sugar; she immediately took a sip. But the coffee's bitter heat did nothing to settle her nerves.

"How do you handle the press?" she asked abruptly. "I mean, obviously you never ended up in photos like mine. But still . . . you never seem bothered by the media."

"Oh, they bother me plenty." Daphne stirred a sugar packet into her cappuccino, then delicately tapped her spoon against the side of the cup. "You think it was fun for me last summer? The paparazzi chased me for weeks after your brother broke up with me, trying to get a picture of me crying. It took every ounce of my self-control to ignore them."

Sam felt suddenly guilty that she'd never considered Daphne's feelings once, not during the entire time Jeff had dated her. It was just . . . Daphne hid her emotions so well—the way Beatrice did, the way Sam was *supposed* to do—that it usually seemed like she didn't have any at all.

A curious silence fell between them. Sam thought back to this morning's confrontation with her mom. Suddenly, amid all the insults and sharp words, one sentence stood out. *Then maybe I should get Daphne to teach me how to be a princess!*

"Would you help me?" She spoke without thinking, the way she always did.

"Help you?" Daphne gave a puzzled frown.

"Teach me how to handle the press, to be more likeable. You know you're better at it than I am."

Daphne seemed surprised by the request—and, really, so was Sam. But where else could she go for help? It wasn't as if she could search *How to be a good princess* on the internet.

Daphne gave a slow nod. "Sure, I'll help."

They both looked up as another figure burst through the back door of the Patriot: Jeff, wearing his favorite state championship rowing shirt and khaki shorts, his hair still mussed from sleep. When he saw Daphne and Sam sitting together, his expression shifted from puzzled disbelief to a sudden, boisterous delight.

"Hey, guys." He came to stand behind them, throwing his arms around their shoulders to hug them close. "Sorry I'm late to the party."

Daphne said something polite, but Sam just gave her brother a playful shove. "I believe the party was last night. Technically this is the afterparty."

"Or the after-afterparty. Sounds like you and Marshall had an afterparty of your own," Jeff teased. Sam stiffened, and he glanced over. "Sorry. Too soon?"

"No, it's okay. Your ability to make me laugh at my own mistakes is one of your greatest gifts." Sam drained the rest of her coffee in a single sip, then reached up to ruffle Jeff's hair, just to remind him which twin was boss. "I'm going to head out."

He and Daphne both made a show of protesting, but Sam knew better than to crash their date.

Just as Sam reached the door, Caleb following dutifully in her steps, Daphne called out, "See you later, Samantha!"

Sam wondered what she'd gotten herself into, asking for Daphne Deighton's help.

DAPHNE

"It's been way too long since we did this," Daphne declared, reaching across the Marikos' counter for another sugar cookie.

For years this had been the two friends' most sacred tradition: Saturday-afternoon shopping, followed by dinner at Himari's house. Sometimes Daphne would sleep over, and they would stay up far too late, talking about everything and nothing at once, the way only best friends can do.

Himari smiled. "Thanks for coming with me. I had a year of shopping to make up for."

"You made a valiant effort," Daphne teased, glancing at all the shopping bags jumbled behind Himari's chair. Daphne herself had only bought a single sweater that was on sale. She did most of her shopping online, where she could stack up coupons or buy couture items secondhand.

"Speaking of which, I have something for you." Himari leaned back in her chair to grab one of the shopping bags, then handed it over.

Daphne pulled off the tissue paper to reveal a supple leather handbag, the same emerald green as her eyes. Its gold chain was so soft that it slipped through her fingers like water.

"Himari—this is far too nice—"

"I saw you eyeing it at Halo," Himari said brightly. "Consider it a thank-you for being such a good friend this year. It means a lot to me, that you came to see me at the hospital so often," she added, more softly.

Somehow Daphne smiled through the wave of her guilt. "Thanks."

"It's nothing." Himari sighed. "I just can't believe you're graduating in a few weeks. I don't know how I'm going to survive all of next year without you."

"Please. You'll rule the school with an iron fist."

"Of course I will," Himari said impatiently. "But who's going to help me make sure the freshmen all know their place? Who will help me steal the best spots in the senior parking lot? Who'll sneak out of Madame Meynard's French class with me to get sesame bagels when we're supposed to be practicing our dialogue?"

There was a touch of sadness in Daphne's smile, because she had spent a year doing all those things alone, too. "I won't be far; King's College is only fifteen minutes away," she pointed out.

"You and Jeff are going to have so much fun," Himari moaned. "I can't wait to come visit you guys."

Daphne smiled. "All the time, please."

She and Jefferson had been texting ever since last weekend, when he'd arrived at the Patriot to find her deep in conversation with his sister. Daphne knew at once that she'd scored a huge point in her favor. Samantha's disapproval of her had always been a source of unspoken tension.

Himari pushed her chair back from the counter. "Want to watch something? I have *so* much TV-bingeing to catch up on."

Daphne's phone buzzed in her purse; she saw that it was her mother and pushed Ignore. She wasn't in the mood to deal with Rebecca's endless supply of plots and schemes.

"Yeah, I'll stay." She made to turn upstairs, but Himari had already crossed the room toward the back door.

"Can we go outside, actually? My brothers have taken over the playroom."

There was nothing Daphne could say without arousing suspicion. She followed Himari despite her sudden uneasiness.

When they pulled open the door of the pool house, Himari sighed. "It's too hot in here," she announced. "Let me get the AC."

Daphne went to sit down, clicking through the TV menu without really registering what it said. The last time she'd been in here, the night of Himari's birthday party last spring, this couch had been unfolded into a pull-out bed.

It was where she'd lost her virginity to Ethan.

Daphne braced her palms on the couch cushion beneath her, trying—and failing—not to think about that night. Of the way Ethan's body had fit against hers, skin to skin.

There was a loud clattering sound from the doorway. Himari had stumbled, barely catching herself from falling to the floor.

Daphne rushed forward, grabbing her friend beneath her arms to steady her. "Are you okay? Should I call your doctor?"

Himari's face had gone ashen, her eyes fluttering shut. "I just need a minute."

Daphne helped her to the couch, then found a bottle of water in the mini-fridge and forced Himari to take a few sips. "You probably overexerted yourself today," she babbled. "Let me help you upstairs. Or do you want me to get your parents?"

Himari's breaths were quick and shallow. For a terrifying moment, Daphne thought she might have passed out or somehow relapsed into a coma.

Then Himari's eyes shot open, and Daphne knew at once that something had changed.

"You were in here last year, weren't you?" Himari asked, speaking very slowly. "With *Ethan*."

The hair on Daphne's arms prickled. She didn't know how to answer. There was no way she could admit the truth, yet she couldn't bear to lie to Himari, either. Not after everything her friend had been through.

The misery must have been written there on her face, because Himari drew in a breath.

"I can't believe it," she whispered. "You and him—I remember now. I saw you!"

Daphne swallowed against the fear in her throat, sticky and hot like tar. "Let me explain," she said weakly.

"Explain what? The fact that you cheated on your boyfriend—Jeff is my friend too, you know—in *my* house?"

"I'm sorry—"

"Sorry that you did it, or sorry you got caught?"

"I'm sorry for *all* of it!"

Something in her tone must have given her away, because she saw the moment of Himari's comprehension, as the last piece of the puzzle fell into place.

"Oh my god. The night of the twins' graduation party. That was *you*."

Daphne leaned forward, but Himari lurched unsteadily from the couch. She stumbled back, to where a row of plastic folding chairs leaned against one wall, and held one before her so that its four legs were stretched out like weapons.

"You stay away from me." Himari's voice bristled with outrage, and even more heartbreaking, with fear. "You slept with Ethan, and when I confronted you about it, you tried to *kill* me to shut me up!"

Daphne's mind was brutally silenced by those words.

"Of course I didn't try to kill you," she managed. "I mean, I guess it might seem that way, but you don't know the whole story."

"You're the one who drugged me that night! Aren't you?"

Daphne glanced down, unable to bear the hurt and disgust on Himari's face, and gave a miserable nod.

Himari set down the chair, but didn't move. "You're unbelievable."

"I never thought—I just wanted you to do something dumb that night," Daphne stammered. "Something I could hold over your head, the way you were holding Ethan over mine. I never, ever meant to hurt you. You're my best friend."

"I *was* your best friend, until I got between you and Jeff." Himari shook her head. "That's the thing about you, Daphne. You always put yourself first. You're completely and utterly selfish."

Daphne winced. It was one thing to know the ugly truth about her choices, another thing entirely to hear it from someone else. "I'm so sorry, Himari—it destroyed me, what happened to you."

"Are you kidding? You don't get to ask *me* to feel sorry for *you*," the other girl hissed. "I could have *died!*"

"If I could take back what happened, I would! It's the biggest regret of my life!"

Himari looked at Daphne for an interminable moment. "I wish I could believe you," she said at last. "But you're too much of a liar. You lie to me and to Jeff, and most of all you lie to yourself."

Sometimes, when Daphne was asleep, she got trapped in a lucid dream—she had the panicked realization that she was asleep but still couldn't wake up. She felt like that now, trapped in some warped, nightmarish version of reality.

"Please," she begged. "Is there anything I can do to fix this?"

Himari shook her head. "Get out. *Now.*"

When Daphne got home, her mother was sitting in the living room. There was only one light on, a brass standing lamp that threw strange shadows over her, emphasizing her cruel beauty.

"Where were you?" she asked, without preamble.

Rebecca Deighton was invariably polite to strangers, especially strangers who might prove useful to her at some point in the future. But she never wasted the effort on her own family.

Daphne's eyes burned. She felt a sudden urge to tell her mother everything that had happened—to let it all spill out and ask for advice, the way other girls did with *their* parents.

Of course, she couldn't do anything of the sort.

"I was at Himari's," she said weakly.

"Not with Jefferson?" Rebecca gave a little tsk of criticism. "Has he asked you to the wedding?"

Daphne shifted her weight. "Not yet."

"Why not?" her mother asked, cold as ice.

"I don't know."

Rebecca was on her feet in an instant, grabbing her daughter by the shoulders. Her nails dug into Daphne's flesh so sharply that she bit back a cry of pain.

"'I don't know' isn't acceptable anymore! If you don't have an answer, then go find it!" Rebecca released her hold on Daphne and stepped back. "Come on, Daphne. I raised you better than 'I don't know.'"

Daphne held back her tears, because she didn't dare show fear before her mother. Fear was a weakness, and if a Deighton knew your weakness they would never stop exploiting it.

"I'll handle it." She headed up the stairs to her room, where she fell back onto her bed and closed her eyes. Her stomach churned with a hot, queasy anxiety.

But amid the tangle of her thoughts, one thing was utterly clear. If Daphne wanted Jefferson to invite her to the wedding, she couldn't keep throwing herself in his path. She needed him to seek *her* out . . . and she saw a way to make him do exactly that.

Daphne hesitated a moment, but Himari's words echoed cruelly in her mind. *You always put yourself first. You're completely and utterly selfish.*

Fine, then. If Himari thought she was heartless and self-centered, Daphne would go ahead and prove her right. This plan would hurt people, but so what? Daphne cared about nothing and no one but herself.

She dialed Natasha, one of the editors at the *Daily News*. The journalist answered on the second ring.

"Daphne. To what do I owe the pleasure?"

When Daphne had explained what she wanted, Natasha let out a low whistle.

"You want me to call Prince Jefferson himself and ask for a quote? Do you realize how angry that will make the palace's press secretary? They'll bar me from royal photo calls for months. Not to mention they'll keep asking how I got his number."

"I'll make it up to you," Daphne said urgently. "Please, you know I'm good for it."

Natasha laughed, a low, hoarse sound. There was a rustling on the other end as if she was writing this all down, her pencil frantically scratching over the paper.

"You *will* owe me—and I mean something big. Like engagement-announcement-big," Natasha warned. "But okay, Daphne. For you, I'll do it."

Daphne hung up the phone and smiled, a bitter triumphant smile that was lost to the shadows.

BEATRICE

Sometime in the last month, Beatrice had started thinking of this as *her* office, rather than her father's.

Redecorating had helped. It was Teddy's idea, actually; he'd stopped by one day and asked where all her things were, and Beatrice had realized, startled, that nothing in here belonged to her.

She'd traded the gold-braided drapes for wispy curtains, which she kept tied back, so she could look out over the lazy gray curve of the river below. And she'd exchanged the oil portrait of King George I that used to hang above the fireplace for one of her father.

Unsurprisingly, Lord Standish had been horrified by her changes. "Your Majesty, that portrait has hung in this room for centuries!" he'd protested when he saw the footmen removing it. "He's the father of our nation!"

"I'd rather look at my *own* father for guidance," Beatrice had insisted. She found it reassuring, as if her dad were silently watching over her, guiding her steps. Occasionally she caught herself talking to the picture aloud. Asking her dad for advice about her duties, about Teddy—and about her family.

Beatrice was relieved that Sam had moved on and was dating Marshall. Yet she couldn't help worrying that the way Sam had let the world learn of their relationship, with those steamy pool photos, was a cry for attention. She wished she could talk to her sister . . . but Beatrice had given up trying.

Besides, if it helped Sam get over Teddy, Beatrice couldn't really argue with it.

She stretched her arms overhead, giving herself a momentary break from the Royal Dispatch Box, which Robert filled each morning with her daily business. By now Beatrice had realized that he put the inconsequential documents at the top and tucked away the items he'd rather she didn't get to, like policy briefings or updates from foreign offices, at the bottom.

The first thing she did when she got the Box was remove all its contents and flip over the entire stack so that she could work through them from bottom to top.

She set aside the Federal Reserve's economic forecast and picked up the next document: an update from the Paymaster General about funding the government during Congress's summer recess. It was a painful reminder that Congress's closing session was in two weeks, and she still hadn't been invited.

Were the members of Congress really going to let the closing session come and go without the monarch's presence?

Yesterday, Beatrice had swallowed her misgivings and asked Robert what she should do. "Nothing," he'd said silkily. "In moments such as these, the role of the queen is to do nothing and say nothing. Anything else would obstruct proper governance."

Her phone buzzed, distracting her from her thoughts. *Guess who sent this one,* Teddy had written, with a photo of matching plaid shirts. Beatrice honestly couldn't tell whether they were outerwear or pajamas.

She and Teddy had divided up the wedding gifts, so their respective secretaries could begin drafting the thousands of thank-you notes they would have to sign. They'd gotten in the habit of sending each other pictures of the most outrageous ones.

She flicked her hair over her shoulder with an impatient gesture and typed a response. *The Prince of Wales. Only the British wear plaid that looks like a carpet.*

Ouch, Teddy answered. *Actually, these are from Lord Shrewsborough.*

My old etiquette master!

She could practically see Teddy's smile as he replied. *Etiquette, what a dying art.*

Beatrice swiveled in her chair toward where Franklin was curled up in the corner. His eyes were closed, his legs twitching as he dreamed some delightful puppy dream. She took a picture and sent it. *We miss you.*

Things between her and Teddy had changed since Walthorpe. Now Beatrice caught herself relying on him, in ways she hadn't foreseen. She would ask Teddy for advice on her problems, and together they'd talk out her various options. They went on walks together, Franklin running impatiently before them on a leash. Occasionally when they were both laughing at the puppy's antics, Beatrice caught herself wondering if two people could fall in love this way—by loving the same thing so deeply that their excess love spilled over and drew them toward each other.

It was the oddest and sweetest and most unexpected sort of courtship, as if they had wiped away everything that had happened between them and met again as strangers.

Beatrice remembered what her father had told her the night before he died: that he and her mother hadn't been in love when they were first married. *But we fell in love, day by day,* he'd said. *Real love comes from facing life together, with all its messes and surprises and joys.*

She glanced back down and sighed at the next paper in her stack. It was the guest list for her wedding.

Robert had compiled the list based on long-standing protocol. He'd added foreign kings and queens, ambassadors, chancellors of universities, members of Congress. *I kept it to fourteen hundred guests,* he'd told her; *which means that you and Teddy each get a hundred personal friends.* Beatrice hadn't bothered protesting. She didn't have a ton of friends, anyway. Plenty of people *claimed* to be her friend, but the only real one she'd ever had was Connor.

She froze. Surely she was seeing things, hallucinating Connor's name because she'd just been thinking about him.

But no, there it was, right in the middle of the guest list: *Mr. Connor Dean Markham,* with an address in Houston.

So he'd left town, Beatrice thought dazedly. She tried not to think beyond that, but some part of her couldn't help wondering what his life was like, whether he was happy. Whether he'd met someone new.

What was he doing on the invite list?

She leaned forward to press her intercom. "Robert? I need to talk to you about the wedding invitations."

A few moments later, Robert's new assistant, Jane, opened the door. She was pulling a wheeled cart behind her—which was laden with four enormous boxes.

"Jane," Beatrice asked slowly, "is that *all* the wedding invitations?"

"Yes, Your Majesty." Jane knelt down to pull a box from the lower shelf of the cart. "I wasn't sure what your concern was, so I brought them all. There are forty blank invitations here; if you'd like to add someone, give me their name and I'll have the calligrapher complete it."

"It's fine," Beatrice cut in. "I just had a question regarding one invitation in particular."

Robert peered around the open door. "Can I be of service?"

Beatrice nodded. "There's a name on the guest list that surprised me. My former Guard, Connor Markham."

"It's tradition that we invite former Revere Guards to a royal wedding," Robert said slowly. "You'll see that some of your other previous Guards were also included."

Beatrice blinked down at the list. Sure enough, a few of her other guards—Ari and Ryan—were listed below Connor.

"I see," she said carefully. "However, I'd like to remove Connor from the list."

"Is there a problem that I need to be aware of?"

Robert held her gaze for a long, slow moment. Beatrice wondered, suddenly, if he *knew*. She had no idea how he might have found out—but if anyone could dig up other people's secrets, it was Robert.

"Not at all." She marveled at how casual her voice came out, despite the hammering of her heart.

Jane looked up from one of the boxes, which read *J–N* on the side in thick black marker. She'd been fanning through the invitations filed inside, and was now holding one of them.

Beatrice's hand darted out to snatch the envelope from Jane's grip.

"Thank you. I'll need to think about this," she declared, with forced calm.

"Of course." Jane bobbed a curtsy and headed out into the hall, pulling the cart behind her. Robert hesitated, his eyes still fixed curiously on the queen, then followed.

Beatrice sank into her chair. Franklin had woken up at all the noise; he ran over to nudge playfully at her legs. She let him climb up into her lap, not caring that he was getting hair all over her oyster-colored pants, and unfolded the envelope.

The invitation was heavy, her royal monogram stamped at the top in bright gold foil. Beatrice had never asked how long it took for the palace calligrapher to painstakingly write out each invitation by hand.

> *The Lord Chamberlain is commanded*
> *by Her Majesty to invite*
>
> ## Mr. Connor Dean Markham
>
> *to the Celebration and Blessing of the Marriage of*
>
> ## Beatrice Georgina Fredericka Louise
> ### Queen of America
>
> *&*
>
> ## Lord Theodore Beaufort Eaton
>
> *Friday, the twentieth of June, at high noon*

An invitation for *Connor*, to her wedding with *Teddy*.

They were two names that didn't belong in the same sentence. Two very distinct parts of her life, about to collide in a spectacular and fiery crash.

Beatrice's breath came in short gasps. She didn't *want* to think of Connor. She had tried to banish him from her mind ever since that night at Walthorpe, when everything with Teddy had become acutely real. But he was still there, a shadowy figure in the corners of her heart.

She couldn't help imagining what would happen if she actually sent the invitation. She could almost see the emotions flickering over Connor's face when he opened it: shock, anger, confusion, and finally a wary uncertainty. He would spend weeks debating whether or not to come, would change his mind a thousand times, and then at the very last minute—right when he'd decided against it—he would race to the airport and make it just in time, wearing his old Guard's uniform—

And then what? Did she expect him to stand there and watch as she married someone else?

Beatrice stared at her family coat of arms, carved in the heavy stone of the mantelpiece: a pair of horizontal lines surmounted by three stars and a roaring griffin. As everyone knew, the stars and stripes of the Washingtons' coat of arms had been the original inspiration behind the American flag.

Stamped below the crest were the words of her family motto: FACIMUS QUOD FACIENDUM EST. *We do what we must.*

Beatrice had always assumed that motto was about the Revolution: that King George I—General George Washington, he'd been then—hadn't wanted to go to war with Great Britain and lead thousands of men to their deaths, but that independence was worth it. Now, however, the motto seemed to take on a new meaning.

We do what we must, no matter if it means letting go of people we care about. No matter what our choices end up costing.

Beatrice nudged Franklin so that he jumped out of her lap, then leaned down and ran her hand along the bottom of the desk. When she felt a latch, she pulled, and the concealed drawer popped open.

There—in a drawer designed two centuries ago, to hide state secrets—Beatrice now kept a single wedding present, tied with a satin ribbon.

It was from Connor. He'd given it to her the night of her engagement party to Teddy. Beatrice still couldn't bring herself to open it, yet she couldn't bear to throw it away, either.

She set the invitation carefully on top of the gift, then shut the drawer with a gentle click.

NINA

The student center was always crowded in the afternoons, full of people who stopped by to watch the massive communal TVs, or make a halfhearted attempt at studying. Nina was currently sitting at a two-person table with Ethan, tuning out the noise as she planned her upcoming essay on *Middlemarch*. When he let out a yelp of excitement, she glanced up at the baseball game. "Who's winning?"

"The Yeti just got a home run," Ethan explained.

She frowned up at the screen. "Is that the team in red?"

He burst out laughing. "Nina, the Yeti isn't a team. Yeti is a *player*—Leo Yetisha, everyone calls him the Yeti? Didn't you pay *any* attention all those times we watched games from the royal box?"

"Honestly, no." She'd either been talking to Sam or stealing glances at Jeff. It felt strange to think about that now. "In my defense, a yeti would be a fantastic mascot. It's way scarier than the Cardinals or Red Sox."

"Of course," Ethan said drily, "the Yeti, famously the most terrifying of all fantastic beasts."

Nina smiled and stood up, slinging her bag over her shoulder. "I'm heading over to see Sam." She hadn't actually warned Sam she was coming, but Nina thought her friend could use a surprise right now.

In the weeks since the party, Sam and Marshall had gone

on a couple of public dates, though it hadn't distracted people from buzzing about their pool photos. Nina wasn't a media expert, but even she knew that a raunchy make-out wasn't the best way to introduce a royal relationship, real *or* fake.

This was precisely why Nina had warned Sam in the first place. Couldn't she have found some easier way of making Teddy jealous, instead of involving the media—and hurting Marshall and his family in the process?

Nina wondered if she should reach out to Marshall, ask how he was handling things. She knew firsthand how it felt to be the focus of that kind of tabloid attention, and discrimination. The headlines might not be overtly racist, but the comments undoubtedly were.

"Have fun with Sam," Ethan said, standing up to give Nina a quick goodbye kiss.

She thought again how *nice* it was, getting to be with someone without any secrets or subterfuge. No more NDAs, no more hiding in the back of a town car, no more seeing her boyfriend in public and pretending that he meant nothing to her.

When she and Ethan walked across campus, Nina would reach out to catch his hand; when they studied together in the library, Ethan would toss her crumpled-up notes that said things like *You're cute when you're focused*. A few nights ago they'd gone out to dinner, to the tiny sushi place a block from campus, and ended up lingering for hours over a bottomless bowl of edamame. Their conversation had veered wildly from music—Ethan was appalled that Nina could quote entire musicals but not a single Bruce Springsteen song: "We are fixing this *now*," he'd moaned, and handed her an earbud—to speculation about their World History professor, and whether he might be secretly writing fan fiction about members of a British boy band.

She'd learned that Ethan and his mom used to go on a

spontaneous road trip every summer. That he could trace all the constellations but didn't know the stories behind them, which was where Nina and her love of mythology came in.

She'd learned that when he slept, he curled on his side, his arms tucked beneath his head as if he were trying to take up as little space as possible, his eyelashes twitching with the movement of his dreams.

The only thing they hadn't discussed was how they planned on telling Jeff.

At first Nina had been confident that they were doing the right thing, keeping it from him. There was no reason to upset him if she and Ethan weren't even going to last. Now, though . . . they needed to tell him. Nina was uncomfortably reminded of how it had felt when she was secretly dating Jeff, and hiding their relationship from Sam.

She headed through the front door of the palace—and there he was, Prince Jefferson himself, clattering down the staircase.

Somehow Nina was unsurprised. In her experience the palace had always worked that way, as if the building were under some perverse enchantment, flinging you directly into the path of the one person you'd hoped to avoid.

"Hey, Jeff." She strove for a casual, friendly tone, more *good to see you again* than *I'm secretly dating your best friend.* "I was just heading up to see Sam."

She started to edge past him, but Jeff's next words made her fall still.

"Is it true? Are you really sleeping with Ethan?"

Nina felt his words like a punch to the gut. She glanced back and forth, then swallowed. This wasn't at all how she'd hoped to have this conversation.

"We're not—I mean—" she stammered. Ethan had been sleeping in her dorm room, yes, but they hadn't actually . . .

"So it's true." Jeff took a step back, a hand braced on the

stair railing. "When the reporter told me, I didn't believe it. But now I do."

"You talked to a reporter?"

Jeff's jaw tensed. "Just this morning, I got a call from some editor at the *Daily News*—I have no clue how she found my number—asking if I'd like to comment on the fact that my ex-girlfriend and my best friend are the new 'it couple' of King's College."

"We're not an 'it couple,'" Nina protested, and immediately winced.

"I told the reporter she was wrong. 'I've known them both since kindergarten,' I said; 'if they were together, they would have told me.' But she'd done her homework—she had a whole story ready to go, complete with quotes from classmates who said they always saw you together, holding hands."

Nina's stomach lurched. She and Ethan should have been more careful. Now that story would go to print, and it would be like last time all over again: her name the punch line of a trashy joke, her parents' house swarmed with reporters—

Jeff sighed, clearly following her train of thought. "I got my lawyer involved, and he convinced the reporter not to run the story."

"Thank you," Nina said softly.

A trio of footmen walked past, carrying an enormous vase between them. They cast the prince and his ex-girlfriend a few looks, then quickly averted their eyes.

"Of course. I wasn't about to let them drag you through the mud like they did last time." There was a pained softness to Jeff's eyes, a pinch at the corner of his mouth. "I just . . . I never thought it would be like this. I knew that you and I would date other people, but I assumed we were on good enough terms that we would give each other fair warning. At least, I was planning on giving *you* that courtesy."

Nina blinked. "Are you and Daphne getting back together?"

"Maybe," Jeff said bluntly. "If we did, I wasn't going to let you find out from the tabloids. I thought we owed each other that much, at least."

Nina squirmed. She couldn't remember the last time she'd felt so small. "I'm sorry. You're right; we should have told you."

"How long has it been going on?" Jeff asked. "Since before the party?"

"Um. Not technically."

He closed his eyes, and Nina knew he was thinking of all the times he'd seen Ethan since then, when Ethan could have brought this up and instead kept his mouth shut.

"I want you to be happy, I really do," Jeff said hoarsely. "But does it have to be with my *very best friend*?"

In that moment, Nina realized the full extent of the hurt she'd caused.

She had always known that dating Ethan would make things awkward. But she hadn't fully grasped that in dating Ethan, she was fracturing Jeff's relationship with his best friend—one of the few people he really trusted, in a world where it was hard to trust anyone.

How would Jeff and Ethan move forward from this? What were they supposed to do, hang out and play video games as if Nina didn't exist? As if she and Ethan hadn't gotten together, knowing full well it would hurt Jeff, then purposefully *hid* it from him?

Jeff ran a hand wearily through his hair. "Nina," he said, in a deflated voice that cut her to the quick. "Are you sure you know what you're doing?"

"What do you mean?" she whispered.

"When you broke up with me, you said it was because you wanted *out* of this world. You told me that you couldn't handle the royal life, with all its scrutiny and publicity. And now you're dating my best friend." He laughed, but there was no mirth in it. "I just had to kill a tabloid story about your relationship. From where I'm sitting, you haven't really gone that far from the spotlight."

Nina's head was spinning. She wanted to call a quick time-out so that she could catalog everything she'd felt in the last few minutes: her anger at being attacked by a reporter yet again; her hurt at learning that Jeff and Daphne might get back together. And her guilt at the realization of how epically she'd hurt Jeff and Ethan.

Was Jeff right? She had worked so hard to distance herself from the royal world, to make people *forget* that she was someone they'd seen in the newsstand tabloids. By dating Ethan, was she letting herself fall into the same mess all over again?

She looked up at him with sudden uncertainty. "Jeff—"

"Whatever. Forget it," he said, and his steps receded down the hallway.

Nina stood there for a moment in cold, shaky silence. Then she squared her shoulders and headed upstairs.

She found Samantha on the couch in her sitting room, her hair twisted back with a clip as she tapped viciously at her phone. There was a blurred shadow in her eyes that set Nina's best-friend radar on high alert.

"What are we looking at?" she asked, sitting down next to Sam.

The princess gave an aggrieved sigh and handed over her phone. She'd been scrolling through Kelsey Brooke's profile page.

"Can you *believe* this girl?" Sam snapped. "I mean, she's nauseatingly fake. I don't know what Marshall sees in her."

Nina flicked through a few photos: Kelsey wearing a denim jacket and short-shorts, rollerblading on a boardwalk; Kelsey's glittery dark nails curled around a green juice, with the caption *Rise and shine, my witches!*

Well, at least it was better than what Nina had assumed

Sam was doing—flipping through the comments section of one of the articles about her and Marshall.

"Did I miss something? Why are we hate-stalking Kelsey?" she asked.

"No reason," Sam said swiftly. "Just that I'll see her when Marshall and I go to LA next month. And he'll want to talk to her, since, you know, he's trying to get her back." Sam rolled her eyes. "God knows why."

Nina pulled one of Sam's pillows onto her lap and began playing with the fringe. "So . . . I ran into your brother on the way up here. He knows about me and Ethan." At Sam's concerned look, she let the whole story pour out, about how Jeff had learned the truth from a reporter.

"It's not entirely your fault," Sam hurried to assure her. "Ethan deserves at least half the blame. Maybe more, since he's Jeff's best friend."

Nina flinched. "Exactly. I took Jeff's *best friend* from him! I can't imagine how I would feel, if you secretly dated *my* ex—"

"That would be slightly problematic, given that your ex is my brother."

Nina choked out a laugh. "You know what I mean. I just . . . I would be devastated, if something like that ever came between us."

"Nothing could ever come between us. I swear it," Sam said fervently.

Sam's phone buzzed with an incoming message. Nina didn't mean to pry, but she instinctively glanced down at the screen—and bristled when she saw who it was.

"Why is Daphne texting you?"

Sam typed out a quick reply. "She's actually on her way over."

"Why?"

Nina had never told Sam the full story of her breakup with Jeff: how Daphne had confronted her in the ladies' room at the palace, and threatened to ruin Nina's life unless she broke up with the prince.

"I know I always complained about her," Sam was saying, oblivious to Nina's inner turmoil, "but—I don't know, maybe she's not as bad as I thought. She's going to help train me for all the stuff I need to do as heir to the throne."

"I thought Robert was training you?" Nina asked hoarsely.

"Robert is insufferable and irritating, and Daphne . . ." Sam shrugged. "Just give her a try, for my sake?"

No, Nina thought plaintively, she couldn't just *give Daphne a try*. She didn't want to be anywhere *near* that girl.

"If Daphne is coming, I should get going," Nina said, rising awkwardly to her feet. "I—next time I come over, I'll call first."

"Please. You don't need to call," Sam scoffed, but Nina didn't match her smile.

Sam had been wrong, when she said that nothing could come between them.

If anyone could, it would be Daphne Deighton.

24

DAPHNE

Daphne waited for Samantha at the entrance to the Brides' Room: a small room on the ground floor of the palace, near the ballroom. She glanced down at her phone, her pulse skipping when she saw she had a new text—but it wasn't from Himari.

We need to talk, Ethan had written.

Tomorrow afternoon, meet me at the alley, Daphne typed back, and let her phone fall into her purse. Of course Ethan was upset about what she'd done—but Daphne knew she could handle him. Himari's continued silence was a far more ominous problem.

She would just have to worry about Himari later. Right now Daphne was due to meet with Samantha, for . . . what, a class on likeability? A remedial princess lesson?

They'd been texting since that morning at the Patriot but hadn't found a time to meet until now. Daphne wondered if Samantha felt oddly self-conscious about her request, if she'd been delaying the inevitable because part of her wanted to back out of the whole thing.

The two of them had never really hung out like this. They'd been around each other for years, thanks to Jefferson, but Samantha hadn't exactly warmed up to Daphne. Daphne always had a sense that the princess could see right through her.

Well, today was a chance to change all that, and win

Samantha to her side. Besides, Daphne never turned down an excuse to get inside the palace.

Samantha appeared at the other end of the hall. "Sorry to keep you waiting. Nina was just here."

Daphne murmured that it wasn't a problem, even as her mind raced at the news. Natasha should have called Jefferson this morning—had Nina come to find him and apologize? Or was she really just at the palace to see Samantha?

The princess tried the handle of the Brides' Room, but the door was locked. She sighed. "Want to go upstairs? My sitting room is more comfortable anyway."

Daphne shook her head. "You need to practice in front of a mirror."

"Why?"

"So you can *see yourself*," Daphne replied, in a slightly impatient tone. Samantha should have known how this worked; she'd been born to it.

Unlike Daphne, who'd taught herself everything she knew. She'd read every etiquette manual she could find, had spent years paying close attention to what Beatrice and Queen Adelaide did. Daphne had mastered her curtsy the way ballerinas learned to dance—by practicing with Velcro gym weights strapped around her ankles.

"So that I can see myself doing what, smiling and waving?" Samantha demanded. "Please tell me you're not going to make me walk around with a stack of books on my head."

"The stack of books is an advanced move," Daphne heard herself snap, with a touch of sarcasm. "Let's get through the basics first."

"Fair enough." There was a self-deprecating, amused note in the princess's voice that, oddly, softened Daphne's irritation.

Samantha went to find a butler. When he unlocked the door for them, Daphne saw at once why it had been shut.

On a seamstress's table in the corner sat the Winslow tiara, the one that Beatrice had always worn as Princess Royal, surrounded by several bolts of lace. It looked like someone had been comparing options for the queen's veil, only to pause halfway through the task.

"Don't touch anything," the butler admonished, before pulling the door shut behind him.

Samantha plopped down onto the love seat. It was the only furniture in the room aside from the seamstress's table, and the massive three-fold mirror against the back wall.

When Daphne was a child, she used to sneak up to her parents' room when they weren't home. Their closet doors had full-length mirrors on them, and if she opened both doors at an angle and stood in the middle, it reflected her a million times over.

Daphne had loved it. There was something heady about walking up to the mirror as a single person, only to find that when you stood a certain way, you were multiplied into an army.

She kept her eyes directed toward the mirror so Samantha wouldn't catch her stealing glances at the Winslow tiara. But the light kept catching on its filigreed knot of diamonds, each of them burning like a small star.

Daphne had never touched a tiara before. Either your family owned one, handed one down through the generations, like the Kerrs or the Astors or the Fitzroys—or they didn't. The Deightons, of course, were tiara-less.

She headed to the love seat and sat down, smoothing her skirt beneath her as she moved. Next to her, Samantha was subtly copying her movements. Their gazes met in the mirror, and the princess flushed.

"Sorry," Samantha muttered. "I mean—this whole thing is kind of weird."

"First of all, a princess never acknowledges when something is weird. She just suffers silently through the weirdness without pointing it out," Daphne admonished.

"Oh my god, who told you *that*?"

"I read it in an etiquette book. Probably the same one you were supposed to read years ago, but never got around to."

Sam shrugged, acknowledging the truth of it, just as the door swung inward.

"Sam? I heard you were in here—" Jefferson broke off at the sight of Daphne. "Oh, hey, Daphne. What are you guys up to?"

"Wouldn't you like to know," Samantha said automatically, but Daphne heard the note of concern beneath. The princess was clearly worried about her brother.

Jefferson leaned an elbow against the doorway. "I was thinking we could get a group together and go to Phil's later. They have that new DJ in from London. I already invited JT and Rohan," he added, pointedly leaving out Ethan's name.

Samantha nodded. "Works for me."

The prince turned to Daphne. "You'll come too, right?"

"I'd love to," she said, gratified that events were playing out exactly as she'd planned.

She had done this: by passing that scoop to Natasha, and insisting that the reporter call Jefferson directly with the news. In one fell swoop, she'd robbed Jefferson of two of the people he'd trusted most.

And the more isolated he felt, the easier it would be for Daphne to win him back. After all, she wasn't the one who'd betrayed him.

Jefferson mumbled a goodbye, and Daphne turned back to his sister. "So. Where should we begin?"

"No idea." Samantha shook her head. "This is probably why everyone thinks I'm useless at being the spare."

"Actually, you were pretty good at being the spare. But you're the heir now, and that's what's causing you problems." When Sam shot her a puzzled look, Daphne tried to explain. "Being the spare is all about being a foil to the heir."

"Are you saying that when I act out, it's a good thing, because it makes Beatrice look better by comparison?"

"I'm saying that when you were the spare, you existed as a counterpoint to your sister. Don't you know that Beatrice is at her most likeable when she's in interviews with you and Jefferson? When she's alone she can come off too . . . rehearsed, and a little stiff," Daphne said delicately. "But when she's with you two, like in those fireside chats your family always does around the holidays, America sees another side of her."

Samantha blinked, as if she'd never thought of that. "Except now everything's changed," she muttered. "Jeff is the spare, and *I'm* the heir."

"Well, yes. Those are different roles. You haven't been trained as first in line—and, really, you shouldn't have needed to be," Daphne added softly.

If the succession had proceeded on a happier timeline—if the king had never gotten cancer, had lived another thirty years—Beatrice would have been succeeded by her own children, not by her sister.

No child who grew up second in line for the throne should ever become first in line. If they did, it meant that something had gone horribly, tragically wrong.

"Let's do a little practice talking to reporters. Here, I'll give you an easy one," Daphne said briskly. "How does it feel, being the maid of honor for your sister's wedding?"

"It'll be fun," Sam offered.

Daphne tilted her head expectantly, waiting for Sam to say something else. When she didn't, Daphne groaned. "That's it? 'It'll be fun'?"

"What's wrong with that?"

"What on earth is a reporter supposed to do with *three words*? Samantha, you have to give them something they can *use*."

"I could have said something much worse," the princess observed, and Daphne let out a breath.

"Here's the thing about reporters. All they want is to write a story that will make them money. While *you* want them to write a story that's flattering." Daphne had figured that out long ago; it was why she and Natasha got along so well. "Your job is to make those goals one and the same. If you can give them a story that makes you look good and sells copies, they have no reason to attack you."

"Maybe," Samantha said, unconvinced. "But they're pretty attached to the party princess version of me. I doubt they're going to start giving me positive coverage anytime soon."

"They *definitely* won't give you positive coverage if all you're willing to tell them is 'It'll be fun.'" Daphne smiled. "All you have to do is be a little bit . . . softer, create a temporary moment of intimacy. Pretend you're excited to be talking to them."

"I'm sick of pretending. There's too much pretending in my family as it is."

Daphne's ears pricked up at that. She tried not to sound too eager as she asked, "What do you mean?"

"Everyone keeps pretending that they're fine when they're not," Samantha said helplessly. "We're all smiling and waving for the cameras, planning this enormous fairy-tale wedding as if it can somehow make everyone forget we had a *funeral* earlier this year. My mom is pretending that nothing bad ever happened to us, and I'm pretending with Marshall, and Beatrice is pretending most of all! She doesn't even love Teddy; she loves—"

Samantha broke off, shaking her head. "I just don't see the point. Why are we trying to convince everyone that things are great, when they so obviously *aren't?*"

Daphne's mind was whirling. What had Samantha meant, when she said she was pretending with Marshall? Did she not actually like him? But what other reason could she have for dating him?

She realized that Samantha was still staring at her expectantly, and hurried to reply. "The monarchy is all about pretending. When the world feels like it's falling apart, your family is supposed to paper over the cracks, and reassure people that it isn't."

Samantha seemed almost sad as she replied, "It sounds impossible."

"Exactly. That's why being a princess is so hard," Daphne said reasonably. "If it were easy, everyone would do it."

The next day when the final bell rang, Daphne didn't follow the stream of students out into the parking lot. She waited for a few minutes, then turned into the alley—the narrow strip of grass between the campus of St. Ursula's and its brother school, Forsythe. She and Himari used to come out here during their study hall sometimes, when they were supposed to be in the library doing homework. But it was so much more fun sneaking out to watch the boys' sports practice instead.

Footsteps crunched on the gravel behind her, and Daphne's blood spiked with adrenaline. She whirled around to see Ethan coming toward her.

"Ethan," she said gratefully, "I'm so glad you wanted to meet up. You'll never believe what happened."

"You mean, how you completely betrayed me?"

Just as she'd suspected, he knew what she'd done. Daphne hesitated, then forged ahead, her voice threaded with fear. "Listen—Himari remembered everything. Now she *hates* me. She accused me of trying to kill her!"

She waited for Ethan to tell her that it was okay, that they would figure out how to handle Himari, together. But his features were as unreadable as stone.

"Daphne—I don't care what's going on with Himari," he told her. "I texted you because I want to know why the hell you tipped off a reporter about me and Nina. Don't bother denying it," he added swiftly.

Daphne took a step closer to the protective shelter of the building, angling herself behind a massive blue recycling bin, even though no one was around. "Look, I'm sorry I didn't warn you," she offered. "On the bright side, now you can call off the whole thing."

"What?"

"You don't have to keep pretending to like *Nina*." She shuddered. "I'm impressed you were able to keep it going for as long as you did. Don't worry, I consider your end of the bargain fully complete."

Ethan stared at her blankly. "Are you serious?"

"Of course," she assured him. "I'm a woman of my word. It might take a while, but I'll make sure you get your title." She paused, tilting her head in consideration. "Maybe one of the vacant ones from the Edwardian era, like Earl of Tanglewood?"

Ethan just stared at her, shaking his head slowly. He'd stuffed his hands into his jeans, but Daphne could see that inside the pockets they were curled into fists. "You're unbelievable."

Her mouth went dry. "I don't—"

"You honestly thought I was angry because I was worried about our stupid *bargain*?" he asked. "My best friend won't speak to me!"

Neither will mine, Daphne thought, shoving aside her sudden guilt. "I'm sorry that Jefferson is angry with you, but it had to be done."

"Oh, 'it had to be done'?" he repeated. "Daphne, some of us actually want to *keep* our best friends, not push them down staircases!"

That was a low blow. But of course Ethan knew exactly how to hurt her, because he knew her so well. Because he was just as dishonorable and selfish and ruthless as she was. Which was why he would understand, eventually. He would have done the exact same thing if their circumstances were reversed.

"Jefferson will come around, I swear," she said earnestly. "Especially after you break up with Nina."

Daphne had known, when she'd planted that story with Natasha, that it would drive the prince and his best friend apart. The best plans always left the most damage in their wake.

She hadn't wanted to hurt Ethan, but what other option did she have? And it wouldn't be forever. Later—after Jefferson had asked her to the wedding, when she was more secure in her position—she would make it right, and convince Jefferson to forgive Ethan. She could convince Jefferson of anything, once they were back together.

Eventually, when they were all friends again, Ethan would see that she'd done what was best for both of them. Things between her and Ethan would be just like before: the two of them scheming and social climbing in tandem, looking out for each other's interests. Except this time, she would be a princess and Ethan an earl. This time, they would have real power to wield.

She looked up at Ethan, but he was staring at her with evident disgust. "You wouldn't understand," he said heavily. "Unlike you, Nina is a good person."

"What are you saying?" Daphne demanded, over the strange twisting in her gut.

"I'm saying that I won't hurt Nina just because you want me to." He gave a mirthless laugh. "I realize this may come as a shock, given that the rest of America is always telling you how spectacular you are, but not everything is about you."

Daphne stumbled back a step. Her heel caught on the

gravel, sending pebbles flying every which way. Ethan instinctively held out a hand, steadying her.

She brushed him aside, trying to regain some semblance of her dignity.

"Of course it's about me. I asked you to date her in the first place," she reminded him.

They both flinched at the sound of a door opening, but it was just a custodian setting a bag of garbage outside the opposite door. Music blared from his headphones, and he didn't even notice them.

When the door shut behind him again, Ethan sighed. "I can't handle your games anymore, Daphne. You never play fair."

"I play to *win*." The words were a reflex, spoken with half a thought.

Ordinarily Ethan might have smiled at that. But now he just looked at her steadily, his dark eyes heavy with fatigue—and resentment.

"Whatever you're planning, leave me out of it."

They stood there for a long moment, their heartbeats chasing each other.

"Fine, then. You can get your title from someone else," Daphne declared.

Her head held high, she walked away from Ethan as serenely as if she were leaving a palace reception. It wasn't until she was back in the parking lot that Daphne let her steps slow, then slumped wearily against her car door.

It didn't matter; she could do this on her own. She didn't need Ethan.

She was Daphne Deighton, and she had never needed anyone except herself.

25

SAMANTHA

"Jeff?" Sam called out, as she walked around the palace's garage. She'd checked her brother's bedroom first, but when he wasn't there, she'd asked Caleb to radio Jeff's Guard, Matt, and find out where he'd gone. She'd been surprised to learn he was shooting hoops at the old basketball net their dad had installed when they were kids.

The sky was a cloudless blue, the air bright with the promise of summer. Sam pulled her sunglasses lower over her face. Up ahead, she heard the steady thump of the ball against the pavement. She turned the corner, and paused when she saw that Jeff wasn't playing against Matt, as she'd thought.

Marshall was with him.

Oblivious to her presence, the two of them kept good-naturedly heckling each other. It seemed like they'd known each other for most of their lives, instead of a matter of weeks.

Sam watched as Marshall feinted to his left, then broke away past Jeff. He sprinted forward, hurling the ball toward the basket—just as he noticed her, standing in the shade of the garage.

Ever since their pool photos, Sam and Marshall had followed the palace's decree and escalated their relationship: going out on public dates, attending a series of cocktail parties and receptions. Sam was desperate to know what he really thought about all this, but he treated her with the same easygoing irreverence as ever. He made her laugh, held her hand when reporters took photos of them—and that was it.

He hadn't kissed her since the night of the party. His grandfather had probably given him the same mandate that Robert had told her: to keep things chaste from now on. So why did Sam keep fixating on it?

Sam strode behind the basket to grab the ball, her eyes meeting Marshall's. "Looks like you missed that one," she observed, and began dribbling between her legs.

His glance strayed to her mouth, and he smiled. "I had a pretty girl distracting me."

Sam rolled her eyes and tossed the ball to Jeff, who took it back to the free-throw line. "Hey," Marshall cried out in protest, "if you're going to join mid-game, then you're on *my* team!"

"I can't go against my twin. It violates the laws of nature," Sam said brightly as Jeff threw a perfect three-pointer. He ran over to give her a high five.

A ringtone sounded from the stone bench where the boys had thrown their stuff. "Sorry, can we take a break?" Marshall asked, jogging over. He picked up the phone and tucked it into his shoulder.

"Hey," he answered, in a low, tender voice. Sam strained her ears, trying to catch the rest of the conversation. Was he talking to *Kelsey*? Marshall hadn't mentioned her since the morning after the twins' party. But—wasn't he going to see her, when he and Sam went to Orange for Accession Day later this month?

Sam tried to smile as if nothing was wrong. "I didn't know you and Marshall were hanging out today," she told her brother, and he nodded.

"I guess I should have told you. I asked Davis if he wanted to come by, since . . ." *Since I'm not talking to Ethan right now,* he didn't need to add.

Sam felt partially responsible for all this mess. Hadn't she encouraged Nina to go for it, then kept the truth from Jeff? And now her brother was hurting.

She remembered how excited she'd felt, back when she'd first learned that Nina and Jeff were dating. Her two favorite people in the world, ending up together—it seemed perfect. She hadn't realized that when they broke up, she would be left in the middle, forced to keep their secrets from each other.

"Besides," Jeff teased, "I needed to decide if I give you and Davis my blessing."

"Your blessing?"

"You can't date anyone I don't like. As your twin, I have final veto power."

A month ago Sam would have snorted and said something like *you certainly ignored my veto when it came to Daphne*. But now that she'd seen a more vulnerable side of Jeff's ex, had asked for her *help*, the comment felt a little petty.

Jeff picked the basketball up off the ground and spun it idly on one finger. "It's cool, though. I approve of Davis. He's funny, and he seems really into you."

No, he isn't. He's just using me to make his ex-girlfriend jealous—the way I'm supposedly using him, Sam thought dully.

Except . . . she wasn't really dating Marshall to hurt Teddy anymore, and she didn't know when that had changed.

"We're not that serious," she mumbled, and her brother laughed.

"Nope. You *like* him; I see it on your face." Jeff's eyes danced. "Please, can you not scare him off the way you usually do? I like having him around."

Of course, Sam thought. Of all the guys she'd been involved with through the years, her brother approved of the one who wasn't actually hers. The one she didn't get to keep.

Later that evening, Sam wandered down the palace hallway. She felt the telltale flush of sunburn on her shoulders; she'd stayed outside with the boys all afternoon, playing basketball and then sitting out on the lawn, soaking in the sunshine.

She knew she should be grateful that Marshall was making this whole charade so easy on her. So why did she feel a hollow ache pressing down on her sternum?

When she noticed the light creeping from beneath the door to the monarch's study, she came to an uncertain halt. Beatrice must be in there, working late.

Sam realized, suddenly, that she was *tired* of being angry with her sister.

For so long she'd held tight to that anger, lifted it before her like a shield, and now she was exhausted. She wanted to lay down her weapons and actually talk to Beatrice, for once.

"Bee?" Sam gave a soft knock. When no one answered, she pushed the door cautiously open, but the office was empty.

And it had changed. Sam could still see traces of her father—in the antique globe, the heavy stone bookends carved like giant chess pieces—yet this was unmistakably Beatrice's space now.

She walked slowly around the desk, running her hands over its polished wooden surface, then plopped down in Beatrice's chair, bracing her sneakers on the floor and wheeling herself idly forward and back. *So,* she thought, with something that might have been jealousy or might have been loneliness, *this is what it feels like to be queen.*

Curious, she pulled out the top drawer of the desk, revealing Beatrice's personal stationery and a neat row of pens. The next few drawers contained stacks of manila folders, a package of dog treats, a series of notes from Robert.

When she was younger, Sam was always sneaking into Beatrice's room: rifling through her drawers, trying on her dresses, rubbing her arms with Beatrice's scented lotion. At the time, Sam hadn't understood that impulse. But she knew now that when she was sifting through Beatrice's things, she'd been trying to understand her sister, and all the differences between them.

Sam leaned farther down, remembering the hidden drawer built into the bottom of the desk. She wondered if Beatrice kept it full of lemon candies, the way their dad had. She found the latch and pressed it, releasing the drawer—only to frown in confusion.

Inside lay a heavy ecru envelope, printed with the swirling handwriting of the palace calligrapher. It was addressed to Mr. Connor Dean Markham and marked with a scrolling *WP* on the top right corner, where a stamp would normally go. One of the privileges of being the monarch, of course, was that you were exempt from paying postal fees.

Connor Markham—wasn't he Beatrice's former Guard, the one who'd been with her at Harvard? Why hadn't his invitation gone out with the rest of them?

There was something else in the drawer, Sam realized: a thin box secured with an ivory ribbon. It looked like an engagement present.

She couldn't help untying the ribbon and lifting the lid.

Inside lay an ink drawing, of snow-covered mountains seen through the frame of a window. On the far edge of the sketch was a fireplace, and next to it, a small figure that could only be Sam's sister.

They're in love, Sam realized, stunned.

Beatrice was fully clothed in the sketch; there was nothing erotic or overtly sexual about it. But Connor's feelings for her were visible in every sweeping line of ink. There was an indefinable bloom to her, as if she had some private secret you could only guess at.

Sam studied the image a little longer, her eyes lingering on the sparks popping from the fire, on the jagged line of the mountains, veiled by a luscious blanket of snow. It struck her that this wasn't an imagined scene. This had really happened. It was a sketch of that night in December, right before New Year's, when Beatrice and her Guard had been stranded on their way to Telluride.

It all made sense now, the various pieces of the puzzle crashing together. Sam's mind flashed back to the night Beatrice had told her she was calling off the engagement. *You're seeing someone else,* Sam had guessed.

Beatrice had admitted that she loved a commoner, and that he was there that night, at the engagement party. Sam had always assumed she was talking about one of the guests, but Beatrice had clearly meant her *Revere Guard*.

She scoured her memory, trying to recall when Connor had resigned. It was right after they'd come back from Sulgrave—when Beatrice and Teddy had set a wedding date.

Loving Beatrice like this, Connor must have decided he would rather quit than watch her marry someone else.

Sam's hands tightened around the paper. She wanted to run to her sister, grab her by the shoulders, and shake some sense into her. *You don't have to go through with this!* she would scream. *You don't have to marry someone you don't love, just because Dad said you should.*

But Sam knew she'd forfeited any right to give Beatrice romantic advice.

This gulf between them was *her* fault. Every time Beatrice had tried to apologize, Sam had turned her away. And for what, *Teddy?* Her own obstinate pride? None of it was worth losing a sister over.

Sam put the sketch back in the box and retied the ribbon, much sloppier than it had been before. Yet, for some reason, she didn't let go of the invitation. She kept staring at it, tracing the loops of Connor's name with her fingertips.

Before she'd fully acknowledged her decision to herself, Sam had turned out into the hallway and dropped the invitation into a gleaming brass receptacle marked OUTGOING MAIL.

NINA

Nina sank onto the picnic blanket, which was spread out on the grass before the open-air stage. The amphitheater at the center of John Jay Park was completely packed, the ground covered in a multicolor quilt of beach towels and blankets. Conversations bubbled up around them, laughter rising lazily into the air like smoke.

"I'm so impressed you got Shakespeare in the Park tickets. What time did you have to get in line?" she asked.

Ethan stretched his arms overhead with an exaggerated sigh. "Six a.m. When you were still in bed, Sleeping Beauty."

Nina smiled, though she worried the real reason Ethan had gotten up early was because he'd been lying in bed awake, his mind spinning with anxiety. She knew that Jeff still wouldn't speak to him.

Though Jeff didn't seem to be losing any sleep over it, from the photos Nina had seen on all the royal-obsessed blogs. He'd been out almost every night this week, in a group that included Sam and Marshall—and Daphne.

Nina and Ethan had been pointedly left off the guest list.

"Thanks for getting the tickets. I'm sure *Romeo and Juliet* in the park wasn't your top choice for how to spend a Friday night," she said, trying to sound upbeat.

"It's okay; next week we can go to a movie. That *I* pick."

"Oh goodie, something with lots of explosions and car chases."

"Hey, give me some credit," Ethan objected. "I like zombie movies, too."

Nina still couldn't believe that he'd waited in a five-hour line for her. Jeff would never have done that, but then, he wouldn't have needed to. He could have gotten backstage passes with the snap of his fingers—and then they would've had to *stay* backstage all night. The Prince of America couldn't exactly sit out here in the middle of a crowd. It would be a security and logistical nightmare.

One of the actors walked out onstage, and Ethan sat up, rummaging in his backpack before emerging with a pair of square-rimmed glasses.

"I love when you wear those," she murmured. He looked so adorably nerdy in glasses.

"Can you keep it down?" Ethan nudged her with his elbow. "Some of us are *trying* to enjoy the play."

Nina had read *Romeo and Juliet* in middle school, had seen the movie version where Juliet wore a ridiculous pair of white angel wings. Tonight, though, the story felt different. Now, instead of sighing over the beautiful language, Nina found herself upset that Romeo and Juliet wanted to be together at all.

Relationships simply couldn't work when people came from opposite worlds. No matter how long they managed to keep it secret, circumstances would eventually tear them apart. And it would be so much worse than if they'd never found each other in the first place.

In real life, love against the odds wasn't *enough*. All it had done for Nina was hurt the people she cared about—caused the paparazzi to harass her parents, gave complete strangers the right to call her ugly names. In real life, impossible love caused more pain than it did joy.

As the play ended, the amphitheater broke out in applause, and Nina came to herself slowly. She'd nearly forgotten where she was. She wiped at her cheeks, a little embarrassed that she'd teared up.

"You okay?" Ethan asked, as everyone around them began packing up their things.

She hugged her knees to her chest. "Ethan. I don't want to hurt you."

"What?" he asked, bewildered. "You haven't hurt me."

"But you are hurting! And we *both* managed to hurt Jeff! We shouldn't have ever . . ."

Ethan leaned forward. "What are you saying, that we shouldn't have ever gotten together?"

"I don't know!" She closed her eyes, her heart aching. She hated that she'd put Ethan in a position where he could lose his best friend. That she'd put Jeff in a position where he already had.

Ethan wrapped an arm around her shoulders. Nina took a deep breath, feeling her back rise and fall beneath his touch.

"Jeff will get over this—maybe not right away, but eventually. We've been friends for too long for him not to forgive this." Ethan sounded confident, but Nina had a feeling he was trying to convince himself as much as her.

"Of course it would have been better if he'd learned the truth from us," Ethan went on. "But I'd be lying if I said I regret that he found out. We would have told him soon anyway. And in the meantime, you and I can stop hiding."

"We haven't been hiding," Nina pointed out. If they had, the reporter wouldn't have ever found out about them.

"I don't mean on campus. I mean with the royal family." Ethan let his hand fall to the base of her spine. "I was thinking we could go to Beatrice's wedding together."

Nina blinked.

"Ethan," she said hesitantly, "do you realize what you're

saying? This will be the most media-heavy event of our lives. If that reporter wanted to make a story out of nothing but campus rumors, think of how much worse it'll be when we're at the wedding together!" She shook her head. "We were both invited; can't we just hang out at the reception without giving everyone a story?"

"I don't think we'll *be* a story," Ethan argued. "The other guests are all more important and gossip-worthy. Who's going to talk about you and me when there are foreign royalty around? Besides," he added, in a lower tone, "I *want* to be there with you."

Nina wanted to be there with Ethan, too. Yet she wasn't ready to be in the spotlight again, her photo printed in the tabloids. She had worked so hard to dissociate herself from all the gossip, and if she went to the wedding with Ethan, it would start chasing her all over again.

"I'll think about it," she promised, and glanced toward the river.

A few hundred yards away, on the edge of the park, stood the oxidized green form of the Statue of Liberty. Floodlights illuminated the statue's face, casting her features in a golden-green blaze. She looked more dynamic from this angle, as if she'd been caught in a swirl of motion—as if she'd picked up the torch and was about to strike someone with it, to defend liberty itself.

Nina knew that when the French had shipped the statue over, it had almost ended up in another city instead: in Boston or Philadelphia or even that regional shipping city, New York. Of course, Congress had insisted that it stay right here in the nation's capital, where it belonged.

"Want to go up?" she asked abruptly.

When Ethan realized where she meant, he groaned. "Right now? Why?"

"Why not?" Nina answered. It was a very Sam sort of reply.

The woman at the ticket office didn't bother charging them for tickets, since the monument closed within half an hour. "This late, you'll have it to yourselves," she said with a wink.

Sure enough, when Ethan and Nina reached the elevator, they ran into several groups of people on their way down, but no one else heading up.

"This is so unbelievably cheesy of you," Ethan muttered, though he didn't actually sound displeased.

"That's me, the queen of all things cheesy and touristy. Get used to it."

No one else was on the circular viewing platform at the top. It was several degrees cooler up here than it had been at the statue's base. Nina stepped forward, the wind whipping her hair.

Washington wasn't a beautiful city, not the way Paris or even London was. It was too messy, having grown through the centuries without much of a central plan. One-way streets tangled and looped over each other in blithe confusion, Revolutionary monuments standing next to clunky new housing developments with rooftop pools.

That was Washington, Nina thought, a city of contradictions: crowded and cruel and thrilling and lovely all at once.

"Behold, my son. Everything the light touches is your kingdom," Ethan growled behind her, and she burst out laughing.

"Aren't you glad I made us come?" She spread her hands out. "I bet you haven't been up here since your fourth-grade field trip!"

"Actually, my mom used to take me up here sometimes. She was always thinking of activities for us to do," Ethan explained. "Dragging me all over the capital to national landmarks and museums—teaching me history, but also teaching me who I was. As if she needed to make up for whatever sense of identity I was supposed to have gotten from my dad."

Nina looked over. The moonlight gilded Ethan's profile, tracing the curve of his upper lip, the straight line of his nose.

"You can tell me about it, if you want." She reached for his hand. Ethan didn't answer, but squeezed her fingers. She took that as a sign to keep going.

"I know what it's like to grow up with a nontraditional family," she said quietly. "To be the person hiding in the nurse's office with a fake headache on Bring Your Dad to School Day. To have people look at us like we're somehow missing a piece. I know what it's like to grow up knowing that your family is different, and sometimes feeling *ashamed* that it's different, and then hating yourself for being ashamed, because you love your family more than anything, even if it doesn't look like everyone else's."

She dared a glance at him. "Sorry. I don't know why I said all that."

Probably because there was no one else she *could* say it to, except maybe Sam. And while Sam would have given her unconditional love, Nina also knew that Sam wouldn't have understood, not really.

"No, I'm glad you did." Ethan's voice was hoarse. "My mom is the best, no question. She's got more energy than anyone I've ever met. But I always worried about her, too. I used to think that it was my fault that my dad left, since . . . well, my mom is so amazing, so there's no way he could have left because of *her*."

"Ethan, you can't blame yourself for your dad's leaving," Nina whispered, her heart sore.

"Yeah, I know that. But . . ." He sighed. "I guess it's one thing to know it, and another thing to actually believe it. To actually *feel* like it's not my fault."

Nina's hand tightened over his. She realized how rare it was for Ethan to speak with such raw honesty.

"I don't know who my dad is," he said clumsily. "The only thing my mom ever says about him was that they loved each other a long time ago, but that he couldn't be part of my life. She doesn't seem to resent him for it."

"I don't know anything about my biological father either," Nina admitted. "Except that he was a medical school student who donated sperm for extra money. Oh, and that he didn't have any family history of disease."

"You don't wonder about him?" Ethan asked.

No, Nina was about to lie, but bit it back. "Sometimes, but I try not to. I *know* who my parents are. That man is just a stranger who helped them find their way to me."

Ethan's gaze was fixed on the horizon. "When I was little, I had all these outlandish theories about who my dad might be. I thought he was a superhero, or an astronaut—that he was off saving the world, and would come back for us eventually." He sighed. "I think I was in middle school when I finally realized that he wasn't coming."

He leaned forward, the lines of his body languid and weary.

Nina turned toward him. "It doesn't matter who your father is. You know that, right? His choices don't determine who you are. Only *your* choices do that."

"I don't always make the best choices," she thought she heard Ethan mutter, so softly she couldn't be certain.

"*Look* at me." She grabbed his head with both hands, forcing him to meet her gaze. "You are not defined by your father. Neither of us is, okay? You are you, and you are a complete person, and you are *good*."

"But I wonder sometimes . . . if I found him, if I knew who he was . . . would I feel like I belong?"

Nina was silent. She'd lived around the royal family long

enough to know how it felt, standing on the outside of something, peering in with lonely eyes.

"But you do belong," she said adamantly. "You belong with *me*."

Ethan's weight shifted. For an instant Nina thought he might kiss her—but instead his arms wrapped around her and he pulled her close.

Nina turned her head to the side, resting it on Ethan's shoulder, and breathed him in. She thought about childhood dreams and grown-up dreams and wondered how and where those two things might collide. She thought about the feel of Ethan's heart, beating steadily against her own.

She wasn't sure how long they stood there, hugging on the top of the Statue of Liberty, but it was long enough for her to realize one very important thing.

This was the same Ethan who, for years, had convinced Nina that he was snarky and arrogant. Maybe he still was those things. But now she appreciated the wicked edge to his humor, knew the arrogance was just a defense mechanism. She knew the *real* Ethan, the one behind all the emotional armor.

Ethan stepped away, looking a little sheepish. His eyes flicked curiously around. "I wonder . . ."

"What?" Nina demanded, as he marched over to the back of the viewing platform, where the spikes of the statue's crown rose sharply overhead.

"I can't believe it's still here," he said with a grin. "I must have done this when I was ten."

"What's still here?"

He pointed, and suddenly Nina saw it: *EB*, scratched out in blocky letters on the metal's surface.

"You delinquent! You defaced a national *monument*?"

"Your surprise is rather insulting." Ethan reached into his pocket for a key, holding it on an outstretched palm.

Nina hesitated, then smiled.

"Give me a boost," she requested. Ethan obediently picked her up, holding her around the waist so she could scratch out *NG* on the furled sheet of copper, right below his *EB*.

When he put her down, the two of them stood there staring up at their initials—binding them together, here on this landmark, for all eternity.

BEATRICE

Normally Beatrice dreaded invitations. She received thousands per year, and while she hated letting people down, she simply couldn't say yes to them all.

But for the past few months, she'd been waiting desperately for an invitation that never arrived.

She knew precisely what it should have looked like, because she'd seen them before, back when they used to arrive for her father: a scroll of heavy parchment tied with a red ribbon. *Most Gracious Sovereign*, it would begin, *your dutiful and loyal subjects in Congress assembled do entreat you to attend our gathering....*

Beatrice knew it would be unprecedented, for a monarch to show up at Congress without an invitation. But no Congress had ever failed to invite the monarch to its closing session, either.

How could Beatrice fulfill her duties as queen if her own legislative branch didn't treat her like one?

And so, this morning, she'd invented an errand that sent Robert far from the palace. To her relief, he'd left without protest.

Now she was in a town car, headed toward Columbia House, the meeting place of both bodies of Congress.

Outside her window, the city rushed past in a blur of gray stone and brightly colored billboards. People in suits streamed up and down the stairs to the metro. Towering over two city blocks was the bulk of the Federal Treasury Building, topped by an enormous copper eagle. Several minutes later, the car turned in to Columbia House's back entrance.

Beatrice's muscles tightened in fear. She wanted to throw open the car door, yet she forced herself to wait until her driver came around to open it for her. She reached up to touch the gold chain of state that hung around her neck. It was so heavy, its weight pressing into the top of her spine—but her father had never bowed his head beneath it, and neither would Beatrice.

She was decked out in the full regalia of her position. The ivory sash of the Edwardian Order, the highest of America's chivalric honors. The heavy, ermine-trimmed robe of state. And, finally, the massive Imperial State Crown. It was all too big for her—especially the crown, which kept falling off the back of her head, or slipping down to catch on her nose.

The trappings of state were heavy and clunky on Beatrice's slender frame because they had all been designed for men.

A young man in a suit, most likely some kind of congressional assistant, sprinted forward. When Beatrice stepped out of the car in full ceremonial attire, he went pale. "Your Majesty," he exclaimed—then seemed to recall himself, and swept her an abbreviated bow.

"Thank you for coming to greet me." She passed him with a few crisp steps, trying not to think about how utterly wrong this all was. She should have been stepping over this threshold with fanfare, not stealing through the back door of her own government like a thief in the night.

"Please, Your Majesty," he breathed, rushing to catch up with her. "I'm afraid we weren't expecting you."

Beatrice's heels made sharp clicks on the polished granite of the floor. She drew in a breath, summoning every last shred of her confidence. "Will you lead the way . . ." She trailed off, waiting for the young man to provide his name.

"Charles, Your Majesty." His eyes drifted to the crown, and his resolve wavered. "I—that is—it would be my honor," he stammered, and fell into step behind her. Of course, he couldn't *actually* lead the way, since no one was permitted to walk ahead of the reigning monarch.

Beatrice started down the long hallway of Columbia House, past various wooden doors, all of them shut. She had to walk with agonizingly slow steps; the robe of state dragged behind her like an enormous velvet rug. It felt like someone had grabbed hold of her hair and was yanking her backward.

At the entrance to the House of Tribunes—the lower chamber of Congress—Beatrice looked expectantly at Charles. "Please knock. Do you know what to say?"

His throat bobbed, but he managed a nod. Then he sucked in a breath and pounded on the door—once, twice, a third time. "Her Majesty the Queen requests the right to address this gathering!"

Utter silence followed Charles's words.

Except it was worse than silence, because Beatrice realized she heard a soft chorus of sounds from within: uneasy whispers, the rustling of robes, hurried footsteps. Everything except what she should have heard, which was a shouted response to Charles's statement, welcoming her inside.

The heavy wooden door swung inward. Beatrice took an instinctive step forward—but when she saw who stood there, she went still.

Robert Standish slipped through the door, his steps surprisingly light for such a ponderous man. "Your Majesty," he hissed. "What are you *doing* here?"

Beatrice had to remind herself to keep breathing—*inhale exhale inhale exhale*, over and over in succession.

"I could ask you the same question," she said carefully. "Are you trying to close Congress *yourself?*"

Through the sliver of open doorway, she could just see

a glimpse of the House of Tribunes: several hundred seats arranged on either side of the aisle, and at the far end of the room, a carved wooden throne.

Three hundred and sixty-three days a year, that throne sat empty. It was purposefully left so: perhaps to remind Congress of the silent presence of the monarch, or perhaps to remind the monarch that they had no say in the legislative branch. Only when the monarch ceremonially opened and closed each session of Congress could this throne be occupied.

And now Robert was trying to keep her from it.

"Of course I am," the Lord Chamberlain replied, without an ounce of contrition. "In any case when the monarch is not able to preside over the opening or closing of Congress, the monarch's designated representative shall do it."

Anger swelled in her chest. "I didn't designate you! And if I *did* designate a representative, it should traditionally be my heir," she added, remembering a time when she was much younger, when her grandfather had been ill and her father had presided over Congress in his stead.

The chamberlain scoffed. "You can't honestly mean that you would have sent Samantha."

"Her Royal Highness, the Princess Samantha," Beatrice corrected.

She was dimly aware of Charles, watching this exchange with unconcealed fear. But Beatrice couldn't worry about him. She had much bigger problems.

"Your Majesty, you're not welcome here," Robert said firmly.

"You can't honestly expect me to—"

"If you don't leave, you could incite a serious constitutional crisis." When she still didn't move, his lips thinned into a frown. "Now is not the time for this."

"You keep saying that!" Beatrice burst out. "I've been queen for months now! When *will* it be time?"

"When you are *married*!"

She drew herself up to her full height, wishing she'd worn taller heels. "I am the Queen of America," she said again. "It doesn't matter whether or not I'm married."

He raised his eyes heavenward, as if silently cursing her stupidity. "Beatrice. Of course it matters. Having a young, single woman as the figurehead of America—it makes the entire nation feel unsettled, and juvenile, and *emotional*. God, most of the men in this room have *children* older than you."

She hated that he'd referenced *the men in this room*, as if all the female members of Congress didn't even bear mention.

"Just . . . wait until you have Teddy by your side," he added. "Maybe then it will be easier for people to take you seriously."

Robert wasn't smiling, but his eyes gleamed as though he was. It reminded Beatrice of the girls who'd made fun of her in lower school, who'd spoken cruel words in deceptively kind voices, their faces underlit with malicious delight.

Until this moment, Beatrice hadn't realized just how adamantly Robert was working against her.

He didn't do it openly, like the people who booed her at rallies or left nasty comments online. No, Robert's way of opposing her was far more insidious. He'd been systematically undermining her: whittling away at her confidence, distracting her with the wedding, twisting the Constitution's intention to keep her from acting as queen.

And her own Congress had let him. Beatrice didn't know what had happened—whether they had withheld her invitation on their own, or whether Robert had *asked* them not to invite her—but did it matter? Either way, the invitation hadn't come.

"Why are you doing this to me?" she whispered.

"I'm not doing this *to* you. I'm doing it *for* America," Robert said stiffly. "You should know that there is no room for personal feeling in politics."

The Imperial State Crown slipped backward, and Beatrice hurried to grab at it before it could clatter loudly to the floor. Seeing the gesture, Robert bit back a smile.

Shame rose hot to her cheeks. She felt suddenly foolish, like a glassy-eyed doll dressed up in a paper crown.

At least the closing session of Congress, unlike the opening session, was never televised. Otherwise, this image would have been all over the newspapers tomorrow: Beatrice, knocking at the door of her own Congress, being told that she couldn't come in.

Later that night, Beatrice sat up with a weary sigh. Moonlight poured like cream over the hardwood floors, making everything feel deceptively peaceful.

Restless, she threw back her covers and walked barefoot to the window.

Earlier, when she'd confronted Robert Standish, her body had been flooded with white-hot adrenaline. Yet now . . . Beatrice just felt exhausted, and unsettled.

And she missed Teddy. It felt like he was the only person she could talk to, lately—the only person rooting *for* her, instead of rooting for her to fail. But he and his brothers were spending the weekend at their Nantucket house, which, true to her word, Beatrice had quietly repurchased.

She hesitated a moment, then pulled out her phone and dialed the palace's air traffic control line. "I need the plane," she said smoothly. "How soon can it be ready?"

The life of a queen had plenty of restrictions, but it had its perks, too. And for once, Beatrice intended to use them.

When she reached *Eagle III*—the smaller of the royal family's private planes, much smaller than the massive *Eagle V*—the pilot didn't ask why she'd insisted on leaving in the middle of the night. He didn't even protest when Beatrice opened Franklin's crate before takeoff and pulled him onto her lap. She sat there like that, letting the puppy nuzzle her face with his wet nose, for the entirety of the ninety-minute flight to Nantucket.

Finally her car pulled up the secluded driveway, and the Eatons' beach house came into view. It was a large home, yet unassuming, with traditional cedar shingles and a white sloping roof. And there was Teddy, waiting on the wraparound front porch, wearing jeans and a Nantucket red hoodie.

The sight of him broke whatever threads remained of Beatrice's self-control. She flung open the car door and ran forward to throw her arms around him, to lean her head against the solid plane of his chest.

When she stepped back, Teddy didn't ask any questions, just grabbed two mugs from the railing of the porch. "Coffee?" he offered, in a normal, upbeat tone. As if it weren't strange of her to have shown up like this, without warning.

She curled her hands around the mug, touched by his thoughtfulness. "Sorry to wake you up so early. I just—I needed to talk to you, and it couldn't wait. Or at least, it *felt* like it couldn't wait."

"I like getting up early. Sunrise is the best part of the day here, you'll see." Teddy glanced toward the ocean. "Should we go for a walk?" He whistled for Franklin, who bounded forward from where he'd been exploring the muddy grass beneath the porch.

When they reached the beach, Beatrice kicked off her shoes. The sky was a dusky purple overhead, stars scattered over its canvas like frozen tears, though at the edge of the horizon she saw the first pearly hints of morning.

Franklin raced ahead to the dark line of the surf and splashed gleefully along its edge. Beatrice and Teddy followed. They sat down in the sand, their feet planted before them, so that the foam-kissed waves just barely brushed their toes.

For a few minutes they were both silent, watching Franklin sprint up and down the beach, his tail wagging furiously. Each time he ventured into the water, he would let out a little yelp of delight before retreating.

"He's gotten so big," Beatrice mused aloud. Putting off the topic she'd come here to discuss.

Teddy nodded. "Puppies grow up too fast. Blink and you miss it."

Everything was happening too fast. When she was younger, Beatrice had thought time moved so slowly, that a year was an eternity to wait for something. Now it felt like physics had twisted and time had accelerated, and she wasn't sure how to keep up.

She used to be so certain of everything, but now she felt certain of nothing. If only she could rewind the clock to before her father died: when everything had been so clear-cut and simple, when everything made *sense*.

The ocean rippled before her, its surface a molten silver. As always, the sight of it calmed her a little. Beatrice loved how small it made her feel, that the sheer size of it dwarfed everything, even America itself.

"I lost a showdown with Congress yesterday. Or, really, with Robert," she said at last.

Teddy didn't interrupt. He just shifted a little closer, letting Beatrice explain the whole disastrous encounter.

"I keep wondering what my dad would say about all this," she finished, shame and resentment warring in her chest. "Would he have understood why I did it . . . or would he say that I've been foolish, jeopardizing the balance of power? That I acted out of pride and put the entire *monarchy* at risk?"

When he spoke, Teddy's voice was thoughtful and steady.

"Bee—I can't speak for your dad. But I, for one, am proud of you."

"Even though I violated the terms of the Constitution?"

"I thought Congress violated the Constitution by failing to invite you," he countered.

Beatrice looked down, tracing a few swirls on the damp sand. "I'd have to check . . ."

"I doubt it," Teddy challenged, giving her shoulder a playful nudge. "Come on, nerd out for me. You know you want to."

He was fighting back a smile, but his dimple gave him away. Seeing his expression, Beatrice couldn't help smiling, too.

"Article three, section twenty-eight," she recited. " 'It is a duty of the King to convene and dissolve a Congress. In the absence of a Crowned King, Congress shall ask the Heir Apparent to preside over its opening and closing: the Legislative Body deriving its authority from the people, but its Action and Competency from the Crown—' "

She was cut off mid-sentence when Teddy leaned over and dropped a quick kiss on her lips.

"Sorry," he told her. "I just, um . . ."

"Have a thing for girls reciting the Constitution?"

"I was going to say smart girls, but yours works too." He laughed, then grew more serious. "Bee, you know you just answered your own question. Congress acted out of line, too."

By now the sky had lightened, the surf curling back from their feet as the tide lowered. The breeze tousled Beatrice's hair. She leaned back on her palms, watching Franklin race through the waves.

Her entire life, she'd been taught to respect the Constitution, to obey the Crown, to venerate tradition.

But now she *was* the Crown, and truth be told, Beatrice was getting kind of sick of tradition.

The future didn't belong to people like Robert anymore. It belonged to her and Teddy, to Samantha and Jeff. To their entire *generation* of people, who were all dreaming and fighting and doing their best to make the world a better place.

She was still clutching at the sand: scooping great handfuls of it and letting it fall through her fingers like the sand of an hourglass. Teddy reached over, forcing her to look up and meet his gaze.

"I don't know what to do," she said bluntly.

"Bee, you're doing a job that only eleven people have done before. There aren't going to be any easy answers," Teddy pointed out. "You should trust your instincts. And stop listening to the people who try to tear you down, because you're going to be one hell of a queen."

"You think so?"

"I know so. You already are."

Beatrice couldn't take it anymore. She turned and pulled his face to hers, dragging her hands through his blond curls, kissing him with everything that was aching and unsettled in her.

When they finally broke apart, she saw that the sun had lifted above the horizon, streaking the sky with color. Beatrice took a breath, inhaling the mingled scents of coffee and sea salt and brine.

Franklin came racing out of the surf. He gave his entire body a shake from nose to tail, spraying water over them both, before plopping his wet head in Beatrice's lap.

She shifted closer to Teddy, leaning her head onto his shoulder, and scratched idly at Franklin's ears.

Together, the three of them watched the sun climb higher in the sky—setting the ocean on fire, creating the world anew.

28

DAPHNE

"I'm so sorry for what happened," Daphne pleaded. "I never meant to hurt you!"

Himari took a step forward. There was no trace of the stubborn, proud girl who'd been Daphne's best friend. Her eyes were pools of darkness, her features as impassive as if they'd been carved from stone.

"Daphne, you are a terrible person. Now you're getting what you deserve." She placed her hands on Daphne's shoulders and pushed.

Daphne realized, then, that she was at the top of the palace's curving staircase.

Her feet flew out from beneath her, and her shoulder hit the next stair with a crack that resounded through her bones. Yet somehow her body kept falling, tumbling ever faster down the staircase. She cried out in agony—

Daphne sat bolt upright, clutching her sheets to her chest, gasping for air. Her hair was a fiery tangle around her shoulders. Reflexively she reached for the phone on her bedside table.

And there was the text Himari had sent last night, the one Daphne hadn't been able to stop thinking about.

Last night, in a fit of anxiety—after weeks of calling and texting Himari, with no response—Daphne had gone to the

Marikos' house. But Himari had refused to see her. Instead Himari had sent her first text in weeks. *Don't come here again.*

Please, Daphne had hurried to reply, *can we talk?*

I have nothing to say to you. You're a terrible person, and soon enough you'll get what you deserve.

It was a real text. Not just part of Daphne's nightmare.

She fell back onto her duvet and closed her eyes. Her body was still shaking with the panicked adrenaline rush of the dream.

Daphne wasn't safe. She'd made so much progress with Jefferson these past few weeks. But if Himari followed through on her threat, it could all come crashing down.

Her former best friend was going to destroy her, unless Daphne found a way to destroy her first.

She glanced back at her phone, wishing she could text Ethan. She could use his sharp, sarcastic mind right now. But she and Ethan hadn't spoken since their confrontation outside school a few weeks ago. So many times Daphne had started to call him—he was the only person she could talk to about any of this—but some stubborn impulse held her back. She told herself that she didn't need Ethan, that she could handle everything alone, just like always.

Except . . . she couldn't, not this time. There was no way she could go up against Himari again without help. Daphne needed an ally, and not just any ally. Someone strong. Someone so powerful that even Himari would be forced to back down.

Suddenly, a memory crashed into Daphne's mind, of something Samantha had said in their first training session. *Beatrice is pretending most of all! She doesn't even love Teddy; she loves—*

And Samantha had broken off, to rapidly change tack.

Daphne's breath caught. Did Samantha mean what Daphne thought she meant—that Beatrice was involved with someone else, someone who was *not* Teddy Eaton?

Whoever it was, it must be someone highly off-limits: a commoner, perhaps, or someone who worked for the royal family. Otherwise, why wasn't the queen engaged to *that* person instead of Teddy?

Daphne reached for her phone again, and typed a quick email to Lord Robert Standish, requesting an appointment with Her Majesty. She held her breath and pressed Send.

If she was right, Daphne had just stumbled across the most valuable secret she'd uncovered in a lifetime of scheming. And she knew just what to do with it.

If she was wrong, then she would lose everything.

When Daphne arrived at the palace for her meeting with Beatrice, the footman directed her not to the queen's office, but to her personal suite. Daphne tried to conceal her surprise. Despite all her years of knowing the royal family, all the countless times she'd been in the prince's bedroom, she'd never actually set foot in here. But then, she and Beatrice had never exactly been close.

As Daphne stepped through the door, she gasped.

The furniture had been pushed aside so that the queen could stand at the center of the room in her wedding gown. A portable mirror was unfolded before her; a seamstress crouched at her feet, making a series of minute stitches on the delicate hem.

The gown was timeless and elegant and so very *Beatrice*. It had long sleeves, with a narrow V-neck and dropped waist that disguised the queen's small chest. But the real showstopper was the enormous full skirt, its ivory silk faille overlaid with delicate embroidery.

Beatrice was standing there with impossible stillness, almost as if she wasn't breathing. Daphne remembered hearing that the late king used to make her do her homework standing up, so that she would grow accustomed to long hours of being on her feet. So much of being the monarch was a job done while standing—attending receptions, meeting people at a walkabout, conducting long ceremonies—that he'd thought it was never too young to start practicing.

"Robert wants you to sign an NDA, but I told him it wasn't necessary. So please don't post anything about the dress," Beatrice said, a smile playing around her lips. Daphne wondered, startled, if the queen was *teasing* her.

"Of course I won't say anything. You can trust me," she said, though the words felt false in her mouth. "It really is beautiful. The embroidery . . ."

"If you look closely, you'll see a flower for every state. Roses and thistles, poppies and bluebonnets, and, of course, cherry blossoms," the queen explained.

Daphne ventured a step closer, and saw that each of the flowers had been painstakingly picked out in diamantés and seed pearls, adding an ethereal shimmer to the gown.

The seamstress finally looked up, and Daphne realized that she wasn't a seamstress at all, but Wendy Tsu—the most famous designer of bridal gowns in probably the entire world. Who, apparently, was lifting the hem of Beatrice's wedding gown *herself*.

"That embroidery took my team over three thousand hours of labor," the designer stated, with no small amount of pride.

Daphne wondered whether her gown would be this intricate, when—or rather, if—she married Jefferson.

"Your Majesty," she began. "There's something I was hoping to ask you. In private, if you don't mind."

She saw Beatrice exchange a look with Wendy. The designer, whose needle had been flying in and out of the fabric with near-impossible speed, stabbed it through the hem to mark her place. She retreated with a quick curtsy, shutting the door behind her.

"What can I do for you?" Beatrice offered, in a curious but good-natured tone.

"I wanted to ask a favor," Daphne said carefully. "I saw that there's a recent opening for an ambassador to the Japanese Imperial Court at Kyoto. I was hoping you would appoint Kenji and Aika Mariko, the Earl and Countess of Hana."

She felt an odd, lonely pang at the thought of sending Himari so far away. It wasn't fair that Himari should wake up from her coma, only for Daphne to lose her all over again.

But what other choice did she have?

"I'm sure the Marikos would be wonderful representatives," Beatrice agreed. "But Leanna Santos has asked me for that position, and I mean to give it to her."

"Please," Daphne said haltingly, her stomach plummeting.

"It was nice of you to lobby me on your friends' behalf. I'm sorry to disappoint you."

Daphne braced herself. Here she was, about to play her very last card. To throw everything she had into what might be the most reckless gamble of her life.

"If you don't do it, I'll tell everyone about your secret relationship."

The queen went gravely still, and Daphne knew her words had found their mark.

"Are you *blackmailing* me?" Beatrice asked, her voice dangerously cold.

"I'm trying to reach an understanding with you. I promise, if you appoint the Marikos, I'll never breathe another word on the subject. But if you won't help . . ." Daphne let the moment of ominous silence drag out, then went on. "How do you think Teddy would feel, knowing you'd been with someone so completely unsuitable? Not to mention the media?"

Daphne had rehearsed her words ahead of time. She

hoped, desperately, that Beatrice couldn't tell how little she actually knew—that, in fact, she had no idea whom the queen had been secretly involved with.

"How. Dare. You." Beatrice's face was illuminated with a regal fury that Daphne had never seen before.

Some deep-rooted instinct prompted her to sink into a deep curtsy, and stay there. She kept her head bowed, trying frantically to plan her next move.

Finally Beatrice spoke into the silence. "I'll appoint the Marikos, as you request."

She hadn't given permission to rise, so Daphne remained in the curtsy. "Thank you," she murmured, almost swaying from sheer relief.

"Oh, get up." Beatrice's voice was laced with anger and disappointment.

Slowly Daphne rose, swallowing the bitter taste of fear. It struck her in that moment that she would never be a *real* royal, not the way Beatrice was.

She'd spent too many years scheming and snatching up privilege. Even if everything went according to plan—if she got rid of Himari, and got Jefferson back, and eventually married him—she would never be as regal as Beatrice.

"Daphne, this is the one and only time I will let you hold this information over my head," Beatrice said tersely. "If you ever again mention what you think you know, to me or to anyone else—if you *ever* try to blackmail another favor from me—you won't find me so forgiving."

"I understand. And thank you. For your mercy."

"You took an enormous risk today," Beatrice went on, her eyes still locked on Daphne's. "And I can't really understand why. I thought Himari was your friend."

"I . . . she was," Daphne whispered.

There was a brush of something softer in the queen's expression, and Daphne wondered if Beatrice had somehow guessed what she was going through. If she knew what it was like, to be famous and publicly adored and yet keep no counsel but her own.

Beatrice reached for a silver bell on a side table, and rang it. Moments later Wendy rushed back into the room, followed by Robert Standish.

When she saw Robert, the queen stiffened. Probably she blamed him for letting Daphne come over and bully her into something she didn't want to do. After all, he was the one who'd granted Daphne this appointment.

"Robert," Beatrice said, gritting her teeth into a smile, "please escort Daphne to the front doors. And do make sure she signs an NDA on her way out."

Daphne nodded and backed out into the hall. She understood what Beatrice was saying: that Daphne had forfeited her trust.

She and Beatrice might never have been close, but until today Beatrice had tolerated her, maybe even approved of her. Now Beatrice would never look at her the same way again.

It was a very high price to pay. But Daphne had no choice except to pay it.

SAMANTHA

Marshall shifted closer to Samantha in the Los Angeles sunshine. "When I said to wear orange, I didn't realize you were going to choose *fluorescent tangerine*," he whispered.

Sam rolled her eyes. "For your information, I like this dress."

"You look like a Skittle." Marshall's mouth twitched. "The cutest Skittle in the pack, obviously."

They were standing before the Ducal Pavilion, the white-pillared building that served as the administrative center of the Duchy of Orange, while Marshall's grandfather delivered his welcome speech. From what Sam could tell, he and Beatrice were going to reenact the moment when Orange officially acceded to the union.

"What's your grandfather wearing?" she murmured, nodding at the duke's black fur cloak, which looked far too heavy for this kind of heat.

"Oh, that's the bear cloak that the Dukes of Orange wore back when they were kings. Apparently my ancestors thought a grizzly-bear pelt was more badass than a crown," he added wryly. "Normally that thing lives in the museum, but they take it out for special occasions."

"It's way better than a crown," Sam agreed. "I wonder if the Ramirezes have anything this cool." As the Dukes of Texas, they were the only other family who had once been kings, but had accepted a demotion to dukedom so that their territory could join the United States.

"I'm sure they have Royal Rattlesnake Boots or something. I mean, it's Texas," Marshall replied. Sam bit back a laugh, aware that a few people, including Teddy, had glanced their way.

They fell silent as Beatrice started up the steps of the pavilion. Like everyone in the crowd, she was wearing orange, though her dress wasn't quite as *loud* as her sister's.

Sam felt a bit guilty that she still hadn't talked to Beatrice about Connor. But how exactly was she supposed to bring it up? Every time she saw her sister, there was always someone hovering nearby. She'd thought she might get a chance this weekend, but of course Beatrice and Sam hadn't been able to fly to Orange on the same plane.

As her sister reached the second-highest step, just below the Duke of Orange, she drew to a halt. Sam felt a sudden burst of pride at how commanding she looked.

"Good people of Orange," Beatrice began. "I come to you on behalf of the United States of America, with admiration for your fortitude, your energy, and your spirit. I come bearing an invitation to join our most beloved union."

Sam watched as Marshall's grandfather reached up to unhook the bearskin cloak. With a dramatic flourish, he whipped it off and settled it over Beatrice's shoulders. Then he pulled her up a step, to stand next to him—where he fell to his knees and kissed her ring.

"On behalf of Orange, I accept your gracious offer," he proclaimed. "Be it known that we renounce our sovereignty; we are the nation of Orange no longer, but become one nation with you, under God . . ."

Sam stopped listening. "Talk about glamorizing history," she muttered under her breath.

"I know. In reality they bickered over terms for *weeks*. Then, when they finally signed a treaty, they got roaring drunk." Marshall grinned in a way that made Sam's stomach do a funny flip-flop. "Which is really what this holiday is about, after all."

"I know. That's why I like Orange," she replied, and he laughed.

♛

The Accession Day official reception was held at the ducal mansion, an enormous house on Sunset.

Sam had murmured her excuses to Marshall and headed straight to the ladies' room. She was standing at the sink, washing her hands, when Kelsey Brooke walked in.

Kelsey was beautiful, but in a fresh-faced, all-American way, not the bold, aggressive beauty that most actresses chased. With her honey-blond hair and pale blue eyes, she looked like a cheerleader from an eighties rom-com.

Sam hated her on sight.

"Samantha!" Kelsey cried out. "I'm so glad I ran into you. I mean, it's *amazing* to finally meet in person."

Sam had a strong urge to correct Kelsey for failing to address her as *Your Royal Highness*. It made her feel oddly like Beatrice.

"Mm-hmm." She started to turn toward the door, but Kelsey didn't take the hint.

"You're here with Marshall, right?" she asked, though of course she already knew. "He's such a great date at these things. He used to always hold my drink when I posed for photos, put his jacket over my shoulders when I got cold. You're in *fantastic* hands," Kelsey added, with an indulgent smile. She spoke as if she'd lent Samantha a pair of shoes, and wanted confirmation of how great they were—but expected Sam to return them soon enough.

"Yeah, he's great," Sam said noncommittally.

Kelsey gave a bright laugh, her eyes meeting Sam's in the mirror. "So are you guys, like, serious?"

"It's, like, none of your business," Sam heard herself say.

She sailed out of the bathroom, wishing she hadn't let that girl get under her skin—but her anxiety calmed when she saw that Marshall was waiting for her.

"I've been looking for you, Skittle. Come on." He grabbed her hand to drag her up a staircase. "There's something I want to show you."

When they stepped out onto the third-floor balcony, Sam's breath caught.

The city unfurled before them, all the way to the dark blur of the ocean. Orange-clad revelers still streamed through the streets, laughing and calling out to one another, stumbling into bars. The lights of the city glowed like the candles of a birthday cake. It made Sam want to make a wish.

"The party doesn't look like it's stopping anytime soon," she observed.

"Oh yeah, people go totally wild on Accession Day." Marshall dragged two Adirondack chairs forward and leaned back in one. "Everyone wears at least some item of orange clothing. If you're caught without one, there's a penalty."

"What kind of penalty?" Sam asked, sitting down next to him.

"Well, you get a choice. You can either sweep the steps of your local post office, or buy a round of shots at your local bar," Marshall explained. "Traditionally, it's supposed to be a round of orange Jell-O shots, which I find absolutely horrifying."

"Somehow I doubt Jell-O is all that *traditional*."

In the streets, a group of revelers burst out laughing, then broke into drunken song. "Can we go down there?" Sam asked wistfully. "That party looks way more fun than the one in the ballroom. Jell-O shots and all."

"I know." Marshall sighed. "Why do you think I escaped up here? The moment they see me, my parents will make a point of reminding me what a disappointment I am."

Sam blinked. "You're not a disappointment," she started to say, but Marshall talked over her.

"Trust me, I am. My parents wish that Rory had been born first," he said, staring out over the city. The streets were turning a brushed gold in the darkness. "Sometimes I do too. If only Rory would put me out of my misery and agree to take the duchy instead. But she doesn't want it."

"I know the feeling," Sam said quietly. "I'm the disappointment in *my* family."

She'd been acting the reckless spare for so long, she sometimes forgot that it had all started like that: as an act. A way to be *different* from her sister. And where had it gotten her, in the end?

Millions of little girls wanted to grow up to be like Beatrice, America's first queen. But no one ever said they wanted to grow up to be like Samantha.

"When I was younger, my dad was constantly giving me American history books," she said into the silence. "About the Constitutional Convention, or the First Treaty of Paris, or the race to the moon. Each time I finished a book, he asked me what I'd learned. Even if what I had learned was that my ancestors were far from perfect." She sighed. "Back then, my dream was to become a lawyer. I thought it meant that I would be like the people I kept reading about, that I could pass laws that *fixed* things. That I could help make history."

"You'd be a fantastic lawyer. You're certainly argumentative enough," Marshall replied, only a little teasing.

"Except I can never *be* one!" Sam burst out. "Eventually

my dad pulled me aside and told me it would never happen. 'You're the sister of the future queen,' he said. 'You can't also be part of the legal system; it would be unconstitutional.'" She blew out a breath, lifting a few stray pieces of hair. "I think that was the moment I finally understood, that was all I could ever be. The sister of the future queen."

She ran her hands up and down her arms, suddenly chilly. Marshall started to slip off his jacket, to tuck it over her shoulders, but Sam shook her head sharply. He'd done the same thing for Kelsey when *she* was cold.

She didn't want to think about Kelsey—and that eager look in her eye when she'd asked whether Sam and Marshall were serious.

Marshall shrugged and left the jacket draped over the side of the chair. "Sam, my parents would have given *anything* for me to go to law school."

"Why didn't you?"

"I was never good at school, unless you count PE," Marshall said, and she heard the pain beneath the seeming lightness of the words. "Reading was difficult for me; the letters were always changing places or turning into black squiggles. I tried to talk to my parents about it, but they just told me to buckle down and study harder. It wasn't until third grade that they finally agreed to test me. That's when we found out about my dyslexia."

Sam remembered what he'd said when they were ballroom dancing: *I know what it feels like to be someone's punching bag.* Her heart ached for nine-year-old Marshall, struggling with a problem he couldn't understand.

"I didn't realize," she murmured.

He shrugged, not meeting her gaze. "I've gotten really good at hiding it. My family was so ashamed, they made me try everything: tutors, therapy, even hypnosis. 'The Duke of

Orange cannot have a learning disability.'" The way he said that last sentence, Sam knew he was quoting someone: his parents, maybe, or his grandfather.

What surprised her most was that Marshall—who was always ready to push her buttons with a new, outrageous nickname, who argued with her for the sheer joy of arguing—had internalized his family's opinion of him.

Someone must have opened a window downstairs—the party pulsed louder and more vibrant beneath them—but neither of them made a move to leave.

Marshall let out a heavy breath. "My parents always wanted me to follow the traditional path of the Dukes of Orange: to go to Stanford Law, graduate with honors, become a constitutional interpretation lawyer—or something equally highbrow—and eventually go into the family business of governing." To Sam's surprise, he didn't sound bitter, just . . . hurt, and weary.

"I never *wanted* to be a lawyer like you did, Sam. But I still tried for years to live up to my parents' expectations," he said heavily. "Eventually it seemed easier to stop trying."

Sam understood, then, why Marshall had embraced his tabloid image as a notorious partier. He acted that way out of self-preservation. Because it hurt less if his family rejected him for something he *chose* to do, instead of something he couldn't control.

Unthinking, she reached out to cover his hand with one of her own. Then she realized what she'd done: that she'd touched him here, in private, when it was just the two of them and they weren't performing for anyone.

Marshall didn't pull his hand from beneath hers.

"Listen," Sam said urgently. "I don't care what your family says: you are going to be a great duke. You're good at solving other people's problems. You think outside the box. You are empathetic, and thoughtful, and charming—when you want to be," she added, which coaxed an unwilling smile.

"Thanks, Sam," Marshall said gruffly.

Sam was hyperaware of where their hands were still touching. It would be so easy to pull him close and kiss him, right there under the broad expanse of sky. A real kiss, not to make anyone jealous or to cause a scene but because she wanted to. Because she wanted *him*.

Yet somehow Samantha—who'd had her first kiss with the Prince of Brazil at age thirteen, who'd marched up to the world swimming champion after the last Olympics and invited herself to his victory party, who'd always gone after what she wanted in the boldest, most direct way possible—did nothing.

And then her chance was gone, because Marshall was pulling her to her feet with a familiar, mischievous smile. "Come on, love muffin. We don't want to miss too much of the party."

Sam rolled her eyes good-naturedly, following him back down the stairs.

She hated to admit it, but she'd gotten used to Marshall's ridiculous nicknames. She was going to really miss them when this whole charade was over.

♛

Several hours later, the ballroom of the ducal mansion was a blaze of chaotic orange.

Sam saw actors and producers, a few tech billionaires and philanthropists, and most of the aristocracy of Orange—including the Viscount Ventura, in his electric-orange tuxedo, and the aging Countess of Burlingame, who was walking around the party with a teacup-sized dog clutched to her chest. The room undulated with shades of pumpkin and persimmon and fiery orange-red.

She'd gotten separated from Marshall almost an hour ago, but had ended up finding his sister, Rory, who was just as smart as Marshall said. She was getting a degree in computer science, and had zero interest in following in her family's footsteps and working in government.

"Orange comes from the *flag*, Sam," Rory was saying, in answer to Sam's question about the duchy. "The original flag we used, when we fought for independence from Spain. It was supposed to be red and white, but the dye kept changing to orange after a few days in the sun. So we leaned into it."

"From what I can see, you've leaned into it *hard*." Sam laughed, glancing around the room—and saw two things that made her go utterly still.

She saw Teddy, standing in a corner with Beatrice, leaning over to whisper in her ear. Beatrice said something in reply, and they laughed.

And she saw Marshall on the dance floor with Kelsey.

The actress's arms were looped around Marshall's neck, her matchstick-thin body pressed up against his. Sam held her breath, waiting for Marshall to pull away, but he didn't. He just kept smiling down at Kelsey as they swayed back and forth to the music.

"I . . . excuse me," she told Rory, and started blindly across the room. When she found an empty table in a corner, she sank down gratefully.

Only then did Sam realize that she wasn't upset about Teddy and Beatrice. She had seen them together—in a moment that was real and intimate and genuinely affectionate—and she didn't especially care. Exhaustion hit as some tether deep within her finally snapped.

She didn't belong with Teddy at all. She belonged with *Marshall*.

Sam forced herself to think back to last year's Queen's Ball, when Teddy had met her at the bar, smiling and easygoing, the light glinting on his blond hair. They'd kissed in a closet, and the very next day, Sam had learned he was going on a date with Beatrice.

In response, she'd flung the full force of her teenage infatuation at him, and called it love.

If she and Teddy had ever gotten a chance to date normally, she would have realized that they didn't make sense together. Sam would have bored of Teddy by the second date, the way she had with every other aristocratic guy she'd dated. Until Marshall.

Marshall, who was irreverent and exuberant and headstrong, like she was. Who provoked her, who galvanized her into being a better person. Who *understood* her. Marshall, who'd seen the messy truth of her life and hadn't run away.

Sam sat there for a numb moment, letting herself adjust to this new strange truth. To the fact that Marshall was the one she'd wanted all along.

It was too late, she thought darkly. She'd lost him to Kelsey after all.

But then, he'd never really been hers to lose.

DAPHNE

Daphne flashed her diamond-bright smile as she sailed through the doors of Tartine, the newest and trendiest restaurant in Washington. She'd gotten her hair blown out and was wearing a painfully chic black dress with cap sleeves. A pair of tourmaline droplets, on loan from Damien, brought out the vicious green of her eyes.

When Jefferson had asked her to dinner, she'd known that she needed to pull out all the stops. If he didn't invite her to Beatrice's wedding tonight, she wasn't sure he would.

"Miss Deighton," the hostess greeted her. "Please, let me show you to your table."

As Daphne followed her toward the back of the restaurant, a few of the diners nudged one another, very unsubtly snapping pictures on their phones. Daphne kept her eyes straight ahead, but she walked a bit more slowly than necessary, her lips softening into a gentle smile.

When they reached the table, she scanned it with expert eyes, trying to determine which seat would cast her in a more flattering light. Then she sat down, smoothing her dress over her legs and tucking one ankle behind the other: arranging herself just so, on display.

Daphne still hadn't heard anything from Himari since that single ominous text. True to her promise, Beatrice had appointed the Marikos as the new ambassadors to Japan;

Daphne had seen the press announcement the moment it went live. Still, Himari maintained her silence.

Was she really going to move halfway across the world without saying anything at all?

It made Daphne feel oddly hollow, that she was so close to winning Jefferson back at last, and there was no one she could talk about it with. Himari was the only person she had ever really trusted... except for Ethan. And there was no way Daphne could discuss this with him, not when *his* relationship with Jefferson was the collateral damage she'd left in her wake.

It wasn't as if Ethan would speak to her right now, anyway.

A momentary hush fell over the restaurant, which could only mean one thing: Jefferson had arrived.

Daphne stood, along with everyone else, as he started toward her. When he reached her table, she ducked into an elegant curtsy. Jefferson waved away the gesture and sat down, and a collective sigh echoed through the room.

"Daphne. Thanks so much for coming," he said, smiling.

His Revere Guard stationed himself a few yards away, leaning against a wall with his arms crossed. He was wearing plainclothes, not that anyone was fooled into thinking he was one of the waitstaff.

"I'm so glad you suggested it," Daphne murmured. As if she hadn't been awaiting this very invitation for months now.

She and Jefferson had seen a lot of each other the past few weeks, but always in a big group setting, or at the palace, on the afternoons Daphne met up with Samantha for media training. She and the prince hadn't really been alone together until tonight.

Daphne hoped she was right about the reason he'd asked her here. But she knew, too, that he needed to work his way around to it. So once they had placed their orders, she looked up with an eager smile.

"You'll never guess what happened after the Feed Humanity gala," she began. "Anthony Larsen got on one of those rental scooters and tried to ride it home, wearing his *tux*! He hit an uneven corner at Durham Street and went flying onto the sidewalk . . ."

As Daphne spun out the story, Jefferson leaned forward, interrupting with occasional questions and appreciative laughter. A typical youngest child, he'd always hated silences, so Daphne made sure she had an endless supply of anecdotes with which to fill them.

They kept on talking like that, trading bits of gossip and reminiscing about past adventures, until they were nearly finished with their entrées. Finally Jefferson looked down, pressing his fork into his scalloped potatoes.

"You've probably noticed that Ethan hasn't been around a lot lately," he said hesitantly.

Daphne knew what he wanted to tell her, and why he felt so reluctant. It wasn't normal to complain about one ex-girlfriend to another.

But she had long ago given Jefferson the right to tell her anything. It was how she kept her hold on him—a hold that cost her, at times, but it was worth it to have his trust. There weren't many people Jefferson could confide in. That was just part of being a prince.

"I assumed he was busy at college," she replied. "Why? Did something happen?"

There was a long silence, and then: "He's dating Nina."

"Nina, your *ex*?" Daphne demanded, with admirable disbelief. "Since when?"

"I don't know. Since the party Sam and I threw, at least."

Daphne edged her chair closer, her perfect features creased in concern. "Did Ethan tell you?"

"That's the thing—he wasn't going to tell me at all! I found out from a reporter. Then, when I confronted Nina about it, she admitted that it was true."

"A reporter? How did she even get ahold of you?" Daphne bit her tongue at that; she wasn't supposed to know that the reporter had been a woman.

Jefferson, not noticing the slipup, merely shrugged. "All I know is that she called, asking if I wanted to comment on the fact that my ex-girlfriend had moved on to my best friend. For a second I thought she meant *you*," he added, "but you would never do anything like that."

There was a slight catch in Daphne's voice as she replied, "Of course not."

The soft noises of the restaurant flowed around them, low conversations and the clinking of silverware. Daphne saw the other guests stealing glances at her and Jefferson, their eyes bright with curiosity or unadulterated envy.

Like always, the attention was exhilarating. It snapped through her veins like a drug.

"Daph, this isn't about Nina," Jefferson said haltingly. "But Ethan has been my best friend since kindergarten. We were in the same peewee baseball league, the same summer camps, the same *everything*. The minute we both had our licenses, we drove all the way down to New Orleans—my parents were so upset with me—taking turns at the wheel, even though my Guard was in the car, just because we could. We got drunk for the first time together, that night we accidentally had all that port and ended up puking our guts out. God, we almost got *tattoos* together, except Ethan talked me out of it at the last minute."

Daphne felt a momentary pang of regret as she realized the full extent of the damage she'd caused. She forced herself not to think about it. *I'll fix it later*, she promised herself, *once I can afford to.*

"Ethan probably thought he was doing the right thing, keeping it under wraps," she offered, but Jefferson shook his head with surprising vehemence.

"I deserved to hear about this from him, instead of being blindsided by a *stranger*." The prince met her gaze, his eyes brimming with confusion and regret. "Anyway, what I'm trying to say is, this has all got me thinking."

Here it was, right on cue, Daphne thought. Now that Jefferson had lost Ethan, he felt alone—like he had no one else but her.

He had wanted her before, but now he needed her. And need was always stronger than desire.

"I owe you an apology," he went on clumsily; apologies weren't something he had to do very often. "You've always been there for me. Even when we weren't dating, you were still on my side—god, you took Nina *dress shopping*, just because you saw she was overwhelmed by it."

"It was nothing," Daphne demurred. That was when she'd canceled Nina's dress order so she would have nothing to wear to Beatrice's engagement party.

"And I know you've been helping Sam lately, teaching her how to handle the media. You're so *good*, Daphne. It means a lot, that you've always stood by me. That you've never . . . taken advantage of me." His eyes flitted down to the tablecloth. "Thank you. I'm sorry that I took all of that for granted."

In a seemingly absentminded gesture, Daphne let her hand rest on the table between them. But Jefferson made no move to reach for her.

"Jefferson. You know I would do anything for you," she replied.

He gave her an easy smile, the type of smile you might give an old friend.

"I need to bring a date to Beatrice's wedding. We'll dance the opening waltz together, pose for pictures, you know the drill." There was a decidedly platonic warmth in Jefferson's voice as he added, "Would you go with me?"

It was the moment Daphne had plotted and waited for, yet it didn't feel romantic at all. Jefferson wasn't looking at her like he wanted to date her or even like he wanted to sleep with her. He was looking at her like . . .

Like he *trusted* her. Daphne wondered with a sudden panic if by cutting Jefferson away from his friends, she'd somehow friend-zoned *herself*.

She could fix this, she thought frantically. She knew the prince's mind better than anyone; surely she could make him change it.

"Of course I'd love to go with you." Carefully, she pulled her hand from the table. "As long as we're going as friends."

"Friends?" Jefferson repeated, and she knew she'd gotten his attention.

Daphne tossed her hair, well aware that in the restaurant's dim lighting, his eyes would follow the curve of her neck all the way down to her cleavage.

"I can't be *casual* about you, Jefferson. We've been doing this for too many years and know each other too well not to be honest with each other."

She saw the expressions flitting over his face, surprise rapidly giving way to a puzzled interest.

"That's what you want, to go as friends? Not as a real date?" he pressed.

Typical Jefferson, wanting what you told him he couldn't have.

"I don't want to be confused about where things stand. I can't keep getting my hopes up about you." She glanced down, so that her gaze was hidden behind the thick fan of her lashes. "Better that we stay friends, rather than confuse things and end up getting hurt all over again. Don't you agree?"

She knew it was risky, the way she had just raised the

stakes—by telling Jefferson that they couldn't get back together if it wasn't serious. It was an invitation wrapped in a rejection, and she knew Jefferson would puzzle over it for days to come. He never could turn away from a challenge.

Jefferson nodded slowly. "Of course. If that's what you want."

"Perfect," she told him, and smiled.

31

BEATRICE

The sky overhead was a dazzling, brilliant blue. It seemed deceptively joyful, the type of sky that should be viewed from a picnic blanket or a sailboat. Not here.

The National Cemetery sprawled along the northern edge of Washington, almost a city itself within the confines of the larger city. No matter the day, there were always people inside: tourists come to see the war memorials, families who'd come looking for an ancestor.

Beatrice walked along the cemetery's main pathway, past rows of military tombstones that gleamed white in the sun. The Tomb of the Unknown Soldier rose in solemn grandeur to her left. Inside its brass urn burned the eternal flame, which was constantly guarded by two American soldiers. They acknowledged her with a quiet salute.

A few visitors saw her walk past, but for once they didn't take pictures or dissolve into whispers. They just nodded their heads in silent acknowledgment of her grief.

The former kings were all buried at the highest point of the cemetery. Beyond a shallow reflecting pool was a series of plots, one for each of America's former kings, set apart by low stone walls. Beatrice passed the massive sarcophagus of Edward I and Fernanda, and the tomb of King Theodore—Teddy's namesake—who'd only ruled for two years before he died of influenza at age fourteen. As always, it was covered in a small mountain of flowers. Theodore's tomb had become a site of pilgrimage for all grieving parents whose children had died too young.

Beatrice turned in to the small plot that was reserved for her family, only to realize that she wasn't alone.

Samantha knelt before their father's tombstone, her head bowed. There was something so intensely private about her sister's grief that Beatrice started to retreat, but Sam's head darted up.

"Oh—hey, Bee," Sam said.

Bee. It was such a small thing, just a single syllable, but Beatrice heard it for the peace offering it was. Sam hadn't used that nickname in months.

Because the sisters hadn't *spoken* in months, not in any real way. Last weekend in Orange, when Beatrice was on the steps of the Ducal Pavilion, she'd thought she'd seen a momentary softening in Sam's expression. But then ceremony and duties had interrupted, as they always did, and she hadn't been able to catch a moment alone with her sister.

And Beatrice had so many other things to deal with right now—like Robert. Ever since their confrontation outside the House of Tribunes, she'd been trying to interact with him as little as possible. She'd started circumventing him altogether: calling people herself instead of asking him to set meetings for her, pointedly leaving him off emails. It felt liberating.

Beatrice lowered herself to the ground, setting her bouquet of white roses by the headstone, next to a spiky green succulent. "Is that what you brought Dad?"

"I didn't want to bring flowers that would go brown and die right away. No offense," Sam said hastily. "But it just felt appropriate."

"Because it's prickly like you?"

"And stubborn," Sam conceded.

They both looked at the headstone before them, so immutable and heavy. HIS MAJESTY GEORGE WILLIAM ALEXANDER EDWARD, KING GEORGE IV OF AMERICA, 1969–2020, it read. BELOVED HUSBAND, FATHER, AND KING.

"I know it's terrible, but this is my first time coming here since the interment," Beatrice confessed. "Being here just makes everything feel so *permanent*."

"Nothing like a three-ton monument to remind you that he isn't coming back," Sam said, trying and failing to be flippant.

Beatrice reached out to brush her fingers over the headstone. The polished granite felt warm from the sun. For some reason that startled her, as if it should have been bitterly cold.

"I keep thinking that I would give anything for just five more minutes with him," she said quietly.

There were so many things she wanted to ask her dad's advice about. More than that, she wished she could tell him how much she loved him.

Sam braced her hands on the grass behind her. "I know what Dad would say, if he were here. He'd tell you that you're doing a fantastic job as queen. That you should believe in yourself." Her eyes cut toward Beatrice with a beat of apprehension, and then she added, "Most of all, that he always wanted you to be happy. He wouldn't have insisted you marry Teddy when you're in love with Connor."

Beatrice's breath caught. "How did you . . ."

It was the second time recently that someone had brought up Connor. Beatrice was still reeling from last week's conversation with Daphne. She wondered what had happened to make the other girl so utterly desperate.

And yet, every time she thought of Connor now, it hurt a little less. She knew he'd left a mark on her—but that was to be expected. Even when wounds healed, they often left a scar tracing lightly over your skin.

"I figured it out," Sam hurried to explain. "I just—I think Dad would want me to remind you that you don't have to go through with this. You can still walk away."

"You don't—"

"I know it's probably not my place, okay? But if I don't say this, no one will!" Sam cried out, then self-consciously lowered her voice. "Bee, you don't have to marry someone you don't care about, just because you think America needs it. Being queen shouldn't require that kind of sacrifice."

"Sam . . ." Beatrice swallowed, rallied, tried again. "I never told you the full story of the night Dad went to the hospital. It was my fault."

Sam shook her head, puzzled. "No, it wasn't."

"Remember how I told you, earlier that night, that I was going to talk to Dad? Well, I did. I told him about me and Connor." Beatrice closed her eyes, but the memories wouldn't stop assaulting her. "I told him I wanted to renounce the throne to be with my Guard! Don't you see? I killed him, Sam! I literally *shocked* him to death!"

"Oh, Bee," Sam whispered, stricken.

Beatrice fell forward, bracing her palms on the grass. Ragged sobs burst from her chest. It felt like a wild animal lived inside her and was angrily clawing its way out. This time, Beatrice didn't fight it.

The tears that poured down her face were months—years, *decades*—in the making.

"Shh, I've got you," Sam murmured, folding her arms around Beatrice.

Beatrice remembered how when Sam was born, she would beg her parents to let her hold her baby sister in her arms. And now Sam was the one taking care of *her*, holding her close and rocking her like a small child.

Beatrice kept on crying her hot, ugly tears, allowing herself the heartbreaking luxury of grief.

She wept for her father and the years that had been stolen from him. For the ordinary life she'd never gotten a chance to live. Her lungs burned and her eyes stung and she was trembling all over, and yet it felt so *good* to cry, as if all her mistakes and regrets were leaking out of her along with her tears.

Beatrice felt like she'd cried out the last traces of the girl she'd been, to make room for the woman she'd become.

Finally she sat back, sniffing. "Sorry. I just got snot all over your shirt."

Sam gripped her sister's shoulders. "Listen to me. It's not your fault that Dad died, okay?"

"But—"

"But nothing," Sam said hotly. "He had cancer, Bee. If the doctors could have saved him, they would have. You can't blame yourself for the fact he was sick." She squeezed Beatrice's shoulders one last time. "He wouldn't have wanted you to carry all this guilt. He wanted you to be *happy*. If he was still here, he would tell you that himself."

Beatrice closed her eyes, casting her mind back to the day her father had died: to the last conversation they'd had, in his hospital room. He'd clutched her hand with his remaining strength, and murmured, *About Connor . . . and Teddy . . .* Then he'd fallen silent.

Maybe he'd been urging her to marry Teddy, as Beatrice had always thought. Or maybe Sam was right, and he'd actually been granting his permission for her and Connor.

Maybe it shouldn't really matter what her dad had wanted.

This was *her* life, wasn't it? Not her father's or the country's, but hers. And no one should make this kind of choice but Beatrice herself.

"I can help you figure a way out of the wedding," Sam was saying. "We'll charter a plane to Mustique and hide out in a villa till it all blows over. And we can make up some scandals about *me* as distraction—maybe that I'm pregnant with Marshall's baby?" Sam's voice caught, but she forged ahead. "Or we can always tell them that Marshall left me for his ex."

Beatrice lifted a tearstained face to her sister. "You would throw yourself to the tabloid wolves for me?"

"I would do anything for you. You're my sister, and I love you," Sam said simply.

Those three words, *I love you*, threatened to break Beatrice all over again.

She tucked her hair behind her ears, trying to gather her resolve. "Sam, as much as I appreciate the offer, I wasn't asking you to help me call off the wedding. Actually . . . I should have told you this a long time ago." She took a breath, wishing she could look away, but forced herself to hold Sam's gaze. "I'm falling for Teddy."

For a moment Samantha just stared at her, her expression flickering with startled understanding. The sunlight bore down on their faces, probably freckling their arms, but Beatrice couldn't move.

"Okay," Sam breathed, and nodded. "As long as you're sure."

"That's *it*? Aren't you upset with me?"

"Were you expecting me to throw a tantrum or something?" At Beatrice's look, Sam smiled. "It's fine, Teddy is ancient history. I'm happy for you. Seriously."

"I . . . okay. Thank you for being so understanding," Beatrice said awkwardly.

Sam plucked a blade of grass, twirling it between her thumb and forefinger. "I *should* be understanding, given the mess I've made for myself." She let go of the grass, which fell listlessly to the ground, and sighed. "That's why I came here today. I just feel like Dad always knew what to do, and I've made so many mistakes. . . ."

"Do you want to talk about it?" Beatrice asked gently.

She listened as Sam recounted a wild and incredible story, about how she'd faked a relationship with Marshall Davis to irritate Teddy, only to realize too late that Marshall was actually the one she wanted.

When her sister had finished, Beatrice blinked, stunned. "Let me get this straight. You negotiated a politically advantageous relationship—even if it was out of spite—*and* manipulated the press into thinking it was real?" At Sam's nod, she let out a slow breath. "Well. I think the monarchy has been underutilizing you."

Sam started to laugh, then seemed to remember where they were, and swallowed it back. "Yeah, you have."

"Why don't you talk to Marshall, tell him how you feel?"

"I don't know," Sam admitted, biting her lip. "I guess the whole epic-declaration-of-love thing isn't really my style."

"If Dad were here, he would encourage you to go for it," Beatrice murmured, and was rewarded with the ghost of a smile.

The two of them sat there together in a quiet, peaceful silence.

Beatrice knew she would never stop missing her dad. Grief like this was messy and brutal and it *hurt*, so much; yet, being here with Sam, Beatrice felt . . . maybe not better, but stronger.

It didn't really surprise her that she and Sam had broken their silence at their father's grave—as if he were here too, quietly nudging them to find their way back to each other.

"Everything is changing," Sam mused aloud. "I feel like the entire world turned upside down this year, and I don't know what to do."

Beatrice reached for her sister's hand and squeezed it. "*We're* not changing, okay?" she said fiercely. "No more fighting between us. From here on out, we'll always have each other. I promise."

32

SAMANTHA

Samantha gave the gravel a sullen kick, sending the stones flying in all directions. The stables were on the opposite side of the grounds from Washington Palace, far enough that tourists usually shuttled back and forth in royal blue trolleys, but Sam had ignored the footman's offer to drive her over. It was a gorgeous day, and she'd thought she could use the walk.

She was so relieved to have cleared the air with Beatrice. But even being reconciled with her sister—they'd spent the weekend together, catching up on all the months they'd lost—wasn't enough to distract her from thoughts of Marshall.

Sam hadn't seen him since last week's trip to Orange. When he'd texted, she'd replied with vague, one-word answers. Sam knew that Beatrice had said to *go for it*, but Beatrice hadn't seen the way Marshall and Kelsey were tangled together on the dance floor.

It had all played out exactly as Sam had predicted. Seeing Marshall with a princess had made Kelsey decide that she wanted him back.

For once, Sam took no joy in being proven right.

When she reached the stables, Sam hurried through the exhibition hall—filled with replicas of old carriages, coachmen's uniforms, even a wooden pony that children could practice saddling—and into the riding ring, which was surrounded by a row of spectators' seats. It smelled of leather and dust and, underneath, the animal musk of horses.

The first thing Sam noticed was the golden state coach, spread out in the middle of the arena in all its blinding glory.

Eight bay geldings stood harnessed before it, enormous white plumes fixed to their foreheads. A postilion in crimson livery was talking to Sam's mother, who was reviewing something, probably the parade route, with Robert Standish. Teddy had wandered behind them to approach one of the horses in the carriage lineup.

He held out a sugar cube, and the horse eagerly licked it from the palm of his hand. It nipped at his clothes in search of more treats, but Teddy just laughed. Sam watched as he greeted each of the horses with low, soothing noises, stroking their necks so that their ears pricked forward in lazy delight.

This, she realized, was what Teddy did best. There was a steadiness to him, an intent fixity of purpose that calmed everyone around him. He was the sort of person you wanted to lean on in a crisis. *He'll be a good king consort*, she decided.

He looked up at her and smiled, the familiar, dimpled smile that used to make her go weak at the knees. Except now when she saw it, Sam felt nothing at all.

She jumped down into the ring, and a puff of light brown dust rose from beneath her sneakers.

At Sam's arrival, Robert looked at his watch and heaved a sigh. "Apparently Her Majesty is running late. So, Your Royal Highness, you'll have to fill in for your sister. Why don't you and His Lordship get into the state coach."

Teddy started forward, but Sam stayed where she was. "Get into the coach? Why?"

"The coachmen will take you around the grounds a few times, to simulate Beatrice and Teddy's procession through the capital. We just want to make sure everything is in good working order," he explained. "This is the first time the carriage has been used in twelve years."

It hadn't been used, Sam realized, since her father's coronation.

She didn't bother pointing out that this carriage was so heavy, the weight of one young woman wouldn't make a difference. Robert clearly wanted a dress rehearsal, and right now she lacked the patience to argue with him.

Sam and Teddy started forward. The carriage was enormous, made of leather and wood but gilded all over so that, from a distance, it looked like solid gold. Sculptures were carved into the sides: a chorus of gods trumpeting in victory, eagles with their wings unfolded.

"No worries, Eaton, I'll go with Sam," said a voice behind her, as Marshall stepped forward to open the carriage door.

He was wearing jeans and a crew-neck shirt, his hair still damp from the shower. Sam's heart lurched at how nonchalantly gorgeous he looked.

"Hey, Marshall. I didn't know you were coming," she said, with admirable disinterest.

"I thought I'd stop by. When the footman said you were at the stables, I caught a ride on one of the tourist carts. I learned so much," he went on, eyes twinkling. "Did you know that your house has two thousand one hundred and eighty-eight windows, but only three of them still have the original glass?"

Normally Sam would have snorted in amusement at hearing the palace called a house. But her mind had whirled cruelly back to last weekend, and she said nothing.

"Lord Davis!" Robert exclaimed. "Do you ride?"

"Yeah, I went to junior polo camp with all the other fancy lads," Marshall said sardonically.

The chamberlain nodded. "Excellent. I was wondering if

you'd like to ride in the wedding procession, as part of Her Majesty's advance guard? Traditionally it's composed of six young noblemen, and—"

"Whatever, I'll do it." Marshall turned to Samantha, gesturing that he could help her up. "Shall we?"

Sam brushed past his outstretched hand and vaulted into the carriage alone.

The interior was very small; they had to sit facing each other, so close that they were almost bumping knees. Sam blinked, adjusting to the sudden dimness.

Neither of them spoke as, with agonizing slowness, the carriage jerked forward.

She felt Marshall's dark eyes on hers, questioning. After a few more beats of silence, he jerked on a leather strap hanging from the carriage's ceiling. "What's this?"

"An old hat cord." At his look, she explained. "It was for men to hang their top hat on, in case they were so tall it didn't fit."

"Of course, a hat cord." Marshall wrapped his wrist around it and tugged himself forward, doing a pull-up. She ignored him.

The horses' steps dwindled to a halt. Sam peered out the window; they had just stepped out of the arena. Queen Adelaide was complaining that she didn't like the look of one of the horses: in the sunshine, its color was too light to match the others. A stable hand sprinted forward to switch it out.

"Your mom is benching one of the horses and putting in an alternate," Marshall pointed out. "Poor guy. His career ended before it even began."

When Sam said nothing, he lifted an eyebrow in concern. "Sam, are you okay?"

It wasn't fair of him to act like he cared. He wasn't her *real* boyfriend.

"I'm fine." She crossed her arms over her chest.

He held out a hand, gesturing to her closed-off attitude. "This doesn't seem *fine*. What's going on?"

Sam wanted to grab him, kiss him, hurt him, everything at once. She wanted him to want her back—and since that wasn't going to happen, she wanted to leave him before he got the chance to leave her first.

"Actually, I've been thinking," she said, though every word cost her. "We should put an end to this, now that we've both gotten what we wanted out of the whole charade."

She thought she saw Marshall tense at her words, but she couldn't be sure. "Have we?"

"Kelsey was all over you last weekend. She clearly wants you back." Sam shrugged, as if Marshall's romantic dramas didn't much interest her. "Isn't it time we ended this farce of a relationship, so we can get together with the people we *actually* want to date?"

He stared at her for so long that her gaze wavered. She looked over at the door handle, wishing she could throw it open and run.

"Sure," Marshall said at last. "We can break up."

"Great."

The silence that settled between them was denser than before. The carriage rumbled clumsily around a turn, and they were both rocked unceremoniously against the far wall. Sam blinked and sat up straight, trying to recover her dignity.

"So? Go ahead," Marshall told her.

Sam blinked up at him. "What?"

"You want it to be public, right?" There was a cold glitter in his eyes as he jerked his chin toward the window. "If we're going to break up, you should do it now. I'd recommend shouting, so Robert and your mom will hear."

Sam dug her nails into the fabric of the seat cushion.

"There's no need to *fake* a breakup," she snapped. "I'll just tell Robert to make a press announcement tomorrow."

"Come on, Sam, you love performing. End this farce of a relationship the way you started it. You owe me that much, at least." Marshall was still speaking in his normal cool drawl, but beneath the words Sam detected a note of something else, fighting its way to the surface. "Then you can go to the wedding with your new boyfriend, or old boyfriend, or whoever the hell he is."

"I'm not going with him," Sam heard herself say. "He's—he's with someone else."

Marshall scoffed. "In that case, I'm surprised you want to call this off."

"Trust me, it's for the best."

"Come on, Sam." Now Marshall sounded almost cruel. "You wanted to make him jealous; let's really make him jealous. That's all I'm good for, right? We can go to some more parties, take a new round of photos—really sexy ones this time, and—"

"Look, I don't *want* him anymore, okay?" Sam cried out. "I don't care about making him jealous!"

Marshall was very quiet as he asked, "What changed?"

Tell him how you feel, Beatrice had said. So Sam braced herself and did exactly that.

"I met you."

When she dared a glance up, she saw that Marshall had gone utterly still.

"Samantha," he said at last. Normally Sam hated her full name, but she loved it on his lips, loved the note of thrilling, territorial possessiveness underneath. "What are you saying?"

"I'm saying that it killed me, seeing you with Kelsey last weekend. I don't want to *use* you to get someone else. You're the one I want." Her words tumbled hastily over one another. "I can't keep acting like this means nothing to me, not when I—"

Marshall stood up in the moving carriage, bracing his hands on the wall behind Sam, and closed his mouth over hers.

Sam arched her back and leaned up into him, looping her hands around his neck as she pulled him down toward her. An eager hunger flared in her core. Marshall's hands slid lower, to cradle her spine—

"Ouch!"

The carriage had hit a bump, slamming his head into the ceiling.

"Are you okay?" Sam cried out.

He slid back onto the opposite bench, rubbing at his skull. "Guess I should've been warned by the hat cord," he said, grimacing.

Sam's heartbeat was still uneven, the echo of an adrenaline rush pounding through her veins. She tucked her mussed hair behind her ears. "You know, I always figured my ancestors got up to some scandalous behavior in this carriage, but now I'm not so sure."

Marshall made a sound that was somewhere between a snort and a wince. "It's too cramped for scandal. Your ancestors all sat here, staring longingly and broodingly at each other." His expression softened, grew more serious. "Which, apparently, I'm about to do."

She bit her lip, suddenly hesitant. "Marshall, are we . . ."

Afternoon light slanted in through the window, dappling half his face in shadow. "Sam, I've liked you for ages now. Probably since the day we met," he told her.

"Then why did you keep telling me that Kelsey was texting you?"

"I was following your lead!" he exclaimed, exasperated.

"After we kissed, you *laughed* and said that we put on a good show."

"I only acted like that because *you* were looking at the crowd!" she protested. "I assumed you'd seen everyone watching, and that the reason you kissed me was because you wanted it to get back to Kelsey!"

Marshall leaned forward, taking her hand in his. Sam wondered if he could feel the leap of her pulse through her skin. "Trust me," he told her. "I have only ever kissed you because I wanted to."

"But last weekend in Orange—"

"I tried to avoid Kelsey. When she cornered me, though, I knew I had to dance with her for a song or two. Otherwise she would have made a scene," he added, sounding darkly amused.

Sam was deaf to the slow rattle of the carriage wheels, the hum of voices outside; all she could hear was the ringing echo of Marshall's words.

"So—you and I—we're doing this for real?"

He grinned. "Sorry, did I skip ahead again? I have a tendency to do that. Hi, I'm Marshall Davis; would you like to go out with me? I'd give you my grizzly-bear pin to mark the occasion, but it's at home."

Sam laughed from sheer delight. "Yes," she declared. "I will go out with you."

And just like generations of her ancestors had probably done, she spent the rest of the drive stealing glances at her boyfriend, wishing this stupid carriage were a little more spacious.

33

DAPHNE

Daphne's bedroom looked out over the driveway, so she was always the first to know when they had visitors. Each time she heard a car pull up, she would dart a glance outside, hoping it was a paparazzo staking out their house—or, better yet, Jefferson. But when she lifted her curtain and saw the blue sports car, Daphne blinked.

Himari had come to see her.

Ever since the palace had announced the Marikos' new position, Daphne had been half-hopeful, half-afraid that Himari would reach out. The royal wedding was next week, and everyone knew that Daphne was going as Jefferson's date—Daphne had leaked it to Natasha herself, as a thank-you for her earlier help.

If Himari wanted to hurt Daphne, she would do it now, while Daphne was on top of the world.

She hurtled down the stairs. Whatever threat Himari had come to deliver, whatever fight she wanted to pick, Daphne couldn't let her parents find out.

She made it to the front door just as her friend was about to ring the bell.

"Himari. What's going on?" Daphne slipped outside, quickly pulling the door shut behind her.

Himari lifted an eyebrow. "You aren't going to invite me in?"

"Not when I have no idea what you're planning," she said bluntly.

Himari shrugged and started toward the edge of the driveway. A cherry tree—one of a vast number in Herald Oaks, planted a hundred years ago in a burst of patriotism—spread its branches overhead, casting their faces in shade. A few stray blossoms had fallen onto the pavement around them.

"You might have seen last week's announcement," Himari began, alert for Daphne's reaction. "Her Majesty appointed my parents as the new ambassadors to the Imperial Court at Kyoto."

"Congratulations. They must be really excited."

"We're moving to Japan in *two days*."

Himari turned to face her, arms crossed. "My parents are ecstatic, obviously. Everyone thought the appointment would go to Leanna Santos. I don't know how we managed to get it instead." She hesitated, her dark eyes locked on Daphne's. "I keep thinking you had something to do with it, except it makes no sense. Your specialty is hurting me, not fulfilling my parents' wildest dreams."

"I have no idea what you're talking about," Daphne said stiffly. But her heart wasn't in the lie, and Himari clearly saw through it.

"So it *was* you. Color me impressed." Himari lifted her hands and brought them together, once, twice, in a sarcastic mockery of a slow clap. "Well played, Daphne. You must really hate me, to make the queen send me thousands of miles away. How did you convince her?"

"I don't *hate* you, okay? I only did it because you kept threatening me! Because you were going to blow my cover and ruin my *life!*"

A hint of pain, or maybe regret, flickered behind the immutable mask of Himari's expression. "I threatened you? What are you talking about?"

"That text you sent, that I was going to get what I deserved!" Daphne drew in a shaky breath. "I thought you were planning something awful, some kind of massive revenge scheme that would destroy me forever."

"Of course you would think that." Himari rolled her eyes. "I guess I should be grateful that you did something nice this time, instead of pushing me down a staircase!"

"*I never pushed you!*"

A sharp, uncertain silence succeeded her words. Daphne glanced around the street. She heard the low hum of a lawn mower from a few blocks away, but here everything was still.

"I never pushed you," she repeated, more quietly this time. "I did put a sleeping pill in your drink—only because I hoped you would drop your guard and do something stupid. You were threatening to tell Jefferson about me and Ethan, and I wanted some kind of leverage over you, like what you had on me. I never thought you would actually get *hurt*."

"I know," Himari said quietly. With those words, all the fight seemed to drain from her.

"I'm sorry," Daphne said again. "I wish I had just *talked* to you. But, Himari, I was terrified of what you might do. You wanted to date Jefferson so desperately—"

"It was never about the prince; it was about *us*!"

Daphne blinked in surprise. Himari pulled her hair over one shoulder, twirling the ends of it.

"Daphne, when I saw you with Ethan, I wasn't thinking about Jeff at all. I was just . . . shocked that you could betray someone you claimed to love, without a shred of remorse." Himari sighed. "After it happened, I kept waiting for you to break up with Jeff, but you clearly had no intention of telling him. And it made me realize—your relationship wasn't sacred to you. *Nothing at all* is sacred to you. The only reason you get close to people is because you can use them as stepping-stones on your upward climb!"

A strange, brittle emotion carved through Daphne like a shard of ice. "That's not true," she whispered. "At least, not with you."

Light filtered through the branches overhead, casting lace-like shadows over Himari's face.

"I didn't have many friends before you," Himari said softly. At Daphne's surprised look she clarified, "I was popular, sure, but only because of my parents' title. You were the first girl I didn't have to *pretend* to like."

Daphne nodded; she'd felt the same.

"But once you and Jeff started dating, I immediately got bumped down to second place. You were suddenly too busy for me. And whenever we *did* hang out, it was still about Jeff—we were going to a palace event to see Jeff, or shopping for something you would wear with Jeff, or *talking* about Jeff."

Daphne's next words were a defensive reflex. "You didn't act like you hated it. Parties at the palace, free designer clothes—"

"I can buy my *own* designer clothes!" Himari burst out. "I didn't care about the perks that came with being in your entourage; I just wanted time with you. I missed my best friend."

Daphne wrapped her arms around herself, feeling suddenly cold. "I always thought you were jealous."

"Of course I was jealous," Himari agreed. "I'd be lying if I said it was buckets of fun playing the quiet sidekick while you became more and more famous. While the press kept gushing on about you, with your perfect face and perfect boyfriend and perfect *life*. Which no longer included me."

"No, I mean—I thought *you* wanted to date Jefferson. That you were trying to break us up so you could swoop in and date him yourself." Daphne's words sounded clumsy even to herself.

Himari shrugged. "I went through a phase of crushing on him, sure. But that's practically required of being a teenager in America. I never actually *liked* him, not romantically." Her eyes cut to Daphne's. "I'm still not convinced that you do, either."

Daphne couldn't afford to acknowledge that comment. "I'm sorry, Himari. For being a bad friend, and hurting you, and . . ."

"And sending me to Japan?"

Daphne let out a ragged breath. "Yeah. For sending you to Japan."

"You never do things halfway," Himari agreed, a note of grudging admiration in her voice. She looked down. "Still, we both know my parents wouldn't have gotten this appointment without your . . . interference," she said delicately. "And honestly, I don't hate the idea of a fresh start."

A fresh start. Daphne wouldn't know what to do with that. For a fleeting instant, she let herself imagine what it would be like: if she wasn't Daphne Deighton, future princess. If she was just . . . Daphne.

But she'd traded away so many pieces of herself, she didn't really know what was left. She didn't really know who she was anymore, underneath the bright, public self she showed the rest of the world.

"Truce?" she suggested, and Himari's mouth twitched in amusement.

"You stick to your side of the Pacific, and I'll stick to mine?"

Daphne nodded, not trusting herself to speak.

"You know," Himari mused, "the more I think about it, the more I like the idea of being friends with a princess. I'm sure there's a favor or two I could call in."

Daphne tried not to reveal how her heart had skipped at the word. "*Are* we still friends?"

Himari scoffed, as if it were self-evident. "What else could we be? Only friends know each other well enough to cause this kind of hurt. Only friends push each other past the breaking point."

"I don't think most people would agree with your theory of friendship."

"So what?" Himari said easily. "You and I aren't *most people.*"

The two of them stood there for a moment in a strange, weighted silence. The wind picked up, raking its fingers through the trees.

There was an unmistakable similarity between the two young women: a stubborn, steely quality that each of them had seen in the other. It was what had drawn them together, and also what had set them against each other, and, in the end, perhaps it made them more like sisters than friends.

Daphne wouldn't know. She'd never had a sister, had never let *anyone* past her guard, except Himari.

And Ethan.

"I'm going to miss you," Daphne heard herself say.

Himari held out her hand. "It's settled, then. No more feuding."

Daphne nodded and shook Himari's hand, struck by the formality of the gesture, as if they were a pair of queens formalizing a state treaty.

Then, to Daphne's utter shock, Himari pulled her closer, and threw her arms around her in a hug.

"I'm sorry," Himari murmured, so softly that Daphne almost didn't hear it. As if Himari was reserving the right to deny she'd ever spoken the words.

"Me too." Daphne blinked back the tears that burned her eyes. "I wish I could go back and do things differently."

"It's for the best. This town isn't big enough for the both of us."

"This *country* isn't."

Himari softened, just a little. Then she stepped away, letting out a breath. "Well—I should get going. I have a lot of packing to do."

"Goodbye, Himari," Daphne ventured. "And good luck."

As she watched Himari get into her car, Daphne knew she should feel satisfied, or at least relieved. Instead she felt oddly hollow.

Her greatest enemy, her best friend—whatever Himari was, she had defined Daphne. And now that she was gone, Daphne knew a piece of her would always be missing.

"Hey, Daphne."

She looked up and saw that Himari had rolled down her window. "You know the Crown Prince of Japan is only two years older than us," Himari went on, an eyebrow raised in unmistakable challenge.

"I'm aware." The ache in Daphne's chest seemed to loosen, just a little.

Himari tilted her head, that old mercurial smile playing around her lips. "So who knows? Maybe you won't be the only one of us to marry a prince."

34

BEATRICE

"Thanks for walking me back." Beatrice held open the door to her suite so that Teddy—who carried the stack of last-minute presents they'd been given at the rehearsal dinner—could follow her inside. As she moved, the antique mirror on her wall caught the swishing of her dress, which was hand-sewn with pearls to match the ones woven into her updo. When Beatrice nodded or shook her head, they gleamed against the silken darkness of her hair.

"You look so pretty tonight, Bee," Teddy told her, and she smiled.

Pretty. Not majestic or elegant or any of the other things that Beatrice thought of herself, but just *pretty*. She knew it was ridiculous for something like that to matter, but it was still nice to hear. It made her feel almost like a real, ordinary girl—one who'd been to high school dances and stayed out past curfew and read magazines that *didn't* have her picture on the cover. As if she and Teddy might be any couple at all, rather than the Queen of America and her future king consort.

She went over to lift the window, letting in the warm summer air as she glanced outside. Hundreds of people were already lining up in anticipation of tomorrow's event. Ten miles of scaffolding had been erected along the parade route—after the ceremony, she and Teddy would drive through the streets in the golden state carriage before returning to the palace for the reception.

Beatrice looked down at the blurred sea of faces, many of them waving miniature American flags, or clutching flowers, or holding posters that said her and Teddy's names. Her heart seized in her chest.

Perhaps alone in the modern world, this was a crowd of people who'd been drawn together out of something positive—not animosity, or anger, but love. For the country, and what it stood for. And for *her*.

She understood now what her dad had meant, when he'd told her that the symbolic aspects of her job were still the most crucial ones. America needed these moments of pure and uncomplicated joy, something outside the ugliness of political rivalries, to bring the nation together when so many things conspired to tear it apart.

Thunder rumbled through the capital. A low mass of clouds gathered in the distance, making the fluorescent glow of the city lights seem even brighter in contrast. The crowds squealed and began to retreat under cover.

Teddy moved toward her. "It looks like it might rain on our wedding day."

Beatrice nodded; she felt the pressure gathering. The sky was swollen, the air thickening in anticipation of a coming storm. It felt like the entire world was holding its breath—waiting for something monumental, something *big*.

"People will say it's bad luck," she agreed.

"Do *you* think it's bad luck?"

"I've never believed in luck. Or, rather, I believe in making your own luck. Besides," she added, "now the souvenir shops can sell all those commemorative wedding umbrellas, the ones printed with our faces."

"Oh good, do we have extras of those? I could use a new umbrella," he joked, and she smiled.

Teddy turned toward the gifts, which he'd stacked on her upholstered blue sofa. "By the way," he went on, grabbing a flat box wrapped in ivory paper, "I have something for you."

Beatrice hadn't realized that one of the gifts was from him. "You didn't need to do that."

"Given that you bought me a house, I figured I should do *something*." He said it lightly, but Beatrice heard the note of emotion beneath. She tore open the box, and her breath caught.

Inside was a pair of Minnie Mouse ears: the special bridal ones, covered in white sequins and affixed with a miniature veil.

Beatrice felt an aching pressure in her chest that pulled her somewhere between laughter and tears. She placed the ears on her head, not caring that they would ruin her updo. Compared to the tiaras she usually wore, they were curiously light.

Teddy reached to adjust them, tucking a strand of hair behind her ear. "I wish we could elope to Disney World, so you'd get the wedding of your five-year-old dreams, but I think a few people might be disappointed. So, since I couldn't bring you to Disney World, this seemed like the next best thing."

His hand was still cupped around her chin, tilting her face up. Moonlight traced the sweep of his eyelashes, caught the startling blue of his eyes.

"I'm so in love with you," Beatrice blurted out.

Her hands flew to her mouth in shock, the way a cartoon character's would. She had just *said* it, had told Teddy she loved him without a second thought, which was so unlike her that she wondered if it had really happened. She *never* spoke without thinking.

Teddy opened his mouth—but before he could answer, earth-shattering thunder reverberated through the room, and the skies split open in a downpour. Beatrice realized with a start that her window was still open. The curtains whipped up in the sudden wind, rain slanting inside to splatter the carpet.

Together she and Teddy grabbed the massive windowpane and wrestled to bring it down. The wind roared into the room like an angry spirit, flinging raindrops into their faces.

Finally the window fell into place with a clatter.

After the violence of the storm, the silence felt suddenly terrifying. Beatrice turned slowly to face Teddy, her heart hammering as erratically as the patter of rain outside. And yet—she knew she had meant what she'd said.

"I love you," she repeated. As she spoke, something seemed to move and settle deep within her; the very tectonic plates of her being shifting, to create space for this new revelation. She loved Teddy, and, of everything that had happened, that was perhaps the greatest gift of all.

"I didn't see it coming," she said helplessly. "I wasn't expecting it and I wasn't prepared for it, and I'll understand if you don't . . . if you can't . . ."

Maybe all that Teddy could give her was the partnership they'd agreed to that night in Walthorpe. He had only ever promised her his hand, not his heart.

Yet Beatrice found that she wanted both.

"Bee—of course I love you."

His hand reached for hers. Beatrice thought she was trembling, but then she saw that *he* was the one trembling. The storm seemed to be raging all around them, and here they were, suspended in the eye of it.

"I didn't expect to fall for you, either," Teddy said hoarsely. "When we first met, I didn't even know *how* to date you. I thought you were . . . not a person, almost, but an institution. I figured that getting engaged to you was either very brave or very foolish," he added, with a smile.

"Probably both," Beatrice managed.

Some of the rain had misted in his hair, turning its strands a darker burnished gold. A few droplets ran down the edge of his jawline. Carefully, Beatrice reached out to brush them away. In the distance, the city lights still glowed in the rain, like sodden fairies.

"It's my fault," Teddy said softly. "At the beginning I didn't try hard enough to get to know you. All I saw was the tiny fraction of you that you show the world—and, for some stupid reason, I assumed that was all there was."

Teddy's hand was still gripping hers. He traced his thumb lightly over her skin, drawing small, invisible circles on her palm. Beatrice's blood turned to smoke in her veins.

"But now I know there's so much more to you than you let on. You're funny, Bee, and driven, and you're smart as hell. Now . . . I like to think I know *all* of you. Even the parts that everyone else is too superficial or impatient to see."

He lifted her left hand, studying the engagement ring that glittered there. Then, to Beatrice's surprise, he pulled that hand to his mouth and kissed it—not gently, the way a courtier might have, but with an urgent roughness.

"For me, tomorrow will be all about the two of us," he told her. "Not the thousands of people crowded into that throne room, or the millions of people watching on TV, but us. As if we were two ordinary people getting married at city hall, or at Disney World, or in a backyard."

Beatrice's heart raced faster and faster. She wished, desperately, that they *were* one of those couples, and their relationship could be just that—a relationship, without the fate of nations or dynastic futures hanging on its success.

She wasn't afraid of marrying Teddy—she *wanted* to marry him—but she feared all the spectacle and ceremony of it, for reasons she didn't understand.

Teddy gripped her shoulders, forcing her to look up into his face. Beatrice softened, breathing him in like summer air.

"I should get going," he decided, and stepped away.

A new, resolute steadiness took hold of Beatrice. Knowing exactly what she was doing, and what it would mean, she caught Teddy's arm and tugged him back toward her—tugged both of them through the door to her bedroom.

"Bee, I don't . . ."

"We're getting married tomorrow." She felt the clasp of her dress trembling at her throat, where her pulse was racing.

"Exactly," he reasoned. "I can wait one more night."

"Well, I can't." When he opened his mouth to protest again, Beatrice brushed a finger against his lips. "Teddy," she said, very slowly. "I'm sure."

She thought back to that night at Walthorpe, when she'd thrown herself at Teddy, out of loneliness and confusion, and perhaps a drunken hope that it might make things simpler between them. It felt like a long time ago, now.

Some of her nervousness must have flickered over her expression, because she saw comprehension dawn in Teddy's eyes. "You haven't ever . . ."

"No, I haven't." She and Connor had never gotten that far—had never really gotten the chance.

"I love you," Teddy said again, and it set Beatrice ablaze. She answered him in the same words, drinking in his love and his kisses and the way his hands slid over her.

Beatrice tore her mouth from his only to tug his blazer impatiently from his shoulders, letting it fall to the floor. Teddy fumbled a little with her dress, struggling with tiny hooks that ran down the back, until Beatrice gave a breathless laugh and just tugged it over her head half-fastened. His breath caught when he saw her in nothing but her ivory lace underwear.

"I love you," she repeated, simply for the sheer joy of saying it. She wondered if either of them would ever tire of it.

They stumbled back together toward the bed, their kisses wilder and more feverish. Beatrice could taste the rain on his skin. The pearls from her hair were falling loose, gleaming on the pillows around them like tiny fragments of moonlight, but she didn't care. Her breathing was wild and fast, and she felt a tingling sensation spreading all the way to the edges of her fingers. No matter how many parts of her body touched his, it didn't feel like enough.

Distantly, with the part of her brain that was still capable of thinking, Beatrice knew that something monumental had changed—that she and Teddy were both changed—here, in this room that had seen two centuries' worth of history. Where her ancestors had loved and reigned and grieved and found joy.

The steady drumming of the rain echoed their heartbeats, the new rhythm between them.

Outside, the storm might be raging—but here, in the pocket of warmth they had created, Beatrice felt safe. And loved.

35

NINA

It had stormed the entire night before the royal wedding, prompting a last-minute flurry of activity as harried staffers began to carry out the contingency plans. But by dawn the rain had fallen off, the only sound the occasional drip of water from the shingles of a roof. Now the sun was out in full force, leaving the world sparkling and new—and utterly transformed.

Nina hadn't seen the city like this since King George's coronation, when she'd been just a child. The streets were hung with miles of triangular pennants, printed in the red, blue, and gold of the American flag. Even the lampposts had been draped in ribbons and crepe-paper streamers.

"You know we need to leave soon," Ethan warned, though his voice held an unmistakable note of amusement.

"Ten more minutes. Please?" Nina's eyes darted to the artist who'd set up at the nearest street corner; he was painting children's cheeks with miniature hearts and tiaras, free of charge. "I wish I could get my face painted," she added, almost to herself.

"You'd get a few looks when we walk into the throne room," Ethan joked, then seemed to fall silent as he realized what he'd said. The two of them would attract plenty of stares as it was, showing up to the wedding as a couple.

It was the reason Nina had begged Ethan to come out onto the streets with her—because she wanted one last moment of normalcy before the chaos descended.

Right now she wasn't an object of fascination or revulsion. She was just another anonymous member of the buoyant crowds that lined the parade route through the center of town. The wedding would begin in a couple of hours, but the celebrations had been going since early this morning—or, in some cases, since last night.

Enormous projection screens had been set up at major squares and thoroughfares, to air the live wedding coverage. Discordant music blared from various directions: pop songs from portable speakers, a piano bar playing the wedding march. Now and again groups of friends spontaneously burst into the national anthem. Those who were lucky enough to live along the parade route were hosting parties on their balconies, everyone already jostling along the railings in search of the best view. The city was at max capacity: hotels fully booked, friends hosting friends as people poured in from all over the country—all over the world, really—to celebrate Beatrice and Teddy.

Each storefront they passed seemed full of more wedding merchandise than the last. Nina saw foil balloons, tote bags, Christmas ornaments, puzzles, jewelry. Not to mention dozens of "official" cherry cake mixes and cherry brandies. She wondered how much money the government was making off all this.

"Bottled water, two dollars; beer, one dollar," shouted a guy who was walking through the street, wheeling a cooler behind him. When Nina met his gaze, he grinned and lifted the cooler's top. Beneath a jumbled assortment of beer cans were a few plastic bottles of zinfandel rosé, labeled with a sticker of Beatrice's face that he'd definitely made on his home printer.

Nina laughed. This was exactly why she'd wanted to come out here—to see the aspects of the wedding celebration that were decidedly not palace-approved.

She held tight to Ethan's hand as they wove through the crowds, keeping well away from the media crews. Reporters were already stationed in the streets, speaking rapidly into their microphones as they filmed pre-ceremony footage. Nina had jammed a baseball cap low over her head, and in the crowds she doubted anyone would recognize her as Prince Jefferson's erstwhile girlfriend. But she wasn't in the mood to answer questions about Ethan. Or about Jeff and Daphne.

She'd seen that Jeff had officially asked Daphne to the wedding. It was impossible to avoid the internet's breathless speculation about whether they were getting back together. Earlier this year, that kind of news would've been painful to hear—but now Nina didn't especially care.

There was nothing Daphne could do to hurt her anymore.

As she and Ethan jostled through the crowds, Nina found herself marveling at the scale of it all. There were so many people out here—young and old, in pairs or in massive groups—and every last one of them was smiling. Thousands of strangers, drawn together by the wedding of two people they would probably never meet.

"Beatrice seems more popular than she was at the start of this year," she observed.

Ethan laughed. "Everyone loves an excuse for a national holiday."

"You know what I mean. People are getting used to the idea of change." She tugged at Ethan's arm, pulling him around a pair of women in hot pink sashes that said QUEEN BEE. "They're starting to *like* having a young queen. It makes the country feel youthful and energized."

"Some of that's because of Sam and Marshall, too," Ethan reminded her.

Nina had been thrilled to find out that Sam and Marshall were together for real now, and not just for show. She didn't know Marshall that well, but she knew one thing for certain: he didn't try to make Samantha into someone she wasn't. Which made him leagues better than everyone else in Sam's life—including, at times, her own family.

They crossed the intersection into Chilton Square. A few soldiers stood at attention, their helmets topped with ceremonial plumes. Nina smiled when she saw that someone had placed a plastic bachelorette tiara atop the statue of Artemis at the fountain's center. Its veil fell over the goddess's features, fluttering a little in the wind.

She thought of what her parents had said last week, when she'd gone to ask their advice. She'd explained everything—her situation with Ethan, her painful conversation with Jeff, Ethan's suggestion that they attend the royal wedding together—and her mom had reached for her hand with a sigh. "Oh, sweetheart. Relationships are never simple."

"You and Ethan have both occupied a very strange and specific position near the royal family," her mamá had agreed. "But . . . you shouldn't be drawn to Ethan simply *because* you understand each other's backgrounds. There's so much more to both of you. And if you think no one else could relate, you're doing the rest of the world a disservice."

Nina hesitated. She thought of all the things she loved about Ethan: his razor-sharp wit, his unexpected softness. The way everything felt more vibrant simply when she was *with* him.

"No," she decided. "It's more than that."

Isabella shifted closer on the couch. "Then there's really only one thing to ask yourself. Is Ethan worth it, or not?"

Was he worth it?

The press would paint Nina as even more of a villain this time. She was the woman who'd moved on from the prince to his *best friend*. The tabloids would probably claim that she was dating Ethan simply out of spite, to punish Jeff for breaking up with her. The world had already resented her, and now it would despise her.

Nina couldn't begin to imagine the nicknames the internet would give her, once those articles were published.

She remembered what her mom had said earlier this year: that Nina should rely on the people who really knew her to stay grounded. *Ethan* was one of those people now. At some point this year she'd come to lean on him, and that was worth fighting for.

He drew to a halt in the sea of people and stared down at her, evidently sensing the direction of her thoughts. "We don't have to do this, if you aren't ready," he said softly.

"No." She shook her head, causing her ponytail to slip loose. "I want to go to this wedding with you. Whatever happens, you're worth it."

"*I'm* worth it?" he said roughly. "Nina, I'm not—I don't deserve you."

"It's not about *deserving*, Ethan. This isn't a sports game. We don't keep tallies of wins and losses. We're together, and I'm ready for everyone to know it."

Relief blossomed on his features, and he grabbed Nina beneath the arms, spinning her around in a ballroom dancing move. When he set her down again, his eyes were bright. "I'm so glad that I met you."

"You met me a long time ago," she felt the need to point out.

"But I didn't know you back then. I thought you were stuck-up and annoying, and impossible to talk to—"

"Is there a compliment in here?"

"—and my reasons for hanging out with you, earlier this year, were totally messed up—"

What did he mean by that? Was he talking about their journalism class?

Ethan caught her hands in his own. "What I'm trying to say is that I was wrong about you. I had no idea . . ." He paused, as if weighing his next words carefully. "I had no idea, Nina Gonzalez, that I would end up being totally crazy about you."

Nina swallowed. "I'm falling for you, too."

Ethan laced his hands over her shoulders, leaning down to brush his lips against hers. A few bystanders, seeing them kiss, let out low whoops of approval. Nina smiled against his mouth, leaning further into the kiss—because now, for a little while longer, it didn't really matter.

A low, droning noise echoed through the air. They both looked up, to see a formation of military planes flying overhead in an elaborate zigzag formation. The aircraft seemed awfully low to Nina.

"Is this some sort of salute?" she started to ask, as the planes swooped still lower—and their cargo hatches flipped open. A bright floral rain fell from the sky: pink and white roses, hydrangeas, and of course cherry blossoms.

The crowds seemed to shout out in a single voice as the flowers fell on their heads, making it momentarily look like the capital had dissolved into swirling pink-and-white waves.

Laughing, Ethan drew a stray petal from Nina's hair. "I think that's our cue to get going."

♛

It was a bit disorienting, stepping from the vibrant chaos of the streets into the palace's cool, beeswax-scented calm. Nina had hastily changed out of her shorts and into a gown, which she'd bought online last month; after the way her last dress had been mysteriously "canceled," she no longer trusted the boutiques in the capital. The gown was beautiful, its lavender silk so pale that it almost looked silver, with a gathered neckline that showed off Nina's bare shoulders. She'd tucked back her curls with bobby pins, but anyone who stood close would smell the sunshine on her hair.

In the crowds of people making their way through the entrance hall, Nina caught sight of Marshall Davis, dressed in a crisp tuxedo and accompanied by a couple who must be his parents. His grandfather, the current Duke of Orange—wearing the scarlet robes of his position, and a ducal coronet, made of gold with eight gleaming prongs—walked alongside them.

To her own surprise, Nina called out Marshall's name. He looked up, startled, then muttered something to his parents and started toward her.

"Nina. Hey." Marshall spoke warily, as if he wasn't sure what she wanted with him; and really, Nina didn't know either. She drew to one side of the crowds, near a massive porcelain vase.

"I just . . . I wanted to see how you're holding up," she ventured.

Marshall's mouth curled with a hint of amusement. "Don't worry, I can handle myself without Sam for a while. Believe it or not, this isn't my first royal wedding. I was at Margaret and Nate's, at the redwood grove outside Carmel—"

"I meant the media attention," Nina cut in clumsily. "Marshall—I know how it feels, being put through the wringer for dating a Washington. I'm here if you ever want to talk about it. There aren't many people who really understand, you know?"

Hearing her own words, she remembered the day Daphne had told her the exact same thing—*Trust me when I say that I understand. I'm probably the* only *person who understands.* But unlike Daphne, Nina thought adamantly, she meant it.

Marshall shifted his weight. Suddenly, Nina caught a glimpse of what Sam saw in him: that behind his swagger—which was more an endearing, boyish charm than actual arrogance—he was startlingly vulnerable.

"I'd be lying if I said it's all been smooth sailing, but Sam is worth it. I really care about her, you know."

"I know." When she'd first heard about this whole fake-relationship stunt, Nina had been so certain it was a terrible idea. She was glad Marshall had proved her wrong.

"Besides," he went on, and now that cheeky tone was back in his voice, "the media coverage has been getting better. I think the nation is starting to fall for me. And really, who could blame them?"

Nina huffed out a laugh, though Marshall was right. She'd seen the tone of the comments shifting in recent weeks. Of course, plenty of people still didn't approve, but more and more Americans were rooting for him and Samantha. Perhaps because they saw the genuine happiness on both their faces, and realized that this was something real. Or perhaps because they, too, were people of color, and liked seeing a Washington with someone who looked like them.

"Speaking of Sam, I was going to find her before the ceremony starts," Marshall added, glancing over his shoulder.

Nina nodded; Ethan was probably waiting for her in the throne room. "Right. See you later."

The foyer had thinned out in the last few minutes. Nina picked up her steps, turning into the main central hallway—just as Prince Jefferson turned the corner.

He was wearing the most excruciatingly formal version of his ceremonial uniform, complete with gloves, and a saber and scabbard that positively glowed. Dressed in all that crimson fabric and gold braid, he seemed unfairly handsome, like the hero of some romance novel who'd stepped out of the pages and into real life.

When he saw her, Jeff sucked in a breath.

For a long moment the two of them just stood there. Nina imagined the silence flowing around them like a river, swirling with invisible eddies and currents as it grew ever deeper.

Looking at Jeff, Nina didn't see him as her ex-boyfriend, or even the handsome prince of her adolescent daydreams. She saw the Jeff who had been her friend, the little boy she used to run around the palace with, hunting for secret passageways with Sam.

She remembered when the three of them had once locked themselves inside a maintenance room. Jeff and Nina had been terrified, but Sam had just held tight to their hands and said, "Don't worry. I'll never let anything hurt either of you." Nina was too shy to voice it, but she remembered feeling that way, too: that she would go to war with anyone who tried to harm Jeff.

Except that was *her* now, wasn't it? She hadn't set out to hurt Jeff, yet she *had* hurt him, maybe worse than anyone.

"Jeff. Hi," she whispered, and took a hesitant step forward. He watched her but didn't move. Nina held out a hand, as if to touch his arm in silent support.

His phone buzzed, and the trancelike thread between them snapped.

"I have to go," he said stiffly, and turned away.

Nina swallowed back a protest and nodded, watching Jeff's retreating form. He would forgive her, and Ethan, when he was ready, she told herself—and hoped desperately that it was true.

She could hear the slap of his saber against his polished boots long after he'd walked away.

Subdued, she headed down the hall to the throne room.

At the doors the usher asked for her name, then showed her to her seat, which was in the same row as Ethan's—they had both been placed in the back, along with other low-ranking friends of the family. Nina glanced around the vast space, wondering where her parents were. The normal wooden pews of the throne room had been removed, replaced with chairs covered in tufted velvet cushions and hung across the back with garlands of flowers. Nina could smell all those thousands of blossoms, light and crisp beneath the heavier scents of perfumes and dry cleaning and body heat.

"There you are." Ethan grinned as she settled into her seat. "You know, I wish you *had* gotten your face painted. A red 'Beatrice + Teddy 4-ever' would have gone fantastic with that dress."

The anxious fluttering in Nina's stomach settled a little. Right now, the important thing was that she and Ethan were here, together.

"If only we'd gotten matching ones," she whispered in reply.

They were inside the palace, but still, Nina reached out for Ethan's hand and squeezed it.

36

SAMANTHA

Samantha longed to collapse onto the love seat with her sister and close her eyes. But now that she was in her gown, she wasn't allowed to sit down, for fear of wrinkling the fabric. Sam would have complained, except that even she was absolutely in love with this dress.

The form-fitting ivory satin was deceptively simple, with a crew neck and cap sleeves. No lace—as Sam's mother always said, lace was exclusively for brides—but Wendy Tsu had added sixty organza-covered buttons down the back. To show them off, and in a nod to Sam's typically casual style, Queen Adelaide had even let her sweep her hair into a chic bouncy ponytail.

Beatrice shifted on the love seat, still wearing her silken white robe. Her hair had been styled into glossy dark curls, and pinned half up beneath the Winslow tiara. In the center of the room, on a wheeled clothing rack, her wedding gown hung in all its glowing splendor.

Sam noticed an unmistakable flicker of sadness in her sister's expression. "Bee, is everything okay?"

Beatrice let out a shaky breath. "I just . . . I wish Dad was here."

Sam crossed the room in two strides, then pulled her sister into a fierce hug.

Neither of them spoke. But it was a soft, easy sort of

silence, because Sam knew they were both thinking of their dad.

"It's hard, doing all of this without him," Beatrice went on. "There's this *hole* where he should be—and no matter how happy I am about everything else, I can't stop wishing he was here."

Sam's throat closed up. "He *is* here, Bee. He's looking down on you and smiling."

Sorrow glinted in Beatrice's eyes. "I know. But I still miss him, so much. I love Uncle Richard, but he's not the first person I would've picked to walk me down the aisle."

Sam stood up a little straighter. "Do you want me to talk to Mom? She should have agreed to walk with you from the beginning." Queen Adelaide was down the hall in the Blue Chamber, along with Teddy and his groomsmen; she'd chosen to let Jeff lead her down the aisle, rather than walk with Beatrice—as her husband would have, if he were still here.

"It's fine." Beatrice shook her head at Sam's expression. "Don't be hard on Mom. Today is supposed to be a joyful day, for *all* of us. I won't ask her to do something that would cause her pain."

Sam blinked. "Bee—what if you walk yourself?"

At her sister's stunned look, she rushed to explain. "Hear me out. You're the *queen*, the highest-ranking person in this country. The only person who can give you away is yourself. So why don't you walk down the aisle alone?"

Beatrice glanced down, her hands twisting in the fabric of her robe. Her silver sequined heels glinted in the light.

"I . . . plenty of people will be angry," she said nervously.

Sam hated that her sister was right. A young woman heading down the aisle by herself—it was a snub to convention, a blatant show of independence.

"Maybe they will," she acknowledged. "But what better way to start changing their minds?"

Beatrice hesitated, then tipped her chin up, her expression stubborn and quietly resolute. Sam couldn't help thinking that she looked startlingly like their father when he'd been on the brink of a decision.

"Okay. I'll do it."

There was a knock at the door, and Robert Standish peered into the room. "Your Majesty, the hair and makeup artists are here to do final touch-ups. Then Wendy Tsu will help you into your dress."

The room was about to dissolve into a small hurricane of hairspray and lipstick. Sam cast a pleading glance at her sister, who laughed in understanding. "You can go, Sam," Bee said. "Just don't stay away too long."

"Thank you," Sam breathed.

Ignoring the curious stares of footmen and security guards, she started restlessly down the hallway. She couldn't remember the last time she'd seen the palace thronged with so many people. The throne room was probably full by now; the guests had been told to arrive almost an hour before the ceremony, for security reasons.

The only place free from all the chaos was the winter garden, a small space tucked into the side of the palace. At the center of its brick courtyard stood a potted lemon tree, which only grew in this climate thanks to the assiduous care of the palace groundskeeper.

"Sam?"

A lean, blond figure unfolded himself from one of the benches, and Sam swallowed.

"Teddy. What are you doing out here?" she asked self-consciously.

A hesitant smile curled over his features. He wore the ceremonial navy and white of the Dukes of Boston, his dress coat complete with tails and stitched in golden thread. Even his white gloves were fastened with gold buttons. Sam knew, in a distant and unaffected part of her mind, that he looked impossibly handsome.

"The same thing as you," Teddy said. "I needed a breath of fresh air before all the handshaking and small talk."

"But you're so good at all that stuff," she observed.

"Maybe." He shrugged. "That doesn't mean I like doing it, though."

The silence that fell between them was less awkward than Sam might have expected. She realized that she hadn't been alone with Teddy since that day at the Royal Potomac Races all those months ago, when he'd told her he was marrying her sister.

"Sam—"

"Teddy—"

They both broke off with a flustered laugh. "You first," Sam insisted, and he cleared his throat.

"Sam, Bee and I . . . I mean . . ."

When had he started using that nickname? Hearing it tugged at something in Sam's chest.

"I know," she said, her eyes burning. "You really love her, don't you."

To his credit, Teddy held her gaze. "I don't know how to begin apologizing to you. I mean, there's nothing in *McCall's Etiquette* about how to handle something like this."

"I think we're leagues past anything McCall could've anticipated," Sam replied, but Teddy didn't smile at her joke the way Marshall would have.

"Exactly," he said earnestly. "I'm sorry I made such a mess of things. I never should have . . ."

At his anguished look, Sam took an instinctive step forward, placing a finger over his lips. "Whatever you were going to say, don't. I'm the one who should be apologizing to you."

She was the antagonist in Beatrice and Teddy's love story, and if she hadn't been in the way, they might have discovered how they felt about each other so much sooner.

"It takes two people to make out in a closet. Don't carry all the blame for this, okay?" She tried to smile at him. "I'm happy for you and Bee. *Really*."

A breeze shot into the garden, rustling the leaves on the lemon tree, lifting the smells of soil and damp and citrus into the air.

Teddy's eyes gleamed with gratitude and relief. "I'm happy for you, too. You and Davis seem really great together."

"You—what?"

"Sam, you're so complicated," Teddy said gruffly. "You're impulsive and brilliant and sophisticated and sarcastic. There is so much *to* you, and I've never seen anyone who complemented all of that, who could *keep up* with you, until Marshall. You two make *sense* together. More sense than you and I ever did."

"I—thanks. That means a lot," Sam said awkwardly. She looked into Teddy's luminous blue eyes and added, "I'm really glad that Beatrice has you."

"I'm glad she has you, too."

They exchanged a complicit smile. In that moment, Sam knew that she and Teddy understood each other, because they shared one very important thing—they both loved Beatrice. Being the queen was a near-impossible job, but between the two of them, they might be able to support her through it.

"I realize this is painfully cliché, but do you think we could stay friends?" Teddy asked.

Friends. Sam didn't have many of those, at least, not friends she could trust. Certainly not friends who knew her as well as Teddy did. "I would love that."

She hesitated a moment, but given everything they'd been through, she figured she could hug Teddy. She started to pull him into an embrace. But before she could, he put his hands on her shoulders, and leaned forward to drop a single kiss on her brow.

There was nothing romantic in the gesture; it was decidedly old-fashioned, and sweet. As if Teddy was quietly acknowledging their messy history, and putting it behind him.

Sam felt all her grief and love and loss welling up in her. She blinked rapidly, trying not to cry. She had made so many mistakes, time and again—but at last everything was clicking into place, the way it was meant to all along.

"What the *hell?*"

Marshall stood in the doorway, looking at them in outraged horror.

Sam and Teddy sprang apart as if scalded. Which, she realized, probably made them look even guiltier.

"Marshall—let me explain," she pleaded, taking a step toward him. He recoiled, and Sam fell back, wounded.

Teddy held out his hands in a placating gesture. "Look, it's not what you think—"

"So *this* is who you've been using me to make jealous," Marshall cut in, his eyes on Sam. "When you told me that your mystery guy was taken, I never thought you meant he was *marrying your sister.*"

Teddy was still talking in a low, urgent tone, explaining that this was all a misunderstanding, that he and Sam were just friends. But Sam's eyes must have betrayed her, because Marshall retreated another step.

"I assume this is why you wanted me as your date? It was all a last-ditch attempt to make Eaton here jealous?" He barked out a sharp, defensive laugh. "What did you think he would do, call off the royal wedding?"

"No, I—I never wanted—" Sam stammered, but Marshall was already gone.

She stumbled into the hallway and saw that he'd taken off in the direction of the throne room.

"Marshall!" she cried out. He heard her, and started walking even faster.

It was so stupid, so completely immature of them to be racing through the palace like a pair of shrieking children. Sam kept shouting for Marshall to please just talk to her, but he broke into a jog, refusing to turn around.

She yanked the skirts of her gown as high as she could, now hurtling down the hallway in a full-out sprint, fighting to stay steady in her satin pumps. Stunned footmen and staff flung themselves out of her path. Sam ground to a halt at the back stairs—had Marshall headed up to the second floor?

As she hesitated, a tall stranger turned the corner.

He walked with bold, tense strides, his shoulders stiff. Sam looked at him for a moment in puzzled confusion, only to remember who he was.

Connor Markham, Beatrice's former Guard.

She stiffened in a hot flush of panic. Oh god. Connor was here because *she* had found his wedding invitation in Beatrice's desk—and sent it.

Sam watched, her lips parting in horror, as Connor lifted a fist to knock at the entrance to the Brides' Room. The door swung open, and Robert Standish frowned up at him with disdain. "I'm sorry," he snapped, "but who are you?"

And then Beatrice, in a faint voice: "Connor?"

Sam edged closer, looking past Connor to her sister's face.

It was a naked storm of emotions. Agony, confusion, and, most tellingly, a bleak sort of uncertainty.

In the silence that followed, Sam realized what she had to do.

She took off running in the opposite direction.

37

BEATRICE

Connor was here.

Shock splintered through Beatrice with an almost physical impact, reverberating in her very bones. She tried to move, to *breathe*, but all she could do was stand there in the Brides' Room and look at him.

She was fully dressed for the wedding, a human mannequin at the center of yards of white fabric. The train of her gown curled around her like a great slumbering animal. A beautiful combination of veils cascaded over it all: the tulle one that her mother had worn and, beneath, a Chantilly lace that had been in the family since Queen Helga. The light caught in the tulle, glittering on the diamonds of her tiara.

"I'm Connor Markham," she was dimly aware of him saying. "I'm here to see Beatr—I mean, the queen."

Understanding sparked in Robert's eyes, and he shook his head. "Well, Connor Markham, Her Majesty can't see you right now. As you might be aware, she's about to walk down the aisle in *twenty minutes*."

"It's all right," Beatrice heard herself say.

She'd spoken numbly, as if in a trance. What else could she do? Now that Connor was here, she had to speak to him alone.

Connor and Robert both turned to look at her. "Robert," she clarified, "we need the room, please."

"Right *now?*" the chamberlain demanded.

Connor let out a low growl. And even though he was out of uniform—wearing a tux, and, unlike all his years as a Guard, not carrying a single weapon—he still looked broad and imposing, every line of his body radiating a fierce, coiled strength. Beatrice saw Robert wilt a little beneath that glare.

"You have two minutes." He pulled the door shut behind him, leaving Beatrice and Connor alone.

This room was already small, with the clothes rack along one wall, the makeup artist's table tucked into a corner. Now it felt even smaller. Connor seemed to take up more space than he should have, as if he'd dragged all their memories in here with him.

Connor was *here*, just a few feet away, standing there with military straightness, watching her. *Connor*, whose arms had held her, whose mouth had kissed her, whose hands had brushed away her tears when she'd learned that her father was dying.

Beatrice couldn't meet his gaze. Her eyes fell to his neck, where—below the starched white of his collar, if she unbuttoned it—she knew she would find the edge of his tattoo, a sweeping eagle that covered the planes of his chest.

She wanted to say how sorry she was, and how hard it had been, telling him to leave. She had daydreamed this moment a thousand times, and still she didn't know how the daydream ended, whether she told him to get out—or kissed him.

"What are you doing here?" she whispered.

"I was hoping you could tell me." At her confused look, Connor fumbled in the front pocket of his tuxedo jacket and withdrew a heavy piece of paper. His wedding invitation. It looked tattered and well traveled, its beveled edges worn down, as if Connor had kept it on his person since the day he'd received it. As if he'd pulled it out again and again to look at it, to check whether it was real.

Beatrice sucked in a panicked breath. She hadn't seen that invitation since the day she tucked it in her hidden desk drawer. She'd meant to lock it away, as firmly as she'd locked away her feelings for Connor; but clearly someone had found it, and mailed it.

"I wasn't going to come," Connor said urgently. "I have no desire to watch you marry someone else. But then I kept wondering why you invited me—and I worried that maybe you *wanted* me to come, that you needed someone to help you get out of all this."

Oh god. He thought Beatrice had personally invited him. Of course he did—how could he have known that his invitation was a matter of protocol, that she'd actually tried to *prevent* him from receiving it?

"Bee," Connor said helplessly. Hearing the nickname on his lips, the amount of history fused into that single syllable, nearly broke her. "I had to see you, just once," he explained. "To make sure that you're okay."

Of course I'm okay, she started to say, but for some reason the words froze in her throat. The bodice of her gown was pressing too sharply into her ribs. She'd thought she was okay, but that was before Connor appeared, unfairly dredging up feelings she'd thought were long buried.

It was too much, happening far too fast—

An angry, high-pitched siren blared through the room. The sound of it lifted the hair on Beatrice's arms.

It was the palace's emergency system, roaring to life.

Beatrice had heard that siren only once before, five years ago, when the palace engaged in a massive security overhaul. Their entire family had done a day of emergency training, learning how to untie themselves if their wrists were bound, how to drive a car backward at high speeds—Jeff especially had loved that one—and, most of all, how to react if the palace was under attack.

This alarm wasn't anything like the alarm that had gone off at last year's Queen's Ball, when someone had accidentally started a fire on the South Portico. This alarm meant a massive security breach. A gunman, or, more likely, a bomb.

Had someone meant to assassinate her at her *wedding*? And, oh god—where was her family? What about Teddy?

Beatrice watched, frozen in place, as Connor's years of training kicked in. He whirled about, his fists raised, his back to Beatrice. He wasn't her Guard anymore, yet here he was, still trying to protect her.

"Connor!" she shouted, finally finding her voice. She stumbled forward, her heels catching in the enormous length of her train.

She saw Connor's gaze whipping around the room, searching for something that might serve as a weapon. The thought was almost funny—what did he expect to do, fight off an assailant with an eyelash curler?—except that she knew Connor's body might well be the only thing between her and a bullet.

Even though he was no longer her Guard, he was ready to protect her life with his own.

Cursing, Beatrice grabbed great handfuls of her skirts and shoved them impatiently aside. She'd thought she loved this dress, but now it was just an impediment slowing her down. She needed to hurry, needed to get out—

A steel-lined security panel shot out of the doorway's top molding. It slammed down into the floor, sealing them in.

38

DAPHNE

Daphne clasped her hands demurely in her lap, trying not to look too pleased with herself.

She'd felt the envy of the other guests as the usher led her all the way to the front of the room. Daphne was seated in the sixth row, next to Lord Marshall Davis—of course, they couldn't actually sit *with* the royal family until they married into it. Her parents, meanwhile, were all the way back in the nosebleed section with the other low-ranking royals.

Behind her, the throne room was a vibrant sea of color. A royal wedding, like a coronation or the opening ceremonies of Congress, was one of the few moments in which the peerage could wear their coronets and robes of rank. When they'd left for the wedding, Rebecca Deighton had been dressed in all the insignia she was entitled to as wife of a baronet; which, unfortunately, wasn't much. Just a six-rayed coronet—done in silver gilt, not gold like a duchess's—and a cloak with one yard of train, its ermine edging limited to the prescribed two inches. Each additional rank, of course, merited an additional inch of trim.

At court, these were things of crucial importance.

For an instant Daphne seemed to almost stand outside herself, to marvel at the absurdity of it all—but then she remembered who she was, what she had done to reach this point, and her vision cleared.

She skimmed her hands over her gown: a crimson one with a sinuous trumpet silhouette and gold-stitched roses that traced down the left side of her body. She stood out like a living cinder. Or, more accurately, a torch.

Daphne was aware that most people said redheads should never wear red, but those people had clearly never seen *her*. The dress had a richer, more purple glow than the fiery red-gold of her hair. Besides, red was the color of power, and Daphne needed all the power she could get right now.

By the end of today, she was determined that she and Jefferson would be back together, officially.

Her gaze drifted forward, to the breathtaking jewels and crowns that gleamed in the rows before her, where the foreign royalty were all seated. Daphne had never seen so many heads of state in a single room. She glanced from the Duke of Cambridge to his wife, who was pregnant with their fourth child, yet managed to look as coolly chic as ever in a high-necked maternity gown. The eighty-four-year-old German king had come here in person, rather than sending his children to represent him: a singular honor, but he'd had a soft spot for Beatrice ever since she lived at Potsdam for a summer, studying German. Behind him sat the Italian and Spanish princesses, who, incidentally, were both named Maria. And finally, there was Tsar Dmitri and his wife, the Tsarina Anastasia: Aunt Zia, Jefferson had always called her, though really she was his fifth cousin twice removed. The Romanovs' famous pink-diamond tiara glittered ostentatiously on her head.

Daphne sat up straighter, flashing her brightest, most social smile—only to freeze as a siren blared into the throne room.

For a split second, everyone was too stunned to react.

No one coughed or rustled their skirts or squeaked their shoes on the floor; no one even seemed to breathe. The only movement was the gentle swaying of the ostrich feather that the Grand Duchess Xenia wore in her hair.

Daphne had been afraid plenty of times in her life. Afraid of Himari, afraid of public shame, afraid of her own mother. But the fear that now sliced into her chest was somehow sharper and more visceral than any she'd felt before.

Her mind distilled down to a single, panicked thought: *Ethan. Was he hurt was he okay what had happened where was he?*

Bulletproof panels slid over the doors to seal the exits. And then the silence broke.

Security guards lunged forward, forming a protective phalanx around the guests. Private bodyguards were sprinting toward the various foreign royals, their movements quick and dangerously precise. The room dissolved into a swirling riot of sequins and diamonds and ragged shouts.

One of the guards fought to be heard above the turmoil, begging everyone to stay calm and remain in their seats, but no one was listening. People hurtled down the aisles in search of friends, tripping over the hems of their gowns, overturning chairs in their haste.

Daphne climbed up onto her chair, for once not caring whether she seemed elegant or princess-like. Shock had broken her perfect veneer and her anxious, pent-up self was pushing through. She craned her neck, scouring the crowds for any sign of Ethan, who was probably far in the back.

When she spotted him, she let out a throaty gasp. He was standing next to *Nina*, her hand gripped tightly in his.

Daphne scrambled down from her chair, yanking up her skirts as she started into the crowds. Muttering breathless apologies, she pushed through the dukes and marquesses and earls, all the way to the lower-ranking peers, trying desperately to avoid her parents. These were all familiar faces, yet they blurred senselessly together in Daphne's brain.

At last, there he was—standing to one side of the room, mercifully alone. Knowing Nina, she'd probably run off to find her parents.

Daphne plowed through the intervening courtiers as if they were so many blades of grass.

"Ethan," she breathed, when she'd reached him. She just barely restrained herself from reaching for his arm.

"Sorry, I don't know where Jeff is," he said curtly.

"I need to talk to *you*. It's important."

"Can it wait?" he demanded, with a touch of his usual sarcasm. "As you may have noticed, we're in a bit of a situation."

"Ethan—*please*."

Something flickered behind Ethan's dark eyes, but his expression was as inscrutable as ever. "All right."

Before he could refuse, Daphne grabbed his sleeve and pulled him along the edge of the room, past the earls and marquesses and dukes she'd just elbowed her way through. Past stone-faced security guards, men tapping frantically on their phones, women in billowing gowns.

Normally Daphne would have worried about being with Ethan like this, in such a public place. Yet normality had crumbled to pieces around her. She felt like she was no longer Daphne Deighton at all, but someone else entirely.

Or maybe this *was* the real Daphne Deighton, and the other one—the polite, impeccable Daphne she'd invented for the press—had shattered, revealing the yearning and anxious girl underneath.

Behind the raised dais that held the thrones, the vaulted space was transected by small side rooms. Candles glowed with long tongues of flame, the same flickering red-gold as Daphne's hair.

She tugged Ethan into a side chapel, where rows of triangular pennants hung from the ceiling. Each was a different color, and stitched with a coat of arms, one for each of the current Knights and Peers of the Realm. The more recent additions—men and women King George had invested with knighthoods at last year's Queen's Ball—were toward the front, while the older peers were at the back, their flags faded with age. When a peer died, their pennant was removed from the throne room so that they could be buried with it.

"What do you want?" Ethan asked warily, his arms crossed.

Already the atmosphere in the ballroom was shifting. Now that the initial moment of fear had passed, people were talking in less hysterical tones: exchanging theories about what had happened, debating whether security had caught the culprit, wondering what the media would say about all this.

"I had to tell you something, and it couldn't wait. I . . ." She hesitated, but all her years of artifice and subterfuge had melted away, and for once the truth fell bluntly from her bright red lips. "I want to be with you."

Ethan barked out a laugh. "Don't be ridiculous. You want to be with *Jeff*. You've spent the last four years chasing him, remember? Speaking of which," he added carelessly, "let me be the first to congratulate you on getting back together. You'll make a fantastic princess."

Daphne flushed. She should have known that Ethan wouldn't make it easy on her, that he would be difficult and sardonic and out of reach.

"I don't *want* Jeff." She looked up at Ethan through her lashes, a hot soft glow in her eyes. "Remember at the museum gala, how you said you couldn't keep waiting around for me? I'm saying that you don't have to wait anymore."

Ethan held her gaze for a moment, then blew out a breath and looked away. "I think I'll pass, thanks."

"Ethan, I *love* you."

What a relief it was to speak the words aloud. Daphne took a step forward, to reach for his hand and interlace their fingers.

Of course she loved him. Ethan, the only person who understood her—who knew what she had done and why she had done it and had remained her ally, her *friend*, in spite of it all.

For years Daphne had taken his support for granted. Countless times she had leaned on him, as easily as she might lean against a wall to catch her breath, before striding out to face the world. She'd let her pride fool her into thinking that her strength came from herself alone, when this entire time she'd had Ethan at her back.

Hadn't some part of her always known that she loved him? But she had shoved that knowledge down deep, because she'd been so intently focused on Jefferson. Because Jefferson had the titles and status, and she'd thought that was what she wanted.

"I won't pretend that I didn't spend years wishing you would say this," Ethan told her at last, pulling his hand from hers. "Daphne, you may not remember the day we met, but *I* do. It was at Sam and Jeff's party over winter break, my sophomore year.

"I had no idea who you were until I saw you that night. You were talking to a group, and damn if you didn't name-drop a Renaissance painter and a fashion magazine in the same breath." His mouth lifted in a ghost of the old smile. "The other girls at court just chase whatever trend the internet tells them to. But I saw at once that you were different. That you actually thought for *yourself*—and that your thoughts were wasted on that crowd." He shook his head at the memory. "I think I fell in love with you then and there."

Daphne held her breath, her every nerve afire with eagerness.

"Later that night, I saw you with Jeff. You dropped a sparkler on the ground and pretended to need his help stamping it out," Ethan went on. "He believed your damsel-in-distress act, but I could tell exactly why you'd done it. It killed me a little, knowing how ruthlessly smart you were, and that you were going to use it all to try to get *him*. Just like every other girl we know," he said darkly. "I wasn't surprised when you and Jeff got together soon afterward. He would have been a fool *not* to go out with you."

There was a sudden raw stinging in her throat; Daphne swallowed. "Ethan—"

"A terrible, jealous part of me wanted to hate him for dating you. But not as much as I hated myself for feeling this way." Ethan sighed. "At first I tried to stay away from you, avoid parties or trips where I knew you'd be. But that was torture, too. I didn't know what was worse, being around you while you were with Jeff, or not being around you at all."

It seemed to Daphne that the pennants of the chapel lifted and fell a little, almost as if they were sighing. The candles flickered but didn't go out.

"I loved you, god help me, and I knew better than to let you ever find out. So I tried to forget you," Ethan said brutally. "I told myself that you and Jeff were happy together. I *wanted* you to be happy, no matter how much it hurt me. Even if I suspected that you didn't really love Jeff, I told myself I had no right to interfere.

"But at Himari's birthday party, when you told me how upset and hurt you felt—what it cost you, being with Jeff— I broke all my promises to myself. I couldn't *not* fight for you, Daphne," he said heavily. "I didn't even feel all that guilty about it. I had loved you for so long that it made it impossible to regret sleeping with you. No matter how wrong it was."

Daphne's heart fluttered in her chest. She'd endured the same confusion: knowing that she *should* feel terrible, yet not being able to muster up more than a shred of guilt.

"When you wanted to meet up afterward, I had this absurd hope that you might have changed your mind about us. I think if you had given me the slightest sign, if you'd taken even a single step toward me, I would have blurted out that I loved you." He shook his head. "Of course, the only reason you wanted to meet was to cover up what we'd done."

"But you didn't say anything!"

"You think it would have changed things?" Ethan asked flatly. "You're so cruel to the people who love you, Daphne. You use their love to serve your own purposes, hold it over their heads like a weapon. You are selfish, and I have always known that. But I used to imagine that someday you might love me, too, and turn that selfishness outward. That you would be selfish for *us*, instead of for yourself."

Her and Ethan, facing the world, together. It was what Daphne had always wanted, if only she'd let herself realize it.

"I *know* you, Daphne, in a way that Jeff could never know you—and if he did know, he would leave you in an instant. Whereas I loved every last part of you: your ambition and your inner fire and your utter brilliance. We could have been so happy together, if you'd ever given us half a chance."

"We can be happy *now*," Daphne protested, but Ethan hardly seemed to hear.

"At the museum, when you suggested this ridiculous bargain, I agreed to it. It was never really about the title—not that I don't want one," he said helplessly. "But, Daphne, I put my heart out there and you flat-out rejected it. Then, to add insult to injury, you asked me to date *someone else*. You made me a pawn in your master plan, just like always.

"So I decided that I would punish you by doing what you thought you wanted." He gave a wry, bitter smile. "I guess I hoped that once you heard that I'd been spending so much time with Nina—because I knew you'd find out; you always know everything that happens in this town—you'd start to feel jealous, and realize that it wasn't what you wanted at all."

"But, Ethan, I *have* realized!" Daphne cried out. "I wish it hadn't taken me so long to see. I was just . . . blinded by things that don't matter."

"Yeah. You were."

Light slanted through the flags of knighthood, making his profile stand out as clearly as on the head of an ancient coin: handsome and prideful and resolute.

He wasn't making this easy on her, but she deserved it, after everything she'd put him through. If he wanted her to beg, then Daphne would do it, and gladly.

"I'm so sorry, but I'll make it all up to you," she swore. "Don't you see—Ethan, *look* at me!—things will be different, now that we finally know how we feel!"

"*Felt*," Ethan corrected. "You had my heart for *years*, and you kept on treating it thoughtlessly."

"I'm *sorry!*"

"It's too late for sorry."

Daphne's hands darted up to grab Ethan by the shoulders. "I love you, okay?" She tightened her grip, her voice hard and furious. "And you just said that you loved me!"

"I *did* love you, for a long time. But even I couldn't sit around waiting for you forever."

He spoke impersonally, as if that love were an emotion that someone else had felt, a very long time ago.

No. Daphne refused to accept that his love for her had just . . . faded away. That it had guttered and burned itself out like one of these forgotten candles. No, if he had loved her that much then there must be *something* left, some ember of feeling that she could coax back to life. Unless . . .

"You fell for her, didn't you." She couldn't bear to actually say Nina's name.

"I did."

Daphne's hands fell to her sides as she stepped back, fighting the urge to stamp her foot like a child. How had the only two men in her life both ended up with the same mousy, unexceptional commoner? "That girl is painfully boring, has no sense of style—and has nothing at all to say for herself—"

"She has plenty to say; you've just never bothered to listen—"

"If you loved me the way you say you did, for as long as you say you did, how can you possibly care about *Nina*?" she hissed.

Ethan didn't blink. "If you wanted Jeff for as long as you claimed to, how can you possibly care about me?"

A strained silence fell between them. Daphne's pulse echoed dully through her veins. She almost wished that Ethan resented her, *hated* her, even. Anything would be better than this smooth, cool indifference.

And yet she loved him in spite of everything: all her flaws, his betrayal, both of their stubborn prides.

Ethan was right; he was the only person who'd ever truly known her, aside from Himari. And now that he'd pushed her away, it was the *real* Daphne he was rejecting.

To think that she'd come to the wedding in triumph, on Jefferson's arm, only to realize in a panicked flash that *Ethan* was the one she'd wanted all along. And now, somehow, he no longer cared.

She felt that she had gained and lost the world in a single morning.

"Well then, it seems like we're done here." Daphne pivoted on one heel and stormed off, blinking back her stupid, traitorous tears.

She'd always thought there was such power in knowing other people's secrets. At court, secrets were even better than money: you could hoard them and guard them and barter them away. But for what?

What did any of it matter when the entire time, she'd been keeping the greatest secret of all from herself—only to discover the truth when it was too late.

BEATRICE

Beatrice's skirts frothed up around her like lace-stitched clouds, probably creasing in countless places, but it didn't stop her from pounding at the door.

"Beatrice, don't," Connor pleaded.

She ignored him, though she knew she looked utterly absurd: standing here in her wedding gown, slamming her fists against the reinforced steel. But that alarm had sent her careening past all rational thought. All she wanted was to get *out*.

Connor stepped forward and caught her hands in his, circling her wrists as he gently lowered them. "It won't do any good, Bee. That door can't open until a full sweep of the palace has confirmed that it's safe."

Beatrice tugged at her hands. Chastened, Connor let go of them, but he didn't step away.

His face was much too close. She could see each individual freckle and eyelash, could hear each shallow breath as it escaped his lungs. He was so familiar, yet at the same time he felt oddly like a stranger, like a shadowy figure from her dreams.

Except that he wasn't a dream at all. He was *here*, real and flesh and immediate. Alone with her in a sealed room.

Beatrice backed away a few steps, and the panic flooding through her stilled a little. Without it she felt curiously uncertain, as if that frantic terror had been holding her aloft, and now that it had ebbed she had no clue what to do. The blaring of the alarm had stopped, but Beatrice imagined she could still hear it, echoing beneath the silence.

"Can you find out what happened?" she asked.

Connor's hands drifted to his waist, then hooked uselessly in his pockets. "I don't have my ERD anymore," he said, naming the encrypted radio used by palace security. "But don't worry; I won't let anyone hurt you."

Beatrice nodded slowly. Her fear had thrown all her senses into confusion; she had no idea how long it had been since the alarm went off.

"You didn't wear your Guards' uniform," she observed softly.

"I wasn't sure I was allowed to wear it, now that I've left."

Beatrice heard the lie in his voice. Connor knew perfectly well that he could wear the dress uniform at state occasions for the rest of his life.

Her eyes traveled again to his tuxedo. It fit perfectly—he'd clearly had it tailored—but the fabric was stiff in the way that new clothes always are, when they haven't yet molded to your body. Beatrice wondered with a pang if Connor had bought the tux specifically for this wedding—if he'd decided against wearing his Guards' uniform because he didn't want to look like a member of security, but instead like a young aristocrat.

Like all the young men her parents had included in her folder of options, the night they'd asked her to consider getting married, what felt like a lifetime ago.

"Connor—where have you been? I mean, what did you do, after . . ."

"I went to Houston. I'm chief of security for the Ramirez family."

"Chief of security for the Duke and Duchess of Texas? That's impressive."

"They know I used to personally Guard the queen."

Beatrice looked away, at the folding makeup table with its brushes and lipsticks laid out on a white hand towel. "I'm glad you're doing so well. Congratulations."

"Damn it, Bee, don't use your cocktail-party voice with me."

Beatrice's mind knew that he was no longer hers, but her body seemed to have reverted to an instinctive muscle memory and couldn't keep up. She fought back an urge to step forward and hold him, the way she used to.

Instead she hugged her arms around her torso. Her dress felt so heavy: all that stiff boning, all the layers upon layers of weighty embroidered silk.

Connor was next to her in a few steps. "Bee, listen—"

She looked up sharply, her vision blurring. "I can't do this right now—"

"But right now is the only time we've *got!*" His gray eyes burned into hers. "When I came here today, all I wanted was to see you one last time, to make sure you're happy. I never meant to say any of this. But here we are, and I'll probably never get another chance to be alone with you. Maybe I'm selfish, but I can't *not* tell you that I love you. Which you already know."

Connor leaned closer. There was an instant when Beatrice knew what was coming yet felt powerless to pull away, as if her mind hadn't yet regained control of her bewildered limbs.

He settled a hand on her shoulder, the other tipping her chin to turn her face up to his. Finally Beatrice seemed to snap back into herself. She opened her mouth in protest— and Connor, seeing her parted lips, leaned in to kiss her.

She didn't resist. It felt so powerfully familiar, because she had *been* here before, so many times: folded in Connor's arms, surrounded by his tensed strength. The sheer Connor-ness of him overwhelmed her senses.

It was as if that kiss had slipped her back in time, to before she lost her dad—back when she wasn't a queen, but simply a girl in love with the wrong boy.

Then reality crashed back in and she pulled away, her breathing unsteady.

A single tear slid down her cheek. Seeing it, Connor lifted a hand. His fingers were callused, yet he brushed away her tear with painstaking gentleness.

"Run away with me, Beatrice. Let me help you get out," he said fervently. "Let me save you from all of this."

It was precisely what Beatrice had threatened to do the night before her father died: to run off with Connor, abandoning all her responsibilities. And yet . . .

Let me save you. Connor didn't understand that Beatrice no longer needed rescuing. She hadn't been forced; she wasn't trapped. If she'd wanted to escape being queen, the only person who could have saved her was herself.

"I'm sorry," she whispered.

"So that's it? You're going to get married, just because you think it's part of your *job* description?"

Her heart broke at how fundamentally he'd misunderstood, and she bit her lip, searching for the words to explain.

Back when Connor had been her Guard, she'd *accepted* that she would someday be queen. Now she *chose* it. Some people might not understand the distinction, but Beatrice knew it made all the difference in the world.

A destiny was something that happened *to* you, that fell upon you like rain no matter how desperately you tried to hide from it. But if you walked toward it with your head held high, then it wasn't your fate—it was simply your future.

Beatrice looked into Connor's eyes and said the only three words that would make him listen.

"I love Teddy."

For a moment she thought he hadn't heard her. Connor's eyes closed, and when he opened them again, they glinted like newly forged steel. "You can't."

She placed her hand, with its glittering engagement ring, over his. "I loved you so much, Connor. Some part of me will always love you." She thought of last night with Teddy, of everything she was still discovering about herself. Her feelings for Teddy might have been the greatest discovery of all. "But now . . . I'm in love with Teddy."

Beatrice had come to understand that the human heart was a magical thing. It had so much room inside it, enough room to contain more than one love over the course of a lifetime.

Connor and Teddy had each given their hearts into her safekeeping. Beatrice imagined she could feel the weight of them in her hands—they were smooth like bird's eggs, like the massive rubies down in the Crown Jewels vault, and infinitely more precious.

It wasn't right of her to keep Connor's heart any longer, not when he didn't have hers.

Connor stared down at their clasped hands. "I don't understand what changed."

"*I* changed. I'm not that girl anymore, the princess who fell in love with her Guard. I'm queen now."

That girl had been lonely, and naïve about so many things. More than anything, she'd been desperate for someone to understand her.

But that girl had died that day at the hospital when the flag sank to half-mast and she realized that she'd spoken to her father for the last time.

"Beatrice—that's exactly my point. You're only with Teddy because you're the queen! If you hadn't been forced into this role, we would still be together."

If her dad hadn't died, *if* she hadn't become the queen, *if*

Connor hadn't left, giving her the time and space to fall for Teddy. If, if, if. It frightened Beatrice a little, that the world was built on so many small *ifs* that decided people's fates.

No, she thought intently, that wasn't true. From now on, Beatrice would choose her own fate.

"I know you've been through a lot this year, and it's changed you," Connor added, his voice breaking. "But can't we find our way back to each other?"

Beatrice shook her head, looking up at him through wet lashes. It had been a long, hard road out of the dark haze of her grief, and she still wasn't entirely free of the shadows. Maybe she never would be. But the only way she'd managed to make it this far was because she'd been leaning on Teddy, and now Samantha, drawing from their seemingly bottomless pool of strength.

She couldn't go back the way she'd come. Certainly she couldn't go back to being the girl she had been, when she was in love with Connor.

He loved her—Beatrice could never doubt that—but he'd never truly understood her, not entirely. Connor's instinct would always be to protect her: with his life, if it came down to it.

Except Beatrice was no longer a girl who needed protecting. Connor wanted to charge in like a knight in shining armor, offering to rescue her. Whereas Teddy gave her the confidence to rescue herself.

"I'm sorry," she whispered. "But I really do love him."

She watched Connor's breathing slow as understanding settled in, his eyes brimming with pain. She still hadn't let go of his hand.

There were no windows in here, not even a clock. It was as if they'd escaped to some pocket of time outside time itself: as if the universe had ground to a halt, so that they could finally say what they needed.

"Teddy—he's good to you?" Connor asked, and she sensed the words were costing him more than she would ever know. "He really deserves you?"

There was no coherent way for Beatrice to answer that, so she nodded.

"I figured. You couldn't have fallen for him otherwise." Connor attempted something like a smile, but it came out lopsided and wrong, or maybe it just looked that way through Beatrice's tears. "I'm happy for you," he said gruffly.

"You don't have to say that," she insisted. "I mean—I'll understand, if you hate me."

"I could never hate you, Bee. I just . . . I miss you." There was no reproach in Connor's words, only a weary, unflinching truth.

"I miss you, too," she said, and meant it.

Beatrice's tears were coming more freely now, but that wasn't surprising. Nothing in life hurt more than hurting the people you loved. Yet Beatrice knew she had to say all of this.

She and Connor had loved each other too fiercely for her to let him go without a proper goodbye.

"I am . . . forever changed by you," she added, her voice catching. "I gave you part of my heart a long time ago, and I've never gotten it back."

"You don't need it back." His voice was rough with unshed tears. "I swear that I'll keep it safe. Everywhere I go, that part of you will come with me, and I will guard and treasure it. Always."

A sob escaped her chest. She hurt for Connor and with Connor and because of Connor, all at once.

This wasn't how breakups were meant to go. In the movies they always seemed so hateful, with people yelling and throwing things at each other. They weren't meant to be like this, tender and gentle and full of heartache.

"Okay," she replied, through her tears. "That part of my heart is yours to keep."

Connor stepped back, loosening his hand from hers, and Beatrice felt the thread between them pull taut and finally snap. She imagined that she could hear it—a crisp sort of sound, like the stem of a rose being snapped in two.

Her body felt strangely sore, or maybe it was her heart that felt sore, recognizing the parts of it that she had given away, forever.

"You're such an amazing person, Connor. I hope you find someone who deserves you."

Again he attempted a crooked smile. "It won't be easy on her, trying to live up to the queen. For a small person, you cast quite the shadow," he said, and then his features grew serious once more. "Bee—if you ever need me, I'll be there for you. You know that, right?"

She swallowed against a lump in her throat. "The same promise holds for me, too. I'm always here if you need me."

As she spoke, the steel panel began to lift back into the ceiling.

Beatrice straightened her shoulders beneath the cool silk of the gown, drew in a breath. Somehow she managed to gather up the tattered shreds of her self-control, as if she wasn't a young woman who'd just said goodbye to her first love—to her best friend.

As if she wasn't a young woman at all, but a queen.

40

NINA

The steel-reinforced doors lifted without a whisper of a sound.

They seemed so heavy that they should have groaned and creaked, like the portcullis of a medieval drawbridge being raised in battle. Yet Nina heard nothing except a low, hissing silence.

A Revere Guard appeared in the doorway. When he lifted his hand, the gossip rumbling through the room was abruptly cut off.

"The palace is secure; there's no need to panic," he began—but his next words were drowned out by a stampede of footsteps.

The guests cried out breathless questions: where was the threat, what about the royal wedding, were they free to leave. The Guard seemed helpless to stop the sea of frightened people rushing past him and out into the hallway.

Nina realized that she was still clutching tight to her mom's hand, and quickly let go. "You all right, sweetie?" Julie asked, glancing over.

Nina's mamá, standing on her other side, rested a hand on her daughter's back in silent reassurance.

"I'm all right." Nina plucked nervously at her gown. Why wasn't there any circulation in here? There were too many people, crowding the room with their shrill complaints. Nina hadn't seen Ethan since she'd left to find her parents; she wondered if he was still toward the back of the room. And where was Sam? The Guard had said the palace was secure—that meant the royal family was all safe, right?

"Sorry, I just need some space," Nina muttered. Her parents nodded in understanding as she joined the flood of people headed out the ballroom's main doors.

She jostled blindly down the hallway, past oil portraits and carved side tables and iron sconces, past Guards and footmen who spoke in low tones, too preoccupied to worry about her. Finally, a few doors down, Nina turned in to an empty sitting room. She collapsed onto a couch, slumping forward and closing her eyes. At least now she could breathe.

"Oh. It's you."

At the sound of that voice, Nina went hot and prickly all over.

"Excuse me." She hurried to stand, but Daphne had planted herself before the door like a human barrier. A strange series of expressions darted over her face: surprise and dismay rapidly giving way to a hungry, avid sort of calculation.

Nina knew that look didn't bode well for her.

"Don't run off just yet. There's something we need to talk about." Daphne smiled like a lion, bold and beautiful and utterly deadly. It shattered what remained of Nina's self-control.

"I already did what you asked, and broke up with Jeff! You're here as his date, Daphne. *You won*," she said acridly. "Can't you just leave me *alone*?"

Daphne made a show of stepping aside. Her smile never faltered, but it became, oddly, more relieved. As if Daphne was secretly thrilled to speak openly, without any pretense at being the polite, well-mannered Daphne Deighton that the world knew and loved.

It struck Nina as oddly pitiful, that she was perhaps the only person with whom Daphne could be herself.

"Of course I'll leave you alone," Daphne sniffed. "I can

assure you that this isn't pleasant for me, either. I just felt like I should warn you, from one woman to another, about Ethan."

Nina wasn't sure how Daphne knew about her and Ethan—whether Jeff had told her, or whether Daphne had seen them holding hands in the throne room. She found that she didn't especially care.

"It's none of your business," she tried to reply, as calmly as she could.

"But aren't you afraid of what will happen once everyone finds out?" Daphne made a clucking, concerned sound. "Nina, for a girl who claims to hate the spotlight, you somehow keep finding it over and over again. America isn't going to be very kind to you, once they learn you've left Jefferson for his *best friend*."

Nina itched to slap her smug, perfect face. How did Daphne always seem to zero in on her greatest fears?

"I'm not stupid. I know it won't be easy," she replied, with more bravado than she felt. "But Ethan is worth it. We have something real."

Daphne gave a sharp laugh. "You fool. *I'm* the one who told Ethan to go out with you."

Silence scraped at Nina's eardrums. She couldn't hear anything anymore: not the muffled sounds of footsteps, not the security guards speaking into walkie-talkies. It had all receded behind a wall of shock.

"Ethan only ever started dating you because of me." Each of Daphne's words was like the sting of a lash, like a knife digging into Nina's side. "You see, I was worried that Jefferson still cared about you. I realized that I would never get him back if you were still an option. So I asked Ethan if he would keep tabs on you."

"You're lying." Nina's reply was automatic.

Daphne rolled her eyes. "I orchestrated the entire thing. I

told Ethan everything I'd learned about you, from your weird M&M obsession to the fact that you love Venice. I wanted him to flirt with you a little, and he did exactly what I said."

Nina's heart lurched with a sick sense of betrayal as she recalled the pleasant glow of surprise she'd felt when Ethan had noticed those things. She'd thought he was so observant, that they were *compatible*.

She'd never really questioned why, after they'd lived on the same campus for months without seeing each other, he'd suddenly shown up in her journalism class and asked to be partners. Had he been following Daphne's orders the entire time?

At the hurt look on Nina's face, Daphne smiled. "Well. It's nice to know he made use of all my intel."

Some stubborn part of Nina refused to back down. "Ethan wouldn't do that to me. He's nothing like you."

"You have no *idea* what Ethan is really like."

Nina's stomach plummeted as she remembered what Ethan had said, just this morning: *My reasons for hanging out with you, earlier this year, were totally messed up.* And that night at the twins' party: *You shouldn't want to be with me. . . . If you only knew.*

Daphne cast her a withering glance. "Don't you see, Nina? Ethan loves *me*, not you. He dated you when I told him to, because he loves me. He's kept secrets so dark you couldn't begin to imagine them—covered up things that would make your blood run cold—because he loves me." Daphne spoke with a terrifying calm. "Whatever you think of me, that I use people and manipulate the tabloids, then you have to think the same about Ethan. He and I are cut from the same cloth."

Manipulate the tabloids. Nina drew in a breath. "You told that reporter about me and Ethan, didn't you? The one who called Jeff?"

"Of course," Daphne said, smirking. "Don't you get it by now? I'm behind *everything.*"

What a fool Nina had been, thinking she could escape. No matter how much Daphne took from her, no matter that Nina had broken up with Jeff, it would never be enough. Daphne had meant what she'd said at Beatrice's engagement party: she would always be one step ahead of Nina, making her life a living hell.

But why did Daphne even care what she did anymore? She wasn't a threat; she was with Ethan now.

Nina sucked in a breath as comprehension dawned. "Oh my god. *You're* in love with Ethan, aren't you?"

Daphne gritted her teeth but didn't answer, which was how Nina knew it was true.

"You've always loved him," she went on, threading the pieces together. "But you wouldn't date him, because you wanted to be a princess more than anything else. Even more than you wanted Ethan."

"You have no idea what you're talking about," the other girl spat. "You don't know me at all."

Nina took in Daphne, the absolute desperation of her ambition, and again felt that disgusted, hollow sort of pity.

"I feel sorry for you," she declared. How could anyone give up a person they actually loved, to mold their entire life around someone they didn't?

"*You* feel sorry for *me*? Who do you think you are?"

"Who do I think I am?" The sheer condescension of Daphne's question made Nina stand up straighter. "I don't have to think about it at all, because I *know* who I am! Unlike you, I am proud of where I came from, of the brilliant, hardworking parents who raised me. They may not have a title, which clearly means everything to you, but you know what? We don't care."

Nina took a step forward to underscore her point, and felt a grim satisfaction when Daphne flinched.

"We don't fixate on how long our ceremonial capes are, or how high we fall in the list of the peerage," she went on fiercely. "We care about the things that matter—integrity, honesty, kindness. We don't look at other people and automatically think of them as our competition; we think of them as our *friends*."

Nina was so deeply tired of court, with its layers of pointless and archaic protocol, its titles and precedence, its utter lack of loyalty.

"You know what, Daphne? You win. You can have all of it—Jeff, Ethan, the titles and tiaras. I don't *care*. Enjoy living inside this gilded cage, being scrutinized and picked apart by every person on the planet. None of it will make you happy, since none of it will be *real*."

Her eyes glinted with defiance as she moved to the door, then turned to deliver one last parting shot.

"No matter what you do, no matter how high you climb, you'll never have anyone to share it with," Nina said coldly. "You'll be completely alone."

41

SAMANTHA

Samantha had never been any good at waiting. But for once she was sitting as patiently as a princess should, one ankle tucked demurely behind the other the way Daphne had taught her. When security came, she wanted to greet them with some degree of dignity.

It had been a split-second decision. She'd seen the expression on Beatrice's face at Connor's arrival—a look of anguish, of agony—and felt a sickening wave of guilt.

She had done this, by mailing Connor's wedding invitation.

Sam didn't know what Beatrice would choose, but she felt certain of one thing—Beatrice needed *time*. Time to process the fact that Connor was here. Time to sort through the tangled knot of her feelings.

Before she could second-guess herself, Sam had sprinted up the stairs to Robert's office and set off the emergency alarm.

She couldn't have done this a year ago; only now that she was heir to the throne did she have the authority. The system still didn't make it easy on her: she had to scan her fingerprints *and* her eyes, and provide one of the emergency security codes that Robert had so irritatingly made her memorize.

At once, steel-reinforced doors had slammed down throughout the palace—doors that couldn't be lifted until security completed a thorough sweep of the property. Sam had done the impossible for Beatrice, and had made time stop.

Of course, the system had recorded her login; the security team would figure out soon enough that she was to blame. Until then, she would sit here in Robert's office, waiting for them.

Sam wondered what Marshall thought about all this. Had he made it to the throne room, or had the sirens gone off while he was still wandering the halls? Were things between them ruined forever, now that he'd seen that stupid moment with Teddy?

At the sound of footsteps in the hallway, Sam stood.

Robert Standish flung open the door. "*You*," he snarled. "Do you have any idea what you've done?"

"I'm sorry for all the confusion I caused," Sam said carefully. The chamberlain slammed his hand against the doorway, and she gave a startled jump.

"Why the *hell* did you set off that alarm, today of all days?"

Sam tilted her chin upward, stubborn until the end. "I had my reasons. What are you going to do, carry me out Traitor's Gate and send me off in exile?"

"I'm taking you to Her Majesty."

He reached out to grab Samantha's arm, but she recoiled. "I know how to walk," she said coolly.

Neither of them spoke as they marched down the staircase and along the main front hallway.

All around them the great machinery of the palace was groaning back to life. Footmen and security guards brushed past, their eyes burning with curiosity when they saw the chamberlain with the princess. Even the historical figures in the oil portraits seemed to be staring. In the ballroom a string quartet were arguing in low tones; the violinist was gesturing rapidly with his bow, underscoring each word with a flourish.

Sam wondered what the musicians had thought when the doors closed, locking them in the ballroom alone.

As they turned the corner, Robert broke into an almost-jog. Sam hurried to keep up, though the narrow cut of her dress constricted her steps.

And there was Beatrice, standing at the entrance to the Brides' Room. She looked like the paper doll versions of herself that they sold at the palace gift shop: pale and crisp, as if her edges had been drawn with a very sharp pencil.

"What's going on?" she asked, gesturing them inside.

"It was a false alarm," Robert said tersely. Beatrice let out a relieved breath, but the chamberlain's eyes fixed meaningfully on Samantha. "Your *sister* set it off."

A beat of silence followed his proclamation: a sticky, strained silence that condensed between them like the sweat dampening Sam's back. Sam longed to close her eyes, but forced herself to hold her sister's gaze.

"I see," the queen said at last.

Robert blinked, evidently startled by the calm of her reply. "Your Majesty, the princess put the safety of thousands of people at risk—"

"Was anyone hurt?"

Sam had never before seen Beatrice like this, in such full, crackling command of her authority.

"Our reputation was hurt! All those guests were sent into an unnecessary panic—not to mention what the media will say when they learn that we halted your wedding without reason. Samantha knowingly engineered a false sense of alarm," he spluttered. "She needs to be punished!"

Beatrice looked from Samantha to Robert and back again. "You're right. Sam should be punished," the queen concluded, and Sam's chest seized. "But the punishment is mine to give."

"Your Majesty—"

331

"What happened today will stay between us. Robert, you'll make a statement explaining that we received a threat and had to halt the wedding, but that you won't be providing any details about the threat as a matter of national security. As for punishment . . ." Beatrice looked at Samantha, her expression unreadable. "Given that she interrupted my wedding, I will decide what my sister has to do as retribution."

Robert blinked. "With all due respect—"

"That is a direct order," Beatrice said smoothly.

It was clear from the set of Robert's jaw that he violently disagreed, but he acknowledged her statement with a stiff nod.

"Your Majesty, almost two hundred of your guests have already departed, including most of the foreign royalty," he went on. "No matter how much we reassure them, they claim that they no longer feel safe. The only one who *hasn't* already headed to his plane is the King of Germany, and that's because he apparently slept through the entire fiasco."

"Who needs foreign royals anyway?" Sam asked, as brightly as she could. "Don't we have a backup guest list? Or, wait—you could go grab two hundred people from the streets! Think of the PR opportunities!"

Robert closed his eyes and released a long-suffering breath, as if silently praying for strength.

"There's no need for any of that. We're postponing the wedding," Beatrice declared.

The Lord Chamberlain nodded. "Of course, but for how long? We could wait a few hours, or I suppose we could restage everything for tomorrow morning, if you'd rather start fresh."

The queen shook her head. "We're postponing indefinitely."

When Robert realized what she meant, his eyes narrowed. "Beatrice. I will *not* let you do this."

"May I remind you to address Her Majesty by her proper title," Sam chided, and he clenched his hands at his sides.

"What is your plan, *Your Majesty?*" he asked, sneering. "You're going to cancel an expensive, intricately planned, *global* event just because you're getting cold feet?"

Sam shot Beatrice a livid glance, desperate to interject, but Beatrice gave her head a tiny shake. And Sam realized that this was a battle her sister needed to fight for herself.

A battle that she'd needed to fight for months, but hadn't been confident enough to, until now.

"It might be a global event, but it's still my life," Beatrice said quietly.

Robert's face was mottled red with outrage. "If you fail to go through with this wedding, you will destroy your family's legacy. After everything the monarchy has done—"

"Excuse me, *everything the monarchy has done?*" Sam cut in. "What part of our legacy are you defending, Robert? The colonizing? The gross human rights violations my ancestors committed in the name of expansion and progress? *Slavery?*" She shook her head so emphatically that her earrings danced. "You can't possibly say that's all fine, but, oh no, if my sister postpones a wedding, it'll destroy the monarchy forever!"

"What could either of you know about legacy?" Robert's tone was blistering, all trace of politeness utterly gone. He narrowed his eyes at Beatrice. "You are just a girl sitting on a throne that is far too big for you, occupying shoes you can never hope to fill!"

Beatrice stood up straighter. "I am the head of state, not just a girl in a tiara!"

Robert laughed, but there was no mirth in it. "Beatrice, you *are* a girl in a tiara! That is precisely your job—to smile and do as you're told and *wear the tiara!* But if you persist in doing this, you won't have a tiara for very much longer. As your chamberlain, and the steward of your family's reputation, I cannot let you go through with it."

"About that," Beatrice replied, with a stubborn ferocity as palpable as heat. "You're dismissed. The Crown no longer has need of your assistance."

Sam gasped at her sister's pronouncement. Robert's brows furrowed in indignation. "You can't mean that."

"You're free to go pack up your things," Beatrice repeated. "I'll let the Undersecretary of the Household know that you're leaving."

"But—the wedding—"

"Is no longer your concern."

Robert's expression was ugly, and twisted with malice. "This country will never accept you ruling alone."

"No, *you* were the one who couldn't accept me ruling alone," Beatrice corrected. "I'm not sure what the country is going to think, but I'm willing to give them a chance."

Robert opened his mouth—but drew to a halt at something in the Washington women's expressions. "Very well, then. *Your Majesty.*" He spat her title with utter disdain and stormed out of the room, slamming the door behind him.

"Oh, Bee" was all Sam could say, as Beatrice threw her arms around her and held tight.

They stood like that for a while, clinging to each other with such force that Sam couldn't have said which of them was leaning on the other. Maybe they both were. That was what you did with family, wasn't it? You grabbed hold of them and didn't let go. You supported each other's weight, held each other up, even when you lacked the strength to stand on your own.

"How did you know to pull the alarm?" Beatrice's question was barely a whisper.

"I guessed, when I saw you and Connor." Sam pulled back a little, so she could look into her sister's face. "It's my fault that he came to the wedding. I'm the one who mailed his invitation."

She felt Beatrice stiffen.

"I went into your office to talk to you one day, and when you weren't there, I looked through your desk. Even the secret drawer that Dad used to hide candy in," Sam confessed. "That was how I figured out that you'd been seeing Connor. I found his invitation and I just—sent it," she said haltingly. "I'm so sorry."

Beatrice considered her sister's words for a long, drawn-out moment, and then she nodded. "Don't be sorry, Sam. I'm not."

She looked so painfully bridal right now. Her pair of veils fell in a cascade around her, the fine net of the tulle catching shadows like water. Yet she'd just called off the wedding of the century.

"So—are you and Connor back together?"

"I told him goodbye." Beatrice glanced down, running her palms over her ethereal shimmering skirts. "Of course, I wish his timing had been better," she went on, with something like humor. "But I can't be angry with Connor for fighting for me. We have so much history."

From the way she'd pronounced *history*, Sam knew that Beatrice saw Connor as a figure who belonged to her past, and not her future. But . . . hadn't she just called off her wedding to Teddy?

"I don't understand," Sam blurted out. "If you're not choosing Teddy, then aren't you choosing Connor?"

"I'm choosing *me*!"

When Beatrice turned, her eyes were lit up with a new, confident glow. Sam realized that in getting rid of Robert, Beatrice had shed a stifling and oppressive weight.

Now that she was free of him, she could step into her own power at last.

"I'm the queen. By definition, I'm different from the eleven kings who came before. But the moment I marry Teddy, I won't be that woman anymore."

"Even if you marry Teddy, you'll still be queen," Sam pointed out.

"I'll be a queen with a king consort. Not a queen ruling on her own." Beatrice sighed. "Dad always reminded me not to underestimate the power of symbolism. What kind of symbol would I be if the first thing I do as queen is get married?"

Her sister was right. There was little imagery as powerful as the Crown. And Beatrice, sitting on the throne, alone—that kind of image could make a real difference.

"Bee. You're a *rebel*," she said, with an incredulous smile.

Beatrice shook her head. "I fell for someone who was in Mom and Dad's binder of approved options. And, by the way, so did you," she added. "That's not especially rebellious."

Sam felt a pang of regret at the reference to Marshall. "It doesn't matter who Teddy is. What matters is that you're choosing *not* to marry him. You're a runaway bride! I can't wait for the made-for-TV adaptation of this," she went on, trying to coax a smile from her sister. "As long as it doesn't star Kelsey Brooke."

"Runaway bride." There was a note of fear in Beatrice's voice, as if she'd only just processed the full extent of her decision.

Sam reached for her sister's hand. "How can I help?"

"Actually . . . there is something you could do for me," Beatrice said slowly.

"Name it."

"Will you do the royal tour that Teddy and I were supposed to go on?"

Sam blinked. "You aren't going on your newlywed tour?"

"As much as I'd like to spend the summer traveling, I need to stay here for a while, figure out how to actually start *doing* my job." Beatrice's eyes were bright. "Besides, I think you're overdue for a royal tour, given that you're my heir."

"I doubt anyone really wants to meet with me," Sam began, but Beatrice shook her head.

"They do, Sam. You inspire people," she said urgently. "Not just because you're with Marshall—though it would be nice if our family looked more like the nation we're supposed to unify."

Sam bit her lip but couldn't bear to interrupt.

"The monarchy is over two centuries old, and I'm the *very first* woman to ever be in charge of it. The world keeps getting more diverse, but our family is changing at a snail's pace! We can't go on like this. If we want to survive into the next century, we're going to have to find a way to stay relevant," Beatrice insisted. "I need *you* to help forge our way forward. You're the one who realized that I should walk down the aisle alone. You're changing the way people view our family. You can see problems that I'm too removed to see."

Sam shifted her weight from one foot to the other, dazed. "Are you sure I'm ready? I never finished Robert's lessons."

Beatrice rolled her eyes. "Forget Robert's lessons. The important thing is that you do exactly what a princess is meant to do."

"Which is?"

"Help people believe in themselves."

Sam shook her head. "I don't know how to do that."

"Of course you do. You did it with me," Beatrice said gently.

Sam had always thought of herself as the black sheep of her family. The one who took a perverse delight in breaking the rules, just to prove how pointless the rules were in the first place.

Was it possible that all her rebellious energy could actually be *useful*?

"I'll do it," she said hoarsely, excitement blossoming in

her chest—though it was edged in regret, when she thought of Marshall.

Seeing Sam's expression, Beatrice stepped forward. The great volume of her gown moved with her, its hem hissing smoothly over the floor. "Is something wrong?"

"Marshall. We . . . got in a fight before the wedding."

Beatrice put her hands on her sister's back, giving her a gentle push. "Well then, what are you waiting for? He's probably still here."

♛

Sam rushed through the sea of people flooding the halls. Now that Robert had confirmed the wedding wasn't taking place—at least, not today—the guests seemed eager to get outside, as if they still didn't quite trust that the palace was safe. When Sam didn't see Marshall in the crowds, she stumbled out onto the front portico.

And there he was, about to step into one of the palace's courtesy cars.

"Marshall!" She hurried forward, still wearing her narrow-cut ivory dress. "I need to talk to you!"

His head darted up at the sound of her voice. "Sam, no."

There was only one thing for her to do.

Sam ran around the front of the car to the driver's side. She hoped she wasn't visible to the flocks of people gathered outside the palace gates, murmuring confusedly about the wedding.

"Get out," she commanded the chauffeur.

"Your Royal Highness, I'm sorry, but I can't."

Sam drew herself up taller, adopting the imperious, queenly tone she'd heard Beatrice use. "That was a direct order."

Startled into submission, the driver stepped out of the car. The keys were in the ignition, the motor already rumbling.

Sam looked up in time to see Caleb hurtling down the front steps of the palace in pursuit. "Sorry," she called out, before getting in the car and throwing her foot on the accelerator.

"Sam!" Marshall shouted from the backseat. "What are you *doing*?"

She tore down the front drive, reaching to frantically adjust the mirrors. Marshall tried to throw his door open, but Sam had enabled the child lock.

"Buckle your seat belt," she informed him. "We're going for a drive."

Technically Sam didn't have a license; she'd never passed the parallel parking section of the driver's test. She was only allowed to drive her Jeep—which she'd lovingly named Albert—on the country roads near Sulgrave, and only if her car was at the center of a formation, with a black security vehicle in front and another behind.

Driving in the capital, without her Guard, was definitely illegal. But it was too late to worry about that.

Sam whipped around another corner. Metro stops and colored pennants passed by in a blur. She wasn't really sure where she was going except that she wanted to get as far from the palace as possible.

"Sam, you have to pull over!"

"I just wanted to talk," she said reasonably, as if it were totally normal for her to commandeer one of the palace vehicles.

Marshall let out a huff of protest. "I have nothing to say to you."

"Good, because you're not the one who's going to do the talking. You're going to listen." Sam's hands tightened over the wheel as she blasted through a yellow light. The windows were tinted, so no one could look through and realize that the wild driver speeding down Cumberland Street was next in line to the throne.

"Look, it's true that I had a crush on Teddy," she admitted. "I kissed him last year at the Queen's Ball, before he even *met* my sister."

In the rearview mirror, she saw Marshall grit his teeth. "This isn't exactly helping," he pointed out, but Sam forged ahead.

"When Teddy got engaged to Beatrice, I felt . . . angry, and rejected. I'm not proud of this, but I asked you to start dating me out of spite. Because I wanted to hurt Teddy as badly as he'd hurt me.

"Then you and I started acting like a couple, and at some point I stopped thinking about Teddy altogether. I really *like* you, Marshall, and it killed me that we were pretending. Before I met you, I never gave any thought to the guys I hooked up with. It was always just meaningless—"

"Still not helping," he cut in, and she winced.

"What I mean is, things with you are different. So different that it scares me. Last weekend in the carriage . . ." They pulled up to a stoplight, and she risked a glance back at Marshall. "I thought we had agreed that it wasn't fake anymore. That we meant it."

"That was before I knew you were using me to get your sister's fiancé!"

"I didn't want him!" Sam burst out. "You have to understand, I never *actually* wanted Teddy. I just wanted him to choose me over Beatrice."

"You're not making sense," Marshall insisted, though his tone was slightly less caustic than before.

"I've always been jealous of Beatrice." Sam kept her eyes straight ahead; they were somewhere in the financial district now, monolithic office buildings rising up on either side of the road. "I fixated on Teddy, because it was easier to think about him than the fact that Beatrice is the future queen and I'm the useless one."

"You're not useless," Marshall said heavily.

"I would say that I wish I could take it all back, but that's not true," she concluded. "Because if I hadn't asked you to fake a relationship with me—no matter how messed-up my reasons were—I would never have realized that I want to be with you for real."

There was a protracted silence. Sam swallowed. It would be okay, she told herself; at least she'd tried.

Then she heard the click of Marshall unfastening his seat belt. He braced a hand on the front seat and began climbing up over the central console.

"*Seriously?*" Sam veered wildly into the other lane, just barely managing to avoid colliding with a taxi. A chorus of angry horns shouted at them.

"Sorry." Marshall lowered himself into the passenger seat. "But if we're really having this conversation, then I need to be able to see your face."

"I—okay."

"Sam, did you really mean everything you just said?" he asked.

She darted a fearful glance over, but couldn't read his expression. "Of course I meant it," she told him. "I'm done with pretending, or performing. And I understand if you can't forgive me. I just . . . I needed to say all of this, before you ran off to Orange and I never saw you again."

Marshall turned to look out his window. For a heart-wrenching moment Sam thought he was done with her; and she steeled herself to say goodbye.

"Pull in there." He gestured to a blue sign down the block that read PUBLIC GARAGE.

"What? Why?"

"Because," Marshall said, and now there was a note of frustration in his voice, "I can't kiss you properly while you're driving, and we already went through this in the carriage, and god help me, *why* do we keep having these conversations in moving vehicles?"

It was the worst driving of Sam's life. She cut across a lane of traffic, then bumped over a curb as she pulled into the garage—driving only with her left hand as her right reached hungrily for Marshall. She found a spot on the second level and pulled in diagonally, wrenching the car into park and killing the engine.

They were both out of their seat belts in an instant. The car's interior lights dimmed, and the parking garage was shadowed, but the darkness didn't slow them down. Sam leaned so far in to Marshall that she was almost in his lap, throwing her arms around his neck to hold him tight. "Oh my god," she whispered, laughing, "where *are* we?"

"I really don't care," Marshall replied, leaning over the central console to kiss her.

His hands tangled in her hair. Sam made a pleading, anguished sound low in her throat, a sound she'd never heard herself make before. She grabbed Marshall's shoulders and pulled him impatiently forward—

The car's horn blared, loud and angry, into the interior of the garage.

They broke apart, laughing and breathless and utterly unselfconscious. Sam glanced up and saw that Caleb was standing behind the car, his arms crossed. He'd clearly tailed them in one of the other palace cars. His jaw was set in what he probably thought was a stern expression, but Sam saw the amused fondness beneath.

She shifted, and the seams of her ivory dress dug into the side of her body. She wondered, suddenly, what came next.

For months her attention had been fixated on this day. First because she'd resented Teddy and Beatrice, and then because it had become a deadline—because she and Marshall had only ever agreed that he would be her wedding date, and she hadn't known what would happen once the wedding was over.

"So . . . we're okay?" she asked, because she needed to hear him say it aloud.

"We're okay." Marshall shook his head, his eyes dancing with amusement. "I can't be angry about your ridiculous quest to make Eaton jealous. Not when it's the reason we found each other."

Relief flooded Sam's chest. "What now?" she asked. How did you start dating someone for real, when your entire relationship had been for show? Did you have to rewind all the way back to the first date?

Marshall glanced over as if he heard the thoughts swirling through her brain. He reached out a hand and Sam took it, lacing their fingers.

"I was thinking, do you want to come back to Orange this summer?" he asked. "There's so much we still haven't done—I want to take you hiking and to the beach in Malibu, and Rory says she wants to hang out. She's a big fan of yours," he added, and smiled.

Sam's heart lifted, but then she remembered the promise she'd just made.

"Actually . . . Beatrice wants me to do a royal tour for her. To take over the one that she and Teddy were supposed to go on."

She'd revealed more than she'd intended to with that statement, but she knew she could trust Marshall. He nodded, not pressing her for details.

"Of course you should go," he agreed. "But your tour will pass through Orange, won't it?"

"I think so." If it didn't, Sam thought, she would just have to add a few tour stops.

"Then I can't wait to show you around." Marshall's eyes glinted with mischief as he opened the passenger door. "In the meantime, can you switch spots with me? Don't take this the wrong way, but you're a terrible driver."

"I know," Sam agreed. "When we cruise to Malibu, you can be the one to drive."

Marshall laughed at that, bracing a hand on the console as he pulled her into one more rushed, rough kiss.

"What was that for?" she asked, a bit dazed, when they broke apart.

Marshall looked at her as if it were obvious. "Because you're *you*, Sam, and I'm completely crazy about you."

Because you're you. She was struck by the utter simplicity of it.

"I'm crazy about you, too, Marshmallow."

He made a sharp sound of protest. "*Marshmallow?*"

"I thought it was time you had a nickname of your own." Sam smiled at him. "Don't let it go to your head."

42

NINA

Nina clattered down the steps that led to the palace's back lawn. A few dozen yards away, at the end of a flagstone path, stood the royal family's garage. Technically Nina wasn't allowed inside, but no way could she face the front driveway right now, filled with outraged guests and bewildered drivers and anxious crowds pressing against the front gates.

She knew how to get into the locked closet where the valets kept the keys. And Sam wouldn't mind if Nina borrowed her car.

"Nina, wait up!"

She stumbled at the sound of Ethan's voice, though she shouldn't have been surprised. Of course he'd found her; he, too, knew all the exits from the palace, knew exactly how she could get out when she felt cornered and trapped.

When she didn't turn around, he began running down the stone steps after her. "Are you okay?" he called out, with unmistakable concern.

She planted a heel and whirled around, her hair flying into her eyes. "Just leave me alone!"

Ethan blinked. She hated him for looking so gorgeous in his tuxedo. Sunlight caught the deep purple-black of his hair, which curled a little at the base of his neck. "What happened?"

"*Daphne* happened! Your secret girlfriend or ex-girlfriend

or whatever she is! By the way, she's the one who told that reporter about us."

"I know," Ethan said quietly. Nina felt a momentary rush of satisfaction that he believed her—unlike Jeff, who'd refused to hear a word against Daphne—but it quickly evaporated.

"Please, let me explain." Ethan hurried down the remaining steps toward her. "Don't run away because Daphne scared you."

"Scared?" Nina repeated, stung. "I'm angry as hell, and I feel betrayed. Don't make the mistake of confusing that for fear."

Ethan faltered, chastened. Sunlight fell over the planes of his face, caught the amber flecks in his eyes. She swallowed, wishing she didn't have to ask this next question.

"Did you ask me out only because Daphne told you to?"

He was silent for a moment, then gave a quick, pained nod. At Nina's expression, he rushed to explain.

"Look—Daphne did ask me to flirt with you. She worried that if you spent too much time around Jeff, you guys would get back together. So she wanted me to run interference. But, Nina, I never—"

"Why would she ask *you*?" Nina cut in. "What made her think that you would do what she said? She claims you've been in love with her for years!"

Ethan closed his eyes. "I *was* in love with her for years."

He'd whispered the words, yet Nina heard each syllable as if he'd shouted them. She flinched away, horrified. "How could you ever have feelings for Daphne? She's awful!"

"She's done a lot of awful things," Ethan agreed, and Nina couldn't help noticing the way he'd shifted her wording.

She was seized by a nauseating sensation of déjà vu. This was exactly what had happened at Beatrice's engagement party, when she'd tried to talk to Jeff about Daphne. Except this time it was almost *worse,* because Ethan knew what Daphne had done, and still he was defending her.

"Nina, please don't blame me for things that happened in my past. It isn't fair," Ethan protested. "I'm not proud of my original reasons for hanging out with you. But everything is different now! *I'm* different!"

"If you spent time with me just because *Daphne* said to, then you aren't that different at all." Outraged pride flamed in Nina's cheeks. "How can you possibly have loved her?"

"I thought we were the same—"

"Because you both move people around like pieces on your own personal chessboard?"

Ethan winced, stuffing his hands awkwardly into his pockets. "Because we were both on the outside, and wanted in," he said miserably. "I saw Daphne's energy, how single-mindedly she went after the things she wanted. It's the same determination that I've always had. Or used to have," he added, more softly. "Nina, you know how much I've always wanted to belong."

"So when Daphne asked you to 'run interference'"—Nina angrily lifted her hands to make air quotes around the phrase—"why did you agree? You didn't stop to think that I'm a real person, with *feelings?*"

"First of all, I never thought it would *go* this far, okay? I figured I would hang out with you a couple of times, just to prove that I had. I hardly *knew* you back then—the only thing I remembered about you was that you could be a know-it-all." Ethan gave a helpless shrug. "But you surprised me, Nina. You weren't at all what I thought you were, and I kept wanting to know more about you."

Nina hated the way her mind kept sifting back through her memories. How many of them were real?

She crossed her arms, feeling cold despite the sunlight.

"That night when you walked me home, and we kissed," she heard herself say. "Was Daphne the one who called you?"

"I—yeah," Ethan admitted. "It was Daphne."

Nina tugged at her neckline, wishing she could get out of this prison of a dress. "So you were thinking of her the whole time."

"I was thinking of *you*!"

At the raw urgency in his tone, she fell silent. Ethan swallowed and continued.

"I was thinking that I don't deserve you," he said quietly. "Nina, I'm not as confident as you. I wasn't able to grow up alongside the royals without always feeling like I was *less* than they were, like I had something to prove. I guess I thought that if I kept moving, kept focusing on the next thing—the next AP class, the next scholarship, the next upward rung in my ladder—eventually I would climb high enough."

"Climb where?" she exclaimed. "What did you *want*, Ethan?"

"I wanted to feel like I deserved things. Like I had earned them myself, and had just as much right to them as everyone else." By *everyone else*, Nina knew he meant Jeff.

"But, Nina, you make me feel like I *do* deserve things. Not because of what I've accomplished, but because of who I am. I've never had anyone look at me the way you do—like you actually like *me*, as I am now, without excuses or complications," he added. "You make me want to be a better person, just because I'm with you."

Nina's heart was straining against her ribs. She glanced away, to where the leaves in the orchard flashed a brilliant gold in the sun. The fragrance of the apples mingled with the heady, earthy scent of last night's rain.

"How long?" When she saw Ethan's confused look, she clarified. "How long were you obsessed with Daphne?"

"A long time," he said bluntly. "How long were you obsessed with Jeff?"

She stiffened. "That isn't fair."

"Maybe not. But, Nina, don't you see? You and I belong together! No matter how foolish this is, no matter how many years we spent chasing other people, we found each other in the end. Please," he added. "Don't hold my past against me. *You're* the one that I want. Not Daphne."

Far off in the distance Nina heard the low rumble of conversation. Probably gossip about the royal wedding, making its slow way through the capital. That was Washington, she thought: so crowded, so hungry, so merciless.

She lifted her eyes to Ethan's. His face was pale and vulnerable in the afternoon sunlight. Nina couldn't help it; she stepped forward into his arms.

Ethan made a strangled noise and pulled her in to his chest. He held on to her tightly—not as if he wanted to kiss her, but as if to reassure himself that she was still here, that she hadn't run off and left him.

"Please believe me," Ethan murmured, and Nina felt her resolve melting. She loved the feel of his breath against her skin.

"I do believe you," she said at last, detangling herself from his arms.

He broke into a broad, relieved smile, but it faltered when he saw the look on Nina's face.

"I believe you, but that doesn't mean I'm ready to trust you," she explained. Not when he'd originally gotten close to her because he was following *Daphne*'s orders.

Ethan shook his head. "Don't you see, this is exactly what Daphne intended. She attacked you like that because she *wanted* to break us up!"

"Just like she broke up me and Jeff at the last big palace

event? I would say that history is repeating itself, but I've figured out by now that this is Daphne's signature move!"

"She can be . . . very ruthless when it comes to the people she cares about," Ethan agreed.

"I think you mean the people who are in the way of what she wants." Nina bit her lip. "You know, I used to wonder why you and Jeff never dated that many people, even during the time he was broken up from her. Now I've figured out why! It's because Daphne thinks she has claim to both of you. Whenever either of you gets too close to someone else, she swoops in to chase them off. And the worst part is, you *let* her!"

That hurt more than anything else: the realization that, in the end, the only two men Nina had ever loved had both been under Daphne's thumb.

Daphne was like a spider, beautiful and insidious, spinning her webs around people with such dexterity that they never realized they'd been caught until it was too late.

"Please don't let Daphne come between us," Ethan said again. "There must be something I can do to prove that I've changed."

Nina's eyes burned, and she stared down at the walkway, tracing a crack in one of the stones with her shoe. "I just . . . I need time."

"Of course," he agreed. "I'll do whatever it takes to make this right, to show you that—"

"I need time without you, Ethan."

Nina had some thinking to do—about everything she and Ethan had done, the mistakes they had both made. About how Daphne and Jeff fit into all this.

It sickened her, how painfully tangled the four of them had become.

"I understand," Ethan told her, his voice surprisingly formal. "Take as much time as you need. I just hope . . . I just hope that you'll come find me afterward."

He took a step back, and the distance stretched out between them. Nina had to fight the urge to step forward and pull him close again.

"I'll see you around," she replied, through a tightness in her throat.

She turned and started across the lawn toward the garage, squaring her shoulders. She knew Ethan was watching, but didn't dare look back at him.

And somehow, as she walked, each step became slightly easier than the last.

43

SAMANTHA

Later that afternoon, Samantha headed up the staircase of Nina's dorm. She was wearing oversized sunglasses and a scarf, though now that the semester had ended, the campus was so empty of students that she almost hadn't bothered.

The last bewildered guests had finally left the throne room, but the palace was still in an uproar. Sam's mom had retreated upstairs to her room, stunned and emotionally drained by the day's events. Meanwhile Robert's assistant, Jane—who'd been abruptly promoted to Lady Chamberlain—kept telling the press the same thing over and over: "The palace is not prepared to make a statement at this time. We will let you know when we have plans to move forward with the wedding." Which, of course, only fueled the rumors.

At Nina's room, Sam tapped out the old one-two-three knock they'd invented when they were children. The door swung open, revealing not Nina, but her mom.

"Oh—hi," Sam said, surprised. She glanced behind Julie and saw that the whole family was here, all three of them packing up Nina's things to move her out.

"Samantha. It's good to see you." Julie held open the door with a faint smile.

Sam loved that Nina's parents always called her by her first name—that they didn't gossip, didn't even ask what had happened this morning to call off the wedding. They just treated her like any other, ordinary friend of their daughter.

"Sam?" Nina was kneeling on the floor, halfheartedly folding a sweater in her lap. Sam noted with amusement that she and Nina had both changed into the same sweatpants, matching leopard-print ones that they'd bought together last fall.

Nina rose to her feet, letting the sweater crumple to the floor. Her mamá—who stood near the window, wrestling tape over a large cardboard box—watched as she pulled Samantha into a hug.

It was a hug that Sam needed as much as Nina. After everything that had happened today, the strange whirlwind of Beatrice's almost-wedding and that tumultuous car ride with Marshall, she felt disoriented. As if she was still reeling from emotional whiplash.

When they stepped apart, Sam scoured her friend's face. Nina looked upset, her eyes wider and glassier than normal, but she attempted an apologetic half smile.

Sam wasn't sure what had happened to Nina earlier, but whatever it was, she suspected that it had to do with Ethan. Or maybe Jeff. All she knew for certain was that Caleb had seen Nina run off, close to tears, before she'd apparently torn out of the garage in Samantha's car.

"Sorry I borrowed Albert," Nina said, reading her mind. "He's parked in lot twenty-three. I can get him now, if you want."

"No, I mean . . . keep Albert. I don't care." Sam glanced around the dorm room. It looked oddly forlorn like this, stripped of everything that had given it personality: the colorful photo boards, the vinyl jewelry boxes where Nina had organized her cocktail rings. Now it was all just bare white walls and unflattering fluorescent lighting, a few stray hangers sticking out of the empty closet.

The whole campus felt listless right now. A few people were still here: parents dragging suitcases to cars, students who'd waited until the last minute to clear out their dorm rooms, before university staff reassigned them to summer school. But mostly, King's College was silent.

"I wanted to check on you," Sam went on. "Is everything okay?"

"Julie . . . ," Isabella said meaningfully, exchanging a look with her wife. "We're going to need a couple more boxes. And packing tape. Why don't we run out and get some?"

"Good thinking. We'll be back soon," Nina's mom announced, slinging her purse over her shoulder before heading out.

When the door shut behind them, Nina climbed onto the bare mattress, pulling her legs up to sit cross-legged. The ceiling fan clicked overhead, lifting the air of the room and letting it settle back down again.

Tentatively, Sam took the opposite side of the bed. "Did something happen today?"

"It's Ethan," Nina admitted, and the pain in those two words set Sam instantly on the defensive.

"Did he hurt you?" she cried out. "Should I have Caleb go beat him up? Or Beatrice could exile him to Canada, or—"

Nina cut her off with a strangled laugh. "Slow down, Sam. Ethan may have hurt me, but I'm not sure I want him gone, either."

"What happened? Did you break up?"

"I don't know." Nina pulled a pillow into her lap and hugged it. "I need some time to figure things out."

"I'm sorry," Sam breathed, meaning it. Even if she'd thought the Ethan thing was weird at first, even if she hadn't fully understood, all she'd ever wanted was for her friend to be happy. It felt especially unfair that Nina should feel such anguished confusion today, when Sam's relationship with Marshall was finally, blissfully clear.

"Do you want to talk about it?" she ventured.

"It's a long story. I'm not sure I'm ready to tell it yet."

There was an edge to Nina's voice that kept Sam from pressing further. She just nodded, reaching a hand beneath her bracelet—the one from the Crown Jewels collection, which she'd forgotten to take off after this morning—and sliding it up and down her forearm. The diamonds felt deliciously cool against her skin.

"I want to forgive him," Nina added, so quietly that it was almost a whisper. "I'm just . . . I'm scared of being hurt again. I wish I was as brave as you are."

"I'm not that brave."

"You're the bravest person I know!"

"It's easy to seem that way when you don't care what people think of you. That isn't courage; it's just recklessness," Sam said quietly. "I of all people know the difference."

Nina glanced over. "But you *do* care what people think of you, Sam. You just *pretend* not to."

Sam sighed. She'd learned her lesson about pretending. "Maybe it's inevitable that we're going to be hurt, when we let other people in. Maybe we can't care deeply for someone without being hurt by them, too," she said softly. Certainly she and Marshall had caused each other pain, alongside all the joy. The same with Beatrice and Teddy.

What was that saying, grief is the price we pay for love?

Nina nodded slowly. She seemed pensive, all her attention curled inward. "It's just . . . it's easier to believe in things, believe in *people*, when you read about them in books. They're so much safer when they're fictional. The real-life ones . . . I'm still not sure how to handle them."

Sam let her head fall all the way back onto her friend's

mattress, lacing her hands tranquilly over her stomach. Next to her she felt Nina doing the same thing.

They both looked out the window at the blue square of sky dotted with fluffy wisps of cloud.

"Remember when we used to go cloud-watching?" Nina asked.

Sam nodded, the hairsprayed coils of her hair crunching a bit at the motion. She and Nina used to sprawl out in the tree house in the orchard and name the shapes they saw drifting overhead—birds, stars, smiling faces that broke apart and reformed on the current of the wind.

Nina shifted so that she was lying on her side. "I always pretended they were ships, like pirate ships far up in the sky. I liked to imagine that someday I would find my way onto one, and let it sweep me off into some epic story."

"Really?"

"Over the last year, I feel like I *have* lived through a story. I dated my best friend's brother—who is a *prince*—and then his best friend!" Nina sighed. "When I daydreamed about getting swept up in a story, it was always *my* story. But that's not how it played out."

Sam kept staring up at the sky, where the clouds—which, come to think of it, did look remarkably like ships—sailed serenely onward. Her chest ached at the realization that Nina still felt this way. Like a supporting character in someone else's narrative.

Nina was far too bright, too fiercely self-assured, to play the role of a damsel waiting around for *anyone*. Nina should be the heroine of her own story.

Hadn't Sam felt something similar? For years she'd struggled with her own identity, because she'd always defined herself in *relation* to someone else—to whatever boy she was hooking up with, or to her brother, or most of all in relation to Beatrice. When, the entire time, she'd needed to figure out who she was, herself.

She sat up abruptly, seized by an idea.

"Nina—will you come on a royal tour with me?"

Her friend pushed up to a sitting position, tugging a hand through her hair. "A royal tour?"

"Now that the wedding is postponed, Beatrice asked me to do this summer's royal tour on her behalf. Just think," Sam pleaded. "You said you needed time to figure things out! What better way to sort through it all than road-tripping with your best friend?"

"But . . . what are you going to do the whole time?"

"Talk to people."

It sounded so simple, yet it wasn't. There were so *many* people out there—in the world, yes, but also right here in this country—people who all wanted different things. Some thrived on uncertainty; some craved stability. Some lived on dreams and some were relentlessly practical. Some wanted the government to take charge of everything; others wanted the government to leave them alone.

Beatrice's job—and now Sam's, too—was to understand them all. Despite all those clashing desires and viewpoints and opinions, she had to find a way to work on behalf of *all* of them.

The prospect sparked a strange feeling in her, as if her bones were stretching and reshaping themselves; or maybe the *world* was stretching, tugging her outward like a rubber band.

The wind rustled through the trees in the courtyard. Sam imagined she could hear it whispering, urging her and Nina to *go go go.*

There were still so many things that she and her best friend needed to talk about. Sam longed to tell her everything—

how she'd set off the emergency alarm, her moment of truce with Teddy, and the misunderstanding it had caused with Marshall. And she wanted to hear what had happened between Nina and Ethan.

"We're overdue for an adventure," she insisted, and saw her friend's eyes sparkle at the word.

"You and me, traveling together, all summer," Nina said slowly, a smile tugging at her mouth. "It's madness."

"Utter foolishness," Sam agreed.

"There's no way I'll be able to keep you in line."

"I'm sure you'll regret it partway through."

"Trust me, I'm *already* regretting it," Nina said, grinning.

Sam let out an actual yelp of excitement. "Is that a yes? Are you coming with me?"

To her relief, Nina laughed. And then they were both laughing—a bright, mischievous, complicit laugh, the way they had laughed when they were children, and knew that they were up to no good.

"Yes, I'm coming," Nina declared at last, wiping her eyes. "You're right about one thing. You and I are overdue for an adventure."

44

DAPHNE

Daphne was in her bedroom when the town car pulled up outside. It was missing the American flags that usually fluttered near its headlights, but she recognized it as one of the royal fleet.

Jefferson had come to see her.

For some reason she didn't move from her spot near the window. The heels of her stilettos seemed to have grown roots, twining down through the carpet and floorboards so that she would be planted here forever, like the tree nymph she'd been named for.

"Daphne!" Her mother flung open the door, and was across the room in a few brisk strides. "You need to get downstairs. The prince is here."

Rebecca's beautiful features were twisted—with hunger, Daphne realized, and ruthlessness. Her father followed in her mother's steps. He cleared his throat, but when neither woman looked his way, he said nothing.

"What's the matter with you?" Her mother's bright green eyes narrowed. "You look terrible."

"I'm just tired."

Rebecca grabbed Daphne by the shoulders and steered her to her vanity, where her makeup brushes and pots of color were scattered, a great tapestry of illusion. She grabbed her daughter's chin and tilted her face up, to darken her lashes with mascara, paint a deep red gloss on her lips. Daphne held herself utterly still. Her mother's movements were as expert and as fast as those of any makeup artist, a legacy from her time as a runway model.

When she stepped back, Rebecca looked at her daughter with cool appraisal. "Better," she said gruffly.

Daphne's eyes lifted to the mirror. There she was, as deadly beautiful as ever, her hair licking down her back like red-gold flame. The sight of her reflection should have steadied her, but for once, it didn't.

When she got downstairs, she found the prince loitering in the entrance hall. "I'm so sorry," she murmured; royalty never waited for *anyone*.

"Daphne! I'm so glad you're here," he replied, following her into the living room. Out of habit, she sank onto the sofa, and he settled down next to her. She felt oddly hollow, as if her insides had been scraped clean by the flat of a blade, and now all that remained of her was a beautiful, empty shell.

Not that Jefferson could tell the difference. He only saw the shell—because it was all that Daphne had ever shown him.

For a while they chatted about the wedding and the security scare. Daphne could hardly follow, but somehow she kept nodding at the appropriate times and murmuring vague responses.

"I'm really glad you were my date today, even if the wedding didn't actually happen," Jefferson was saying, and she snapped back to attention. "I know you wanted to go as friends. That you didn't want to date again unless we were serious. And . . . I've been doing some thinking."

Daphne's mouth, which her mother had so helpfully lip-glossed for her, fell open in surprise. She quickly shut it. Outside the doors to the hallway, she heard a muffled footstep, a hiss of excitement. Her parents clearly felt entitled to listen in on this conversation. After all, it was the moment of their family's great triumph.

"You have?" she managed.

Jefferson flashed her his brilliant, princely smile. "You're amazing, Daphne. You're so good to me, and to everyone I care about. I know it wasn't that serious between us before—I mean, *I* wasn't that serious," he amended clumsily. "I was young and stupid. I took everything for granted, especially you. But after everything that's happened, I know better. I'm ready now," he added. "This time, I'll be serious about *us*."

Daphne didn't understand why her throat had gone sandpaper dry. But Jefferson didn't seem to notice—because he was busy slipping off the gold signet ring he always wore on his pinkie finger.

It was small, much smaller than the massive Great Seal ring worn by his father, and now by Queen Beatrice. This was a family signet, its flat round bezel marked with the Washingtons' coat of arms: a script *W* below a row of stars. The only other man entitled to wear one was Jefferson's uncle Richard.

The walls seemed to shrink in on her. No matter how hard she sucked air into her lungs, Daphne felt like she couldn't breathe.

Jefferson started to reach for her hand, then paused, as if realizing he should ask her permission. "I love you, Daphne," he told her, and she knew that in that moment that he meant it—*really* meant it, so much more than all the times he'd said it back when they'd dated in high school. "I was . . . I hoped . . . Would you wear this?"

She felt herself teetering on the edge of some great precipice, as if she had finally scaled the top of a peak she'd been climbing her whole life. And now that she was finally cresting the top, she wasn't even sure why she was here.

Once she stepped out into the world wearing that ring, everyone would know that she and Jefferson were back together—more than that, even. That they were *sworn* to each other, that they had reached an understanding. A signet ring wasn't an engagement ring, yet that script W unquestionably marked her as one of the Washingtons.

The moment the paparazzi snapped a photo of Daphne in that ring, her entire world would change.

People would start taking bets on everything from their engagement to future baby names. Porcelain companies would surreptitiously begin their designs, in hopes of being granted the commission for her commemorative wedding china. Daphne would become the center of a whirlwind of breathless speculation.

And someday when she and Jefferson were married, she would soar to the top of the social hierarchy, and become the third-highest-ranking woman in the realm. Everyone would be obligated to curtsy to her. Except, of course, for Samantha and Beatrice.

It was everything she had struggled for all these years—her greatest moment of triumph. Yet Daphne's lungs had frozen. She didn't know how to say yes. To accept the ring, and everything that came with it.

As if she were a marionette being pulled by a string, she lifted her right hand. It trembled only slightly.

Daphne sat absolutely still, powerless to move, as Jefferson slid the signet over her ring finger. It slipped easily over her knuckle to settle at the base of her finger. The ring still felt warm from the heat of his skin.

"Thank you," she managed, though it came out almost a whisper. "I didn't . . . I wasn't expecting this."

Jefferson laced their fingers and squeezed her hand. "I love you, Daphne," he said again. "I'm sorry it took me so long to figure out—and for everything I put you through—but I promise that things will be different this time. We have each other, and that's what matters more than anything."

We have each other. Jefferson no longer had anyone else, because Daphne had taken them all from him—had torn his best friend from him in a fit of spite.

And to reach this moment of triumph, Daphne had ensured that she was just as alone as the prince now found himself.

Dimly, she realized that she hadn't actually told Jefferson *I love you* in return. She needed to. She should open her mouth and say it; it would be easy, just three simple words. Hadn't she said them countless times before without meaning them?

The afternoon slanted through the windows, to fall in a play of light and shadow over the planes of the prince's face. His Highness Jefferson George Alexander Augustus, Prince of America, was still waiting for her answer.

Since she was fourteen her life had revolved around him: winning him, keeping him, trying to hurt anyone who got between them, hurting herself instead. Daphne had plotted and schemed and manipulated, had burned bridges and scorched earth in her efforts to draw him back to her side. And now he was here, and it was all over at last, and the only thought running through her head was what an utter fool she had been, to build her life around the wrong boy.

It was too late to change course. Her chance for a future with Ethan was gone. And now that Daphne was here, confronted with the future she'd spent all those years striving for, no one could ever know what it had cost her.

No one could ever know that the smiles she gave Jefferson were smiles she should have showered on Ethan, the boy she'd loved, only to realize it too late. No one could know that she had paid for the highest of titles with the greatest of heartbreaks. And she would never tell them.

She remembered what Nina had said this morning: that

Daphne would get everything she had ever wanted, only to find that she was completely alone.

Daphne looked at Jefferson and gave him the answer he expected, the answer her parents wanted her to give—the Deighton answer.

"I love you, too," she assured him, her face frozen in her beautiful, perfect smile. "And I'm so very happy."

45

BEATRICE

Beatrice had never seen the palace in such upheaval. Especially not when she was the cause of it.

Security and footmen and party planners swarmed the halls, searching for something to do, for an answer that no one seemed able to give. In all their centuries of history the Washingtons had never experienced anything like this: a royal wedding that wasn't. It was especially chaotic given that the Lord Chamberlain had just handed in his resignation, leaving his assistant in charge.

If only Beatrice had been confident enough to fire Robert months ago. He'd never really been working for her; he'd been working for an outdated notion of what her role should be. And she could never become the queen she needed to, not with him undermining her efforts.

She remembered, suddenly, what her father had said that final morning at the hospital: *It won't be easy for you, a young woman, stepping into a job that most men will think they can do better. Harness some of that energy of yours, that stubbornness, and stick to your beliefs.*

Her father wouldn't have wanted her to be a puppet queen, her every movement dictated by Robert and the palace establishment. King George had understood that change was an integral part of America's DNA, that change was *crucial* to the nation's success. If the monarchy was as stiff and inflexible as Robert wanted it to be, it would never survive.

"Franklin," Beatrice called out. The puppy emerged from beneath a marble coffee table, his tail wagging furiously. At her voice he bounded toward her. She settled onto the rug, smoothing her skirt over her legs, pulling his warm puppy weight contentedly into her lap. If only everything in life could be this simple.

The two of them were alone in the second-floor sitting room known as the Green Room. It had originally been named in the theatrical sense, since it was where the royal family gathered before their famous appearances on the Washington Palace balcony. But forty years ago, Beatrice's grandmother had decided that the name should match the setting, and redecorated. Now the room looked like something out of the Emerald City, all forest green and gold.

Curtains looped over the enormous floor-to-ceiling windows that lined one wall. Through the gap between them, Beatrice saw the crowds still gathered outside the palace. They milled about restlessly, clearly wondering whether she and Teddy were still going to come out onto the balcony, even though they hadn't gotten married today. It didn't help that the palace still hadn't confirmed when the wedding would take place, and refused to release any details about the so-called "security scare" that had delayed it.

If Samantha had never pulled that alarm—if the wedding had moved forward as planned—Beatrice and Teddy would be standing out on the balcony right now: waving down at crowds who were bright with excitement, instead of murmuring in confusion. The newlyweds' balcony appearance dated to the reign of Edward I. He'd thought it the easiest way to introduce America to its new queen, only recently arrived from Spain. By now the balcony appearance was arguably the most beloved of all the Washingtons' wedding traditions.

Beatrice had appeared on that balcony so many times in her life—in smocked dresses and ribbons as a child, in tailored skirts and patent-leather heels as she grew older—smiling, waving, presenting a meticulously curated image of herself to the world.

A memory rose to the surface of her mind, of one of those annual Fourth of July appearances. Beatrice had leaned her elbows over the balcony's iron railing, craning her neck to see the military planes that soared in formation overhead. Then strong hands had hoisted her upward: her father, propping her onto his shoulders so that she could see.

When he'd gestured, it wasn't upward, to where the planes were leaving great trails of smoke like messages in the sky, but to the sea of jubilant, shouting people below.

"They're cheering for you, you know," he'd told her. "Because they love you, Beatrice. Just like I do."

Her vision blurred, and she twined her fingers in Franklin's fur to steady herself. Her father's words rattled around her empty head like pebbles in a jar. What would he say if he could see her now, hiding from her people instead of facing them?

A knock sounded at the door, and Beatrice wiped furiously at her eyes. "Come in," she called out, her voice surprisingly steady.

Teddy stepped into the room, shutting the door behind him.

He was still wearing his outfit from this morning, the white button-down shirt and striped blue trousers of his ceremonial dress uniform, though he'd taken off the matching jacket. His shirt was untucked, and unbuttoned at the throat, revealing a small triangle of his tanned chest. Beatrice forced herself to look away as she stood, smoothing her dress against her thighs.

"You took off your gown." Teddy nodded to her royal blue dress, with its elbow-length sleeves and pintucked waist.

"It's a lot of gown" was all Beatrice could say. It hadn't seemed right to keep it on, not after the decision she had reached.

Teddy lingered near the doorway, not making any move toward her. The new distance between them, when just last night they had been twined together in bed, made her chest ache.

"Beatrice," he said heavily, and it struck her that he'd used her full name. "What happened earlier?"

"That security breach spooked everyone," she began, automatically launching into the explanation she'd given all day: that after the jarring chaos of the alarm, she'd felt too on edge to move forward with the ceremony. Surprisingly, Queen Adelaide hadn't objected—probably because she could tell that her daughter's mind was made up. Even Jane had agreed, especially once Beatrice had clarified that her family would personally cover the cost of today's events, leaving nothing to the taxpayers.

"We both know it takes more than a security scare to change your mind," Teddy interrupted. "If you'd still wanted to get married after the alarm, we would have. Please, Beatrice—we promised each other secrets, but no lies. Remember?"

She opened her mouth to protest, then closed it, shame silencing her.

"You know why the alarm went off, don't you," Teddy went on. It wasn't really a question.

"I do."

At first Beatrice hadn't been able to believe what Sam had done. But then, seeing her sister's quiet composure as she'd confessed, Beatrice had realized that it was the right decision.

And she'd realized, too, how much Sam had changed.

Her irrepressible mischief was still there, but the loss of their father had transmuted it into something else: a bold self-possession that turned heads. Where she had once been willful and rambunctious, Sam now let her inner confidence carry her along. And the world was taking notice. Certainly Beatrice was.

For the first time, she felt truly glad that Samantha was next in line for the throne.

"Samantha set off the alarm," she confessed, meeting Teddy's gaze. His bright blue eyes went wide with shock.

"Sam?" he asked, bewildered. "Why?"

"She was . . ." Beatrice trailed off, but the truth must have been written on her face, because Teddy's features grew grave and closed-off.

"He was here, wasn't he."

Teddy didn't use Connor's name because he didn't know it, but it hardly mattered. Beatrice could tell exactly who he meant.

"How did you know?"

"Because I know *you*. I've seen that look you get when you're thinking of him," Teddy said hoarsely. "You know I'll support you, whatever you decide. But if you want to be with him—"

"I told him goodbye."

Teddy ran a hand distractedly through his hair, mussing its perfect golden waves. Combined with the untucked shirt and cuffed sleeves, it made him look young, and boyishly disheveled. "Then why did you cancel the wedding?"

"I didn't cancel it; I'm delaying it," she clarified. "Teddy, everything between us happened at lightning speed. Our relationship and engagement, the wedding planning—it was all a whirlwind. When that alarm went off today, I realized that I had gotten lost in it all." Beatrice took a hesitant step forward, willing him to understand. "We deserve to get married when we want to, on a timeline that makes *sense*. I don't want our wedding to be some kind of reaction to what we think America needs. I want it to be for us."

"It would still have been for us, if we'd held the ceremony today." Teddy reached for her hand.

"Would it?" Beatrice pressed. "Half of America thinks I'm marrying you because I need you to do my job *for* me. I'm the *first* female monarch," she said helplessly. "What kind of example am I setting for the women who come after me—for all the women in America—if I don't do it alone for a while, before you join in?"

"Let me get this straight," Teddy clarified. "You wanted to marry me when you didn't love me, because you thought it would help manage public opinion. And now you *don't* want to get married even though you *do* love me, because you want to manage public opinion?"

"Public opinion is a fickle beast," she said lightly, and let out a breath. "If I marry you now, I'm validating the claims of all those people who say a woman can't rule alone. I want to prove them wrong."

Teddy nodded slowly. "I get it," he assured her. "Still . . . I'd be lying if I said I'm not disappointed. I *wanted* to be married to you. And to go on our honeymoon."

"We should still go!"

His eyebrows shot up with surprise and unmistakable amusement. "The Queen of America, sharing a honeymoon suite with a man who *isn't* her husband? Are you sure?"

"Like I told Samantha, we're dragging this monarchy into the twenty-first century. People are going to have to get used to it." Beatrice stepped forward into his arms, nestling her head against his chest for a moment. She'd grown so addicted to his strength and solidity, to the warm familiar scent of him.

"I promise we'll get married someday. And that when

I propose again, it'll be better than the last time." She saw Teddy's mouth curl into a half smile at the memory. It was strange to think of how different things had been back then, how little they'd known each other.

Beatrice paused, fumbling for the right words to explain. "When I marry you, I want to do it as *me*, not just as the queen. And I'm still figuring out who that is. Who *I* am."

Teddy's blue eyes were very soft as he said, "I know exactly who you are."

"I know. You believed in me, even when I wasn't brave enough to believe in myself." She tilted her face up to his. "But there are so many things I still want to *do*. I want to see the world and have adventures and learn, so that someday when we get married, I'm ready for it. And most of all . . ."

She looked out at the balcony, and the teeming mass of people still gathered below. Their phones winked at her like a million dancing fireflies.

They were *her* people. If her father were here, she knew precisely what he would say: that he was proud of her, that he loved her. That she had the power to change history.

"Most of all?" Teddy prompted.

Beatrice tugged her hands from his and stepped toward the balcony. She was suddenly glad that she'd taken off her wedding gown; she didn't want to look like a bride right now, but like a sovereign.

She was going to make a balcony appearance—to step out into the warm June night, alone.

"Most of all," she told him, "I am going to be the queen."

ACKNOWLEDGMENTS

For reasons I still don't understand, sequels always seem to cause more trouble than their predecessors! I am so grateful to everyone who devoted their time and talents to making this book a reality.

To my editor, Caroline Abbey: thank you for your endless patience, for your ability to laugh, and mostly for being so ridiculously good at your job. There is no one I would rather be on this royal journey with.

A huge thank-you is due to the entire publishing team at Random House, especially Michelle Nagler, Mallory Loehr, Kelly McGauley, Jenna Lisanti, Kate Keating, Elizabeth Ward, Adrienne Waintraub, and Emily Petrick. Noreen Herits and Emma Benshoff, thank you for your boundless energy and your willingness to publicize this book in all kinds of unexpected ways. Also, special thanks to Alison Impey and Carolina Melis for these truly magnificent covers.

Joelle Hobeika, this story is so much stronger because of your guidance. Thank you for never giving up on it. I am lucky to work with an incredible team at Alloy Entertainment: Josh Bank, Sara Shandler, Les Morgenstein, Gina Girolamo, Kate Imel, Romy Golan, Matt Bloomgarden, Josephine McKenna, and Laura Barbiea.

Naomi Colthurst, thank you for the editorial breakthrough that saved this plot—you understand Samantha in a way that no one else does! Thanks also to Alesha Bonser and everyone at Penguin UK.

I am constantly in awe of my foreign sales team, Rights People. Alexandra Devlin, Allison Hellegers, Harim Yim, Claudia Galluzzi, and Charles Nettleton—thank you for bringing *American Royals* to so many languages around the world.

I don't know how I would do this job without my friends. Meaghan Byrne, you were the perfect partner in crime at Mount Vernon. Sarah Johnson and Margaret Walker, I can always count on you to debate the finer points of my alternate-history timeline, translate Latin, and generally act as on-call historians. Emily Brown, thank you for letting me vent each time the story got the better of me. Sarah Mlynowski, I am always grateful for your creative help. And Grace Atwood and Becca Freeman, thank you for being *American Royals*'s earliest cheerleaders, and for proving it's possible to make real-life friends through the internet.

I would be nowhere without the unwavering support and guidance of my parents, who are still my greatest champions. Lizzy and John Ed, I love you both so much. Sorry for all the times I've stolen details of your lives and put them into a book—I would promise to stop, but we all know that's a lie.

And finally, Alex: none of this would be possible without you. Thank you for carrying me when I need it most.

A QUEEN DESPERATE FOR ALLIES.
A PRINCESS CLINGING TO FREEDOM.
TWO FORMER RIVALS FIGHTING FOR THEIR FUTURE.

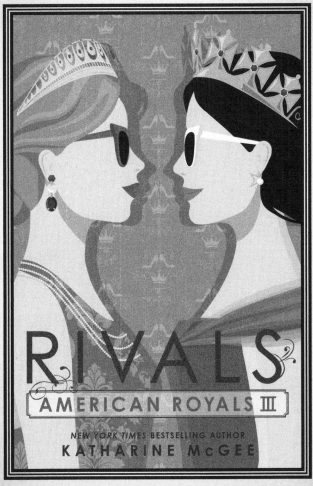

**Turn the page for a sneak peek at
AMERICAN ROYALS III: *RIVALS*.**

American Royals III: Rivals excerpt text copyright © 2022 by Katharine McGee and Alloy Entertainment. Cover art copyright © 2022 by Carolina Melis. Published by Random House Children's Books, a division of Penguin Random House LLC, New York.

NINA

"I can't believe I'm going to a royal event without you." Nina propped her phone against her shoulder and bent down to adjust a strap on her chunky red heels.

"It's a *library* event. This is the exception that proves the rule," Samantha pointed out. A horn blared a few feet from Nina, and Sam sighed. "Please tell me you didn't take the subway in a cocktail dress."

"Of course not." Nina's outfit wasn't actually a cocktail dress, but she didn't bother correcting Sam. "I walked."

"That's even worse!"

"Why? It's nice out, and it was only a quarter mile."

"That's not the point! You'll show up at the event with sweat stains," Sam spluttered. "And messy hair!"

"Like you just said, it's a library event. No one will care what I look like. I'm just here to get Makayla's signature and pig out on hors d'oeuvres." *And see Jeff*, Nina didn't say aloud.

Samantha groaned. "You brought books with you, didn't you?"

"Only one book!" Nina said defensively. "What else was

I supposed to do? I'm not going to be one of those weird fans who ask an author to sign a body part."

Sam chuckled. "Nina—I hate to cut this short, but I actually need to go. I'm having dinner with Marshall's family later."

"That's great!" Nina was excited for Sam and Marshall; their relationship was clearly getting more serious.

"Anyway, have fun nerding out! Love you," Sam told her before hanging up.

When Nina reached the library's front steps, she paused. The building felt different than usual tonight, its iconic stone steps bathed in the glow of the party lights, making it all seem like a mirage. Inside, Nina heard the raised voices and laughter of the usual gala crowd—bored and glamorous young people, all vying to outshine and outtalk and outmaneuver one another.

She'd been surprised when Jeff invited her to tonight's event. It often felt like the two of them were enrolled at completely different schools. The prince belonged to the part of King's College that was carelessly privileged and painfully exclusive—populated by the same people he'd known at his all-boys high school, and at court, and in every other corner of his wealthy, royal life. Nina's version of King's College, on the other hand, involved working an on-campus job, eating free pizza in the student center, and attending parties in dorm rooms, not enormous white tents.

Nina much preferred her version of King's College. At least she could be certain that her friends liked her for her own sake, not because of what she could *do* for them.

She didn't really know where that left her and Jeff,

though. How could they stay friends if the only place their lives overlapped was this weekly lunch?

"I have this event coming up for the Young Patrons of the Public Library," Jeff had explained as they took their seats in the dining hall. "Do you want to come?"

"That's okay." Nina had attended enough of these parties with Sam to know that the Young Patrons—of every organization, whether it was the library or the museum or the wildlife conservation fund—were people who wanted to see and be seen. They rarely cared all that much about their so-called cause.

"Are you sure? The guest of honor is Makayla Oyeney," Jeff had told her.

"*What?*" Nina's voice came out as a barely audible squeak. Makayla was the author of Kingmaker, an epic fantasy series that had just been adapted into a hit TV show. Now the world was anxiously awaiting the series' sixth and final book.

"So you'll come?" Jeff had asked.

Nina chuckled. "For the record, this is shameless bribery. But yes, I'll be there."

Now, as Nina glanced around the entrance hall, she felt acutely aware that she didn't know anyone here. Women in couture dresses clutched champagne in thin-stemmed flutes; men in tailored suits laughed as they snatched Gruyère tartlets from passing trays. Nina's flowy skirt and top felt too casual; she thought of Sam's admonishment and resisted the urge to check her armpits for sweat stains.

"Nina!" Jefferson wove through the crowd toward her,

and Nina relaxed into a smile. "I was just talking with Makayla. Want me to introduce you?"

"Absolutely." She followed him toward the center of the atrium, brimming with questions—but when she finally caught sight of the author, she saw with horror that Makayla was deep in conversation with none other than Daphne.

"You didn't tell me Daphne was coming," Nina blurted out.

A sheepish, half-hopeful expression darted over Jeff's face. "I know it's uncomfortable between the two of you, since you and I—I mean—because of our history," he got out. Nina imagined that this conversation must be as awkward for him as it was for her. "But I meant it when I said that I hope we can all hang out. Can you try to get along with her? Please?"

It was the *please* that got her. Nina's relationship with Jeff had been through so many ups and downs; she couldn't bear to risk damaging it, not now that they were finally, tentatively, friends again. Daphne wasn't worth that.

Makayla smiled in greeting as they walked over. "Your Highness, your girlfriend was just telling me that the proceeds from tonight's event will fund the renovation of the children's wing."

Nina gave an involuntary gasp of outrage. "The children's wing? They can't get rid of the pirate ship!" The pirate ship–shaped playhouse was an iconic part of the library; Nina used to spend hours there as a child, reading up in the crow's nest.

"Makayla, I'd like you to meet my friend Nina," Jeff interjected. "She's the one I told you about."

Nina felt a little curl of warmth in her chest at his words. She waited for Daphne to excuse herself—surely she wanted to work the room, filled as it was with the wealthy and titled—but for some reason Daphne stayed put. Nina looked at Makayla, trying to ignore Daphne's lingering presence.

"Ms. Oyeney, I'm such a fan of yours." A million questions vied in her head, and she blurted one out. "I have a theory that Luke is really Nymia's son. Am I right?"

Makayla smiled. "If you're as voracious a reader as Jefferson says you are, then you'll know I can't reveal any plot secrets. Not when I have another book to write."

One of the librarians bustled over to interrupt. "Ms. Oyeney, the photographer was hoping to get a photo of you and His Highness with the library's chairwoman. Are you free?"

"Please, before you go—can you sign my book?" Nina was too eager to be embarrassed as she opened her tote bag and pulled out the third Kingmaker book, *Of Sea and Sky*.

Makayla unearthed a Sharpie from her pocket, scrawling *To Nina* on the title page. "It was lovely to meet you. Have a great rest of your evening."

Once Jeff and the author had left, Nina turned aside. She refused to acknowledge Daphne with even a single syllable. So she was utterly floored when Daphne muttered, "You're wrong about Luke. He can't be Nymia's child. His mother is clearly the Lady of the Rivers."

Daphne was still staring pointedly down into her champagne. But she had to be talking to Nina. Jeff and Makayla were already halfway across the room.

Nina couldn't tell what surprised her more: that Daphne had spoken to her or that Daphne knew anything about the Kingmaker series. "The Lady of the Rivers?" Nina said slowly. "How would Luke have gotten earth magic if his mother is a water nymph?"

"But is it *really* earth magic?" Daphne glanced up, her eyes glinting in challenge. "He can transfigure. No one knows where that power comes from. And it fits the words of the prophecy."

Nina listened, dumbfounded, as Daphne recited the prophecy from the first book. "Wow," she said at last. "I never pegged you as someone who reads Kingmaker."

"We all need a little escapism, don't we?"

It bothered Nina, knowing that she and Daphne were fans of the same series. "I just figured that you're too busy painting your nails and planting stories in the press to bother with books. Aside from Machiavelli, of course."

Daphne didn't flinch. "Really? I'm shocked that *you* like the Kingmaker books. They're about a cunning, devious princess who plots and kills people in order to regain her throne."

When Daphne's words sank in, Nina barked out a disbelieving laugh. "The books aren't about Alina. She's a coldhearted, scheming manipulator. She's the villain!"

Daphne shrugged. "Villain, hero; isn't it just a matter of perspective?"

Nina felt herself getting increasingly angry, at Daphne and—irrationally, ridiculously—at Alina, though she was a fictional character. They just steamrolled through the world, taking what they wanted, tossing aside anyone they couldn't use. Letting their whims dictate their actions.

"You're wrong," she said hotly.

Daphne smirked. "Nina, I can't be wrong about my favorite character. That's a matter of personal opinion, definitionally."

"It's still wrong of you to like her! But you don't see her as evil, do you? Anything is acceptable in pursuit of a crown, isn't that right?"

Nina's blood was pounding, the rest of the room receding to a blur as she stared at Daphne. And yet . . . there was something oddly refreshing about speaking like this. With Daphne she could say exactly what she thought, no matter how viciously unfiltered. The only other person she could talk to with such brutal honesty was Sam.

"I respect that Alina is clearheaded in going after what she wants," Daphne countered. "And I still don't understand why you insist on calling her evil. Luke has killed people over the course of the series, too—a lot of people. Yet he is brave, and she is evil?"

"Because Luke was defending his throne!" Nina burst out.

"Alina thinks it's *her* throne," Daphne said quietly. "They can't both have it."

She wasn't talking about Kingmaker anymore, was she? This was about the two of them—about Jeff.

"Jeff and I are friends again, okay? That clearly bothers you, but guess what? I don't care."

Daphne's voice was low and significant. "That's all you want with Jeff? To be *friends*?"

"I know this won't make any sense to you, given the way your mind works," Nina scoffed, "but some of us actually hang around Jeff because we *like* him. Not because we want to be a princess."

It was probably time to head home; she had already gotten her moment with Makayla. But Rachel had looked up the tickets to this benefit online, so Nina knew that they'd cost six hundred dollars apiece. For that much money, she should at least try one of the cheese tartlets that were being passed around. And whatever expensive beer was served at events like this.

Nina started to move away, but Daphne's voice chased her. "Where do you think you're going?" She sounded outraged that Nina had dared to leave mid-conversation. As if Nina owed Daphne anything.

"To the bar," Nina snapped.

Daphne elbowed past her. "Not if I get there first."

Chris Bailey Photography

KATHARINE MCGEE

is the *New York Times* bestselling author of the American Royals series and the Thousandth Floor trilogy. She studied English and French literature at Princeton University and has an MBA from Stanford. She's been speculating about American royalty since her undergraduate days, when she wrote a thesis on "castle envy"—the idea that the American psyche is missing out on something because Americans don't have a royal family of their own. She lives in her hometown of Houston, Texas, with her husband and son.

katharinemcgee.com

Underlined

A Community of Book Nerds & Aspiring Writers!

READ
Get book recommendations, reading lists, YA news

DISCOVER
Take quizzes, watch videos, shop merch, win prizes

CREATE
Write your own stories, enter contests, get inspired

SHARE
Connect with fellow Book Nerds and authors!

GetUnderlined.com • @GetUnderlined

Want a chance to be featured? Use #GetUnderlined on social!